FOLLOW
THE
SHADOWS

FOLLOW
THE
SHADOWS

THE TALES OF MOERDEN BOOK 1

ROSEMARY DRISDELLE

SPARKPRESS

Published by SparkPress, a BookSparks imprint,
A division of SparkPoint Studio, LLC
Phoenix, Arizona, USA, 85007
www.gosparkpress.com

Published 2023
Printed in the United States of America

Print ISBN: 978-1-68463-218-3
E-ISBN: 978-1-68463-219-0
Library of Congress Control Number: 2023906292

Interior design and typeset by Katherine Lloyd, The DESK

For my parents,
Ursula Grigg and Martin Thomas,
who each in their unique way
helped shape me as a writer.

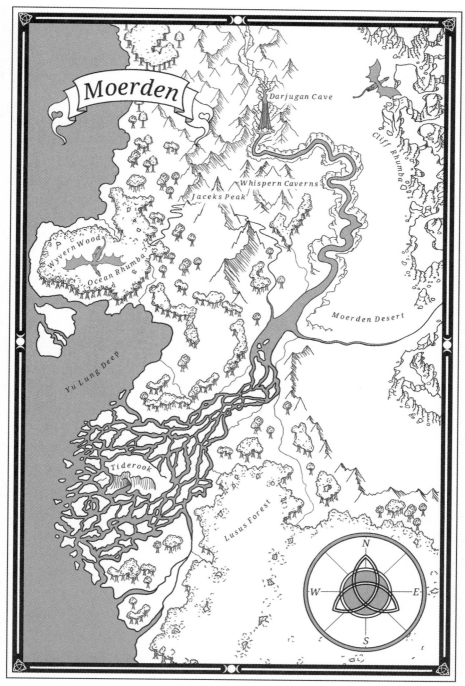

Map by K. Bates

PROLOGUE

The jeong leader's nostrils quivered at the pungent reek drift-ing in the air: birds roosting in the evergreen branches above, the lingering odor of deer now far to the east, and unmistakably, dragons. At least two of them were a few valleys to the south and drawing nearer.

Dragons seldom traveled in the foothills at dusk, though they could sometimes be seen riding the high airstreams, especially when the moon rose early.

The jeong could overtake the deer before midnight, but the dragons were closer, and they were a rare treat. The pack leader hesi-tated, weighing the choice. Even a large jeong pack usually had little chance against a fully-grown dragon. Indeed, they had plenty of respect for the little ones as well.

Hunger and curiosity prevailed. A pair of dragons wandering outside their colony—their rhumba—at this time of day was too enticing. The leader looked for the softening light that signaled sunset. He turned with a growl and led the pack south at a trot.

In the hush of twilight, the autumn hillside faded into shadow. A male dragon emerged from the brush at the edge of the trees, mov-ing with uncertain steps. His head drooped, and his tail dragged through the tall grass. A juvenile peered out from the shelter of his father's leathery wing, alert and chittering softly.

The two crossed the slope, leaving a crooked trail of flattened grass. The father moved tentatively, sometimes halting or taking a few steps backward. His head swung from side to side before he turned on one scaly four-toed foot, pivoting in a full circle. His long tail curved around him so its bulbous tip came to rest below his chin. The younger dragon sheltered, encircled within.

The little one popped out every half minute or so from under the canopy of his father's wing, more agitated and vocal as the minutes passed. He repeatedly looked at the opening where they had left the wood, extending his long neck in that direction.

Shadows under the sweeping branches deepened with the dying light.

The youngster pressed his nose against his father's chest, as though trying to get the older dragon's attention. He scooted to the side, spread his wings, and launched into the air with a couple of strong thrusts. When his father didn't follow, the little dragon dropped to the ground again and crept to his father, who pushed him in under his wing with a gentle nose bunt.

As the older dragon rocked from side to side, his nostrils spouted bursts of flame, scorching the grass and raising a curtain of smoke. He slumped, oblivious to the rising panic of his son. The youngster darted out of the tail's safety to look about the gloomy hillside and scurried back to nudge his father's ribs with his small snout.

Darkness gathered at the wood's edge.

Here and there, the green glint of a wild eye reflected the thin moonlight. A soft panting gathered strength.

Wind rattled the forest canopy. Wolfish faces and bulky shoulders emerged—hardly a gap between trees was empty. As one, the jeong crept from the trees. A cold collective howl rose to the waxing stars.

The little dragon clambered onto his father's back and faced the jeong. He spouted his own small flame, blowing defiant jets into the deepening night. The swollen tip of his tail glowed white. His anxious chittering intensified to a staccato rattle.

Wary, the jeong hesitated, retreating each time the big dragon's flaming maw swung near. They hung back, avoiding patches of smoldering turf. Nonetheless, it looked like easy pickings here. The adult dragon was behaving oddly—sick, perhaps. Maybe the little one would get away—or maybe they would feast on parent and pup this evening—but feast they would. They had their prey surrounded.

The youngster scrambled about, his claw tips slipping and skidding on smooth scales. Wings tucked in tightly, he tried to guard all sides, tail swinging like a mace. His high-pitched whining alternated with weak jets of smoky flame.

The circle of jeong drew tighter.

The juvenile stood and extended his wings. Despite his youth, his wingspan was well over ten feet, and the wide bat-like leathery wings cast shadows on the attackers. He threw back his head and shrieked—a rising wail that traveled for miles. The pack drew back, but the older dragon stayed slumped on the ground.

Voicing a collective snarl, the jeong lunged.

The leader went for the soft tissue below the jaw. His fangs tore out the large dragon's throat in an instant. In the spray of blood, the pack swarmed the quivering dragon, tore with claws and teeth, and roared with the thrill of victory.

A jeong leaped up, claws slid on scales, and the terrified juvenile took flight, the tip of one wing moving out of range just as razor teeth snapped.

Hovering for a moment, he shrieked a second time and brought his glowing tail around. Its bulging tip struck the jeong's forehead, smashing the skull and driving bone fragments into soft brains. The youngster retreated as the body slid away, gaining altitude and distance with a few wing strokes.

He flew to the edge of the wood and found shelter in the boughs of a hardwood tree. Clouds now blocked the moonlight, and the meadow lay deep in shadow, but the sound of cracking bones and tearing sinew dragged on for hours. He clung to his high perch until sunrise.

When dawn came at last, he edged along a sturdy limb, then dropped into the meadow. He crept through tall grasses into a blackened strip trampled flat and littered with gnawed bones. The odor of smoke rose, mixed with the reek of blood and wild musk.

A bristling bloody heap—the single jeong he'd killed—lay rigid, untouched, in the jumble of dragon remains. A host of kreel, glossy creatures like living pearls, were already cleaning up, one blade of grass at a time.

The only other thing that remained of the old dragon was a glassy orb, bloodied but gleaming in the rays of the dawn. The young dragon pushed it into clean grass and rolled it in the dew before swallowing it whole. Then he spread his wings and flew off over the wood.

Chapter
One

THINGS THAT
DON'T CONCERN YOU

mm u hear nything about dr. bonner? mom sez he disappeared on sun and his wife called the cops!!! u think he got killed or what? call me bb

Marise stared at the text message. Her biology tutor disappeared. She tapped a quick reply, *No way! Asking Mom,* as she headed for the home office where her mother sat at the computer.

"Mom—Mom, did you hear anything about Dr. Bonner? Cel says he's disappeared."

Carol Leeson swiveled and looked at her with raised eyebrows. "Dr. Bonner is gone? No, I don't think so. It's probably just a rumor. Wait. There *was* something about a missing person on the news. I wasn't listening." With Marise watching over her shoulder, she turned back to the computer, moused across the monitor, and clicked to bring up the front page of the *Cadogan Daily News.*

"Look." Marise pointed to a small block of text and read out loud. "Elderly Cadogan Mills resident missing, feared lost. Seventy-six-year-old Earl Bonner of Castle Hill was reported missing Sunday evening after an absence of almost twelve hours. Police fear the retired biology professor may have wandered into woods behind his home and got lost. Ground Search and Rescue combed the immediate vicinity throughout the night but found no sign of the missing man. The search is expected to.... It continues on the next page."

"We don't subscribe, so we only get the front page. How awful. His wife must be out of her mind with worry. I wonder if there's anything we can do."

"*Hmmm*." Marise was already calling Celeste as she left the room.

"Merry meet."

"Merry meet. Cel, it's true. It's in today's paper. He disappeared yesterday, and they were looking for him all night. They think he's lost. In the woods."

"In the woods? Aren't there bears and wolves and stuff?"

"I don't know. Maybe. Why wouldn't there be? Cel, are you thinking what I'm thinking?"

"What?"

"About the crystals? Remember?"

"Yeah, but what if he comes back? I mean, I hope he's okay! He's not dead, right?"

"But if they don't find him, I want to try to get those crystals if he doesn't come back. He said he'd leave them to me in his will. He said! I'm going to get them. You can have one. They'll be perfect for scrying. They're better than anything I've seen at The Cupboard."

"They're not really crystal balls, though, are they? They're not quartz. You said they're clear like glass."

"I don't know what they're made of. Bonner wouldn't tell me. I don't think they're quartz; I just know they're special—I knew it as soon as I saw them. How long do you think we should wait, you know, to see if he's coming back?"

"I dunno. Wait till they call off the search, I guess. I feel kinda bad talking this way. It's like we want him to be dead. I like Dr.

Bonner—he's cool. Now we'll have to find another tutor. Um, if he's dead, I mean."

"Yeah, I know. I don't want him to be dead or suffering or anything. I'll be happy if they find him. But he's really old, Cel. He's really, really old. Maybe he just went for a walk and had a heart attack or something." Marise looked out a window and pondered the expanse of forest in the distance. "If he's not coming back, I can't see why I shouldn't have those crystals. I don't think he'd mind. It wouldn't give them negative energy or anything if I took them. I don't think. He'd probably want someone to have them who'd use them."

"Right." Celeste paused. "I guess. I'm gonna look up scrying in my Wicca books. Okay, but wait till they give up looking for him or whatever. Wait, okay? I gotta catch my bus. Blessed be."

Marise glanced at her watch as she pounded down the hall toward the office. "Mom! Remember, you said you wondered if there was anything we could do. I thought of something. Can I take the day off school to help look for Dr. Bonner?"

Carol Leeson pointed out that Marise was inexperienced and might be more of a hindrance than a help. She handed Marise her backpack and shooed her out the door as the school bus turned the corner.

But nothing could keep her mind off Bonner, though her thoughts were split between wondering what had happened to him and wondering whether the crystal balls she had seen in his office drawer were still there. She listened for news, daydreaming about having one of his crystals.

Days went by without any sign of Earl Bonner.

For Marise, the time brought worry and sadness. Something had happened to him. It looked as if he wouldn't be back. She imagined him shivering in the night, in the forest, or torn apart by wolves. Even in her dreams, she had the urge to find the crystals before someone else did.

Over and over, she relived the moment when she had discovered the crystals. Bonner had asked her to get a pen from his desk. She'd found only pencils in the top drawer and moved on to the second one, then to the deep bottom drawer, which slid so easily she almost pulled it right out of the desk. Two objects rolled forward as the drawer tilted toward the floor, shedding their tissue paper wrappings and thumping on the wood. Marise's eyes widened as she beheld two perfect crystal balls.

"Whoa!" she breathed, seizing one and holding it to the light. It was about four inches in diameter, transparent, perfectly smooth, and flawlessly clear.

"Marise!" Bonner leaped from his chair and snatched it from her. He thrust the ball back into its tissue nest and re-wrapped the second one as well.

"Now, now, that's not a pen, is it?" He glared at her over his reading glasses.

"You mustn't touch things that don't concern you." The long curly white hairs of his eyebrows, contrasting with black frames, made him look like a kindly grandfather, but his tone was stern. Producing a small brass key from his lab coat pocket, he closed the drawer before locking it and sliding the key back into his pocket.

Marise knew the value of a good crystal ball. Priced far beyond her budget at The Witch's Cupboard, they were like gold. But she believed magical tools find you, and she'd been waiting patiently for a crystal to come to her.

"Are those crystal balls?" she asked.

"No."

"What are they? Glass?"

"I don't know."

"What do you use them for?" She tried imagining Bonner gazing into one of the balls with a sprig of mugwort in his hand and almost laughed. She was sure he wasn't a witch.

He took his glasses off and rubbed his eyes. He cleaned the lenses with a tissue and replaced the specs with exaggerated care before giving her an answer. "I'm using them for some scientific research. They're unusual, yes? But they're not what you think." He eyed the small silver pentagram hanging from a chain around her neck. "Forget them."

Forget them? Impossible. "Will you be finished with them sometime? Would you sell me one? When you don't need it anymore, I mean."

After another pause, Bonner threw her the promise that repeated itself in her head. "Tell you what—I'll leave them to you in my will, okay? Now, can we get back to cell structure?"

Now, it was as though Bonner perched on her shoulder, whispering to her, *Time is running out. Go for the crystals.* Still, she waited, wondering where he was.

On Thursday, Search and Rescue scaled back, and Marise overheard her parents agreeing that, at this point, they were only looking for a body. On the following Monday, the search was called off. They had found no sign at all of Earl Bonner.

She tucked her last biology assignment for the elderly scientist away with a sigh. She had finished it—a concession to the part of her that wanted everything to return to normal—but wouldn't be handing it in. The exercise hadn't been a waste of time, however. It had given her an idea.

That same evening, Marise rang the doorbell at the Bonner house. She held a macaroni and cheese casserole, still warm from the oven.

She didn't know the woman who answered the door.

"Hello," Marise said with uncertainty. She was unprepared for a stranger and wondered what to say next. "Is Mrs. Bonner home?"

"Yes. Can I tell her who's calling?"

"Oh," she stammered, "of course." She suddenly felt horribly guilty. "I'm Marise Leeson. Dr. Bonner is—was—is my biology tutor. I wanted to tell Mrs. Bonner how sorry I am, about Dr. Bonner I mean. I brought her a casserole." She shoved the dish into the woman's hands and started to go.

The woman smiled. "That's very kind of you, dear. I'm her niece, Kathleen Bonner. Look, there's a lot of family here this evening. You know they called off the search this morning?"

Marise turned back. Nodded, looking at the casserole, thinking this had been a big mistake.

"Why don't you come in, and I'll tell Ellen you're here. She'd probably like to thank you. Or perhaps you'd like to join us in the family room?"

"No! That's okay," she said. "I'll just go. I—I still hope they find him." She turned again. *This was stupid. Celeste was right. I came much too soon.*

"Marise," Kathleen called. "Please come in for a moment. Just a moment?" She held the storm door open wide. "I'll go tell Ellen you're here. She's quite well, actually, all things considered. I know she'd want to thank you."

Marise kicked off her navy-blue sneakers on the porch. In the living room, she perched on the edge of an overstuffed chair with her hands clasped in her lap. From her position near the arched doorway, she watched the door to Bonner's study, but she didn't have long to ponder before Ellen Bonner came slowly down the hall, pushing her walker.

Ellen Bonner was a tiny, almost elfish woman. A peacock blue cardigan flapped around her like a scarecrow's rags. She looked all angles with her padded shoulders, skinny arms and legs, pointy slippers, and a chain of square stones around her neck. When Ellen smiled, her skin folded neatly into crevices and creases around her eyes and mouth, but she looked as alert as a ten-year-old. *A lot like her husband,* Marise thought, *except he was much taller.*

"Hello, Marise. Thank you for coming, and thank you for the casserole. I'll return the dish to your mother, shall I? It's very kind of you."

"It was nothing, really. I'm sorry about Dr. Bonner. Do you think . . . ."

"Do I think he might still turn up?" Ellen smiled again. "Well, I suppose he might, but no. I think he's probably gone, bless him. He was six years older than me, you know. Seventy-six in February. When you get into your seventies, you know that anything can happen, any day. I'm glad it ended this way rather than some dreadful medical emergency or lingering illness. I always worried about that.

"At least, I'm telling myself that this is better. The uncertainty is hard, of course. And we won't completely give up hope. Still, I suppose your biology lessons are probably over, *hmmm*?"

Marise glanced at the office door again, and Ellen followed her gaze. "Was there anything of yours that you wanted? Since you're here, you might as well get it now."

"Oh! Well, there were a couple of things he was supposed to give back last week," Marise said, "and my lab coat, I guess." She struggled to hide her delight as her plan fell back into place.

"Yes, that's what I thought. You go on in and see if you can find them. They may not be where you expect because the police went through the office pretty thoroughly. They left it tidy, though."

She followed Ellen and waited while the elderly woman reached over her walker to turn the knob and push the door ajar.

"I've no idea where they'll be, but check the desk first. I'm going to get back to the family, okay dear? You can let yourself out if you like. Thank you again for coming." Ellen carried on down the hall, her walker rolling silently on the carpet.

Marise couldn't believe her luck.

When she crossed the threshold, a familiar smell struck her— like dust and vinegar, she'd always thought—the scent of old cardboard boxes and pale dead things pickled in bottles. Shelves lined the walls on both sides of the room. Boxes labeled with black scribbly writing filled their bottoms. The top shelves bristled with lab glassware, photographs in plain black frames, jars of lab specimens, and all manner of other odds and bits. Books and disheveled papers lay crammed between the shelves.

A long table stood at the far end of the room beneath a window. A microscope surrounded by a scattering of glass slides, coverslips, forceps, and a couple of small brown glass dropper bottles took up one end. Mr. Bonner's desktop computer occupied the other. In the center of the room, facing the door, stood a small oak desk marred by stray ink marks and circular stains from coffee mugs. Otherwise, the desk was bare.

She looked over her shoulder to confirm that Ellen really had left her alone, then pushed the door almost closed. *It'll look suspicious if I close it,* she thought. Then she hurried around the desk and tugged on the bottom drawer. It was locked. She circled the table to where lab coats hung, only to find that Bonner's was not among them.

It struck her that this was peculiar, and it shook her confidence. She'd have to break into the drawer to get the crystals, and she wasn't sure she would go that far. *I'll look for the assignments while I think. Maybe there's another key! Or maybe he moved the crystals.*

She grabbed her lab coat and Celeste's. There was a third labeled Tom Saunders. She didn't know him, so she left it but checked everyone's pockets.

Marise looked through the two upper desk drawers. No assignments, and no key either. She searched through some of the papers on the shelves and ran her gaze along the top shelf, checking for crystals or anything that might be a good hiding place for a key. Warming to her search, she pulled a chair over and stepped up, keeping a firm grip on the nearest shelf edge. Being a couple of inches over five feet tall when her hair was especially curly, she could just see the items at the back if she stood on her tiptoes.

She examined the face of a pickled animal fetus in a tall bottle labeled CERVUS ELAPHUS, 100 DAYS, and shuddered. Beside it sat a photograph of a young Earl Bonner, dressed in a university gown and holding a dead chicken by the feet. She took it down, studied it, checked its dusty footprint on the shelf, and placed it back on the shelf.

Marise stepped down and moved the chair along. As she clambered back up, the murmur of voices down the hall grew louder. She listened for a moment before returning to her search.

There was another odd photograph, a framed newspaper clipping showing a group of men in scuba gear. The caption read, "Boston Volunteer Fire Department diving team." Though the men weren't wearing masks, it was hard to recognize Bonner given the blurry photo. She scanned the list of names at the bottom and found Bonner, second from the left in the back row. He was easily the tallest man in the photograph.

Glancing beyond the space the photo had occupied, she spied a chunk of driftwood, and tucked behind it, a snow globe with a miniature castle inside. She slid the photograph back onto the shelf sideways and reached for the toy. Blowing the dust off revealed a tiny fire-breathing dragon perched on the highest castle turret.

She turned the globe upside down and back and chuckled at the glint of sparks swirling in the liquid. Even more amusing were the tinkling notes of *Puff the Magic Dragon*. She tipped the globe again.

"Marise?"

"Oh!" Marise almost dropped the globe. She spun around on the chair and clutched the shelf.

Ellen stood in the doorway, and Marise jumped down, her face flaming red. "Oh, Mrs. Bonner, I'm so sorry. I shouldn't have. I got distracted. Oh, I'm sorry." She hastily put the globe on the desk and rubbed her hands on her hips as though she could wipe away her embarrassment.

Ellen pushed her walker over to the desk and picked up the globe. "You know, I'd completely forgotten this. Earl was reading dragon mythology one year, and I gave it to him as a little joke. It is clever, isn't it?" She shook it. Sparks rained down while the music played. "I always thought it wrong that the dragon is so obviously unfriendly. Puff was a friendly dragon, *hmmm*?"

Still stricken with embarrassment, Marise expected Ellen to lecture her about not touching 'things that don't concern you,' as the professor would have done. But Ellen merely looked at her again and then up at the top shelf with all its curiosities. Her free hand idly pushed the second button on her bright cardigan back and forth through its hole.

"It is delicious, isn't it?" Ellen mused. "All this stuff is like attic treasure. If we'd had grandchildren, they would have loved it, I'm sure." She shook her head, and her eyes met Marise's again. "Have you found the assignments?"

"Uh, no," she stammered. "I took my lab coat. Did you know his lab coat's missing?" She stopped short. She hadn't meant to bring it up.

"No. Really?" Ellen frowned. "That's odd. Why would he take his lab coat? Well, maybe it's in the laundry—I'll look. That *is* strange." She started to turn away but returned, taking her left hand off the walker and carefully reaching into the voluminous pocket of her sweater.

"I've forgotten what I came in for. Look, the police gave me this key." A small brass key dangled from her fingertips. "They found it on the carpet by the window. Officer Brown said it fits the desk's bottom drawer, which is full of papers. I'm sorry I didn't think of it earlier. Kathleen reminded me. I bet you'll find your assignment there, locked away from prying eyes." Ellen smiled.

She looked up at the cluttered shelves again and around the

room as though seeing it for the first time. She said nothing for a long while as Marise stood frozen, key in hand. Then Ellen shook the dragon globe again, slipped it into her pocket, and left. In a moment, Marise heard the tinkling notes of *Puff the Magic Dragon* receding as she stared at the open door.

The crystals seemed to be toying with her.

The bottom drawer hadn't been full of papers the day she'd seen the crystals. Perhaps they weren't there now. If they were, the police would have found them. She bent to unlock the drawer and gave the handle a tentative yank. It barely moved. It was much heavier than the last time. She pulled harder. The drawer opened a few inches. As Ellen had said, it was crammed full of papers.

Her heart sank.

She extracted a handful of papers and poked through them. "Landing of the 'Anita' at Cremeliere harbor in ice, December 1907, with 300 reindeer from Norway," she read. The next piece was "The Reindeer Trek." Then there was a battered map of New-foundland, Canada, and under that, "The Parasites of *Anolis* Lizards in the Northern Lesser Antilles." She dug deeper. A print-out from the Ontario Ministry of Agriculture and Food on diseases of cervids. A paper titled "Terrestrial Slugs: Biology, Ecology, and Control." A photocopy of a page of the *Compendium of Pharmaceutical Specialties*.

Marise reached for more. Slugs and snails, amphibians and reptiles, deer, parasites, Canada, drugs, and finally, many pages of handwritten notes with no apparent organization. No assignments. There were lots more papers, but she didn't think it was worth going through them. She pulled the drawer open a little farther, peering into the back.

There, nestled in a space at the back, a glossy crystal sphere spar-kled in the light of the overhead lamp.

One crystal.

Marise grasped it. She hastily wrapped it in the lab coats and felt around in the back of the drawer again to make sure the second crystal wasn't there.

Straightening, she took one last look at the collection of treasures on the bookshelves. She scanned the rows of books and the boxes, opened the other two desk drawers, and looked into their gloomy depths. The second sphere was not to be seen, and she didn't really care about the assignments. She was giddy with relief at finding the crystal, but she was jumpy, her nerves frayed from the stress of deceiving Ellen.

She stuffed the papers back into the drawer and locked it. In the top drawer, she found a pencil and a piece of scrap paper. After chewing thoughtfully on the eraser for a moment, she scrawled a note.

> *Thank u, Mrs. Bonner. I didn't find the assignments, but that's ok. It doesn't really matter, I guess. If u find them, u can send them with the casserole dish. I'm sorry 4 for your loss. Marise Leeson.*

She dropped the key onto the piece of paper, placed the pencil beside it, and fled through the door and down the hall. She shoved her sneakers on without untying them, bundled lab coats under her arm, and bolted for home.

Chapter
Two

WITHIN THE
CRYSTAL BALL

Marise gazed into the eye sockets of a grinning skull above her. A row of carved masks hung like garish crown molding—leering faces of wood and clay with pools of darkness behind them. Some had bold stripes of color. Some had hair or earrings. Dangling from one, a pair of bird skulls turned. She tried not to look, but the eyes watched her, following her around the shop. They gave her the creeps. She imagined real eyes pressed to peepholes.

The Witch's Cupboard, tucked into a curve of a backstreet in Cadogan Mills, smelled like patchouli and looked like the recesses of a sorcerer's storeroom. Amulets, bundles of smudge sticks, and bunches of dried herbs hung from hooks on rafters and shelves. A wall of pigeonholes held many different sized and shaded corked bottles, offering ashes, marigolds, and wolf's hair—all powerful substances. Small crystals and stones heaped in baskets glinted in sunlight filtered through a dusty rose-tinted window. A crooked stack of cauldrons in a back corner slumped against a brush pile of broomsticks.

The book section, where she and Celeste scanned the titles with careful nonchalance, took up one side of the center aisle. The new and used books were divided into three sections—Wicca, self-help, and fantasy fiction—but many appeared to have wandered from their spots to visit another section. Marise glanced over a fiction series sitting smack in the middle of the Wiccan books. Stylized dragons slithered up their spines, reminding her of the pewter dragons in the locked glass case at the front of the store. That case also held a magnificent quartz crystal ball.

Marise snapped her attention back to the Wiccan books. Celeste already had one open.

"About Divination and Crystal Balls," Celeste read softly. "Listen to this! 'Like other magical tools, a crystal ball has only the power and significance that you give to it. It is a symbol that you use to connect to the forces of the universe and to the power within yourself. Real spheres of quartz crystal—the traditional crystal ball—are costly and difficult to find. However, spheres made of other materials can be just as effective if used correctly.'

"Do you think she cares if we look at the books?" Celeste's eyes darted to the side to indicate Lupin, the store owner. The tall violet-haired woman, who looked oddly like her name, wasn't paying attention. She appeared to be fiddling with something behind the counter.

Marise shrugged and took the book. She scanned the page. It says all you need is a reflective surface. "Historically, various surfaces have been used. Water, ink, quartz crystal, even a thumbnail that has been polished to a glossy finish. The material is less important than the technique."

Celeste grinned. "Ha! You don't need a crystal ball! I'll just polish my thumbnail and gaze at that. Do you think that'd work?"

"No." She chuckled. Sliding the book back onto the shelf, she took another that Celeste had already partly pulled out. "Maybe if you'd been scrying for a hundred years—not the first time. And you'd need better nail polish. Maybe black."

Marise looked up to see Celeste examining her chipped pink

nail polish with arched eyebrows. Something drew their gazes back to the front of the store, where the chair by the cash register stood empty. Celeste nudged Marise as she scanned the shop, peering through openings into adjoining aisles.

Marise remained unruffled. "What? We're not doing anything." She scanned the titles on the shelf again, laid aside the book in her hand, and chose a slim black volume titled *Nostradamus: Master of Divination*. She opened it at random and read silently for a moment.

"What's primal knowledge?"

"I think it's, like, knowing stuff about your ancestors or something."

"*Hmmm*. This says that when you scry, the optic nerve tires and stops transmitting information from the outside world. Instead, it releases information from within the brain, allowing us to tap into knowledge and experience what is . . . subconscious . . .. The resource that scrying taps into is universal, or primal, knowledge, and knowledge acquired through personal experience—knowledge that already lies within you." Marise pointed to an illustration of an enormous tree on the page.

Celeste's eyebrows shot up again. "Like stuff you know that you don't know, you know? Ouch! Hey!" She smacked her hand on the top of her head. Both girls wheeled to find Lupin holding a red hair up to daylight.

"*Exactly*," Lupin stated. "Nostradamus was an educated man and widely traveled. He had political interests. He didn't even *begin* to make predictions until he was my age—middle-aged—he would have known a *lot* by that time." As she spoke, Lupin appeared more interested in the hair than in the famous diviner. She seized it at both ends and tugged, testing its strength.

Celeste and Marise looked at each other. Marise was unsure whether to ask about divination or address the attack on Celeste's head, but finally broke the silence. "Do you think that's right? About the optic nerve getting tired? That's your eye, right?"

Lupin glanced at her, turned, and, lifting a lock of hair with one palm, casually chose a second hair. With a jerk, she plucked it.

"Ow! Quit that." Celeste pulled her long hair back over her shoulder.

"Yes, the optic nerve carries messages from the eye to the brain, and the brain interprets them as what you *think* you see." Lupin held the two hairs delicately between thumb and forefinger. "And yes, I believe that the nerve might become tired and confused. Brains often make *mistakes*. Perhaps a trained mind could pull buried information from within—supposing *something* is buried." She looked at the girls as if she thought this unlikely in their case. Her pale blue eyes strayed back to Celeste's head.

Celeste backed up against the bookshelf with her arms folded. "How do you know so much?"

"*I* went to medical school." She dropped this information as though it was obvious and explained everything. "Studied to be a surgeon. Didn't finish. It drained my life force." She turned toward the front of the store, motioning for them to follow, continuing in her strange monotone. "Divination requires gazing into a substance with a reflective surface for long periods. The surface mustn't reflect images from the *surroundings*—only points of light. The visual point of focus—what you think you're looking at—is *within* the crystal ball. If you see images or shadows, follow them."

Lupin walked behind the counter. She moved a piece of needlework from the chair to the countertop, brushing aside a pile of desiccated citrus peels—possibly part of her inventory. But Marise guessed by the look of it that it was more likely a remnant of yesterday's lunch.

She studied the needlework. A face peered out of the center—two eyes, a wide nose, and a straight mouth in shades of gray, silver, and black—stark against a white background. A wavy pattern surrounded the features in gold and brown tones.

Lupin stretched Celeste's hair across the fabric, studying the color contrast. "You have to remember that you are *receiving* energy rather than sending it. If you try to control the process, you will fail." Lupin looked directly at Celeste. "I want a lock of your hair."

"What?" She backed away from the counter. "Why?"

"The *Green* Man," Lupin said. "I'm stitching his picture with human hair. It's a bit like blackwork, you know."

Both girls stood speechless.

Lupin leaned toward Celeste. Shadows under her eyes made them look enormous. "There are not many colors to work with. It could *use* a bit of red. I'll take it from the side, underneath—no one will know."

"Why would I let you cut a hunk out of my hair?"

"Because you *can*." Lupin placed one hand on the counter and held up three fingers with the other. "Do you know the rede? What you send out comes back times three. Let's make a deal. You do me this favor, and I'll do you three. But not stuff from the shop without my approval. What do you say? A small lock of your hair."

Celeste stared at Lupin.

"You can have a lock of my hair," Marise blurted. "What's so special about her hair? What kind of favors?"

Reaching over, Lupin riffled through her chocolate brown curls, letting them slip through her long fingers. "A bit short," she mused, "and curly hair is difficult to work with, but the highlights are pretty. Yes, I'll take it." Her eyes swung quickly back to Celeste. "And *you*?"

Celeste gave Marise a venomous look but relented with a shrug. "Well, okay, I guess."

The haircut took only a moment. Soon a lock of red hair and a pile of brown curls lay side by side on the counter. "Until later, then,"

Lupin said. "Three favors each." The girls turned to go, now in a hurry to get away.

As Marise gripped the door handle, she heard, "Divination is a solitary endeavor. Ritually cleanse the crystal ball and yourself, especially if the ball has a *history*. You'll need mugwort and anise." Running her eye along a shelf above the cash register, Lupin tossed them two small plastic bags of dried herbs. "Charge the ball in moonlight. Remember to focus *within* the ball and be receptive. Tuesday is a good day. The full moon at the beginning of Taurus. There, that's *one*. Each. Blessed be."

They fled the shop before Lupin could bestow any more favors upon them.

On Tuesday, the full moon rose a few minutes after 9 p.m. Marise had bathed in warm water treated with sea salt and bath oil and donned a green hooded cape over blue jeans and a powder blue cotton tank top. Deliberately ignoring her mother's ban on shoes in the house, she stepped into her sneakers with bare feet.

Her parents were out; she had the house to herself.

The crystal ball, cleansed with an herbal infusion and charged for three nights in the light of the waxing moon, waited on a small table wrapped in black velvet. On the floor, a circle of alternating yellow and silver candles surrounded the table.

Seated in darkness, she laid her hands loosely on her thighs with the palms turned up and closed her eyes. She imagined the chair back and her spine as the trunk of a tree, drawing power through deep roots from the earth below. She imagined tree limbs sprouting from the top of her head, sweeping down like a curtain of weeping willow branches. Green fingerlike leaves brushed the carpet. She transformed the branches into cascades of blue light and sat for a moment, enjoying the turquoise glow. Then she opened her eyes, savoring the moonlight filtering through the sheers.

Relaxed and focused, Marise stood and lit the candles, proceeding clockwise. A soft scent of lemon drifted up. She unwrapped the ball, letting the velvet drape over the table edges. The crystal awaited her, speckled with points of light. Leaning toward it, she cleared her mind of all thoughts and focused on the depths of the ball, alert for images.

Something moved in the glossy depths, something big.

Surprised at her quick success, she tried focusing on the image, but it slipped away like a wisp of smoke. She saw it again—shifting, formless. Remembering Lupin's words, 'if you see images or shadows, follow them,' Marise waited, breathless and fixated on the center of the ball.

A black reptilian eye gazed back.

She jerked away. The eye blinked and disappeared.

"What was that?" Fascinated, Marise picked up the ball, gazing deeply into it, searching the dark interior. She forgot about candles, points of light, and meditation.

Where is that mysterious eye?

A wave of vertigo washed over her. Her feet left the floor, and then she was spinning, hurtling through space.

Marise slammed onto the ground and slid, careening down with debris. She tasted dirt and had grit in both eyes. She plunged feet first, down, down on a wave of dirt and stone. All around her, chunks of rock bounced and rolled. The roar faded far below. Rubble rolled over her, halting her descent.

She heaved against the weight, struggling to sit up, shedding the layer of pebbles and flakes of rock. They showered off her while more shifted to fill the hollow she'd left.

Where am I? What happened? Marise sat with her face cupped in her hands, fighting the urge to rub her gritty eyes. *The house collapsed! An earthquake? An explosion?* Tears leaked from under her eyelids. She wanted to see but didn't dare open her eyes. Not yet. Was she trapped in the ruins of the house?

A slight breeze came, but it was warm, too warm. *Fire?* she wondered.

But fires make noise, and all she could hear was her own ragged breathing. Grit scratched her eyelids as she rubbed her face with the cape's fold. *I have to see. I have to get out of here.* She scrubbed harder. Using her hands, she rubbed her eyebrows and wiped away tears, daring a quick blink now and then.

There was light.

As she clenched her teeth, sand ground between them. She spat, shook her head, and ran her fingers through her hair. Finally, she dared to open her eyes.

A layer of small reddish and ocher stones covered her legs. The white rubber tip of one sneaker poked through. She bent her knees and worked her legs free. Then lifted her head and looked around.

Marise gasped. She was perched precariously on a steep pitch, far above a broad desert floor of reds, yellows, and browns. There were steep screes, towering cliffs, and a jagged skyline. This was not Cadogan Mills.

"Where am I?" she said as her thoughts tumbled about, trying to sort it all out.

A shadow blocked the sunlight. She looked up and stopped breathing.

An enormous flying creature hovered over her. Only yards away, the terror had acres of wings stretching out and a tapering neck as long as the rest of its body. A sinuous blunt tail lashed the air and struck the scree to her left, sending rock shards flying. The rubble around her lurched into motion once more.

Marise threw up her arms to shield her face. She whimpered, peering past her arms to keep the monster in view. Against the bright sky, it looked black, with a flash of brassy gold along the ridge of its neck. Alert black eyes looked straight at her. A spout of fire belched from gaping jaws.

The air shimmered as the beast plunged.

Marise rolled to the left, instinctively curling into a ball. She cried out when the loose gravel shifted underneath her.

She slipped a few inches, remaining cupped in the hollow that her body had made. There was no escape, nowhere to run. She squeezed her eyes shut and clenched every muscle.

Time slowed.

Nothing happened for what seemed an eternity. Then a wave of intense heat rolled over Marise. Her fingers stung, and she smelled burning hair. She sucked in a breath, holding it, keeping every muscle taut.

A deafening bellow thundered above her, and she jerked into motion.

Debris slid on the slope as she unfolded, kicking her legs as though she could run from the blistering air. She knew she was screaming but couldn't hear her voice over the din. Tears streamed from her eyes as her fingers, still interlaced behind her head, trembled and cramped.

The bellow cut off, making her shrieks the deafening sound until she stifled them and curled up again, terrified. In the sudden hush, she heard a thud and a wild snort, then nothing.

A cool breeze wandered over her ear's edge and clenched fingers. She sucked in a breath and tried to look about through slitted eyes. Another bellow rent the air, and she jerked again.

This time, though, the sound came from high above. Silence returned.

She remained huddled in a tight heap on the rocky scree.

That was a dragon. No way. No. A dragon. A dragon almost killed me. There are dragons? Dragons are hunting me. No. No.

The ball has some hypnotic power. I'm imagining this. Lupin drugged me somehow with the herbs. This is what I get for stealing the crystal ball. What ye send out comes back times three. I'll never look at it again. I'll return it. I will. I swear.

But the sand between her teeth told her this was real, and she was not in her bedroom. She realized something else as well—the crystal ball was gone.

Perhaps it lay buried on the mountainside. Or perhaps it had rolled and bounced into the desert valley. If the sphere had brought her here, as it seemed to have done, it wouldn't be taking her home.

She peeked past her folded arms. Between her elbows, the slope dropped below her at a sickening pitch. Tracks left by landslides ran down to the distant base and buckled into foothills. She would never get down there without being badly injured, or worse, buried.

She lowered her arms and turned to check the sky, half expecting to see a dragon. Nothing but the blue expanse stretched overhead, devoid of both clouds and flying creatures. Only a desert sun hung suspended above nearby peaks.

Disbelieving, Marise tipped her head back to get a better view of the heights. The mountains were rough and jagged, as though someone had walked through with a sledgehammer randomly smashing them. Rock staggered from splintered peaks, often plunging down a vertical face for hundreds of feet.

At the foot of each, the stone shifted slowly toward the plain below. A greenish haze on the lower slopes stretched into the plain, suggesting vegetation, but nothing moved out there. It seemed the land was endless bare, dry, sunbaked rock. Even if she could reach the plain, there was nowhere to hike. There was nothing familiar.

Something moved in her peripheral vision.

Marise turned her head. Something bulky lodged on the slope just above and to her right. It balanced on the slope, one scaled leg extended downward, with four toes driven into the rubble. A wing flapped lazily, fanning the expanse below. The other wing lay folded tight.

Reptilian and avian at the same time, it could only be a dragon. If the wings weren't enough to prove it to her, a tendril of smoke curling from prominent nostrils removed all doubt. A brassy spiked crest rose between spherical black eyes, snaking along the sinuous neck and down the spine toward the tip of the tail, which lay somewhere out of sight. The hide, sage green like verdigris, looked scaly but smooth, and the leathery wings joined its torso.

She stared at the dragon, and the dragon stared back. She was sure this was not the monster from a few moments ago. That dragon had been far bigger. There were likely more of them about, and if two of them knew about her, others would as well.

Its menacing head glided forward.

Marise shrank back. The sudden movement made her slide farther. As her cry of alarm split the silence, the head jerked back, hovering above its shoulders, mimicking her expression—eyes wide and jaw slightly open.

She dared to look away for an instant, scanning for anything that might provide shelter. There was nothing. But instinct told her she had to get away. Like a crab, she inched across the slope.

The ground shifted. She stopped.

The dragon watched, its head creeping toward her again.

With a shudder and a shriek, she scrambled away from the dragon. Gravity took hold of her and everything around her. Tons of rock swept into motion, churning, and gathering speed. Dirt and debris slid, bounced, and roared in a rush to the foothills far below.

Marise flipped over on her belly, arching to keep her head up while she cast her arms about fruitlessly for something to hold on to. Debris slipped through her fingers and dragged her down with its own relentless grip. Her cloak, still fastened firmly around her neck, slipped up past her head, turning inside out. She wondered how long she would plunge before the tumult smashed her to bits or buried her forever.

Something plucked her out of the chaos.

Hoisted into the air, she gasped and dangled, swinging, and catching sickening glimpses of a hillside through the opening of the cape. Debris rained through folds of fabric and fell to the din below. She bucked like a fish in an osprey's talons.

In seconds, she passed the base where rubble piled up on itself as more crashed from above. Her abductor swept low over the crest of a foothill and down the far side, where a gentler and smoother surface sloped. She fell, hitting the sandy hillside and rolling a few feet before coming to rest in a tangled heap on the edge of the gully.

She felt something near, but the cape wrapped around her head, stifling and blinding her. Struggling to her knees, she clawed at the fabric, searching at her throat for the ties. Her fingers slipped across the knotted cords but made no sense of them. She gasped for air and sobbed in desperation. At last, she pulled the cape over her head with brute force just as a shadow passed.

Marise drew in a panicked breath and swallowed a scream. There was nowhere to run. She searched the sky, pushing down pain and nausea, and looked for a rock or anything to arm herself. Seeing nothing, she tried standing.

The shadow passed once more before the bulky creature heralded its arrival with a low hoot and settled in the gully directly below. Marise stayed upright long enough to turn her head and look into its bottomless black eyes. Her vision went dark, and she bent over the dusty ground, retching as her knees buckled. Firm, warm sand underneath her felt like the only real thing for a heartbeat before she surrendered to the darkness.

Chapter
Three

USELESS GRISTLE

M arise cupped her hands to scoop water from the river, longing to bring cool, clear water to her lips. *Water!* The sun shone warm on her back as she inched her hands closer to the river's surface. Her fingers wouldn't stay together—the liquid ran between them, rushing away until not a drop remained. Something coarse scratched her cheek, and she raised a hand to brush it away.

She woke to the chill of a desert sunset.

The sun had already dropped behind the nearby peaks and chilly air pooled in the gully. A coolness spread over her arms and face, but her back still felt pleasantly warm. On the slope above her, she saw a rabbit. She blinked, and the rabbit transformed into her crumpled cape, lying just out of reach.

Forcing a swallow past her parched mouth and throat, Marise wondered where she might find water, then realized there was no hope of water. Now fully awake, she realized there was no sun to warm her back either, and she remembered the last thing she had seen—a large scaly reptile that looked remarkably like a dragon. A fearful suspicion crept into her mind.

She pitched away from the warmth, then pulled herself up with a groan. She dared to look back. A scaly head rose on a sinewy neck, returning her gaze.

Marise scrambled backward a few more yards. When the dragon didn't follow, she crouched, wary, watching. As the seconds ticked by, she tried to think, tried to figure out what to do. This dragon could have killed her, but it had not. It appeared more curious than ferocious—but what would happen once curiosity was satisfied? The other dragon had wanted to kill her. Of that, she was certain.

The desert evening quickly sucked her body heat, leaving goosebumps on her arms and legs. She considered reaching for her cape. It would not be very warm. She wished she could cuddle up against the dragon's warm hide again, but she dared not.

The creature moved. Its head sank to her eye level and glided forward. Marise drew back, but too slowly. The square snout bumped her cheek. A broad forked tongue darted out, flicking over her face. She flinched and gasped. Her heart hammered in her chest, and her breathing quickened.

The snout bumped her shoulder, but gently, like an encouraging nudge. She risked looking into those black eyes again and wrapped her arms around herself, trembling only partly from the cold.

The dragon laid its head down on the sand and looked at her, so like a hopeful dog that the last of her reluctance faded. Friendly dragon or deadly, it was the only source of heat—her only hope in this cold, wild place. As she drew near, its back leg moved to create a hollow, and she tucked herself into it.

The skin of the dragon's leg felt pebbly, like the peel of an avocado, but soft and pleasant to touch. Underneath, she felt firm leg muscles. At her shoulder, a ridge marked the beginning of its ribcage. Scales began there too. Each the size of a dollar coin. Above, a claw flexed on the second joint of the dragon's folded wing, jutting forward like a hand; four digits combed the air as the wing adjusted.

Marise felt warmer already. She drew in a deep breath, and a peculiar odor reminded her of dust, dry dust like the attic in her grandmother's house. *Or maybe books. Like the old, yellowed books in The Witch's Cupboard.* Reminded of Lupin, she wished she could claim one of her favors, and for a moment, she hated the woman. *This is Lupin's fault. I did what she said and now look.*

She sneezed.

The dragon's head whipped around, and Marise pressed herself back into the crook of its leg. All the beast had to do was open its mouth and bite her head off or roast her like a sausage—but it simply watched her.

She reached out tentatively, and leaning forward, touched the scaly cheek. The scales felt cool, smooth, and dry.

The dragon jerked away. She pulled back with a gasp as an eerie shriek drifted down from the cliffs. "Keeyah, keeyah," like the cry of a hawk. Then it changed, taking on an urgent tone and a shape, like a name. "Javeeeer, Javeeeeer."

The dragon tensed, raising its head. It looked briefly down at her and back at the darkening sky as if scanning the shadowy hillside.

"Javeeer."

"Keeyah!" the dragon answered. The cry sounded like a call and a whistle, a shriek so piercing that Marise covered her ears.

She hid, curled in the shelter of thigh and wing, wishing again that she could run away or burrow into the sand, but there was no time. Something was coming. The dragon slapped its wing down like a lid, blocking her view.

"Keeyah," the dragon shrieked again, and a moment later, Marise felt the thud of something landing nearby. Low hoots punctuated the silence, terminating in another sharp whistle. The wing above her lifted, and she gazed into the face of yet another dragon. An immense dragon.

She gaped and shrank back, raising an arm as though it could protect her. Her dragon was surely a young one, only half grown.

The newcomer was massive by comparison—easily the size of a bull elephant, but much more elegant, with graceful curves outlined against the darkening sky. She wondered if it was her dragon's mother. *Does she think I'm a threat?*

Marise peered out at the head poised above her, hardly daring to breathe.

The dragons were silent, but she knew something had passed between them. Her dragon's muscles twitched and tensed. The larger one flexed its neck into an *S* and reached for Marise with a wing claw. She threw her other arm up to cover her face as the smaller dragon pulled his leg in, squeezing her into the soft recess behind his ribs.

She gulped for air and struggled to see. A blast of flame lit up the hillside. The larger dragon shrieked and drew itself upward until it towered over them both. The young one looked down at Marise, then heaved to its feet, spread its wings, and stepped away. She forced her bruised limbs to straighten and, hugging herself to conserve heat, stood helpless before the dragons.

The adult was magnificent—bat-like in the dusk, yet powerful, with a wingspan over fifty feet. With a few quick flaps, it launched over her head, tail snaking back and forth. It roared and spouted flame, and the youngster stretched its wings in response, lifting off in the opposite direction, and flying low to the ground for a few strokes.

Shivering, Marise watched it return. As it passed, it looked at her and banked left toward the rising ground.

The end of one wing cut into the sandy slope, and the dragon jerked off course. She barely saw the bulging tip of its tail coming before it hit her in the chest, knocking her wind out and smashing her head against the sand. She writhed and gasped, struggling to breathe. The yelps and whistles faded into the rushing sound of her own blood roaring through her ears. Once again, she slipped into darkness.

It was dark, though a patchy glow shone somewhere, as though patio lights had been turned on. Far above, Marise could just make out a rocky ceiling patterned by cracks and shadowy hollows. The only thing she saw clearly was the scaly, mysterious face of her dragon.

The dragon nudged her shoulder with its nose.

She sat up with a wince and groaned. Her head throbbed, and a mosaic of scratches and bruises covered her arms. Worse, she felt sickeningly thirsty, and a dull ache in her belly told her she hadn't eaten in many hours. She tried to remember if she'd had breakfast that morning—or was it the day before? She had fasted before her scrying attempt.

The dragon settled back, watchful, as Marise looked around. The cave was vast, its far walls lost in gloom. Patches of sand and pebbles scattered over an uneven floor while larger rocks were heaped against the walls. The air felt warm but not stuffy. In the dim light, it was impossible to tell which of the distant shadows marked the entrance, but two things pushed everything else from her thoughts: water flowed nearby, and there were dragons. Lots of dragons.

The trickling sounded sweeter than she could imagine. Her throat ached at the thought of a drink. Searching for the source, she spotted a spring flowing from a crevice in the cave wall. Water spilled over the edge of a jutting rock, falling into a small natural basin.

She longed to rush over, hold her mouth under the little stream, and duck her head in the pool, but four enormous dragons stood between her and the waterfall. And they were all watching her.

She thought the closest and largest, standing apart from the others, was the one from the foothills. A second had a long white scar running down its neck. The remaining two hung back in the shadows, perhaps as uncertain of her as she was of them. None of them, she thought, looked hostile.

Thirst overcoming fear, Marise heaved to her feet. The most direct route ran between the dragons, and she was torn between it and the longer route through the shadows beyond them. Drawing a deep breath, she took a step toward the tinkling waterfall. No one moved. She took two more steps, placing each sneakered foot carefully, trying to watch all the dragons at once.

A scaly head appeared in her peripheral vision, and she ducked away, raising her arm in defense. It was the young dragon. Their eyes met, and she smiled though her lips trembled. Suddenly, she felt more courageous. She raised her chin and walked to the pool with her dragon beside her. The others turned their heads as she passed, but none came any closer.

Water. Water!

It filled the basin and spilled over the rim, draining away through another opening in the rock. Her lips found the little waterfall, and she drank until she couldn't drink anymore. She dipped her head under the stream and splashed water on her neck and shoulders. She scrubbed her arms with her hands, heedless of the stinging and the blood that beaded on her many scratches.

With her hair dripping and her clothes almost as wet, she turned to face the watching dragons. Perched awkwardly on the edge of the pool, she endured the scrutiny of five pairs of black eyes.

It was astonishing to see the glow illuminating the cave came from the bulging ends of their tails. Each dragon had its own light, which varied in brightness. Her dragon's orb, lying near her feet, shined brightly, lighting her from below like a spotlight. A ridiculous mental image of herself on stage, with an audience of dragons, sprang into her mind.

Marise was overwhelmed. She slid to the floor and leaned against the wall.

The largest of the dragons moved in. It paused a few feet away, lifting its tail and swinging it around at eye level like a miniature wrecking ball. She ducked and raised her arms, but the dragon merely dropped the tip into her lap. The light went out.

She noticed that the end of the dragon's tail looked like a claw with three talons permanently fixed around a sphere. The bony black ridges of the talons held the sphere securely but left most of its surface exposed.

Marise felt the damp hair on the back of her neck prickle with recognition. The sphere looked exactly like Bonner's crystal balls, except this one was part of the dragon. Questions raced through her mind. *Did Dr. Bonner's spheres come from dragons? Did the professor know what they were? What was he doing with them?* She gazed up at the dragon and wished it could answer her.

Seconds ticked away, yet the dragon didn't withdraw its tail. She wondered what she should do. *If the sphere really is the same as the one that brought me here, this one will take me home. Is the dragon offering me a way out of here? Can I go home? Just like that? That must be it!*

She reached for the sphere. The fine bones at the end of its tail made it flexible, and she picked it up easily. She cupped the orb in her hand. It felt the same as the one she'd lost. The talons were like cool metal against her palm, but the sphere itself was warm and, somehow, friendly. She looked back at the dragon.

Now what? Gaze into it and visualize home? Think, like, there's no place like home? Abracadabra?

'You can't travel with a sphere that's attached to someone else. The sphere goes with you!'

Dropping the sphere, Marise gaped at the dragon. *Of course. The sphere goes with you.* She imagined appearing in her bedroom, clutching the dismembered dragon's tail. Her face grew hot and red. *Great. I just thought about ripping a dragon's tail off.* But at the same time, she tried to understand how she heard the dragon speak. It had sort of been inside her head—like a thought. She shook her head in confusion.

The tail rose out of her lap, hovering in front of her as though handing the sphere to her again. She took it between shaking hands, her eyes moving from sphere to dragon and back.

'You are injured. We're sorry. Javeer is young and sometimes clumsy.' A series of images flashed unbidden through Marise's mind, memories from an alien mind of the shadowy scene in the foothills viewed from the air. A body lay writhing. A dragon crash landed beside it, raising a cloud of dust. He righted and bellowed at the sky, nudging the body and blowing spurts of flame. Marise saw the ground rushing toward her. Enormous talons wrapped around the now motionless figure; the weight of her own body was secure in the dragon's grasp. They banked sharply and flew up and over the hilltop.

Marise looked at her dragon. She tentatively patted the side of his neck, and he tilted his head. *Why didn't Javeer talk to me earlier?*

'He didn't know he could. You didn't talk to him, did you?'

Bemused, she shook her head. *'That's true. I didn't really try.'*

'Javeer has only spoken with dragons. Most animals in Moerden don't talk to dragons. And,' the dragon paused, *'he's still learning to use his sphere to do more than just knock things over. He'll need some practice talking with you. It will be mostly images at first until he gets better at it.'*

Marise sensed amusement through the orb, so she dared to ask more. This time, she directed her question at the sphere. "Moerden? What's that? Where am I?"

'You don't know?' The dragon sounded surprised. *'You are at the cliff rhumba, Honedrai, a desert dragon colony in Moerden.'*

Shaking her head, she asked, "Are there people here?" The sphere cooled noticeably between her palms.

The dragon glared at her and was silent for so long that she thought no answer was coming.

'Beings such as you cannot survive in Moerden. Dragons would kill you. You are in danger as long as you are here. You must stay with one of us.'

Another scene leaped into Marise's mind, but for a moment, she wasn't sure if it came from her own thoughts or from the dragon. It was almost as if she was once again perched on the scree with a dragon attacking her. But it seemed she was in the air, rushing toward the fire-belching monster, bellowing as the other dove. A wave of dizziness rolled over her as two heavy bodies collided with a great jolt, then ascended in a rush, clawing and hissing. A second defiant bellow split the air as the tiny figure on the slope below faded from view.

She put a hand on the rock floor to quell her dizziness. *'So, this dragon saved me from that dragon. But then it tried to leave me in the desert.'* Before she could ask more, a snort from beyond the group made everyone turn.

A red glow illuminated a section of wall.

Now Marise saw the cave entrance, a wide tunnel to the right. She only had an oblique view of the illuminated arch, but she clearly saw the enormous dragon that rushed through it seconds later. The beast came spouting flame and dangling the carcass of an animal from its wing claw. She felt tension in the sphere and the dragons around her.

Another dragon burst in, carrying a kill.

Forgotten for the moment, Marise had a chance to compare the dragons. The new arrivals were easily the largest. Their crests looked sharper, their bodies wider. The biggest reminded her of a cougar, eyeing its surroundings, bristling with power and energy.

She noticed Moerden dragons came in two colors. The four adult dragons near her were a dull reddish-gold hue, as though plated with a mixture of brass and worn copper. Javeer and the new-comers, however, were a dusty green, with a polished gleam on worn edges, like weathered brass.

Males, she thought. *Green dragons are males, and Javeer is one as well.*

The lead male turned to those gathered around Marise, and his malevolent gaze immediately fell upon her. She flinched as he hurled his kill to the floor, thrust his great nose upward, and blew a blast of flame that lit every crevice of the high ceiling. She dropped the sphere and scrambled sideways to lean against Javeer.

A bellow echoed off the surrounding walls, continuing on and on. Marise covered her ears, cowering as more dragons joined in. The cave reverberated with the din and flashed red with fire. A smell like hot metal filled the air.

As the tumult died, Marise risked a quick look past the curve of Javeer's neck. The big female and the lead male faced each other. She was planted like a wary lioness, low and tense. He towered over her, tail lashing.

It was him. She was sure of it. He was the dragon that had tried killing her.

The tail sphere lay within reach, and she eyed it. She longed to know what was being said. She stretched out on her belly, still shielded by Javeer, and grasped the orb. There was a voice, but it was not the one she'd heard before. This voice was harsh, threatening, and unmistakably male.

'. . . *tenderheartedness will be the end of us all, Kuvrema. First, you take in the juvenile. Now this useless gristle, this human. Do you think she arrived at the rhumba by chance? Trouble is coming. Haven't we seen enough of it? Kill her now, or I will.*'

'*Korpec, she doesn't know where she is or how she got here. She wants to return home. Her arrival is an accident. We will help her.*'

He fumed. '*You believe that, do you? She cannot return! Where do you think you'll find a relic sphere? If she wants to return, where's the one that brought her here? Cut from the bleeding tail of some wretched dragon dying in Wyvern Wood, I imagine. Where is it now? Does she not have it? You know there are no relic spheres in Moerden. I will end this. Now.'*

Korpec advanced upon Marise, butting roughly past Kuvrema. Marise struggled backward, retreating until she came up hard against the cave wall. Trapped, she could only stare down the endless crimson tunnel of his throat as he drew in a great lungful of air.

Chapter
Four

SPHERE RULES

The cave echoed bellows and shrieks. Marise stayed pressed against the stone. She glimpsed a flash of light from Kuvrema's direction as Javeer leaned back but held his ground. He threw his wings open, creating a barrier between her and Korpec.

The noise quieted. She knew the silence must be full of conversation, but she could hear none of it. Drawing in an uneasy breath, she dared to peek past Javeer's wing. The older dragons towered over them. Kuvrema blocked Korpec. Her tail snaked slowly back and forth, a subtle suggestion of violence held in check. Other dragons had withdrawn to the shadows.

Kuvrema's sphere passed in front of Javeer once, twice, three times, moving just above the ground. On the fourth pass, Marise reached out to intercept it but changed her mind, afraid she might draw attention to herself or distract Kuvrema.

Javeer must have noticed the gesture, however, because he promptly tucked his tail along his left side, putting his sphere where she could reach it.

She seized the orb and focused, listening. She heard Kuvrema's voice, in what she might have mistaken for a calm tone, had her tail not passed again, moving noticeably faster. *I am rhumba henne here, and I say we will try to help her return.*

Korpec responded with a defiant flame, and her tail whipped around, striking him smartly on the shoulder. He snorted and stepped back. Kuvrema reared up and aimed a blast of fire just over his head while her tail hovered menacingly beside her, poised. She whistled, and the other females responded moving in toward their henne and forcing Korpec back toward the cave entrance. The other male had already moved in that direction.

Korpec belched a defeated flame at Kuvrema. *'Don't leave her alone, Kuvrema,'* he growled. *'If I find her on her own, I'll kill her. You can do what you like to me afterward. We're all as good as dead.'*

She produced another blast, and he turned away. He left the cave at a run, moving with a snake-like rhythm that made Marise's skin break out in goosebumps. His glowing tail drew a great circle in the air, then disappeared. The other male hesitated, looking back for a moment, then followed him out.

Javeer drew in his wing, and Marise felt the tension in his tail relax. She pondered Korpec's words: *'You think she arrived at the rhumba by chance? Trouble is coming.'*

There was something going on and Korpec thought she was part of it, but what? *Why were they all "as good as dead?" What did humans and spheres mean to these dragons? And did Dr. Bonner's crystal balls have anything to do with it?*

She had no chance to ask her questions because the five remaining dragons converged on the carcasses the males had left. They tore the animals apart and devoured them with an audible rending of cartilage and snapping of bone.

Revolted, Marise looked away, trying not to acknowledge the growl in her own belly. She longed for something to eat. But not raw meat. The odor of hot rock still filled the cave, and it gave her an idea.

Javeer was working on a limb he had dragged to the side. She picked up his tail sphere and visualized a steak roasting over an open flame. He paused and looked at her. She sensed confusion, and his tail light dimmed. She focused on her hunger. "Hungry. Very hungry." Then she switched back to her mental image of red meat, this time cooking in a dragon's flame. To her delight, he tore a chunk of muscle off the leg, laid it on a rock, and torched it vigorously.

The smell of cooking meat drifted over to her, mixed with smoke and heated rock. She reached for the meat, gingerly flipping it over with her fingertips. He torched it again, and the other dragons paused their meal to watch.

When she judged the meat done, she bowed to him, and he, like the others, went back to his meal. She waited for the meat to cool before devouring it with gusto.

Some of it was charred black and crumbly, but she didn't care, and if it was a bit pink in the middle, she couldn't tell in the dim light. She thought she'd never tasted anything so delicious. Even the odd bit of rock between her teeth didn't slow her down. Soon, she wiped her mouth with the back of her hand and walked to the spring for another drink.

When the dragons finished eating, they burned away the bloodstains and scraps on the pebbly cave floor, raising the familiar odor of a backyard barbeque, then stretched out with their heads together. Marise wondered if they were settling down to sleep or talking among themselves. If there was a conversation going on, she couldn't hear it. She needed a sphere. As she sat beside Javeer, she wondered how far she dared to go.

She stood, walked over, and picked up Kuvrema's tail. She tried keeping her mind blank and waited for Kuvrema to speak. The light in the orb dulled.

'Hello?'

She had Kuvrema's attention but hesitated. "Thank you, ah, thank you for saving me from Korpec back there." She paused. "Is it true what he said? I'd have to kill a dragon to get a sphere?"

'I suppose so. Life without a sphere would be difficult, if not impossible. But Korpec has an overactive imagination. You didn't kill any dragon.'

She nodded, but she was still confused. "So, where did the sphere I used come from?"

'From a dead dragon, of course. But relic spheres are rare. When a dragon dies, it dies too.'

Sensing Marise's confusion, Kuvrema continued. *'You can preserve a sphere if you take it quickly and protect it from the sun, only exposing it to use it. They need to be handled if they are not in the dark. If a sphere's not handled, it will cloud and become useless, even in indirect light, though much more slowly then. But it's a desperate and sick dragon willing to take a sphere from a corpse. We don't do it!'*

Kuvrema's revulsion came through clearly, and Marise shuddered. An uncomfortable feeling grew on her. Unless she found the sphere, she might never get home. *What if it's the only one in Moerden?* she worried. She imagined herself as Korpec saw her, hacking the tail off a living dragon. *Gross. No way I could do that. Kuvrema's right. I wonder how often a dragon dies. Maybe they'd help me get one from a bad dragon like Korpec.* She pondered how two relics might have arrived in dragonless Cadogan Mills.

"Can dragons travel by using the sphere?"

'Yes, it's possible. But we don't, ever. There are certain . . . limitations. And we fly long distances without difficulty.'

"Can you travel to other worlds? Like where I come from? With your spheres, I mean."

A long silence followed, during which she sensed fear and perhaps sadness from Kuvrema. Finally, the dragon replied. *'I think so. I don't know. It's likely dragons in the past have done it, but none alive today has tried. Why would we want to?'*

Marise pictured a dragon materializing anywhere in Canada

and agreed that travel to her world would not be a great idea. Then she decided to get straight to the point. "I need to find my sphere, so that I can go home. Do you think I can get it back?"

'We've looked already—to get it out of the sun. We didn't find it. It must be buried. In time, it may surface. We might stir things up and see if it appears, but that must wait for daylight. Meanwhile, I suggest you rest. You're safe here if you stay with one of us and avoid the older males. They are dangerous! Stay with Javeer.'

"I will." She had no intention of wandering into Korpec's jaws. "You read each other's minds and talk to each other without making any noise. Can you tell everything I'm thinking?"

Kuvrema snorted. *'No! We don't read each other's minds. What a hum that would make.'* Her eyes strayed over the group. *'We direct our thoughts. It's focused. To read someone's mind, to hear thoughts that are private, I'd have to work hard unless the thoughts were strong, emotional.'*

"And me? Can you read my thoughts?"

'It's the same, but we need the sphere. I can't understand what you say aloud, although I know you focus your thoughts better when you speak them. That's curious. I hear what you consciously direct at me, and a bit of your focused thought. I know, for instance, that your next question is about whether you can speak to the others through my sphere.'

Marise gasped. "You're right! Can I?"

'It is possible, but you must concentrate on the group, not on me. Direct your thoughts outward.'

Like a microphone, Marise thought to herself.

'I think you could master it in time. I can help, of course, by repeating your thoughts and directing them at the group.'

Like an interpreter. "Okay. Yes, I see. One more question?" She tried to keep her thoughts muddled to see if Kuvrema knew before she spoke it.

'You learn fast. Sometimes, it's good to keep your thoughts to yourself, but remember, all you need to do is put down the sphere. I can't hear you without it. What is the question?'

"Can I talk to dragons with one that isn't attached? With the one I lost?"

'No!' Kuvrema's response was almost a growl. *'A relic sphere retains many of its properties, but that is not one of them. That would be talking through the dead!'*

The tip of Kuvrema's tail resumed its glow. The conversation was over. Relic spheres were clearly a touchy subject, and she resolved not to bring it up again. She wondered what the other *properties* were, though. Traveling between worlds was obviously one.

Gingerly, she put Kuvrema's tail down, then returned to Javeer, who lay stretched out with his own sphere glowing dimly at his shoulder. The light intensity increased as she drew near.

Marise plunked down cross-legged and looked at the sphere. It dimmed again, and the light from other spheres reflected off the surface—points of light, like she'd wanted for scrying at home. *Great Mother, that didn't go as I planned. I wonder if anyone's noticed I'm gone yet? Celeste will be waiting to hear about the scrying. How am I going to get back?*

She gazed into the sphere's center, wondering if she'd see anything this time—some other part of Moerden, perhaps—but all she saw was a deep orange glow, as though a fire burned in its core. Pulling herself away, she looked at Javeer. His eyes were closed.

She realized she was exhausted as well. It had been a few minutes after nine in the evening when she'd started scrying, but it was daylight here when she'd arrived—probably at least six hours earlier, so it would be early morning at home now. And she hadn't really slept. The thought of sinking into her comfortable bed to ease her bruised and aching body was bliss, but there was no soft bed in the cave. The floor was flat and unyielding. If she slept, it would be on rock.

"Javeer?" she whispered. The dragon's eye opened a crack. She crawled over against him and stretched out on the stone. Even that felt good for a moment. She reached for his sphere and brought it close. She visualized herself sleeping in bed, covered with blankets.

After a moment, an image of a dragon in the bed, covered with blankets, shot into her head. She chuckled and put a green and yellow striped stocking hat on the dragon. Another pause.

He didn't get it.

'Cold?' he asked. He looked as surprised as she was that they were talking.

Marise thought about it, then spoke slowly. "The ground is cold and hard. Not good for me for sleeping."

'I'm warm.'

She got an image of herself tucked into the shelter of his leg, as she had been in the desert. She wondered if she could sleep propped up like that. He shifted, making room for her to snuggle in. She backed into the crevice and leaned back, still holding the end of his flexible tail. His supple, warm skin supported her like a hammock. Breathing in that odd, bookish smell, she closed her eyes for a moment.

Marise directed her thoughts to the sphere again, holding it up in front of her face. "Nice!" She sighed. "Thanks!"

'Sleep. Safe.' His sphere glowed for a moment, then dimmed, leaving scant light in the cave.

Now that she was warm and comfortable, she let the sphere drop, one hand curled around it. She listened to the little waterfall's distant tinkle but noticed another sound, rhythmic and seemingly far off, like a mill wheel turning. It was a familiar sound, and she tried to remember where she'd heard it. Then she realized it was a dragon heart, beating steadily just a few feet away.

As she drifted off, she had the sensation of flying in the night sky, wheeling in the light of the full moon on the back of some great, powerful beast.

When Marise woke, she found that Javeer had gone.

Curled up on the sand, she tilted her head back to look around and winced as pain raced down her neck and back. Her legs felt leaden. Her muscles had stiffened and knotted while she slept.

She rolled slowly onto her back, stretching, pushing through the soreness. She rolled the other way and struggled to her knees.

Daylight filtered through the cave entrance. Two dragons stood drinking at the pool, but otherwise, the cave was empty. Groaning, she staggered to her feet and stood, holding her head between her hands. Pain surged through it, punctuated by five or six rushing heartbeats.

She took a cautious step forward. No one took any notice of her, so she shuffled toward the cave entrance. A sharp twinge in her left hip made her limp, but already movement was easier.

She arched her back as she walked, stretching muscles experimentally. A muscle cramped in her right calf, and she doubled over with a cry. She rubbed the leg till the pain faded and moved on.

Sunlit rock and distant cliffs came into view, framed in the wedge-shaped opening of the entrance tunnel. A moment later, she stepped onto a broad ledge high in the cliffs.

Vertical drops plunged down, while sheer rock faces climbed all around. A panoramic view of the desert floor to the left revealed a wide flat plain stretching for many miles until another line of mountains reared up. Ahead and to the right, a leg of the mountains jutted out into the plain.

Cliffs ascended in layers of multihued rock. Swatches of dusty reds, yellows, and browns contrasted with creamy pink, light gray, purple, and green. Rounded blocks of varying sizes lay stacked one atop another. Others were more finely textured with deep grooves where water might once have trickled.

Up here, you might not see a dragon until it was right beside you. She scanned the cliffs opposite her, looking for more ledges, when something out on the plain caught her eye.

Like the previous day, the sky was clear and blue from horizon to horizon, but in the distance, she saw a gauzy curtain of mist or smoke. She studied it for a moment, squinting, her eyes following its crooked course down the middle of the plain.

It's a big crack in the earth, giving off steam, or maybe smoke. She looked away and scanned the ledge for a way down. She stepped to the edge, but jumped back at the sight of a terrifying drop of hundreds of feet. With a groan, she flattened herself on her belly and stuck her head over the ledge, clenching her teeth against a wave of dizziness. It felt as though her body was turning to liquid, poised to flow over the edge and splatter on the slope below.

The cliff face plunged, vertical and rough. There was no way down. She retreated and stood, grateful to be on solid ground. Looking for a way up instead, she faced the cliff and found it equally unyielding. A few small piles of rubble hugged the rock wall. The only way off the ledge was to fly.

A dragon burst from below. Too late, she remembered Kuvrema's warning and lurched into motion, trying to gain the shelter of the tunnel. Her sore muscles responded much too slowly. She jerked to a halt as she found herself face to face with a second dragon.

She opened her mouth to scream, but the sound caught in her throat as she recognized Kuvrema. Out of the corner of her eye, Marise saw a third and smaller dragon draw near, carrying something in its wing claw. The object swept up and down with the motion of the wing, like a giant feather in the morning sunlight.

Javeer thumped on the ledge, folded his wings, and produced a branch laden with gleaming purple fruit. He held it up with a flourish. Her expression of alarm turned to one of relief and she stepped toward him, her mouth watering. He raised his claw, opened his mouth, and torched the branch with a hearty gust of flame.

Leaves shriveled and turned to dust. The fruit emitted a high whining sound, like a potato in a microwave. Dry twigs burned like matchsticks, while tendrils of smoke rose. First one, then another of the dangling fruit exploded, spraying sizzling juice and fruit pulp in all directions.

Something struck Marise in the forehead and she cried out, smacking a hand over the burn and ducking jets of hot liquid. Falling fruit landed beside her in wet, steamy plops. The smell of hot strawberry-rhubarb pie filled the air. A hissing seed shot straight into Javeer's down-turned nose, planting itself in the soft tissue at the back.

He squealed and dropped the branch, lumbered about, trampling what remained of the fruit. Dark pulp smeared the rock like blobs of paint, and juice ran toward the cave entrance in crimson rivulets. He shook his head violently, coughing flame and blowing fluid out of his nostrils.

Marise, on all fours in the middle of the ledge, looked up to see Kuvrema close her eyes briefly and cock her head at the other female, indicating the tunnel entrance. The two of them disappeared within while Javeer made horrible gurgling sounds, sneezed thunderously, and sneezed again.

Several pale seeds the size of almonds stuck to his cheek. One slid down to dangle from his chin as the sneezing and fluid dripping from his nose and eyes continued. Shiny purple goo oozed between his toes and streaked his verdigris belly. His lashing tail snaked over the rock ledge, spreading the pulp about like jam.

Marise knew she looked no better. She'd put a hand down by accident and then smeared the pulverized fruit, mixed with ash, across her face. Wiping a sticky hand on her jeans, she threw back her head and laughed, flopping full length on the ledge. Javeer drew a breath between sneezes and shuffled forward.

She guffawed, heedless of the mess she rolled in. Sore muscles everywhere protested. She clutched at her stomach, groaning between chuckles. She could not stop laughing. Tears streamed down, cutting a pale streak in the purple pulp from her right eye down into her ear.

Javeer bent over her, watching her convulse. He raised his head and howled.

Chapter
Five

LEARNING TO FLY

Marise straightened up. She hiccuped and giggled, putting sticky fingertips to her lips. Javeer towered on her left, his belly smeared with a camouflage pattern of purple and green. A glistening drop of liquid fell from his nose, splashing onto her collarbone.

A dragon emerged from the tunnel entrance and stopped short. Kuvrema slammed into her from behind. Marise thought they looked more like one dragon with two heads and giggled again.

Specks of dark fruit dotted her tank top, and purple stains spread through the fabric. Glistening patches on her dark jeans looked almost black, while most of the white rubber on her sneakers had turned a mottled plum.

Marise drew in a deep breath and pondered the fruity odor surrounding her. She watched the pair of female dragons sorting themselves out. They made low growling noises that sounded to her like mutters of disapproval. Javeer was silent and watching her.

She crawled to the end of his tail and picked it up. "I'm okay," she said, trying to look past the purple haze coating his sphere. Another hiccup rocked her, met with a surge of alarm from him. She directed her thoughts at all three dragons. "I'm okay." She giggled, rubbing her face with her free hand. "I was only laughing, and

I've got the hiccups. It's nothing. I'm fine." She looked up at Javeer. "What a mess."

Marise sensed relief rolling in from Kuvrema's direction, while Javeer radiated confusion. The sphere must work even covered with purple goo. She tried cleaning it by licking her fingertips and rubbing it, but this merely redistributed the fruit.

Javeer tugged his sphere out of her hands, but gingerly returned it. *'Don't.'*

"Don't what?"

'Don't do that.'

"This?" She rubbed at the fruit again.

He shuddered and yanked his tail away.

"Are you ticklish?" She reached for it, and he allowed her to pick it up.

'Don't do that!'

"Okay! You're ticklish! Is there any fruit left?" She put the sphere down and looked around.

Miraculously, one plump fruit lay intact near the edge, and she crept over to pick it up. Pleasantly warm in her hand, it oozed plum-colored liquid from a split down one side. She brushed it off and bit into it. Juice oozed between her fingers, dribbling down her arm, but she didn't care. Another bite. *Yes, like strawberries and rhubarb, but not as tart, and sort of flowery.* The center held a pair of glossy white seeds, which she tossed over the cliff's edge.

She turned back to the dragons. The females had gone. Javeer still nursed a runny nose, shaking his head and blowing as he kept one eye on her. She laid a hand on the side of his neck, pointing to the tunnel with her other hand as she led the way to the pool.

He dropped his sphere into the water, where it glowed more brightly as the current washed it clean. He dipped his head under, one wing claw gripping the rock. Shaking his head as he lifted it, he showered them both with droplets.

Marise rinsed off and wiped down his belly as best she could with wet hands. She fished his sphere out, careful not to tickle him, and perched on the lip of the pool. "You okay? Does your nose hurt?"

His nose dripped. *'Okay. You okay?'*

She received an image of herself lying on the ground holding her stomach, and a feeling of confusion.

"I'm not hurt! I was laughing! It was funny! Like crazy. I don't know—like this." She rubbed his sphere for a moment, and he shivered. She wasn't sure if dragons laughed, and she knew it was not a perfect explanation, but it would have to do. "Not hurt, right? Tickly."

'Okay.' He sounded tentative.

"You're hurt. I'm okay! It was nice of you to cook my breakfast." She giggled, touching the burn on her forehead carefully and wincing. "Fruit is okay raw. Right off the plant. You don't have to cook it." She imagined herself biting into a juicy ripe raw plum. "Cooked fruit is really hot. Dangerous!" She reached up to pat his nose. "Where did you get it? I didn't think anything grew around here."

'Fruit?' Javeer sent a picture of a plant growing up a vertical rock face. Horizontal branches clung to the rock, loaded with dark globes. The image expanded to reveal a lush green canyon with water flowing through it. *'Not in Honedrai. The river. Lots of fruit.'*

"That's beautiful. Wish I could go there. Maybe you can get more?"

'Go there.' He lowered his head and looked her directly in the eye. She saw a dragon flying with a person seated on its back, just in front of its outstretched wings. Rocky screes rolled past in the background.

She drew in a sharp breath. *'Ride a dragon? Oh no. No, no, no. Way up in the air like that? With nothing to hold on to? Not a chance.'* She had already been picked up twice, carried, flung to the ground, bruised and battered, frozen and scorched. She could hardly move; she was so sore. Riding through the sky on any dragon was out of the question. Marise wasn't deliberately directing her thoughts at Javeer, but he got the idea.

'*Easy to ride. Safer.*' Marise got another shot from the air, looking down at the rushing ground below. '*Not far up.*'

She remembered falling onto hard desert sand. She didn't want that to happen again. But she did want to go. It would be great to get out of this cave, go to the river to pick fruit, maybe even look for her sphere. *Ride a dragon? Is it really possible?*

She put his tail down and walked around to look at his back. He hitched up on his powerful legs as though he meant to take off, but this put his spine so far off the ground she couldn't see. She climbed onto the pool's edge and stood on her tiptoes, leaning against Javeer. She still couldn't see well, and what she could see didn't look good. There was no way she could sit on that ridged back. She climbed down, shaking her head.

Javeer looked dejected. He looked around the cave and walked toward the entrance, where a lone female crouched by the door.

Marise sighed and sat down, trying to rub the mulberry color off her sneakers with wet fingers. Her giggles had fled, and now she felt glum. How could she get out of this cave and go home?

Her thoughts were interrupted by his return with the other dragon—the female with a scar on her neck. That scar, which she now saw was actually a long strip of pale skin bereft of scales, throbbed inches from Marise's face as the older dragon looked menacingly down from above, her neck arched like a cobra. Marise drew back.

Silence. Then the female offered her tail. '*I am Eschla. Javeer wants you to ride.*'

"I can't. I'll fall. There's nowhere to sit, nothing to hold on to. It's not possible." She sounded sulky and stubborn.

'It is possible. You must accept it. Otherwise, you can't leave here. There's no way down, and it's dangerous to carry you—the ledge is too small. Kuvrema was right. She shouldn't have brought you here.' Eschla looked at Javeer, then back at Marise. *'You two will make it work. With any luck, he will be steady and not drop you. You will ride. Today.'*

Her words heightened Marise's feeling of being trapped, but it was clear the dragon meant every word. Marise continued to rub at a stained sneaker, pretending to think it over, but knew she was only delaying.

"How can I ride him?" Her tone remained stubborn.

'Javeer will return to the river and bring back waever.' Eschla made a derisory snorting sound and looked sideways at him. *'Can you manage that?'* She returned her attention to Marise. *'Waever is a vine that binds with itself. We'll use it to make something for you to hold on to. Then we'll talk about flying.'*

Eschla turned to Javeer. *'Go to the bend. Straight there and straight back. Let's not waste the day. Get two long stems. Long ones, long as you. Don't tangle them! Snap them off with your teeth and hold both at the cut end, letting them trail so they don't rub each other the wrong way. You know? Understand? Don't come back with a big useless knot.'*

Marise winced at Eschla's gruff tone, but Javeer didn't look bothered. He glanced at her as she reached up to pat the end of his nose with her free hand in an attempt to be encouraging. She winced again and rubbed the slippery liquid onto her hip. She waited until he left the cave before rinsing her hand in the pool. Turning back, she found Eschla glaring at her.

"Sorry. I've still got your tail."

'Why are you here?'

"What? Uh, it was an accident."

'You're here by accident, and it's also an accident that you can't go back?'

"Yes!" she paused. "I lost the sphere. I want to go back! I have to find the sphere I lost in the rocks on the slope. Kuvrema said we could look for it."

'Where did you get this relic sphere?'

"From my . . . my biology professor gave it to me. Well, he left it . . . to me. I thought it was a crystal ball." Her voice trailed off.

Eschla delivered another derisive snort, and Marise thought she glimpsed a tongue of flame lick the dragon's lip. *'No one who knew anything about that sphere would have left it in the hands of a child. Something isn't right. I've been out to the slides with Kuvrema this morning searching and stirring up the surface where you landed. We found no trace of it. It was careless to let go of it—it may never be found. So, whether you're here by accident or design, we must put up with you—since Kuvrema seems determined not to let Korpec deal with you.'*

"I didn't know! I didn't know what was happening. I didn't know it did that . . . don't even remember letting go of it. I want to go home." Tears welled up in her eyes.

'A pity. If you're telling the truth, you are no use to anyone. This is a colossal waste of time. I'll come back to help you with the waever vine when Javeer returns. I hope for your sake that Korpec doesn't arrive first. He'll be back, you know, and Kuvrema can't protect you every minute. Sooner or later, he'll get his chance.' She reclaimed her tail sphere and stalked away, leaving Marise in semidarkness.

She slumped with her back to the pool and rubbed at the tears tracking down her cheeks. "Why do all the dragons hate me except Javeer?" she wondered. *Why do they think I'm here for a reason, like I'm part of some plot? It's strange. It's like these dragons are used to talking to humans. They understand humans can use relic spheres. They believe humans can ride dragons. But Kuvrema said there are no humans in Moerden!*

Marise tipped her chin up and closed her eyes, hearing

Kuvrema's words again. *'Javeer has only spoken with dragons. Most animals in Moerden don't talk to dragons.'*

No. It was after that. She thought harder. *'Beings such as you cannot survive in Moerden. Dragons would kill you. You are in danger. . .'* That was it.

Her eyes popped open. *Kuvrema hadn't exactly said there were no humans in Moerden. What had she meant? There had been humans, but dragons had killed them all? Or there were humans in Moerden, but the dragons were at war with them. That might explain why Korpec wanted to kill her, but why did the females—especially Kuvrema—disagree?* While waiting for Javeer, she turned everything over again and again in her mind. The more she thought, the more certain she became that she wasn't the first human these dragons had seen.

Something blocked the light in the tunnel, and she leaned forward, watching the archway, poised to dash toward Eschla despite her unfriendly manner. She recognized Javeer's small frame as he crossed the space between them, trailing two thin leafless vines from a wing claw. He offered the cut ends to her, and she took them curiously. The dark brown stems felt soft, furry, and flexible in her hands, like the thick tail of some small animal.

Eschla joined them then, barking commands, and Marise soon found herself fashioning a bridle of sorts, alternating holding Eschla's sphere to get instructions and putting it down to free her hands. She kept glancing at the cave entrance, tensing whenever a dragon came in or went out, until Eschla snapped at her.

'Pay attention! Turn one piece around so they lie opposite to each other. Don't let them touch! Pull one back so it's overlapping along half its length. Now bring them together.'

The two vines clung to each other as though they'd been joined with super glue. *Like permanent Velcro.*

'Now, pass that end to Javeer. He'll pass it over his head, so it hangs down on both sides. Make the two sides even.'

'You need to keep going around with the free end there. Make a complete circle. Not too big! You're going to be hanging onto it. Not too tight either! Don't let it touch until you're ready.

'Javeer, hold it forward!'

Anxious to avoid the sharp edge of Eschla's tongue, she went around with the waever on the right, handing it to him and taking it back. She did the same with the other length, working in the opposite direction. When she finally ran out of vine, he had a furry necklace as thick as a broom handle, a bit uneven in places but otherwise neat and strong. She was convinced the waever stems, which fused the second they touched, would never part again, and she wondered why a plant would grow like that.

Eschla nudged her tail into Marise's hands once more. *'Sit on Javeer's back. The clefts between his ridge spikes are softer than they look. You just have to choose the right one. Hold the waever, and he will lift you.'*

Marise looked up at Javeer's back, then back at Eschla. Her stomach churned.

'Go on! Don't stand there looking terrified. Get up there. We can't babysit you in this cave forever. Do you want to be trapped here alone when Korpec comes back? He will. Soon.'

Marise swallowed. Looking desperately for a way to climb up, she put down Eschla's sphere and grasped the waever. His wing claw wrapped around her torso and lifted her off the ground. She squawked as she lost her grip on the vine, then scrambled for balance, looking down his long spine. Just as abruptly, she was wrenched off the other side and thumped to the ground. She staggered, waiting for her stomach to catch up to her.

Eschla poked with her sphere until she got the message and grabbed it.

'You have to face the other way. Your back to Javeer when you grasp the bridle and let Javeer lift! You don't face backward when you're

riding a dragon.' She swung her head toward the young dragon. *'Javeer, think! Get this right. One fall, even in the cave, will kill her.'*

Marise felt sick. Eschla's sharp words were met by a wave of misery from Javeer and a lump at the back of Marise's throat. She stubbornly swallowed it. No way was this cranky dragon going to make her cry again. She threw Eschla's sphere down and crossed to Javeer's left, turned from him, grasped the waever with her right hand, and jerked it. "Up!"

This time she was ready, and soon she was perched on his back, steadied by his wing claw and clinging to the waever, which had slid around as she came up.

She realized there was more room in the clefts between the spikes than there appeared, and she maneuvered into one of them. She hitched herself forward one spike and let her legs relax on his sides. He looked at her and let go.

Her muscles protested, but his back was surprisingly comfortable, if a little slippery. She found, if she hugged his body with her thighs, the edges of his scales gripped her jeans. The bridle in her hands felt comforting, but she wondered how long she could dangle from it if she slipped.

Javeer waited and Eschla, thankfully, kept quiet as well, standing off to one side. When Marise stopped shifting about, Eschla passed her tail sphere up. Marise took it, braced for another verbal battering.

'Well done.' Eschla's tone was grudging. *'But the hardest part is still to come. It's dangerous taking off from a high point. Focus on staying on Javeer's back!'*

Eschla twisted round as if to go, then turned back. When she spoke again, the harshness had gone from her voice. *'Be very careful until you get used to it. After a day or so, you'll think you were born on a dragon's back. Javeer needs his tail for balance while he is lifting off, but at other times, he can give you his sphere so you can talk. Javeer, stay near the ground and go gently. No crazy flying! The first thing,'* she looked directly at Marise, *'will be getting away safely.'*

Apparently, that was all the flight instruction they would get. Eschla departed, leaving Marise and Javeer to work it out. They looked at each other silently for a moment, then Javeer faced forward. He took a few tentative steps. Pausing, he scratched at something on the floor and ducked his head. When he raised it again, three plump purple fruit dangled from his jaws.

"Firefruit!" She hadn't noticed he had them when he'd returned from the river, but she was hungry and took the cluster. When she bit into one, the skin popped between her teeth and a sweet flowery scent hit the back of her nose. It was just as good raw as cooked, and considerably less messy. She ate two and offered the third to Javeer, who crushed it between his jaws and added a satisfied slurp.

His sphere landed in her lap. *'Go?'*

The question jolted Marise back to the prospect of leaping off a cliff on a dragon's back. "No! Uh, walk around a bit, okay?" Her voice trembled. "Slowly. No flying, I mean, don't fly yet. Okay? Don't just take off."

'Not till you say. We'll go down near the ground, then to the river.'

He circled the cave, giving Eschla a wide berth. By the time he came back to his starting point, Marise knew her sneakers had to go. They slipped against his scales and had no grip at all. He waited as she took her shoes off, tied the laces in a knot, and hung them around her neck without dismounting. Her bare feet braced her against the smooth surface, much better than unyielding rubber.

They did another lap. *'If you slide off . . . if you do, hang onto the waever. I'll land.'*

"Would you be able to catch me if I fell?"

'Maybe. Better to hold on. Go outside now? We can come back.'

"Okay." Her heartbeat thumped in her ears.

As they emerged on the ledge where pulped firefruit had dried to black varnish in the heat, Marise scanned their surroundings and thought it was a perfect time for Korpec to return.

Javeer must have caught her nervousness. *'I'll watch. If anyone comes, we'll go back inside.'*

She looked past the edge of the rock and felt her stomach lurch. A chill swept over her, draining the warmth of the morning sun. His sphere suddenly felt slick between her palms. She gripped it to steady her hands.

She couldn't do it.

I have to do it. I have to do it. I have to.

She remembered her father's account of the time he'd gone skydiving.

"Jumping out of that plane was the hardest thing I've ever done," he'd said. "I was terrified, hanging onto the edge of the door for dear life. They had to push me off the wing."

Now Marise knew what he meant. And she didn't have a parachute.

She fought for calm. She closed her eyes and focused, recalling the Wiccan meditation exercises she'd practiced with Celeste. Her friend's oval face hovered in her mind's eye, with serious blue-green eyes and freckles. Celeste, the cautious one. *I never listen to Celeste. Great Mother, I wish she was here. I wish I was there.*

Another memory surfaced. Celeste's voice chanted, "Perfect love—breathe in. Breathe out—perfect trust. Perfect love—breathe in." The meditation exercise they'd practiced before creating a sacred circle. It had quieted thoughts and helped them focus. Marise let the memory go and opened her eyes, looking down at Javeer's sphere, consciously relaxing her cramped fingers.

"A minute more," she said, her voice more confident. "Listen for my thoughts. When I say 'Now,' you go. I trust you. We're gonna do this. Okay?"

'Okay. I'll be careful.'

She gripped the waever with her right hand, cupping Javeer's sphere in her left. She closed her eyes and felt his spine beneath her, a gentle breeze combing the curls at the nape of her neck, warm sun on her forehead. Remembering her dream from the night before, she allowed herself to feel excited. It was about to come true—she would fly on a dragon's back.

She took in a breath through her nose, thinking *perfect love*, and let it out through her mouth, *perfect trust*. She focused on sunshine being drawn deep into her lungs, and fear flowing out, again and again. *Breathe in—perfect love. Breathe out—perfect trust.* She imagined floating weightless, looking down on the desert panorama. Her breathing slowed, and she focused on it.

"Now, Javeer."

The sphere lifted, and she automatically wrapped her free fingers around the bridle and opened her eyes. Muscles worked beneath her. Wings cocked, stirring the air.

The sense of peace she had summoned blanketed Javeer as well. He launched, spreading his wings as soon as he was well away from the cliff face.

She gasped as the desert opened beneath her. Gliding, they dropped toward the valley.

Chapter
Six

FORBIDDEN

Marise floated in the air, then her body caught up with Javeer's. The sensation made her heart pound and breath catch. Her eyes clenched shut for a few sickening seconds, then opened wide.

He made a smooth descent to the foothills and the plain beyond. When he leveled off, perhaps ten feet above the ground, he flew smoothly, the movement of his wings a lazy wave.

Marise felt the slow roll of his shoulders, the sinuous rise and fall of his spine. She crouched on his back, convinced the slightest movement would pitch her off. White hands pulled the bridle taut, as if she meant to strangle him. Her stomach lurched when she looked ahead, cartwheeled if she looked down.

His sphere came around and hovered in front of her. She stared at it, too paralyzed to take her hand off the waever. Pressing her knees against his scales, she slid her clammy fingers around the sphere without letting go.

'Okay?'

"Okay?" Her voice was a croak. "Nothing to it, huh?"

'Relax. You're like a boulder on my back. Don't pull on the waever! Float. Fly with me.'

"Oh. Sorry." She forced herself to slacken the bridle a little and then consciously relax her muscles, starting at her toes as she'd learned in meditation. She was dizzy and couldn't relax fully, but reached a stage where she thought she was moving with him and not clinging to him.

'Better. Going to the river.'

Javeer winged straight out into the plain. After a few minutes, he turned his head slightly. *'Marise, can you see behind us? I think someone is following.'*

"Look behind? Are you kidding? Turn around? Oh, I can't. I can't." She heard a shrill note in her voice and tried calming it. "You think someone's there? Korpec?"

'Maybe. It's better if you look back. If I look, I might tilt and dump you. Just hold on and look behind for a second.'

She turned her head to the right, felt a wave of dizziness, and looked forward. Trying again, she got the same result. She wasn't sure what was worse, the thought of twisting around and losing her balance, or the fear of meeting unfriendly eyes behind her.

"I can't do it. Maybe you could turn around. No, wait."

Still gripping the sphere so Javeer would know what she was doing, she raised her elbows, leaned forward, and peeked back under her left arm. The desert sped beneath them. Her eye was drawn to a commotion in the sand below—an indistinct shape darting off to the side and then disappearing in a puff of dusty air. Whatever it was, it either blended perfectly with the sand or hid below the surface.

She swallowed and forced herself to look.

The stone foothills had diminished to rolling sand dunes dotted with brushy sage green vegetation. The sand flashed with vibrant reds and yellows. Marise gripped with her knees and leaned farther to get a wider view.

She gasped in alarm.

Off to the left, yet close behind, a dark form sped across the sand. The pursuer continually changed shape and size, like an amoeba. As she watched in horror, it darted toward them, then retreated. She couldn't see it clearly, but it reminded her of a grotesque hunchback dragon.

"Javeer, there is something! It's close. Over there." She sent him an image of their hunter.

'Shadow,' he said calmly. *'That's our shadow.'*

"Oh Goddess." She sighed, then giggled and straightened. "You're right."

'Look for another one.'

"Oh." Marise took a deep breath and bent over again, putting one hand on the back of his neck. She searched for another shadow. She couldn't be sure. At times, she thought she saw something, but it winked out, only to reappear a moment later in a different place.

"I'm not sure. Wait till the ground levels out behind, and I'll look again."

The land was flatter. The scraggly bushes were spaced farther apart, most of them partially ringed by a groove in the sand. Javeer's shadow was solid and distinct.

Cautiously, she gazed far ahead for the first time, and saw the wide valley in both directions, bounded by craggy peaks. On the right, it closed in gradually; left, it grew steadily wider to a flat horizon. She thought the river must flow that way. She searched for the curtain of mist she had seen earlier, but there was no sign of it.

The earth below cracked open, and she stiffened with a yell. Suddenly, they were ten stories up, cruising over a canyon with a blue ribbon of water winding at the bottom. Javeer made a slow turn to the left and glided for a moment, taking a careful look behind.

'Korpec.'

With that single heart-stopping word and image, Javeer plunged. Marise cried out as he fell from beneath her, then pitched her forward before she could brace herself. The hand that grasped the bridle clutched a ridge spike. Her swinging sneakers nearly knocked it away again, and her other hand released the sphere to grab at them. Clenching thighs and knees against his hide, she struggled for balance as the dragon's long tail straightened out behind. Fighting an adrenaline rush and a stab of dizziness, she panted, her body shaking, her only thought to stay on his back.

Marise pitched to the left, screaming, as he cut a hurried circle and shot upriver. She hunched, holding the bridle close to his scales, and pulled tight against his neck. He accelerated, whipping around several turns in quick succession, hugging the right-hand canyon wall. With a series of gut-wrenching swoops, they descended toward the river.

Staring ahead with wide eyes, she tried ignoring the red blur of rock on both sides. Instead, she took in a carpet of color and movement on the canyon floor. A canopy of mottled green swayed like gently rolling waves, dotted with brilliant splotches of yellows and reds, purple, and white. The greenery rioted up the canyon walls, in some places climbing almost to the plain above. To Marise, those walls seemed to close in on them as they raced past.

Javeer dipped and sliced into a dense thicket, folding his wings against his body. They crashed in the understory.

Marise flew forward into a tangle of plant stems and slid down to land at his feet with a grunt. She scrambled up, panting, and saw him pull the canopy closed above them with his wing claws and teeth.

She sprawled on a carpet of dead leaves, sick with relief, and glimpsed the blue sky through gaps in the foliage. The air was alive with swarms of bright insects, glittering like crystals in the sunlight. A shadow dimmed the light for a moment, and she sucked in a breath and held it. They remained still for a long time before he cautiously raised an overhead leaf with his nose and looked up.

Marise crept to the edge of the thicket and peered out for her first good look at the canyon. She had never seen such a place.

Rising a hundred feet or more, the cliffs framed a broad flood plain lush with vegetation. The river wandered from side to side, wide and slow, then rapid and boulder strewn. Water gurgled between the rocks.

Plants rambled over rocks and riverbanks and climbed the canyon walls as though trying to escape. Some had leaves a yard wide, their fleshy expanse turned out to catch the sunlight. Vines trailed in the stream, and yellow, purple and white flowers blossomed everywhere, suspended in air or bobbing in clusters along the riverbank.

She breathed in warm humid air, finding it spicy and soothing. A patch of ground along the far shore caught her eye. Sand blanketed the vegetation there—flowers thoroughly grimy and leaves weighed down until it looked as if their stems might snap. As she watched, a big leaf tipped, dumping its load on the plants below, then bounced up, triggering a series of smaller landslides from leaves all around. She wondered where all that sand had come from. Everywhere else, the banks of the river were green.

Marise held out her hand for the sphere, hoping it was safe to talk. Unsure if Korpec could hear them, she spoke softly. "So beautiful! So green. All the flowers. Like a jungle. Why don't the dragons live here by the river? Where did you get the fruit, you know, the firefruit?" She chuckled, not waiting for an answer. "I want to put my feet in the river. I'm so dirty! Is it safe to go out?"

Javeer stuck his head out through the canopy. *'Yes. Korpec has gone, but watch! He might come back. Canyon grals—firefruit?—grow on the other bank. I'll find some.'* He pushed his way onto the beach. To her surprise, he splashed through the water rather than flying.

She watched him until he disappeared, then summoned enough courage to step out, eyes on the sky. She stayed close to the vegetation as she walked along the river, ready to dive for shelter. Korpec didn't appear, and the beautiful setting calmed her despite her worry.

Immersed in greenery, a universe away from civilization, she would hardly have been surprised if the Goddess or the Green Man himself stepped out of the shadows. She remembered a ritual she and Celeste had performed in the woods on the summer solstice. The wild glade they had chosen had been pale and bare compared to this.

Marise lifted her sneakers from around her neck and tossed them down as she luxuriated in the feel of sand between her toes. She rolled her jeans up and stepped into the clear water. It felt deliciously warm, and she splashed around, letting the sand and stones massage her feet, and poked at the shiny pebbles with her toes. She plucked a yellow blossom bigger than her hand and buried her face in it, breathing in a scent like chocolate and cinnamon. She set the flower adrift in the river like an offering.

Once more, she checked the sky, then stretched out on the bank and dunked her head in the river. She splashed water over her face, arms, and shoulders, and squeezed most of it out of her hair before sweeping her curls back off her face. Seeing movement out of the corner of her eye, she twisted around.

Javeer dropped a cluster of firefruit and added a pile of fuzzy brownish nuts that looked like kiwi fruit with a shell. He cracked one between his teeth and spat it out on the sand.

She looked doubtfully at the glistening mess. Gooey pulp, like undercooked egg white, oozed from inside a thin shattered casing. She rinsed a firefruit in the stream with one hand, holding the nut to her nose with the other.

Smells like . . . antiseptic ointment? Apple juice? I can't eat something that has dragon spit all over it, she thought. *Anyway, this doesn't look too good. But I don't want to offend him.* With sudden inspiration, she picked up the nuts and arranged them on a flat bed of pebbles. She wrapped a hand around Javeer's sphere.

"Can you flame them? Cook them?" Marise backed away. "But be careful. Stay back!"

He directed a jet of fire at the nuts, turning them a deep golden brown. One split with a snap, and a smell like roasting chicken wafted through the air. The cooked nut had a spongy cream-colored center. She leaned forward and easily removed it from its shell. It tasted remarkably like chicken but sweeter, with a rubbery texture.

Marise grinned at Javeer. "Moerden chestnuts!"

'Argar seed,' he said, and roasted a few more. Marise sat down to eat with her feet in the water.

Finally, Marise felt full. Her thoughts turned to the mysteries of the desert dragons. She reached out to touch his sphere. "Why don't dragons live here by the river? It's so beautiful, and there's lots to eat, and water."

'No caves. Desert dragons live in caves.'

"There are other rhumbas? Do you know what they're like?"

'I was hatched in Wyvern Wood, the ocean rhumba. I remember it's more like this. Coastal dragons use caves for shelter, and keep things there, but they live in the forest, near the mountains.'

"Really? You were born at the coast? Why are you here in the desert?"

'My parents are dead. I couldn't go back.'

Marise's breath caught in her throat as an image of what looked like a very large snarling wolf with blood dripping from its muzzle flashed by and faded.

"Wha—what was that?"

'Nothing.'

The image and the tone of his reply left her shaken.

When I get home, I'll bring him fruit and nuts, and a barbeque grill to cook me a steak. But first I have to find a way home. If I could just get back to the cliffs . . . the sphere must be there. Somewhere. But first I want to see more of this canyon.

She suggested a walk, using the river as a path since it was shallow and not choked with plants. She rinsed her hands and face again, and put her sneakers on, then they headed downstream, side by side. Javeer's tail draped around her shoulders like a shawl.

Conversation came more naturally. She hardly noticed his words came mixed with images, except when images took over.

She pulled a length of trailing plant festooned with white blossoms out of the water as they splashed past and tied it around Javeer's tail. She snapped off another piece for herself, yanking on the vine that snaked onto dry land. Something lurking in the undergrowth scuttled away through the greenery.

"Great Mother!" She jumped back, bumping into him. The vegetation shook in a straight line all the way back to the cliff wall.

'Bojert.' He looked down at the blossoms tied to his tail and ate the largest ones.

Marise laughed. She wasn't sure if the plant or the fleeing animal was the bojert, but she guessed it was the animal. "Is there anything you don't eat?"

'Bitterbush from the sands,' Javeer replied immediately. *'And cilirum.'*

"What is cilirum?" She suddenly felt as if she had a mouthful of sand, and she spit.

'Cilirum live in the sand. They eat sand. They are sand. Not good to eat.'

She saw an image of a hump of sand moving among the brush in the plain. The gritty feeling in her mouth faded. "I think I saw some on the way here! They were moving in the bushes. Do they bite?"

'In the bitterbush, yes. There are lots. They don't bite, they slime. It makes them slippery and the sand sticks to it, so they disappear. The females catch them sometimes and rub the slime onto wounds.'

"Yuck."

'No cilirum where you live?'

"No! No desert where I live. I live in a town. Cadogan Mills it's called. But it's in the forest, I guess. There's fields and woods all around." She concentrated on sending him pictures of Maritime Canada. Forested slopes of mixed hardwoods and evergreens, wooded trails, farmer's fields, lakes, and streets. *He must find it even stranger than I find the desert.* The thought saddened her.

They arrived at a bend in the canyon where the river turned rapid and rocky. It was harder to walk on the riverbed and plant growth on the shore was still dense and tangled.

"Javeer, let's fly back to the cliff rhumba and look for my sphere, okay? I want to go home. I'm sore and dirty. My parents don't know where I am. I need a shower and some sleep. In a bed! Can we go look for it?"

'Okay.' Javeer sounded reluctant. He hunched down in the water, though, and she grabbed the bridle to be lifted up. This time, it all went smoothly. He strolled upstream, while she took her sneakers off and hung them, dripping, around her neck.

He paused to harvest another cluster of Moerden chestnuts and a bunch of orange berries, which he passed up to her. He chose a spot where the river was wide enough to spread his wings and lifted almost straight up with a few powerful flaps.

They rose above the canyon rim and headed back toward the rhumba. Though she scanned the terrain carefully, she saw no other dragons on the plain.

Now, Marise saw the distant wall of the valley. Mountains stretched in endless peaks, cliffs, and screes, descending to the foothills like tiers of a many-layered wedding cake. Everything looked desolate and lifeless. She knew the caves of Honedrai were somewhere in that expanse of rock, but without the dragon, she'd never have found her way back.

Javeer hadn't given her his sphere, so she reached back and rapped on the ridge spike behind her back, hoping he'd take the hint. A few seconds passed before his tail dropped into her lap.

"Where's the rhumba?"

'Straight ahead. In the second layer of cliffs.'

Marise couldn't see any tunnel openings. She scanned the heights again, visualizing the cave entrance, and remembered that Kuvrema's cave opened sideways onto the ledge, facing an enormous outcropping of stone. It would be almost impossible to see until you were right on top of it.

"How many caves are there in the rhumba?"

'Many on this side of the valley. And the peaks beyond. Many dragons live here. There are four caves on the north face. Kuvrema's, where the older females live, the male cave, Korpec's, and another female one. Young dragons live in that one. And one where we keep things. Most caves are in the Sauria Valleys beyond the Face.'

Marise wondered what kind of *things* dragons might keep. *Treasure?* She smiled, thinking these dragons didn't seem the gold-and-jewel sort. *Relic spheres?* Even Korpec said there were no relics. But the mention of males made her think of other concerns.

"Why does Korpec want to kill me?"

He answered after a long pause. *'Korpec would kill me, too. He thinks we bring danger to the rhumba. I'm from another rhumba and not one of his bullies. I'm a threat. And he's always feuding with Kuvrema. Anything she wants, he hates.'*

"Then why does Kuvrema want us alive?"

'Kuvrema is different. She found me starving at the edge of the desert. She knew I would die. She brought me back to the rhumba and looked after me, protected me from the males.' Almost as an afterthought, Javeer added, *'Kuvrema's son died—about two years ago.'*

"How long have you been here?"

'Almost a year.' He veered right as they came near the scree, winging low nearer the bottom. *'This is where you appeared.'*

"Can you see the sphere?" She leaned forward to look down. "Do you remember exactly where it was?"

'*See that hollow in the rubble there?*' He dipped. '*It's probably above that.*' He turned away and circled, coming back in higher up.

There was no sign of the sphere among the stones. "Unless it rolled."

'*If it's lying in the open, it'll be ruined. Maybe it's buried. Maybe we can start a slide to see if that uncovers it.*' Javeer dropped and ran a claw through the scree.

Marise grabbed his crest as the jolt half unseated her. A mass of loose rock lurched downward, and she realized that this approach would likely bury anything lower down deeper in the rubble.

"This isn't going to work." She couldn't help sounding disappointed. "Why don't you just fly down toward the bottom so we can look for the sphere on the surface? Even if it's ruined, at least we'd know."

She was growing more convinced she was trapped in Moerden, maybe forever.

They spent the next fifteen minutes crisscrossing the slope. She found she was able to lean forward and look down if he flew up the slope or across it, but vertigo defeated her if she tried it while he flew down. Despite a careful search, neither saw any sign of the sphere.

At last, Marise gave up. The sphere was buried and only fate or luck would return it to her. She resolved to ask Kuvrema for advice.

Curious to learn more about the cliff rhumba, she asked Javeer to show her the other caves. He left the scree and climbed with obvious relief.

'*We're safer close to the rhumba. We won't go too near the male cave.*'

"Of course! And we'd better look out for Korpec."

Javeer flew along the second level of cliffs, pointing out cave entrances one after another. He circled close to both female caves, and she recognized Kuvrema's entrance by the smeared firefruit.

He dipped near the unoccupied cave. She dubbed it the storage locker. When they drew near the entrance to the male cave, which lay a long distance from the others, he merely pointed with his nose and circled back.

Marise wanted to see the Sauria Valleys, where Javeer had said there were more caves and dragons, but she could see they needed to be higher up to pass between the peaks. Plucking up her courage, she asked him if they could go.

He climbed well above the second level and glided close to the cliffs, which revealed the entrance to a fifth cave, concealed in the alleys and convolutions of the third level.

"Look, Javeer! Look! It's another cave, isn't it? Do you know about this one?"

'Kuvrema has shown me three. I found the fourth myself. I thought there were others.'

"Let's go explore it! Do you think the others know about it?"

'Sure. Honedrai has been here a long time. They've probably used this cave. Maybe they do now.'

"Can we go see?"

Javeer winged past, and she viewed the entrance from the air. A layer of fallen rubble cluttered the ledge, suggesting no one had landed there for some time. He came in gently, tucking his wings as he neared the cliff and landed. He kicked most of the rubble away, sending rocks rattling down the cliff face.

Marise peered down from her high perch, eyeing the edge of the platform uneasily. "Javeer? How do I get off? Jump?"

'Maybe I could lift you down? Or hold the waever and slide?'

She got an image of herself with one hand on the bridle and the other on the edge of his wing while she slid down, feet first. *That'd work. It's not that far.* But she was worried about going over the edge.

"Can you turn around? So, we're facing the rock?"

With her back to the precipice, she swung her right leg over and paused, looking down. She considered putting her sneakers on, but it would be awkward. The surface below looked smooth, so she dismissed the thought. She reached for Javeer's wing. He cocked it up and forward, and she wrapped her fingers around the bony ridge on the leading edge without letting go of the bridle. Taking a deep breath, she shoved off, letting her hand run along the wing, which tipped forward as she descended in a rush, sliding over the slippery scales. She landed in a heap and winced at the shock to her sore muscles.

In the cave entrance, there were only shadows, but somehow she was certain something watched them. She could feel it. She turned to look at the cliff faces, searching ledges and crevices. Javeer, too, shifted uneasily and lifted his head to the sky.

Trying to shake off the sensation, Marise turned to the entrance, thinking it would help to get out of sight. Inside, she still sensed another presence, and her skin broke out in goosebumps despite the heat. Javeer, meanwhile, hung back.

Bare feet made no sound on the layer of decaying vegetation that covered the floor. The passage ran off to the side, like Kuvrema's cave, opening into a space where darkness reigned.

Standing in the dim light of the tunnel, she scanned the shadows, looking for movement. *Was that something over there?*

There was a noise behind her, and she snapped her head around to see Javeer poking his head into the tunnel.

"Light," she called. "Light!" But then, remembered she wasn't holding his sphere. She beckoned, moving toward him. His large body blocked what little daylight there was. "Light," she said again, despite the futility. She reached for the waever.

They moved into the cavern together. As soon as there was room, Javeer brought his sphere up and set it aglow. The light was faint at first, growing brighter as they advanced. The sense of being watched faded, but Marise still looked over her shoulder every few seconds, seeing nothing but the outline of the tunnel. After about a dozen steps, they stopped.

The shadows around them stretched away. The floor was level and sandy, walls near the entrance worn smooth. Bones lay about, half buried in sand, along with piles of dry, dead vegetation. Her eyes were drawn to a large mound lying just at the edge of their light.

"What's that?" She pointed, and he lifted his tail higher.

The mound looked like a pile of dust and rocks, its gray features indistinct. Marise saw a ridge lined with deep web-like cracks. Here and there, something poked crookedly out of the mass. She ran her eyes back and forth over the ridge. The hair stood up on the back of her neck, and she sucked in a sharp breath.

"Dead dragon!"

Javeer uttered a shriek, turned tail, and bolted, leaving her in darkness with the corpse.

Yelling his name, she wheeled and followed, hurtling for the patch of light on the far wall. She tripped and fell, her outstretched hand closing on something cylindrical and smooth. She held it up in the dim light. A bone.

She screamed. The noise circled the cave and flooded back, seeming louder. Her mouth snapped shut. She threw the bone into the darkness and lurched to her feet, scrambling for distance between herself and the corpse. She hardly slowed when she gained the tunnel and dashed for daylight. Bursting onto the ledge, she threw herself against the cliff wall.

Javeer flashed past and plunged off the ledge with Korpec blazing flame in pursuit.

"Javeer!" she cried out. "Javeer!" Korpec turned and came at her, advancing with shocking speed.

Marise ducked into the shelter of the tunnel but hesitated, trapped between the terror in the darkness and the dragon who had sworn to kill her.

Korpec landed on the ledge, breathing fire.

She scrambled away, closer to the darkness within. Dimly, she heard herself sobbing.

He thrust his head down the tunnel but jerked back, growling, and snaking his neck around to the rear. His head scraped along the rock wall with a terrible grinding sound.

Marise caught a glimpse of Javeer's jaws clamped around Korpec's tail. Korpec reared up, flexed his tail like a whip, and flung the younger dragon off the ledge.

Javeer's wing struck the edge of the rock as he fell, his feet turned skyward. Korpec turned again with a snarl, advancing into the tunnel mouth and belching flame.

Marise rushed into the cave and dodged to the left, pressing herself against the wall where Korpec's blazing breath couldn't reach her, her own breath coming in gasps between whimpers of panic. Eyes searching the blackness in front of her, ears listening for his advancing footsteps, she waited. There was nowhere to hide.

The air and the stone at her back grew uncomfortably warm. Gusts of fire illuminated the cave to her right, revealing more bones, more piles of branches—but Korpec did not come.

Daylight filled the tunnel entrance again, and Korpec's bellow of rage receded like the whistle of a passing train.

Marise hugged herself, sobbing.

After a few moments, she stepped from the wall and dared to peek around the corner, shaking. A familiar dusty green snout and dark eyes peered in at her from the ledge.

"Javeer? Javeer." She knew he had no idea what she was saying, but she babbled on as she rushed out. "Oh, Javeer, you're okay! I thought you were dead at the bottom of the cliff. Great Mother! I can't believe . . ." She flung her arms around his neck.

Gradually, she became aware of another dragon sitting silently nearby. *Kuvrema.*

Javeer offered her his sphere. She freed one hand to take it, then the other to wipe tears from her face.

'This cave is forbidden. We shouldn't have gone in.'

She nodded.

'We have to leave. Now.'

"I know. I want to get away from here, but I'm shaking. I'm afraid I'll fall."

'You won't fall. We fly well together. I'll catch you if you fall, or Kuvrema will. We have to go. Quickly.'

"Okay. Okay, I'll try." She leaned on him, wrapping her hand around the bridle. She gripped it like a lifeline. As he lifted her onto his back, she clung with two hands, feeling sick, and trying not to think when he dropped off the edge.

Kuvrema flew ahead, close but higher, and Marise could see a pair of blue sneakers and a cluster of orange berries dangling from one wing claw.

Chapter
Seven

FLIGHT FROM
CLIFF RHUMBA

The only sound in the cave was the trickle of water. Even Javeer's sphere, cupped in Marise's hands, was silent. She looked toward the entrance, where Eschla hunched like an enormous vulture. The curve of her neck gleamed bloodred in the late afternoon light, and a flicker of flame around her lips hinted at suppressed rage.

Where's Korpec? Marise wondered. She started as two pairs of eyes gleamed from the far reaches of the cave, but when she stared at them, they blinked out. She brought her attention back to Kuvrema, just yards away.

Sitting cross-legged with her back against Javeer's shoulder, she sensed his misery. He had already recounted the day's events to Kuvrema, but now, as her silence dragged on, he spoke to Marise. *I left you in the cave. I panicked. Then Korpec was there. He might have killed you—if Kuvrema hadn't come just then, he would have. I'm sorry.*

She shuddered at the memory of being left in the dark with a dragon corpse, but the dreadful image of Korpec flinging him off the cliff lingered as well. She had believed him broken and dead.

"Well," she said, stiffening, startled by the sound of her own voice, "if we'd come running out of the cave together, we might both be dead."

'I'd have fought him.'

'It may be my fault,' Kuvrema interrupted, breaking her silence at last. 'I never told you about the cave, Javeer. We don't speak of it, but I should have known you'd discover it.' Her tone grew sharper. 'But you were poking around the rhumba when you were supposed to be at the river!'

Kuvrema's glance fell on Marise and lingered. She thought if a dragon could frown, Kuvrema would be frowning now. Marise's chin came up, and she directed her thoughts to the adult dragon. 'It's not my fault. I didn't know.'

The dragon's disapproving look lingered. 'Now we're in trouble, and we must decide what to do . . . I must decide what to do.'

Marise had had enough of mystery, silence, and danger. Something strange was going on. Something dangerous. She wanted answers. She gripped Javeer's sphere tighter with her cold fingers, fighting her uneasiness. "Why are we in trouble?" she demanded. "What have we done, exactly?" She feared the answer—wasn't sure she was ready for it.

Kuvrema looked steadily at Javeer, whose mind remained curiously blank. Marise wondered if they were deliberately blocking her out or if they had simply forgotten her.

"How did Korpec know we were there? How did you, Kuvrema?" she persisted. "Was someone following us?"

'Kuvrema and Korpec have both been keeping track of us,' Javeer responded. 'They heard when I pushed rocks off the ledge and guessed where we were. Both checked the cave with spheresight and discovered us.'

"What's spheresight?" Marise felt the trap closing. Dragons watching her every move. Dragons waiting to attack her. Dragons wanting to kill her. And no way home.

'You can see what's happening somewhere else by looking into the sphere and thinking about that place. I don't really look into mine. I just think about the place. I look through the sphere in my head, sort of.'

"Is Korpec watching us now? Does he hear what we're saying?" She took a deep breath. "Can I do that, too? Can we see what Korpec's doing now?"

This time, Kuvrema answered. *'No. If you look while I'm using spheresight, you see what I see. We cannot watch dragons, only places. If we concentrate on the male cave and he is in there, we can see that, but we can't watch him if we don't know where he is. And if we watch for more than a moment, he'll know. It's rude to watch!'* Kuvrema's tone turned softer. *'For you, if you used a relic sphere, you could see places you've been. But I think, if you hold the sphere while you're looking, it will take you there.'*

Of course. Yes. That's exactly how I ended up here—except I wasn't imagining anything, just looking for images in the sphere. I probably could have ended up in outer space. Maybe I am in outer space! Despite the tension, she chuckled.

'Javeer,' Kuvrema said, *'Have you told Marise how you came to Honedrai?'*

'Only that I was born at the coast, and you found me.'

'I think it would help to show her what happened.'

He stiffened, pulling his head back.

Marise felt his mind empty abruptly. Holding the sphere was like listening to a disconnected telephone line now. She gave Kuvrema an anxious look.

'Javeer, you're not the only one upset by these events.'

"Right," Marise said. Her voice had lost its defiant edge, sounding thin and wobbly.

'Marise has endured a lot, and her own family is lost to her. She's been strong. You haven't been easy on her—not that you meant it. She needs to understand the rhumba better. The dragon in the cave died from the same thing that killed your father—the stagger, not jeong. Can you think of a better way to explain?'

There was a flicker of something from Javeer, then nothing. He shifted back and forth on his feet. After a moment, his eyes closed. Gradually, an image began forming in the emptiness, one that felt flat and controlled at first.

I wonder if dragons can lie. Then his memories rolled over her. She stumbled through the woods at sunset, frightened and confused. She wandered into a grassy hillside meadow. Pressing anxiously against his father's warm hide, she peered out from under his father's wing. Danger stalked them. Invisible. Deadly. Close. Very close.

Horror gripped her as the older male slipped in and out of rational thought. She felt desperate to get away, but he was oblivious.

She was helpless as a pack of monstrous wolf-like creatures emerged from the trees. Marise stared at their massive shoulders and broad heads, white fangs, and hungry eyes, gleaming in the last rays of sunset. Panting, she smelled their musky, wild odor.

She braced for the attack. Everything blurred to blood and teeth and swarming red fur. Her heart raced; breath quickened. She stifled a shriek, flew up from his father's corpse, and felt the jarring impact of his sphere smashing the skull of a jeong. She fled to safety high in the trees, and time stopped.

Marise fought to separate herself from the memory, eyes focusing slowly on the cave again. She raised her head to look at Javeer, beads of sweat on her face. Javeer was silent.

Kuvrema's somber voice filled the void. *Javeer's father had the stagger—a sickness that kills every dragon who gets it. Every one. It is horrible. Dragons lose their minds, become confused, and stop looking after themselves. They wander away and get lost in the forests, in the desert. Some die that way. Others stop eating and waste away, stumbling about, turning in circles. Their legs are useless. They drag themselves with their wings.* Her tone changed, and her next words were laced with horror. *'They lose control of their spheres!'*

A chill swept over Marise. Her eyes darted around the cave, to the other dragons lurking in secluded shadow. "The dragon in the cave?" she asked, though she knew the answer.

'Half the dragons at Wyvern Wood have died. Desert dragons are luckier. We don't get it here—only if we go to the coast. But he was from there. He wandered out of the forest and was floundering in the bitterbush, half starved. Didn't know his own name.' Kuvrema bowed her head. *'My son Jigmae found him. We got him into that cave, and at first, he had moments—flashes of clarity—but they came further and further apart. We brought him food and water, but he blundered around in there until one day he lay down and died. Everyone was terrified he had brought the stagger to the desert.'*

"So, you left him there." Marise shook her head. *They should have put him out of his misery and flamed the whole cave.* "Now I've been in there, breathed the dust, touched stuff." Looking at her palms as though the infection might be visible, she wondered how long she had before she'd be mindlessly dragging herself around, perhaps in the same dark cave.

'Once he was in the cave, no one would go near him, and they still don't. No one ever goes there. Ever. Now Korpec and other males spend their time patrolling toward the coast, making sure no others get close.'

"And that's really why Korpec hates Javeer. Because he came from the coast, and he might have it too?"

And because, well, mostly because of the stagger. But Javeer doesn't have it.

"And why does Korpec hate me? He thinks I have it?"

'Some believe humans brought the stagger to Moerden. Korpec fears you have brought it to the desert, yes. And the fact Javeer has befriended you makes him more suspicious. It makes no sense, of course.'

So, I'm not the first human to visit Moerden. She wanted to know more about that but decided not to ask just yet. "What do you believe, Kuvrema?"

'I don't think humans or dragons spread the stagger. Javeer was

with his father for a long time while the disease took hold. His mother was already dead, and Javeer doesn't have it. No one got it here after the sick dragon arrived. It only seems to spread at the coast, and only half the coastal dragons have died. But it does spread, and it spreads even when humans aren't around. I don't think it's easy to catch. I don't believe you bring the stagger. But I wonder if you might be able to help. Maybe you came to us for a reason.'

"What? I can't help! I don't know anything about this. I'm just a kid. Like Javeer. I don't know anything. This is just a big accident." She folded her arms, pressing his sphere against her ribs. *So maybe I don't have it. Maybe you can't get it in the cave.*

"No way am I getting mixed up in this," she said. "I'm not having anything to do with dying dragons."

Kuvrema nodded. *'Possibly. But you've been in the cave with the mummy, and now I think Korpec will pursue you until you are gone— or dead.'* We have to get you out of here. Both of you. Soon.

'First, we need food. The males will not bring noubria tonight. Because of Korpec, they will not come here. We must hunt for ourselves. And we'll do something about that sun.' She gestured at Marise with her wing claw.

She looked down and noticed her shoulders and arms were flushed and hot. Her face felt hot, too. Pulling back the edge of her tank top, she gasped at the stark division between scarlet and white skin. She wondered what Kuvrema had in mind, but the henne had already moved to Eschla.

Javeer lifted his head off the sand and got to his feet, forcing Marise to sit up. She heard *'I'll be back'* before he pulled his sphere out of her hands. He strode across the cave and out through the tunnel. No one moved to stop him. Kuvrema and Eschla exited as well, leaving Marise sitting in the dark. Two or three other females clustered in a dim sphere of light, as far from Marise as they could be.

Moments later, Javeer returned. He dropped a bundle, and

Marise recognized her green cloak, left in the foothills since yesterday. It felt like years since she'd torn it off over her head. She shook it, feeling sand rain down on her toes. She nodded her thanks to him. *Yes. The cloak is thin. I can wear it to keep the sun off.*

Javeer passed her his sphere and the berries he had gathered in the canyon. He popped the chestnuts, which they shared in silence.

Eschla returned next, clutching something in her wing claw. It looked like a giant rolled tongue, fleshy and rough. A frothy white liquid dribbled from one end like spit.

"*Ugh*. What's that?" she asked Javeer in a whisper.

'Cilirum.'

"Cilirum? I thought you said you didn't eat them." She watched Eschla cross to the waterfall.

She dropped the cilirum into the pool, and water splashed over the rim as the creature tried escaping. She flicked it back into the water a few times, then reached in and extracted it. Again, it rolled itself up. It was shiny now, the color of dried blood. Eschla turned and advanced upon Marise.

'Take the garment off.'

"*Ohhh*, no." Marise remembered now. Javeer had said they used cilirum to treat wounds. "Oh. No, no. You're not touching me with that thing." She clutched his sphere as though it could shield her.

Eschla thrust her nose close to Marise's face. *'Take off the garment or I will tear it off.'* A drop of cool white liquid landed on Marise's toe, and she jerked her feet away.

"Gross! That's disgusting. Javeer!"

He snorted. *'It will help.'*

"Oh, my gaw—Goddess!" She glared at Eschla, who glared back, holding the pulsating cilirum as though she might hurl it at her.

"*Mmm.*" Marise jittered, shifting her feet. Then in a rush she dropped his sphere, pulled her tank top over her head and faced

Eschla, naked to the waist except for her lacy black bra. Self-consciousness filled her, and she looked to see if anyone was watching, but her attention quickly returned to the drooling tongue approaching from above.

She jumped and gritted her teeth as Eschla plunked the slimy cilirum onto her shoulder. It spread out to the size of a dinner plate but fleshy and pliable, thick in the middle. It felt smooth and cooled her sunburn.

Clingy. Like being in mud. She groaned as muscles rippled inside the mud pie, and it moved.

The cilirum kneaded her shoulder and collarbone as it tried crawling away. It adhered so tightly she thought it would suck her skin off. Rippling edges fingered her hairline, and it crept into her armpit, but Eschla kept her grip on the beast, pushing it methodically over the sunburn—front, back, and down Marise's arms. Everywhere, it left a glossy film. An odor reminiscent of paint thinner wafted up. Then it started up her throat and enveloped her chin. She longed to pull away, but she clenched her jaw, held her breath, and kept still.

Undulating muscles explored her lips and nostrils, nibbled at her ear, and plucked at her eyelashes. It felt like her eyelids were first glued shut and then stretched like elastic. Her cheeks pulled away from her teeth, and her eyebrows seemed to be traveling up her forehead toward her hairline. She imagined herself with a face distorted and bulging in every direction, pulled and plumped and rearranged. She could not breathe, but she held still.

Finally, a corner of her mouth slipped free and Marise sucked in a deep breath, pungent with that odd chemical smell. It sped like menthol down her throat and into her lungs. Suddenly, she felt wide awake, tingling with life. *Wow. That actually feels nice, like a cucumber facial and a massage all at once.*

Eschla peeled the cilirum away. It let go of her forehead with a soft smooching noise. The dry sting of the sunburn had faded, and when Marise worked her facial muscles, she was pleased to find everything seemed to be in the right place.

Eschla finished off the tops of Marise's feet and left with the cilirum curled in her claw.

Marise marveled at how good she felt. She looked toward the cave entrance and picked up Javeer's sphere. "Will she let it go?"

'She'll take it back to the bitterbush.'

"That was gross. Gross! But it felt so good. Even my sore muscles and bruises feel better." She flexed her shoulders and stretched her arms, regretful Eschla hadn't cilirummed her entire body.

Her skin had dried already, so she put her tank top back on, and soon Kuvrema came in with one of the goat-like animals, which Marise assumed was a noubria. A large quantity of Moerden chestnuts dangled from her other claw.

After they had eaten, Kuvrema sat and told them what had been decided. They must leave the rhumba before dawn and not return.

'Get some rest now so you won't have to sleep outside tonight. But go well before daybreak. I don't want Korpec to know which direction you've gone, though I think once you leave, he'll go back to patrolling and hunting and not look for you. Go northeast, away from the coast, and head for the source of the river. You'll find caves there. I'll look for you in a day or two. Eschla and I will watch tonight. Now sleep.'

Overcome with apprehension, Marise pressed against Javeer's side and clung to his sphere. "We're banished. What will we do?"

Kuvrema woke Marise and Javeer long before the sun climbed past the eastern peaks. Marise sat up and stretched her stiff limbs. She visited the pool to drink and splash cold water on her face.

It was warm in the cave, but she knew it would be chilly outside. She slipped her green cloak over her shoulders and drew the hood up around her face. Then she slung her sneakers around her neck and put the bridle over his lowered head.

On the ledge, they paused for a minute as Kuvrema and Javeer said goodbye. Their scales made a clicking sound as they brushed against each other.

Kuvrema's last words were so soft Marise barely heard them. *'You'll be okay on your own, Javeer. You're old enough. Follow the river. Watch the skies and stay out of sight. I'll come to find you in the caves at the head of the river.'*

At last, Javeer hoisted Marise up, and they were off. The full moon set, casting little light. Marise hoped her dark cloak and his greenish scales would make them almost invisible against the dark plain below. Honedrai quickly fell behind.

Marise knew her chances of finding the sphere and getting home were more remote now than ever, and they were going somewhere where it would be just her and Javeer, a desert away from where her sphere lay buried.

"How far is it to the head of the river?" Marise asked.

'I don't know. Cliff rhumba dragons don't go in this direction. I thought there wasn't really anything up here.'

He flew about a hundred feet up, a comfortable altitude for Marise now that she'd grown more confident on his shoulders. The chilly air, stirred by the steady beat of Javeer's wings, poked its way inside her cloak, but Marise didn't really mind. He felt warm beneath her, and despite their situation, it was exhilarating to be flying under the fading stars, watching the mountains emerge in the sky.

As the sun cleared the horizon, she saw foothills and peaks stretching on until they dwindled in the distance. She spotted the crooked line of the river ahead, a curtain of morning mist rising from its warm waters. Soon, Javeer flew over the lip and dropped into the misty depths.

The air was cold on the riverbank where the sun's warmth

hadn't yet penetrated, so Marise stayed on his back as he strolled through the plant growth, breaking off branches laden with fruit. At a bend where the river formed a deeper pool, he scratched with one foot and plucked up something that looked like a small loaf of sourdough bread. He ate it, then he scraped another out of the gravel. He grabbed it with his wing claw, and the loaf dripped as he rose into the sunlight and headed north.

They picnicked on a sunny slope, where they had a good view of the southwest. The sourdough beast was a shiny brown creature with a series of spiral grooves, like adjacent galaxies, across its upper surface. Marise decided it was Moerden's version of a giant clam but lacking a shell. Javeer called it an *houra* and said there were many of them in the canyon river pools.

He obligingly roasted it when Marise impaled it on a forked stick, and he even tried a bit of the cooked meat. She thought it tasted more like peppery walnuts than clams. It didn't go well with fruit, but she ate it anyway.

They set off again, hurrying northeast. The sun was higher in the sky now, driving the temperature up mercilessly. Even the breeze from his wings felt sullen and heavy. Her legs stuck to his hide, and she rubbed the perspiration off her face with the hood of her cape. Droplets of sweat tickled down her spine. Still, the river zigzagged across the desert.

The sun shone directly overhead before Javeer announced he heard the roar of a waterfall. Soon, she heard it too.

He followed the river upstream. The canyon veered north and eventually cut between vertical walls that towered high above the plain. Beyond a narrow passage, cliffs curved away, creating an enormous chimney. Clouds of swirling vapor rose within it like steam from a kettle, dissipating high above in dry desert sunlight. As Javeer drifted through the haze, cool beads of moisture formed on scales, skin, and clothing.

He flew straight ahead, then circled left, passing across the face of a thundering waterfall that plunged to the base of the chimney. In the center, the mist was thick and the air itself seemed liquid. Marise tipped her face up and closed her eyes, welcoming the moisture.

Javeer climbed above the fog, and when Marise opened her eyes again and looked down, she gasped with delight. He had turned his back to the falls and a shimmering rainbow hung in the passage. The perfect circle seemed solid enough to touch. She imagined what it would have looked like when she and Javeer flew in through its eye just moments before.

Marise looked away from the spectacle to search for somewhere they could set down. To her right, plants clung to the rock face and tumbled over the edge of a narrow shelf below. Flourishing in the humid air, some reached proportions that dwarfed even the lush growth of the canyon.

As they winged around full circle, Marise could no longer see the rainbow, but she imagined herself floating above it. The mist thinned, and she spotted a wide ledge to the right of the main falls. A smaller chute had carved out a large pool there with a sloping pebble beach. Water plunged down from above and then raced over the pool's rocky brim to rejoin the river.

Above the beach, a tangle of vegetation as dense as that on the far side of the chimney defied their passage, but there was ample space to land by the water. He settled, and she slid off, hardly noticing the sting of the stones' sharp edges when her feet hit the ground. She threw off her cloak and dangling sneakers and stretched, crossing her arms above her head. The air smelled earthy and green. It felt wonderful in her parched throat.

Javeer drank at the water's edge, and she went to stand beside him and picked up his sphere. Water lapped at her toes but roared and roiled by the cliff where it slapped the rocks and spilled over them. The pool looked deep and tempting.

"Do you think anything lives in there?"

'I don't think so. Couldn't be anything big. What would it eat?' He dunked his head, then shook the water off.

She walked into the pool until it covered her feet. The water felt pleasantly cool. She eyed farther out. In constant motion, the water itself looked alive. "You really think there's nothing in here?"

Javeer walked in beside her and felt about with his feet. He went deeper, stuck his head under, and looked around. *'Nothing. Just rocks.'* His voice sounded the same even when his head was underwater.

Marise let go of his sphere, walked back to shore, and stripped down to her underwear. She looked at Javeer, who had also retreated, and took her jeans and tank top down to the water to wash them. She rubbed her jeans vigorously over the pebbles, then tossed her clothes back on the beach.

Javeer had climbed the slope and was grazing on vegetation, paying no attention to her. She gazed at the dark water, thinking how sticky she felt. She waded up to her knees and plunged in.

Water rolled against her skin, rinsing away sand and sweat, dried blood, and cilirum slime. Tentatively, she put her feet down and found a fine, gravelly bottom. She sat where the water was deep enough to wash over her shoulders and tilted her head back. "*Ahhh,*" she breathed, letting her arms float below the surface.

A shrill cry drifted down, and she thought for a moment they'd been followed, but the only thing moving was a trio of birds wheeling above her. They dipped and swept past, flashes of yellow and green. With a fading shriek, they were gone.

Marise ran her hands over her arms and legs to remove any remaining grime. There was no sting of sunburn. There wasn't even much of a tan left. She marveled at that, but the pool felt too inviting to think about it for long.

Lounging in the shallows, she rinsed her hair and washed her face. She swished at the surface with her feet and threw handfuls of pebbles, watching them splash and sink. Then she pushed forward and dove into deeper water, opening her eyes to look around.

As she neared the falls, she saw the pebbly bottom change to smooth rock and plunge into green darkness. Recalling her fears something might live deep in the pool, she turned to rise.

Something cold and slippery brushed her leg.

Marise yelped, sending bubbles to the surface. She twisted around to look, but there was only shifting gloom. She kicked away from the cliff and emerged near the curtain of water.

When she turned toward the beach, she didn't find it where she expected. She was moving with the current, and its relentless pull grew stronger with each passing second, carrying her toward the edge. Wet rocks and white foam sped past as the beach receded and the roar of the main falls swelled. She spun and opened her mouth in terror.

Just yards away, water plunged over the cliff and plummeted into the canyon. In seconds, Marise would go with it.

Chapter
Eight

BEYOND THE FALLS

"Javeer!" Marise cried. She saw him at the top of the beach, fanning himself with half-folded wings, but knew he wouldn't hear her over the roar of the falls. The current swept her past rocks, and she reached out, flailing for a handhold. "Javeeeeeer!"

"Javeer. Javeer! Help me."

She saw him glance in her direction, stiffening as he took in the scene. His wings spread, and he launched.

Marise clung to a rock for a moment, but its slippery surface was impossible to grip. The water's unrelenting pull loosened her hold and dragged her away.

She bumped along, scraping past half-submerged boulders. They slipped out of her grasp one by one. She gasped for breath as the falling water pushed her down. Screams turned to swirling bubbles.

One outstretched hand found a jagged stone and locked around it. She pulled herself up for a quick breath, but the torrent hammered from above. The current seized her again.

She pushed her feet down. Nothing. She reached blindly for anything solid but found only water. Another shriek was cut off as she went under a second time, and the undertow sucked her down and away from the rocks. She felt herself spinning, rushing for the cliff edge, for the long fall on the other side. Helpless, she went limp, oddly detached as she waited for gravity to take her.

Something pushed her back to the surface, back toward the smaller falls. She sucked in a lungful of air and opened her eyes, spluttering and coughing.

Javeer hovered, holding place with steady wing strokes. He thrust his head under and gave her a hefty push with his nose, tossing her toward the rocks.

Gasping at the impact, she clawed at the exposed rock as he shot backward. He came back once more, giving Marise another push, this time heaving her out of the pool and straight through the curtain of the side chute.

She put her hands out, bracing for a collision with the cliff wall, but instead she slid across a rock shelf. She struggled to her knees, wincing at the sting of new grazes, and twisted around.

Javeer, visible through a break in the curtain of water, tilted, too close to the river. One wing sliced the surface, and the current spun him around and dragged him down. A second later, he disappeared.

"Javeer. No!"

She reached out as though she could pull him back. Then she remembered seeing Korpec toss Javeer from the ledge outside of the cave. He had been fine.

That won't hurt him. He's a good flier. He'll be back any moment. She waited, perched behind her curtain like a mermaid spying on dry land, biting her lip. The seconds stretched into minutes.

"Come on," Marise said, chewing her fingertips. "Come on!" She strained forward, focusing beyond the edge, searching for a dragon shape in the curls and eddies of mist.

"Come on, Javeer."

Something approached, gliding through the haze, but it was the flock of yellow and green birds she'd seen earlier. They wheeled and plunged close to the falls, shrieking and hissing.

Marise slumped, but eyed the shifting curtain, the ever-changing swirls of vapor beyond, the play of sunbeams glancing through misty air. She wondered if the rainbow had gone or was just invisible from where she now sat. As minutes passed, her thoughts wandered skittishly around the possibility that he wasn't coming back. A lump formed in her throat.

He should be back by now. The fall killed him. Or he can't fly.

She imagined him floundering at the base of the falls, broken, drowning. *What'll I do? I'm trapped here. No sphere, no clothes, no food, and no way home. I can't even get off this ledge.* She smeared a tear into the beaded water on her cheek.

"Okay, Cerridwyn," she said, invoking one of her favorite Goddesses. She thought Cerridwyn would like this wild and natural place. "The rule of three has played out. What you send out comes back times three. Was it really *so* bad to take the sphere?"

Her voice grew louder. "I'm sorry, okay? I need some guidance here, some help. I need to go home." At the end, she was shouting, but her words merely faded into the roar of the falls.

An ugly thought crept into her mind, the beginnings of a plan both welcome and dreadful. She felt terribly guilty, but at the same time, practical. She whispered "Javeer." *If he's dead . . . but maybe he's just injured and needs help. But if he's dead . . . if he's dead, there's a sphere. I can't help it if he's dead! I could use his sphere. Even if he's only hurt, I should try to get down there.*

She wondered if it would actually be fatal to go over the falls and decided if it had killed Javeer, it would kill her, too. She'd have to find another way down.

Swimming back to the beach was impossible. She turned and looked behind her. The rock curved away, revealing a turbulent hidden pool behind the falls and a funnel-shaped opening in the cliff face.

"Is that a cave?" She climbed to her feet.

After only a few steps, Marise saw it was a cave, or at least a tunnel, and it connected with another space beyond. She continued forward and found herself standing behind the main falls.

She turned away and gasped with surprise. The falls concealed a cavern easily the size of Kuvrema's cave at Honedrai. Though shadows gathered in its far reaches, the center glowed with sunlight that plunged down through a natural chimney. Where the column of light hit, it illuminated a mosaic of colored rock set into a floor of square red brick.

"What's this?" She studied a strangely familiar pattern laid out in thousands of small flat pieces of desert rock—reds, ochers, and browns. Darker shades were concentrated at the center, fading gradually to yellows at the periphery.

A series of glossy black curves divided the mosaic: three ovals arranged in a triangular shape with a circle at the outer edge woven through their tips. Surrounding it all, a wide band of smooth rock carved with pairs of back-to-back, serpentine dragons marked the edges of both mosaic and sunlight.

Trying to remember where she'd seen the pattern before, she looked about for clues. Light reflecting off the mosaic illuminated much of the cave, but to the right, a dim light filtered around a corner, as though another tunnel led to the open air. She scanned the cave, saw nothing, and started up the second tunnel. As she rounded the first bend, she came upon a small spring bubbling from a cleft near the ceiling and running along a trough in the floor until it disappeared through a hole. Beyond the hole, Marise saw two cardboard boxes and what looked like a pile of clothes.

She hurried over and peered down at the collection of items— two boxes and a small backpack. They seemed so out of place she reached out to touch the nearest box to be sure it was real, then picked up the backpack.

The bag was a small one for hiking or schoolbooks. Its dull

shade of brown blended with the rock, but strips of diagonal reflective trim flashed as she turned it in her hands. She pulled open the drawstring at the top and turned it upside down, dumping the contents. A dozen small empty glass jars with white lids clattered to the brick along with a marker, a tangle of latex surgical gloves, a small pair of scissors, a black cylinder that looked like a pocket flashlight, and a bundle of folded white fabric.

She stared at the cloth for a long moment before picking it up and slowly turning it over in her hands. She held it at arm's length, giving it a shake. It was a clean white lab coat, and before she found the breast pocket, she knew what she would see there neatly printed in black marker: EARL BONNER.

Of course. He came here. That's why the second sphere was gone. He's here somewhere. He has a sphere, and all I have to do is find him.

"Goddess! I'm naked, and Bonner might come around the corner at any moment! What am I doing?"

She hastily donned the lab coat, which fell to her ankles. As she fumbled with the buttons, she heard an immense splash from the direction of the waterfall.

Unsure whether to run from the sound or toward it, she froze. She had only seconds if someone, or something, was approaching. Marise flattened against the wall of the tunnel, where she would not immediately be seen. She inched up the slope, her gaze turned in the other direction, her heartbeat loud in her ears.

A breeze swept past, smelling of wet rock and water weeds. She heard heavy footsteps and held her breath, flattening herself against the rock behind her.

A lumpy shadow expanded on the tunnel floor.

Javeer's head appeared around the corner, followed by the rest of him. He looked at Marise and shook like a dog, spraying her liberally, then handed her his sphere. She gaped at him.

Her delight at seeing him alive, and apparently unharmed, was tempered by indignation that he had been gone so long. "Where have you been? I thought you were dead. I thought you were smashed on the rocks at the bottom of the falls."

'No. I got distracted. There's lots to eat at the bottom. And more caves. Nice down there. I stopped to explore and eat some kr—what's this?' He nosed the boxes and the scattered backpack contents.

Her heartbeat slowed as she ran her hand through her hair. *What the heck? Distracted? I knew he was a better flier than that.* She shook her head, sighed, and patted Javeer's neck.

Turning to the nearest box, she pulled open its crossed flaps. "Crackers. *Ugh*. Moldy bread. Peanut butter! That's okay. Sardines? Moosehead beer! Water. Canned milk. Looks like a picnic." She opened the second box—granola bars, a couple of rotten apples, and a package of baby carrots in an advanced state of decay, a small camp burner, a box of tea bags, and a mug. Javeer sniffed the apples, then sneezed.

"It's food from home. My home, I mean. It's been here a while though because a lot of it's bad. Don't eat anything. Well, the crackers are probably okay—they're in a tin—if it's even crackers." Marise pulled the lid off. One of the four sleeves of crackers had been opened, but the rest were intact. She opened one and sniffed the contents. "Smells okay. Want one?"

'Yes.' He sounded excited. He took the cracker gently with his lips and flipped it into his mouth with his tongue. A thoughtful look crossed his face. *'Small. Can I have another?'*

She gave him two, then nibbled on one. "Cheese."

'Dry.' He took a deep breath. The breath came back in a cough like a thunderclap, then he drew in another.

She watched him warily as he clamped his jaws tight and stared at her. She saw his belly slowly contracting. Still holding his sphere, she felt an explosion growing behind her ribs. Just in time, she realized the sensation came from his chest, not hers. She ducked and pitched away an instant before a blast of flame shot from his mouth.

He whipped his chin up, but not before he'd set the side of the larger box ablaze. Marise twisted and grabbed the opposite end to drag it toward the stream. The bottom gave way, leaving a trail of tins and bottles, and flakes of blackened paper. In the end, she simply held the smoldering cardboard in the water until it was wet through. Behind her, Javeer belched gouts of flame at the ceiling, then finally grew quiet, looking sheepish. The smell of burning cardboard drifted in the tunnel.

She picked up his sphere again, probing for any sign of another explosion. "You okay?" She studied his expression. "It was the crackers. They *were* dry, weren't they? But the fire?"

'Sorry.' He sighed. *'It happens when I cough.'* He looked mournfully at the scattered contents of the box. *'Fire makes it stop.'*

Marise thought this over and nodded. "That's cool. You burn up whatever's stuck down there. I wish I could do that. When I choke, I cough and cough." She chuckled. "You know, being a walking torch has advantages." She tossed the wet cardboard to the side and scanned the items scattered on the floor. No sphere.

Her mind had been working on the implications of her discovery. Now, the facts came together. If Bonner was close by and he had the second sphere, it still could only get one of them home. And he certainly wasn't likely to give it to her. She'd stolen, then lost his other one. But he wasn't there. The food had been sitting untouched for days. She and Javeer might find the professor's body around the next corner, or they might find nothing at all, but she knew they wouldn't find him alive.

No, Bonner's missing in Moerden like he's missing in Cadogan Mills. Wherever he is now, he has the sphere. This hasn't changed anything.

'What about all this stuff?' Javeer set a tin of milk rolling with

his wing claw. It bumped into her toes, and she stooped to pick it up without really seeing it. She wondered how to explain.

"All this belonged to someone I know." She sent a memory of Bonner in his lab coat. "I don't think he's here, though. Let's check the rest of the cave, then get out of here. Okay?"

Happily, her fears of finding Bonner's remains didn't come true—there was nothing in any of the remote corners of the big cave, except a large coil of waever vine so ancient it turned to dust when she touched it. As they explored, she told him about her tutor and the sequence of events that had landed her in Moerden, beginning with the day she first saw what she thought were crystal balls in Bonner's office. She took care to visualize events clearly.

Javeer mostly listened, but he asked a question now and then. *'Who is Puff the Magic Dragon?,'* and *'Do you light candles because you can't breathe fire?'* When Marise described seeing the dragon's eye in the sphere, he interrupted again. *'It was me! I felt you looking. I was flying along the cliffs where you appeared. You fell out of the air!'*

Remembering her difficult landing and Kuvrema's statement that the sphere takes you to the place you're looking at, or visualizing, she wondered what would have happened if he had been flying any higher. She decided she didn't want to think about it, and paused by the mosaic, once again pondering its curious symbol.

"What do you think of this?" she asked. "Look, those are dragons carved into the outer circle. Back-to-back. See?"

'No. Dragons? In the floor?'

"Yes, carved in the rock. The pattern, see, this is a head spouting flame." She squatted to put a finger on a dragon's snout. "Here's the rest of it. Neck, body, tail." She traced the length of a lanky, stylized dragon with a finger, but its tail didn't seem to end. It went on in loops and curves until it tangled with the dragon behind it. "Look. They're linked. The tail of each dragon is so long it ties knots with the one behind—like a Celtic knot. Oh. A Celtic knot! Yes. That's why the pattern in the center looks familiar."

She turned her attention to the central pattern again. "Javeer, there's a circle, and three eye shapes sticking out past it from the middle. There's a name for those, but I can't remember. Together they make a triangle. Look." She stuck her hand into the sunlight, using the shadow of her finger as a pointer to join the three points. "In Wicca, the three symbolize the Maid, the Mother, and the Crone, but for the Celts, I think it was earth, sea and sky?" She tried to remember what she'd read about the symbol. "Yes, that's it. All three of them are right here in this cave. It's a protection symbol! And the circle's for eternity." She looked at Javeer.

'I see the dragons. They are not like us. I don't like them. But the rest is a picture of the earth, sea, and sky? Eternity? Dragons didn't do this.'

"No, people made it." Marise sighed. "This meant something to whoever made it. It has a message."

'What's the message?'

Marise sighed again. "I don't know. Maybe it's supposed to protect us from something." Let's go up the tunnel. "There might be more stuff."

The tunnel climbed, curving counterclockwise, opening out into another chimney with the path spiraling up its walls. "Widdershins," she muttered, hitching up the lab coat as they ascended. "Bad luck." She watched the path ahead carefully, but nothing frightening appeared.

They emerged on a sunlit plateau, where the river poured out of a cliff face before widening and roaring over the edge of the falls. The top of the chimney, above the mosaic, was surrounded by a short thick wall of red brick. Its top was notched like a castle turret.

"Look at the view! You can see for miles. It's like a lookoff." Marise studied the plain in the direction of the rhumba and saw nothing moving but a flock of birds flying toward them. *But if I wanted to approach without anyone seeing me, I'd go down into the canyon.* She dragged her eyes away and directed her thoughts to Javeer. "I wonder if we can see where I left my clothes."

He craned his long neck over, peering down like a gargoyle. *'Yes. It's hazy down there, but I see them. Is that something crawling on the beach? Only a shadow, I think.'*

She looked at him with eyebrows raised. She'd caught an image of a distinct form moving too fast to be a shadow—long and dark, not unlike an alligator.

'The waever is there too.'

"That's right. Without the bridle, I can't fly. The only way back to it is through the falls. But you can fly," she said. "Javeer, I'm hungry. Let's go to the canyon to dry off. How about if I go down and put some crackers and stuff in the backpack, and you fly down for our things? I'll meet you back here."

'Is it safe for me to leave you? What if . . .'

"You'll be all right by the pool on your own, won't you? You're not afraid of any *shadows*?"

'I'd know if Korpec came in through the falls.'

"Kuvrema said he doesn't know about this place. Be as quick as you can, okay? Grab everything and come right back. If I'm not here, come find me." Marise hitched up the lab coat and sprinted down the path.

When she arrived at the boxes out of breath, she looked around, rubbing the goosebumps on her arms as if she could soothe her uneasiness. It felt spooky without Javeer, and the pool was only a short distance away. She stuffed the rest of the opened sleeve of crackers, the peanut butter, and two bottles of beer into the backpack. As an afterthought, she added the black cylinder.

What was that? A snuffling? A slithery sound. Maybe. Not Javeer this time, for sure. Marise straightened with the backpack in her hand, turning to run as the noise came again. From above.

Javeer ambled around the curve, stretching out his long neck in greeting. She jumped with fright, then wrapped her arms around his neck and hugged him. She reached for his tail sphere as he brought it round.

"Did you see anything?"

'Something lives in the pool. I don't know what it is.' Javeer gave her a brief image of a shiny dark tail disappearing under the surface. *'Better not swim there again.'*

She couldn't wait to get out of the cave after seeing that.

Up on top, she found her sodden clothes and sneakers, the green cape, and Javeer's bridle. She took off the lab coat and donned the cape. Then she rolled up her clothes, stuffed them into the top of the backpack, and strung the sneakers through the straps. Soon they were flying to the canyon out in the valley to find some lunch, dry Marise's clothes, and warm themselves in the afternoon sun.

Marise sat with her back against a rock, dangling one foot in the river. She turned Bonner's handheld microscope over in her hands. It was the object she'd mistaken for a flashlight. Switching it on, she looked through it at the back of her wrist, first at 60x magnification, then 100x. The endless shield of skin cells knit tightly together reminded her of Javeer's scaled hide.

She glanced up to see him nibbling berries near the canyon wall, and thought, *We are so different, yet we're so alike. But Korpec doesn't think so.* She eyed the open sky above, thinking for the hundredth time if Korpec appeared directly above, there would be little they could do. But she saw nothing but blue.

Turning her attention back to the microscope, she plucked a leaf from a grassy tuft at the water's edge, laid it in her hand upside down, and peered at it through the eyepiece. She saw a forest of spiky plant hairs, plump and pale green. Clouds of tiny water droplets lay trapped among them. Then, at the edge of view, there was movement. A bristly jointed foot withdrew when she focused on it.

Pulling the lens from her eye, she changed the view back to 60x and found the creature connected to the foot. She thought it looked like a louse but with ten legs instead of six, and a green hue like the flesh of an unripe apple. A horizontal sickle-shaped head burrowed in the forest of plant hairs.

Marise called to Javeer, who turned from stripping the leaves of a trailing ground plant and wandered over. She spread the strap-shaped leaf on a rock. Then, picking up his sphere, she passed him the microscope.

"Look at this. Hold the microscope like this, then put your eye to the lens on top. Not right up against it. Close, so you're looking through it like it's a tunnel, or a hole in the rock." She mimed the action. "Move it back and forth, nearer or farther away. You'll see blurry shapes. When you get it right, you'll see the leaf." She pointed at the green strip.

Javeer held the microscope in his wing claw and bent over the rock, putting his eye to the lens. With his wing partially extended, cloaking his shoulder, Marise thought he looked like Dracula bent over a meal. The image made her uneasy. She scanned canyon and sky.

A stab of frustration brought her attention back to Javeer. He sent an image of fuzzy red.

'*I don't see anything.*'

"Move the lower end around. It has to be right over the grass." She was careful not to look at his sphere as she tried to guide him, worried she might be miniaturized and pitched into the world of the sicklehead.

She saw a flash of green. "There! There. No. It's gone. Did you see it? Go back."

He found it—a solid green field.

"There. But it's fuzzy." She glanced at the microscope. "Slowly move it closer. Slowly. Don't hit the rock." A sharp image of pale green carpet flashed past, and she felt his surprise and excitement.

'I saw something! There it was again! There. What is this? Where's the leaf? All I see is grass.'

Marise saw it too—an endless plain of pale green plant hairs. "That's the leaf, the parts too small for us to see with our eyes. Move toward the end." Fields of curling hairs slid past, and her stomach did a flip-flop, but she kept watching.

The sicklehead bug came into view. With ten feet planted in the downy surface, the creature held its head up, so it appeared ready to thrust its face right up through the microscope. Its dark green, slit eyes were set vertically and far apart. An even wider mouth gaped, full of long, tightly packed teeth like bristles on a brush. She thought it looked like a sickly green Halloween jack-o'-lantern with an evil grin.

"Oh!" The sight made her jump, but the effect on Javeer was worse. He lurched away from the rock with a strangled cry, crushing a bush underfoot. His sphere whipped out of her hands, smashing another plant on its way down and sending a flock of yellow flower petals and seeds downriver on the breeze. Javeer chattered. Smoke curled out of his nostrils.

Marise laughed at them both. She laughed harder at the terror on his face and remembered the exploding firefruit incident. Leaning against the rock, she tried to stifle her laughter. She felt his concern as he shuffled back toward her and returned the sphere.

Patting his scaly chest, she reassured him. *'It's okay. Funny. Happy. Okay.'* When her giggles subsided, she said, "It's okay. That monster is very, very small. It's so small we can't even see it without the microscope. Smaller than a grain of sand! It can't hurt us. Only scare us with its horrible face." She giggled again. "Aren't you glad it isn't big, like whatever's in the pool?" Javeer nudged her shoulder with his nose.

'I'm not afraid of that.' He leaned over and devoured the leaf.

"Oh! You ate the monster." Marise guffawed. "You probably eat them all the time. There may be millions of them here."

'Ugh.' Javeer apparently accepted the inevitability of microscopic creatures in his greens, though. He returned the microscope to her and went back to grazing, starting with the remainder of the tuft of grass by the water's edge.

Marise sat and rested her head against the rock. She looked up at the crooked strip of sky visible from the canyon floor. The sun rested on the canyon lip and shadows gathered on the far bank. *I'll relax here for a few minutes*, she thought, closing her eyes. *Enjoy the last of the sun.* She listened to the burbling river, water slipping over and swirling around rocks, circling in eddies.

She tried to think about where Bonner might be, what small life form he might have been interested in, but her thoughts kept slipping to hungry sickleheads and the innumerable tiny creatures all around her too small to see. Breathing in the warm and faintly musty air reminded her of the cave where the dead dragon lay stretched on the rock.

The dragon corpse lifted its head and looked directly at her, as if expecting some profound announcement. Chunks of dried dragon hide broke away, exposing tendons and bone, a smooth skull, and a chain of knobby vertebrae. Debris struck the floor, raising a cloud of dust that wafted toward the cave entrance.

She was worried about Javeer. She needed to warn him about the dust, had to get him away from it. But she must finish her task here first. She tried to remember what it was. There was something she needed to do at once.

The corpse slowly crackled to its feet. Dust billowed, drifting toward her. She knew it was a wall of deadly germs. Soon, it would break out of the cave. Then it would be too late.

Marise clutched the microscope, feeling ridges on the dial dig into the heel of her hand. It was all up to her, but she didn't know what to do. Where was Professor Bonner? He'd have the answer.

The crumbling dragon towered over her, lurching forward, descending. She gasped in the sickening cloud, raised her hands to shield her face, thrust the microscope into the side of its jaw, and heard the crack of metal on bone.

Javeer pushed the microscope aside gently and nudged Marise's forehead. She came fully awake, realizing two things: Bonner had a job to do in Moerden, and a sandstorm had rolled over the canyon edge from the plain above, raining blankets of sand and dust.

Scrambling to her feet, more revelations rolled over her. *That's why there are always patches of vegetation loaded down with dirt.* That's *why dragons live in caves, rather than in the canyon where there's so much food. We have to get out of here.*

Marise's eyes stung. She held her breath and pulled the green cloak around her. Then tossed the microscope and her dry clothes into the backpack and slung the bag over her shoulders.

Javeer lifted her, and they bolted for clean air above the sandstorm. Marise's sneakers, still entangled in the backpack straps, kicked her in the ribs as though urging her to hurry.

Only yesterday, she'd have been terrified, but she was much more comfortable on his shoulders now. Once clear of the billowing dust, she shook sand out of her hair and cloak, then reached behind to pat his flank. He brought his tail around, and she grasped the sphere.

"Javeer! Professor Bonner knew about the disease. I'm sure he was studying it. That's what the microscope is for! I think he had the answer, but I have to go home to find out for sure. Javeer, I need a sphere. If I can get back to Cadogan Mills and find out what Bonner knew, maybe I can stop the stagger. We have to find a sphere. There must be one somewhere!"

Chapter
Nine

SECRETS
AND REVELATIONS

Marise hardly paused for breath as they flew back to the lookoff. "Dr. Bonner was doing research with spheres. He told me! And he had all those little bottles and rubber gloves in his backpack. I'm sure he was trying to figure out what causes the stagger.

"What was all that stuff in the drawer with the sphere? I can't remember. Papers and maps. Stuff about lizards. Which are kind of like dragons. And deer. And parasites! He must think it's a parasite. Oh, parasites can do awful things to you, like crawl out of your mouth, and like, make you act possessed and stuff."

She sent him an image of her principal with a pallid, fanged worm as thick as her arm protruding from his mouth.

Javeer pulled his head back and yanked his tail away.

"Oh sorry," Marise reached for the sphere. "Sorry, actually I made that up, but I know parasites are bad, and I'm certain Dr. Bonner came here to catch one—to prove it causes the stagger. Remember that sicklehead by the river? It might be something like that, but we have to find out what. If I could get back to his office, I'd look at all those papers again to find out what he knew. There were notes there—he must have been on to something. Maybe he was close to finding a cure. Javeer! We might be able to cure the stagger forever. If I could just get home."

She continued babbling all the way to the cave. When they landed, Javeer pulled his tail away and went toward the falls. Plants festooned the walls near the opening, soaking up the mist and filtered sunlight. Some even clung to the roof, sending down long leafy tendrils like a ragged bead curtain. He sat with his back to her, framed by the vegetation and the shifting cascade of green and blue water.

Marise wondered what he was thinking. She dressed and paced the carved dragons framing the mosaic. She scanned the cave walls as though she might find a sphere tucked into a crevice, then peered down the tunnel leading to the smaller chute and froze. A damp zigzag trail ran the length of the tunnel between round wet patches that looked disturbingly like footprints.

An evening breeze stirred by the falls carried the odor of wet rock and something else that reminded her of burnt sugar. She reached down to touch a wet patch and brought her finger to her nose. Yes, like burnt sugar. She hugged herself, rubbing her arms to smooth down goosebumps.

Which way was it going? she pondered. With Javeer so near, she felt only mildly uneasy about the pool creature, but she didn't like the idea that it might be lurking in the cavern.

Finally, Javeer rejoined her, illuminating his sphere light and dispelling the gathering shadows. He arched his neck. Then he heaved like a cat coughing up a furball, his stomach contracting repeatedly.

"Javeer? You okay?"

He retched. His round belly disappeared under his rib cage. He made a gargling noise.

Marise picked up his sphere but kept her distance. "Javeer?"

"Aghghghghghgh."

His belly contracted again. He shook, produced a deep wet

cough, and spat an object onto the mosaic. Relaxing, he looked at Marise.

Her mouth dropped open. A flawless transparent sphere sat in a puddle of froth.

"You've had this all the time? In your stomach? Where did it come from?"

'My father. I kept it.'

"Oh. You took it when he was . . . you swallowed it, and it's been in your stomach ever since? More than a year?"

'I kept it. I don't know why. It was all that was left.'

She stroked his neck. "How sweet." Her sad smile remained for a few seconds before it faded. "Oh, wow. Javeer, this is it! You solved it. We might be able to save the dragons." She brought a hand up to touch her forehead. "But I'd have to use it. I'd have to take it home. Is it okay?"

'If you really think you can do it. You'll come back?'

Until this evening, Marise's only thought had been to find a sphere and go home. Now she needed to come back, and that would be difficult, especially as she had no believable explanation for her disappearance. She either had to return to Cadogan Mills and figure out a way to find all Bonner's research without being seen, or she needed to explain to Javeer she might be gone a long time.

"I'll come back. I promise. I have to think. We need a plan."

She picked up the sphere as though it might shatter in her hands and walked up the tunnel to wash it in the stream. Javeer turned up his sphere light, illuminating their way. After his father's sphere was clean, they continued to the lookoff where they settled by the brick wall.

He stretched out with his nose pointed toward the canyon and Marise leaned back against his ribcage, his sphere resting in her palm. The sun crept down a crimson sky toward peaks that glowed like embers.

"How long have I been gone?" she mused. "Two nights at Honedrai, and a day here. It was night when I left home, so it's probably, like, two in the morning there now. It's almost Wednesday. How am I going to explain? They're probably searching for me like they did for Dr. Bonner."

She continued silently. *The whole town probably knows I'm missing, and mom and dad will be really upset. I'm in big trouble, I guess.*

'Use spheresight to see what they're doing. Remember what Kuvrema said? You look into it without touching and think about what you want to see. Think about your rhumba and look.'

She smiled at the thought of her house being a rhumba. "That's a good idea. I wonder if there's enough light." She pulled herself into a cross-legged position, placing the relic sphere on the ground in front of her.

"I'd better not be holding your sphere while I do this. Who knows what might happen. I'll tell you what I see after."

She draped his tail across her thigh and laid her hands on her knees. Gazing into the center of the relic, she pictured her house on Montrose Lane.

Nothing. Darkness. Complete at first, then softened by a white glow, like moonlight shining on freshly fallen snow. There were mounds of snow, punctured here and there by splintered pillars. The ground was undulated and uneven, as if ruins lay buried beneath. She blinked in confusion.

What am I looking at? This isn't working. That's not my house. It's like I'm seeing some place where there's lots of snow. But it's April! She looked away and tried again, building layers of detail in her mind's eye, then turned back to the sphere.

Shadows and snowdrifts slowly took shape in its core.

Marise studied the image. Towering walls framed the winter scene on both sides, lit by the glow reflecting off the snowbanks.

The walls looked familiar somehow. She concentrated on the one on the left, and her stomach squirmed. She recognized a large window and the bamboo blind inside. It was the Koh's house, number 16, next door to hers. Her gaze snapped back to the space beside it, filled with snow drifts where her house ought to be.

A police officer appeared. He shuffled his feet and looked over his shoulder. He turned full circle, searching the area with his flashlight, and backed toward the police cruiser parked across the driveway. With his back to the car, he swept the flashlight beam back and forth, the other on his gun. She knew that unsettling feeling of being watched when someone used spheresight.

At another time, Marise might have enjoyed making him squirm, but just now she was too confused. Where was her house? Was this the future? The past? The longer she looked, the clearer the image in the sphere became. Yellow caution tape stretched between the houses on both sides. A wide area of black slush blanketed the ground where the front yard used to be, and the stump of a brick chimney pointed at the stars. For an instant, she thought she smelled wood smoke.

The truth dawned, raising hair on the back of her neck. Her house was gone. Burned down. Nothing left. But how? Why? She stared at the caution tape, and the scent of wood smoke turned to the sulfurous smell of a match and a whiff of lemon. *Lemon-scented candles.*

A second wave of dismay rolled after the first. She had done it. She'd left candles burning when the sphere pitched her into Moerden. No one else had been home. All those candle flames must have ignited the velvet cloth she'd draped over the table.

Marise stared into the sphere without seeing. She let tears well in her eyes and roll down her cheeks.

"Why is this happening?" she asked the gloom. "Why can't I just go back?"

She looked at Javeer as though seeing him for the first time and picked up the relic sphere with distaste. Holding it in one hand, she sprang to her feet and walked toward the edge of the cliff.

When she turned, her words came in a torrent. "I wish I'd never seen this sphere, or any sphere! Because of this *thing*, I'm stuck in this damn desert with dragons trying to kill me. My house is gone. My parents may be dead. And it just keeps getting worse and worse and worse. Why is this happening?" Her voice rose in pitch and her fingers turned white around the sphere. She pointed at Javeer with it.

"You had this the whole time, didn't you? Hidden in your stomach. You had it, and you knew you did. I could have gone home right away, when I first landed, right after Korpec tried frying me."

'Didn't want—'

"But no, you kept it to yourself. You kept it hidden. You threw me down the cliff and just about killed me—"

'Didn't mean—'

"And everything since is all *your* fault. I've been beat up, flamed, starved, terrified, banished, and sunburned, and slimed . . ."

'Tried to be—'

"And now, now you cough this thing up, after all this time, and it's too late! It's too late. I can't go home." She screamed at him, gesturing wildly with her free hand.

'Go.'

"Why now? Now, because you want me to do something for *you!* All of a sudden you cough up a sphere after we've been searching and hunting for days. You never wanted to find that sphere in the landslide at all, did you? Did you!"

'We looked—'

"Now I finally have a sphere and what good is it? You might as well have just kept it in your slimy stomach. It's gross!"

'Just go.'

"I can't go—"

'Don't come back.'

"—because home is gone, and it's all wrong now . . . you know? Nothing's the same."

'Go.'

" . . . and I'm all mixed up." Her voice faded to a whisper. Tears traced a silvery line past her jaw and down her throat.

The sun had set, and she stood under a waning moon and a panorama of twinkling stars, holding the sphere in one raised hand and gesturing at Javeer with the other.

He slumped. Eyes half-closed, neck slack, scaly hide sagging to the ground. He looked as if he was melting. Misery flowed over her like oily smoke.

Marise's eyes widened, her lips formed an O, and she lowered the sphere till her arm hung slack. She gaped at him for a dozen breaths. She turned the sphere up and looked at it, then back at Javeer.

"You can hear me, can't you?"

He half-opened an eye.

"I can hear you. You can hear me. Kuvrema was wrong. We *can* talk with a relic sphere." She put it down. "Can you hear me now?"

There was no response. She picked up the sphere again and let the events of the past few days race through her mind.

She sank to the ground facing him, grasping the sphere with both hands. "No. Javeer, no. I'm sorry. Everything I just said was wrong. It's all *my* fault. I stole the sphere from Dr. Bonner's office in the first place. I knew it wasn't a crystal ball, and I didn't even try to find out what it really was. I burned the house down. I lost the sphere! I made you go to that cave with the dead dragon in it. If I hadn't showed up, you'd still be happy living with Kuvrema and the others." Tears welled up again in her eyes.

"I have no right to this sphere at all. It's yours, your father's. I understand why you didn't tell me about it. If you gave it to me, I'd use it to go home, and you'd lose it. It's not your job to get me home. I'm sorry, Javeer, so sorry." Sobbing, Marise tucked the sphere under his slack wing and flung herself onto her back.

"What am I going to do?"

He said nothing, but after a moment, he draped his wing over her.

Through teary eyes, Marise saw the moon rising and felt the chill of another desert night creeping over her, but she didn't move. Eventually, Javeer nudged her with his nose, and she climbed wearily to her feet. He picked up the relic sphere in his mouth and led the way down into the cave. Once well inside, he lit his sphere and blew a few blasts of flame to warm the space. She slumped against the wall, well away from the mosaic, and he rolled the relic sphere to her like a bowling ball.

'We can't hide here forever.' His voice was firm.

"What can we do?"

'You can take the sphere and go, and I'll fly back to the coast and hope for the best. Or we can fly into the mountains, find a nice cave, and eat firefruit and houra till we die of old age—several hundred years for me.' He tilted his head at an odd angle. *'Or we can do what we said—try to find out what your doctor knew about the stagger.'*

Surprised by his businesslike tone, Marise came out of her funk. She sat cross-legged and returned the look. "I can't go home," she said. "At least not to my family, if I want to come back. Everyone thinks I burned the house down. I did burn the house down. They probably think I'm dead."

When she thought about her parents wondering what had happened to her, looking for her remains among the ashes of the house, a lump formed in her throat. She wanted nothing more than to go straight to them. But then she thought about trying to explain where she'd been and how she'd caused the fire, and she wanted to stay in Moerden forever.

She imagined Javeer and Kuvrema, and all the rest dying from the stagger, losing their minds, littering the desert with their desiccated corpses. Her eyes brimmed with tears, but she impatiently smeared them away.

Everything was different now. It wasn't possible to just go home. But it would be difficult to come back once she reappeared in Cadogan Mills. She needed a plan.

"I don't need to go home to look at those papers," she said after a few minutes. "I need to go to Bonner's office. I can go there and come back, and no one will ever know. I guess my family will have to wait longer to find out I'm alive. I don't think they're dead because they weren't home when I, um, when I left."

Marise grew excited. "You know what? Maybe Bonner's there! Maybe he went home. If he's there, maybe he can come back, and I can go home." Seeing Javeer's crestfallen expression, she hastily added, "But I'll come back later, after things are, uh, normal, again."

'Look at Bonner's rhumba. See if you can see him.'

"Right. Good idea." She put the sphere down in front of her and methodically constructed Bonner's office in her mind. She looked within the sphere and saw only gloom. "Stupid! It's about four in the morning there. Bonner's in bed if he's anywhere. Javeer, I'm tired too. We need to sleep. We'll have to wait until morning. Will we sleep here? Do you think it's safe? What about the pool grue?"

'Pool grue? The thing in the pool? Yes, it's too cold up on top and too visible. Dragons don't travel much by night, but with Korpec, you never know. We'll stay here, move away from the falls and the tunnel, where it's warmer. That creature won't bother us. I'm bigger, and I'm sure it won't like fire. I could kill it if I had to.' He aimed a burst of flame in the direction of the pool. *'I think it's afraid of us. Do we still have crackers?'*

Marise chuckled, retrieved the backpack, and fished out an

empty beer bottle, the peanut butter, and a few crackers. She'd opened the beer in the canyon, feeling naughty, but its bitter taste and yeasty odor had surprised and disappointed her. Javeer had tasted it too, and spat it out, so she'd poured the rest on the sand and used it as a water bottle.

Javeer went up the tunnel with the bottle, returning with water and the two remaining sleeves of crackers from Bonner's boxes, and they sat down for a late-night snack. Afterward, they tucked themselves into a back corner of the cave, where nothing could sneak up on them. She reclined in the hollow of his leg.

Even though she was comfortable and warm, she couldn't sleep at first. She kept imagining she heard the soft splishy sound of wet feet approaching from the pool. The noise never came close, if it was a noise at all, and eventually she dosed off and dreamed of snowdrifts burning under a full moon. The smoke that curled up smelled of lemons and burnt sugar.

Marise woke, curled in the warm pocket of air surrounding Javeer. She stretched and yawned, awakening sore muscles. As she sat up, she put her hand down in something dry and gritty. She opened her eyes to see bits of cracker all around and the mangled remains of two cracker sleeves. She gripped the relic sphere. "Javeer, you sure love those crackers, don't you? You ate the rest of them, huh?" He made no comment but ran his nose over the crumbs and plastic as though searching for some he'd missed.

Seated in front of the relic sphere, she built an image of Earl Bonner's office in her mind again. The room appeared at once, lit by early afternoon sunshine and looking just as it had when she had last been there. In fact, she thought she saw the pencil and the note to Ellen she'd left on the desk. Only the key was gone. With a sinking feeling, she realized this probably meant Bonner hadn't returned, but at least the room looked empty and untouched. She let the image dissolve and tipped her head back to look at Javeer.

"You saw it?"

'Yes. Did it look all right?'

"It looks exactly the same. I don't think he's there." She sighed. "So, I suppose I'd better go. I've never done this. Not on purpose, I mean. I'm scared. I just imagine the place while I'm holding the sphere, right?"

'I think so. Dragons don't do it. Young dragons are forbidden to try. I don't really know why. Maybe they get lost, like you did.'

Marise didn't feel any better. She rolled the sphere from one hand to the other and rubbed a sweaty palm on her jeans, then put the orb down. Her sneakers were beside the backpack, and she walked over to put them on. She dumped out the pack, putting only Bonner's lab coat back in, and slung a strap over one shoulder. She stood thinking for a moment, then put the other arm through, settling the pack securely on her back.

Nodding to Javeer, she retrieved the sphere. "Javeer, I'll be back. Soon, I hope."

He bumped her shoulder with his nose. *'Good luck. I'm going to use spheresight to look for Kuvrema. If I can find where she is, she'll feel me looking and maybe come to find us. We need to tell her.'*

"She said she'd come. Maybe she doesn't know about this cave, and she won't be able to find you."

'I'll check the canyon and anywhere I think she might be. I'll come back here.'

"Okay. Here goes then." Now that she couldn't delay any longer, she was reluctant. Crouching for stability, she balanced on her left knee, her right foot flat on the floor. She took a deep breath and imagined her destination as though she stood between the door into Bonner's office and his desk. She breathed deeply to calm herself, waiting until the image settled solid and clear.

Holding the sphere, she focused deep within it. Marise glimpsed Bonner's office in the sphere. She saw a brilliant flash of peacock blue and felt herself flung through the air.

A stabbing pain shot through her right foot, as though she'd slammed a door on her toe. Instinctively, she pulled it back. Pain raced up her leg.

For a heartbeat, she found herself looking into Ellen's astonished eyes before she crashed to the floor. Only then did she realize the folly of having crouched while visualizing the room as though she was standing.

Chapter
Ten

MYSTERY OF
THE MOERDEN PLAGUE

Marise slammed down on her back. Her head bounced off the rug and she rolled to the side, grimacing.

"Not again," she groaned, but in truth, this time, her landing was easier. Seconds later, she was up and focused on her throbbing foot. A quick glance confirmed her fears. The toe of her sneaker had been torn away and blood seeped out of the opening. "Ouch!" she said, but there was no time to investigate the injury. She looked up to meet Ellen's gray eyes, fixed on her from across the desk.

Ellen shifted forward, gripping her walker with one hand and slowly buttoning her voluminous peacock blue cardigan with the other.

Neither spoke. Marise limped around the end of the desk and leaned on it with one hand. Ellen's eyes flicked up and down as though trying to determine what, exactly, she was looking at.

Marise knew she must be a sight—hair uncombed, tank top ripped and blotched with fruit stains, blue jeans stained as well, and a chunk torn out of one sneaker. She was scraped, bruised, and bleeding.

"Well," Ellen finally broke the silence. "Marise Leeson isn't it? You're too bedraggled to be a hallucination, and I don't believe in ghosts—though you have arrived in a rather spooky way. So, I guess we'd better call the police and tell them you've turned up."

"No! No, Mrs. Bonner, I can't go home yet. Don't call the police. I have something important to do first."

"What?" She sounded shocked. "Everyone thinks you're dead. Your family is in a terrible state. I've no idea where you've been, but you must go home at once. You know your house has burned? It's a right mess, I can tell you." Ellen moved toward her.

"Mrs. Bonner, I know where your husband went," she said, desperate to stop her from making that phone call. "Look, I've got his backpack. And his lab coat!" She hastily shrugged the backpack off and, dropping the sphere into the top, dragged the crumpled lab coat out. She showed Ellen Earl's name on the pocket.

Her eyes went wide. "You've seen Earl? Are you saying he's alive?"

"Well, no. I haven't seen him, and I don't know he's alive, but I think he might be. I know where he went."

"And are you going to tell me?"

"Yes," she paused, "but it's a long story. First, will you tell me what happened here since Sunday night? Are my parents okay?"

Ellen glared at her but nodded. She looked down. A pool of blood spread from the damaged sneaker. "Yes, to the last question, but perhaps we'd better have a look at your foot first."

Her foot throbbed excruciatingly. She limped around Ellen and sank into the desk chair with a sigh. Her tailbone protested, but she ignored it, bending forward to remove the sneaker. She pulled it off and cried out. The tip of her second toe was missing, cut clean off as though trimmed with a meat cleaver. She'd always hated that toe, jutting out longer than the rest.

"Good gracious! How did you do this?" Ellen leaned in for a closer look.

"I don't know." Marise felt faint. "It happened just now."

"We must bandage that. Wait here."

Mercifully, Ellen wasn't long. She returned with a wet cloth and a first aid kit, and Marise leaned back, putting her foot up on the walker.

Ellen's forehead furrowed while she worked. "I gather your parents came home to find the house completely engulfed. Much too late to save anything. The neighbors had called 911 only a minute or two before. The fire trucks weren't there yet. Everyone assumed you were still inside." She glanced up.

"*Mmm*. I wasn't. Ow."

Ellen cleaned the stump with hydrogen peroxide. "Sorry, dear. At least it's clean.

"It took them till morning to put the fire out, and by then it was snowing. And it *snowed*! Imagine! Twenty centimeters of snow in Cadogan Mills in April. It was a good old storm, too. Winds and blowing snow. They couldn't even begin sifting through the ashes until the streets were cleared, and they got some snow removal equipment in. They're still looking for your remains, my dear. So, you see, everyone believes you're dead. Killed in that fire."

Marise sucked in a breath through clenched teeth as Ellen wrapped gauze saturated with antibiotic ointment around her toe. With a bit of sticky transparent tape, the job was done, and she gingerly lowered her foot. "Thank you, Mrs. Bonner."

"Call me Ellen. I think we're friends now, *hmmm*?"

"Okay," Marise said uncertainly. "Now, I'll tell you my story." Despite her pain, she rose and motioned for Ellen to take the seat, limping back to the table near the window to drag another chair over. After gathering her thoughts, she began.

"Did you ever see Dr. Bonner with one of these?" She reached into the backpack and pulled out the sphere.

"Well, that's a fantastic story," Ellen said. "And clearly some of it is true, else how would you have Earl's backpack and his lab coat? And how would we explain the state you're in, not to mention the peculiar way you arrived? If I hadn't been looking straight at you when you fell out of thin air, I wouldn't believe it." She pointed at the sphere.

"This is all Earl's fault, isn't it? Even your part in it. We are in a bind, thanks to him. If it's all right with you, I'll make myself a cup of tea. Will you have one? I've got some hot chocolate if you'd rather."

"Oh yeah, hot chocolate would be awesome." She looked up as Ellen stood. "Are you calling the police?"

Ellen sighed. "How can I? Assuming this is really happening, and I'm not having a nightmare, if you go back to your parents, you abandon your dragon friends to their deaths. If I send you back, I may abandon my husband to his. Damned if you do, damned if you don't. We are on the horns of a dilemma." She briskly wheeled her walker around the desk and left.

Marise glanced down at her bandaged toe and saw the key inserted in the lock of the bottom drawer. She tugged at the handle, and it opened, revealing the deep stack of papers. Grabbing thick handfuls, she lifted them out and stacked them on the desktop. She was sorting through them when Ellen returned with two steaming mugs on a tray clipped onto the front of her walker.

As she came through the doorway, she did a double take. "What's this?" She leaned over to examine something just below the desktop. Then she looked at Marise with a horrified expression.

"What is it?" Marise half rose from her chair.

"Good Lord. I do not believe it. How can this be?" She lifted a trembling hand to her brow, while Marise limped around the desk, afraid the elderly woman might faint.

Marise looked at the back of the desk and frowned. She saw a flattened semicircle of white plastic embedded in the oak grain, with a roughly circular dull reddish object inside it. A drop of dark liquid had dripped down the wood and dried.

She felt a rush of adrenaline and goosebumps broke out on her arms. The end of her sneaker and the tip of her toe were embedded in the wood. She brought her hand to her mouth and looked at Ellen.

Marise stood frozen as she thought about what would have happened if she'd appeared a bit further forward, or a few feet lower down.

"I think we know why your dragons don't use spheres for travel," Ellen said. "There must have been some dreadful accidents. Dreadful." She reached past Marise and ran a fingertip over the patch. It came away peppered with specks of dried blood.

Marise fought to shut down her growing panic. Now she understood what it might truly mean to "get lost" while traveling by sphere. She had to go back to Moerden, and now she didn't know how to do it safely. She looked at the stacks of papers on the desk and wondered whether there was any point in reading them.

"I don't know if I can do this." Marise swallowed hard. "I don't think I can go back. But I can't just disappear from there as well. Deliberately this time! I promised Javeer. And I have his father's sphere. Dr. Bonner is there somewhere, and he might be in trouble. And dragons are dying."

"Perhaps there's nothing you can do. You might throw your life away for nothing."

"No, I really want to go back. I have to. But I can't. I don't know how. I'm scared." She winced, looking past Ellen through the window, into a familiar world where dragons existed only in fairy tales, and it was impossible to materialize inside a rock.

"Describe to me again the pattern on the floor of the cave," Ellen said, and Marise explained the mosaic ringed by dragons in as much detail as she could remember.

"Curious. Curious. It's not like Earl to make a habit of doing anything so dangerous. I wonder." She looked out the window, but her thoughts were obviously far away.

After a moment, she moved toward the window. "I feel odd harboring a missing person. Runaway? Arsonist?" She sighed. "Well, don't worry. We're in this together now, but if I'm going to get into the criminal life at my age, I'd better be smart about it. Let's draw these sheers so no one sees you. We've already been here much too long. If my nosy neighbors get a glimpse of you, the police will be all over us."

She pulled a cord and sheer curtains swept across, joining neatly in the middle. Sunbeams slanting into the room dimmed and filled with swirling dust motes. "Earl never used these," Ellen said. "Doing this may draw attention." She turned back to Marise.

"If you're sure you need to go back, there's something I want you to see. I think it must be part of this puzzle. Come, we must go to the kitchen." She handed her a cooling mug of hot chocolate as she set off. Marise limped after her, careful not to bump her bandaged toe.

The kitchen, at the back of the house, looked as if it had been remodeled recently. It was a U-shaped room with a double sink under a window at the end. The window stood slightly ajar, admitting a spring breeze freshened with the smell of budding leaves and melting snow. Marise took in oak cabinets and granite countertop, wondering what Ellen had to show her.

"The floor," said Ellen softly.

Marise looked down and nearly dropped her hot chocolate. The entire floor was a stunning mosaic in tile of earthy colors, fading toward the periphery. A Celtic knot and a wide border carved with twining roses.

"Is this the same as the circle you described?"

"Yes! Except for the roses. In the cave, it's dragons around the outside. But the rest is exactly the same. Exactly."

"What do you think it means?"

She stared down at the mosaic, struggling to understand. "I've no idea. Why would this be here? How did it get here?"

"Earl designed it. Ever since you told me about the one in Moerden, I've been wondering what the significance of this one is. It's important, obviously. Earl clearly needed it for something." Ellen paused.

"What if it has something to do with sphere travel?" she said. "Like a launching pad? To help you visualize your destination precisely, so you don't go wrong and wind up inside a mountain. Don't you think so? Earl used this to travel to Moerden safely. I think."

Marise nodded slowly, pondering the suggestion. "It could be."

"The crafty old bastard!" Ellen exclaimed, making Marise jump. "I thought he designed this kitchen for me."

Marise stared at her.

"Well," Ellen said, her chin tipping up. "Like so many women, I'm discovering after he's gone that my ordinary conventional husband led a double life. The cheek! I'm thinking perhaps we should just leave him there, wherever he is. He deserves it.

"But it's not as if there was another woman, *hmmm*? Just another world." She rolled her eyes and gestured at the floor. "Do you think this would work to get you back in one piece?"

"Yes, I think so. Maybe." She was happy to turn her attention back to the floor. "I'd just stand on it and use it to envision the exact same pattern in the cave in Moerden? Easy."

"You think it's safe?"

"I think so. Yes, I think so."

"All right then," Ellen said. "We'd better get to work on that stack of paper. Let's see if we can solve the mystery of the Moerden plague."

Back in the office, Ellen took the handwritten notes because she knew her husband's handwriting, while Marise sifted through the rest. She found herself looking at scientific papers and government documents she could make no sense of. A map of Newfoundland was easier to interpret, but she didn't know what to look for.

"This isn't working," Marise said after about ten minutes. She pushed the map under the desk. "I don't know how to read this stuff. It's all gibberish."

Ellen looked up from her reading. "I'm not finding much either, except this in his notes from two years ago. 'May 2006, young male, turning in circles, difficulty holding wings against the body and flaming uncontrollably, hind leg paralysis.' That has to be a sick dragon. There's some other stuff and then he says, 'Something is affecting the voluntary muscle function.' So, you're right, I think Earl was studying the disease." She riffled through the papers in her hand.

"Here's what I think we should do. We need to start at the end of his notes and work backward. If he was close to an answer, it'll be at the end. Let's turn this pile of scribbles upside down and look at it together." As she flipped her stack of paper, the chime of a doorbell startled them both. Their eyes met.

"Stay here. Whoever it is, I'll get rid of them. You'll be alright in here. No one comes into the office." Ellen headed for the door, fiddling with her sweater buttons.

Marise realized the room was scattered with signs of her presence. Bonner's lab coat, her sneakers, the backpack, and bloody gauze in the garbage can. The first aid kit lay open on the desk. Papers were everywhere. She snatched up the gauze and rubbed the trail of blood that circled the desk. It had already stained the wood floor.

She dumped all the bits and pieces of the first aid kit into the metal box, snapped it shut, and shoved it into the empty desk drawer. She heard the front door open, and Ellen spoke loudly.

"Good afternoon, Officer Wheaton. What brings you here? Is there some news?"

Marise spun around, searching for a place to hide. There was no closet, no hidden corner, no furniture she could crouch behind. If she went into the hall, she'd be seen.

"Sorry, Mrs. Bonner. No. Nothing new at all. I am so sorry." Wheaton's deep baritone carried easily. "I was just returning some items we took from the office. Dr. Bonner's maps and trail guide and so on. I apologize for keeping them so long, but what with the storm and the Leeson house burning and all, I've been busy. Let me put them back in the office for you."

Marise grabbed the lab coat and sneakers and stuffed everything into the backpack on top of the sphere. She rushed for the door but jerked to a halt when Ellen said, "Just leave them there, dear, on the bench. I'll put them away. Have they found that poor girl? The Leeson girl?"

"It's no trouble, Mrs. Bonner. I'll carry these down. No, they've not found any human remains in the ashes. It's a mystery. We're starting to wonder if there's more to this fire." Wheaton's voice drew closer.

Marise darted behind the door and pulled it around in front of her, flattening herself against the wall. The bulky backpack kept the door out too far, so at the last moment, she put it down on the floor beside her, seizing the doorknob and pulling the door close. She didn't dare breathe when a tall man in a black uniform and Ellen passed the gap where the hinges held the door to the frame, just inches away. A faint whiff of cologne reached her.

"Ah, sorting through things?" Wheaton's tone was sympathetic. "It's a tough job when we lose someone. Going through their belongings, remembering all the things they were interested in. This must be difficult for you."

"Yes. Yes, it is. Earl kept busy with his projects even after he retired. I'm just now discovering some of them." Her voice betrayed none of her double meaning.

A strap on the backpack shifted, flopping out past the edge of the door. A plastic buckle hit the baseboard with a click.

"Ah. What's that now? Did you find the missing backpack?" Wheaton's voice came from right on the other side of the door.

Marise held her breath and pushed harder against the wall. Her hand tightened on the doorknob. Horrified, she watched a male hand reach around to grasp the strap of the backpack and pull it up and into the open. The other strap touched her bloodless fingers as it brushed past. "Is this Mr. Bonners?"

"No, actually, this one's mine. It's similar." Ellen lied so smoothly, Marise almost believed her.

"I don't remember seeing it here when we searched the office. You say it's similar?"

"Yes, it's very like Earl's. It wasn't here before. I've been putting a few items in it to take over to my niece's house. Mementos, you know."

Mementos! Marise winced. *The sphere! And the lab coat. If he finds the lab coat . . . .*

"I wonder if I should take it down to the station and get them to photograph it for the file."

Ellen said nothing. Marise's heart raced. Seconds passed.

"Would you mind, Ellen?"

"Not at all. If you think it's necessary." Again, Ellen sounded convincing. "I have other bags. Let me unpack it. It will only take a minute."

"Well, now I think about it, you gave us a good description and these bags are a dime a dozen, eh? Everybody's got one. And like you say, this isn't exactly the same." Wheaton sighed. "I guess there's really no need. Probably overkill. Oh, excuse me. That was a poor choice of words. Very poor choice. I'll—I'll let you get back to what you were doing. Sorry to trouble you." He swung the pack down against the baseboard again, making no effort to tuck it behind the door. Marise eyed it, longing to reach down and snatch it before he changed his mind. She held still, breathing, waiting.

"No trouble," Ellen said lightly, but Marise thought her voice sounded strained. A blaze of peacock blue left the room. As Wheaton followed her out, his arm swung around to grasp the doorknob and pull the door closed behind him. Just in time, Marise let it go. The door swung away, leaving her staring at the empty room, pressed against the wall like a squashed fly.

It seemed to Marise they were trying to decipher a code or a foreign language, since Bonner never completed a sentence or finished a thought. Some pages had only a few words on them. Others contained lists of Latin names or bibliographies of scientific books and articles. The amount of work he had done was amazing, but Marise couldn't fathom a word of it.

"Look here," Ellen said. She had turned up a diagram, a circle with gaps in it. A handwritten scribble filled each gap. "'Female muscles in limbs lay eggs in blood.' Doesn't make much sense. 'Eggs carried to lungs hatch.' This is a life cycle diagram for something, but we don't know what." She turned up the preceding page to reveal another list. Halfway down, '*Elaphostrongylus cervi*,' was circled in red.

Ellen frowned, shifting her gaze from the diagram to the list. "Are these connected? Marise, flip through your stack of papers and see if this name is in any of the titles. Eee-laff-oh-strong-eee-loos serv-i. I probably didn't say that right. I'm going to turn on the computer." She reached for her walker.

"I'll do it, Ellen." She limped back to the desktop computer and pressed the power button. A memory nudged its way into her thoughts but slipped from her mind again. Something about the long, convoluted scientific name was familiar. *Eee-laff, what?* She turned, and her eyes strayed up to the clutter on the top of the shelving.

"Come away from the window, dear."

Marise took a step toward the shelves. It felt like a lifetime ago she had poked through the clutter, but she remembered the day clearly. Pictures, knickknacks, bottles with things floating in them. *What was the thing in the big bottle? Eee-laff? Eee-laff something?* She dragged a chair over and stepped up with her good foot.

"Ellen! Look." She lifted the bottle and lowered it toward Ellen, pointing to the label. "It's like the other one. They're the same, but different. Do you think?"

Ellen looked puzzled. "*Cervus elaphus* there, *Elaphostrongylus cervi* here. You might be right. There's some connection. I'm going to Google these names and see if I can find out anything."

Marise climbed down. Pain shot through her foot as it touched the floor, and clear liquid sloshed about in the jar, making the dull white dead thing inside thump against the glass. She plunked it down on the desk and regarded it with disgust. She returned to going through the stack of papers they had abandoned.

"*Cervus elaphus* is the scientific name for elk or red deer," Ellen said. "*Hmmm.*" She tapped at the keyboard again, talking softly, "Oops, spelled it wrong . . . there, try this one . . . larvae of elapho . . . yes. Marise, the other is a parasite of the red deer, a worm, but what does this have to do with dragons? Have you found anything?"

"Well, there's stuff here about reindeer, caribou, red deer. Here's a story about an eee-laugh-oh-whatever raunge-ell. I can't say it. But it's something that made caribou sick in Newfoundland."

She looked down at a picture of a young caribou standing with its hind end twisted and its back legs pointing forward at such an extreme angle it appeared about to sit down. She crept toward the window, staying low, and showed the picture to Ellen.

Ellen looked at the sick calf and then at Marise. Her lips pursed. "I think we might be on to something."

"So, if Earl was right." Ellen rubbed her eyes. "This worm, or a worm like it, is killing the dragons. The larvae go to the brain and grow. Then worms move to the muscles and release their eggs in the blood. Eggs hatch in the lungs and larvae crawl up to the throat. Eventually, they get passed in the animal's droppings. Slugs and snails eat them, and the deer eat the snails, or whatever. But this time it's not deer, it's dragons."

"Gross," Marise said from her position on the floor.

They had been reading and surfing the internet for several hours, and they had learned a lot about *Elaphostrongylus cervi*, but she wasn't sure any of it was useful.

"But we don't know if this is even the right worm or if he was just guessing. I don't know if there are deer in Moerden. All I saw was some kind of mountain goat the dragons ate. Could they have it and dragons get the worms from eating the goats?" She covered her face with her hands. "I ate some! Anyway, there's no cure. We've found all kinds of stuff that says there's no drug to kill the worms. There's no cure, Ellen. They're all going to die!"

Ellen put down the paper she was holding. "Wait a minute. I don't think it's the mountain goats because it's too dry in the desert. Not the right place for slugs and snails! And you said the desert dragons don't get sick. No, this worm is being spread at the coast. You'll have to go there to figure out where they're getting it."

"But I don't even know if this is the right worm. I bet that's why Dr. Bonner took all those little bottles in his backpack. He was trying to prove this. *He* didn't even know if he was right. What was he going to collect? Why did he start in the desert?"

"Perhaps he thought there might be something there, at the

falls, or maybe that was the only place he could get to. It's where the mosaic is."

Marise nodded. "There's no cure."

"No," Ellen admitted. "It seems there isn't." She turned to the books in her husband's collection. "Damn him. What was he up to?" Her hands moved to the buttons of her cardigan. Starting at the top, she undid them. Then she buttoned them back up again.

Marise turned the information they had over in her mind. She thought about what she might put in all of Dr. Bonner's little containers. *Dragon dung? Deer droppings? Then what would I do? Look for microscopic worms with the little microscope.* She remembered using it in the canyon, and her dream of the mummified dragon turning to dust in a cave in the desert. Her eyes strayed to the pickled red deer embryo on the desk.

Marise and Ellen spoke at the same moment.

"The dragon!"

"But you can stop it."

"What?" Marise didn't see how she could stop the stagger if she didn't know for sure what caused it.

"Suppose it is this *E. cervi*, or something like it. There seem to be a few similar. Deer don't get it from deer, dragons don't get it from dragons. They get it from something they're eating, something that doesn't live in the desert. It's safe for the coastal dragons to move to the desert. They're not contagious."

Marise spoke slowly, trying to follow. "Right. But they could never go back. Or would the worm die out after a while?"

"That depends on whether another animal is spreading it at the coast. I think probably there is an animal involved. A deer of some sort—whatever the dragons are eating. What were you thinking? You said something."

"Yeah. The mummy. I was thinking if the worm really causes the stagger, there should be mummified worms in that dragon's skull.

They'd mummify too, wouldn't they? If I got back there, I could prove it really is a worm like that."

"Brilliant," Ellen said. "I think we have the bones of a plan. *Oops, no pun intended.*" She laughed. "You can go back, get to the dragon mummy, and take its head apart. If you find worms, you can go to the coast, look for deer—and Earl—and tell the coastal dragons to move to the desert." Her smile faded. "Simple, eh? Easy as getting everyone on Earth to stop smoking." She shook her head.

"Great Mother." Marise sighed. "If I don't get killed going back, Korpec will probably get me, or the coastal dragons will kill me. I don't even know how far it is to the coast. Javeer will help, I guess, and maybe Kuvrema." A knot twisted and squirmed in her stomach.

"You're right, dear. It may be impossible. Foolish. Earl has probably already died trying to do this. Do you really still want to go? We could put your sphere outside in the sun and send you home to your parents where you belong. Forget about Moerden."

The knot of fear exploded like hot firefruit. "No! No, I can't leave Javeer waiting like that. Not go back because I'm afraid! Let them die not knowing what I know. I've done enough damage everywhere. I have to go back! But," Marise paused and lowered her voice, "I need a little time. Can I take a shower, maybe eat something? And think about what I need to take with me?"

"Yes, of course! Dear, dear, what am I thinking? You do need a shower. Let's put a plastic bag over that foot. Do you need something for pain?" She rose from her chair and offered Marise a hand.

"While you're getting cleaned up, I'll make us some snacks. We'll fill the backpack with food and pain relievers and anything you want. Anything you want, dear. Now take your time. Relax. When you're ready, if you still want to, you can go."

Chapter
Eleven

CANYON RATS

Earl overlooked the delta from a rocky escarpment. He weighed his options. If he climbed down, he'd be out of the canyon, but he'd be exposed to the sky until he reached the swamps near the coast. It would take a day or two to get under cover again, maybe longer if he got lost in the winding channels. If he stayed near the canyon mouth, however, the jeong would soon find him. A brown twig between his teeth flicked up and down as he studied the terrain below and wondered if he had already come too far.

The Darjugan River rumbled down from higher ground, splitting into two as soon as it leveled off. In the distance, the streams joined again, creating a long thin island, but not before each gave rise to several smaller streams that fanned out across the plain. Little grew there, but gaunt knots of bitterbush lined up twenty paces from the riverbank as though they dared come no closer.

Earl turned to look upriver. *A man could live forever up there, if he could tame those cursed bojerts. But do what? This is the only way out if you can't fly. Still, it might be better to stay up there than perish in that miserable marsh.* Delaying his decision once again, he leaned against a rock and closed his eyes, letting his thoughts run back over two and a half weeks spent in the canyon.

It was daybreak in Moerden when he arrived on the mosaic. He shrugged off his backpack and deposited it in the tunnel beside two boxes he'd left the day before. With his fist, he shaped a depression in the top of the bag, nestled the sphere there, and turned to the falls.

He gazed at the glittering curtain of water, hoping to catch a glimpse of the rainbow beyond. The roar of the waterfall was deafening, but a prickly feeling soon replaced the pleasure of the moment, and he hunched his shoulders, wondering what had changed. A breeze touched the back of his neck, stirring the fine hairs there. Goosebumps broke out on his arms, and he wheeled around.

A monstrous gray-green dragon blocked the passage. *Korpec.*

By reflex, Earl raised his right hand, but it was empty. He'd left the sphere in the cave. He was trapped.

Korpec arched his neck and looked down at Earl, clearly pleased with the situation. Croaking, he glided nearer.

Earl looked around. The delicate plant growth in the mouth of the cave and the plunging water offered no shelter. If he gained the side tunnel, he could jump through the falls at the end, but Korpec could follow. He looked up at the dragon and opened his mouth to plead, knowing it was pointless.

Korpec crowed gleefully and drew a breath, pulling his head back and opening his jaws wide.

Poised to dash for the side cave, Earl saw a crimson glow in the monster's throat and scrambled backward instead, heedless of the precipice. The rock floor grew slick and curved downward. He felt himself starting to slide as the spray of the falls enveloped him. He pitched forward, unable to find a handhold as he careened toward the cascade, but instead of going over the edge, he slid to the side, toward a dark opening at the base of the wall. Earl gripped the edge of the opening for a moment, but the surface was slimy. The mountain swallowed him.

The cavity led to a natural chimney, steep, twisting and perpetually slick. He scrabbled at the rock face as he swept past, slowing his descent. In moments, he saw daylight rushing toward him and the chimney dumped him into a tangle of lush plant growth. He reached out, wrapping arms and legs around the fleshy stems. They caught him like a web and held him, dripping and gasping, while below his feet, rivulets of moisture seeped down the cliff face to a jumble of rocks and frothing water.

Plant roots and tendrils tore from the cliff face, but the greenery held and concealed him. He froze as Korpec winged past, watched as the dragon made a couple of passes over the base of the falls before emitting a shriek and soaring out through the opening in the cliffs. The cry echoed off rock walls all around.

When his heart rate slowed, Earl descended through the tangle until he stood on rock near the base of the falls. He immediately disliked the place. Gusts of spray and mist buffeted him, but they didn't hide an odd unpleasant smell and a brooding atmosphere. Water roiled violently under the deluge from above, but the river was the only way out, and he didn't want to stay another moment. He skirted the worst of the cascade, tucked his head between his arms, and sliced into the water, calling up skills from years of competitive swimming and diving.

The turbulent water dragged him deep into the pool, tumbling him over and over until he lost all sense of which way was up. He held his breath, curled into a ball, and let the water take him. Moments later, he popped to the surface, gasping for air. He was at the mouth of the channel, where swift currents plowed through a narrow opening.

He sped into the canyon beyond the cliffs.

The fury of the falls faded, the river spread out, and Earl could relax and drift. He was exhausted. A dull pain throbbed relentlessly in the center of his chest. Before long, he was shivering in spite of the desert heat, and he knew he had to get to shore.

He spotted a wide pebbled beach where the river was shallow and lots of vegetation grew. Canyon grals climbed cliff walls on either side, laden with fruit, and he thought he saw a patch of waever vine as well. He crawled out and sprawled on smooth beach stones that were hot from baking in the sun.

The pain in his chest faded, and though his bed was hard, he grew drowsy. He thought he should take his clothes off and let them dry in the breeze, thought he really needed to get under cover where Korpec wouldn't see him, but he hadn't the energy to move. Soon, he was softly snoring.

Earl rested in the little glade all the next day. There was no point going back. He couldn't get back up to the cave, and even if his food and supplies were still there, his sphere was lost. "I won't be finding what spreads the stagger now," he told a nodding pink blossom. "The only way is downriver. There's only desert up above, and I can't climb out."

He kept an eye out for dragons in the sky, and at night, he curled up in the vegetation at the foot of the cliff, with broad flat leaves above him. Nothing troubled him, except an occasional small flock of flycatchers passing over, dipping and wheeling, sometimes diving into the canyon to snap insects out of the air.

His exhaustion and scrapes healed. The canyon provided food in abundance—ripe fruit, berries and nuts, creatures he saw living in the water that he might eat raw if he had to, and lots of edible plants. Canyon grals were particularly plentiful and at their peak. Earl ate one after another, piling glossy white pits on a ledge in the cliff wall. He cracked large argar seeds between rocks, cleaned out the mild filling with his tongue and tossed the empty shells on the beach.

He had no reason to stay put. No one would come and save him. He'd run out of food eventually and be forced to move on. But he knew the canyon zigzagged through the desert valley for many miles before flowing into the delta near the coast. It was a long journey with a vast, treacherous swamp at the end.

On the third morning after his narrow escape, he pushed aside the greenery and squinted at the empty sky. He peered through the forest of plant stems and picked out three whiskery faces with enormous eyes and sharp pointed noses watching from the shadows.

Earl knew there were more bojerts around. The brown and tan stripe running up each cheek helped the creatures blend with their surroundings. The day before, he'd seen only one, and it had fled, shrieking and agitating the plant growth for some distance upstream. This morning, they were bolder, retreating when he shook the vegetation and shouted, but then they closed in again. He figured it was time to go.

He filled his pockets with argar seed and hacked down several lengths of waever vine with a jagged rock. These he wound into thick coils, taking care not to tangle them. The shorter lengths, he laid down in opposite directions, making a wide brim for a hat, and he propped it on his head to shape the cap. It was a tangled mess, and the brim flopped down around his ears. He wove some sticks through to give it more structure and decided it would do.

Earl wedged his watch, ruined in the river, between rocks at the water's edge so its crystal reflected the noon sunlight. "There. If Korpec sees you, he'll think you came off my dead wrist. But then again, friendlier eyes might see, and know I was here for a while." He slung the coils of waever vine across his chest and set off downstream.

He made slow progress. The river was too deep to walk in easily, and the plants on the banks grew so thickly it was even harder to push through on land. The nagging pain in his chest returned. He had to pause often to rest. As afternoon shadows gathered at the foot of the cliff, he had to stop, though he thought he'd only progressed a mile or two.

The next day, he fared no better. When the canyon opened up into a broad swale with a small lake in the center and dotted stands of tall bamboo-like canes along its shores, he stopped. At midafternoon, he sat throwing stones into the clear water, weighing whether to stay or move on.

There were houra in the shallows. He saw the slow vortices where they drew water in through their spiral grooves, and an occasional puff of sand when one flushed itself.

"Lots of food here, but I'm not sure I fancy them raw." Earl said. "Any chance houra are what's spreading the stagger?" He thought about it. "No. Whatever it is, it lives at the coast." He watched as a sliver of wood drifted in and got caught in a vortex. It turned lazily, so buoyant on the water. Earl hit it with a rock, and it scooted away.

"Like a water boatman. Like a boat or a raft."

He got up and strode along the shore to the nearest clump of canes. He seized a stem and yanked it toward him. To his delight, it came out of the mud with a slurp and a whiff of sulfur. He tossed it into the water, and it floated.

By sundown the following day, Earl had a raft long enough to lie down on. He'd lashed it together with waever, and he could roll it up and tuck it under his arm. It easily held his weight when he'd tested it on the lake.

He cast off early the next morning, poling straight across to the far side where the flow grew turbulent, and the river roared out of the lake. The raft pitched and bucked until he sat down and gave up trying to do anything but keep it off the rocks. By the time the current slowed and he could focus on steering, he was soaked and shaken, and he'd lost his hat.

In midafternoon, a sandstorm rolled over the edge of the canyon, dumping sand on everything in its path, but the pull of the current carried him clear. He turned to look back at the boiling clouds of dust until a bend in the canyon blocked his view.

Hours later, the raft rode up on a pebbly beach, miles downstream. The storm was a dim memory, and Earl felt extraordinarily tired. He foraged along the riverbank for some supper, only to come upon his hat, waterlogged and crusted with sand. He washed it, then lay down, concealed in a thicket of plant growth at the bottom of the cliff. As his breathing slowed, he noticed a damp musky smell lingering near the ground but dismissed it and sank into a deep sleep.

Earl jerked upright with a yell. Lashing out with his arm, he succeeded only in sending the leaves above him into a quivering dance. A bojert squealed and retreated into a burrow at the base of the cliff, kicking sand out behind it in its haste.

"Bloody. Rats!" Earl yelled, clapping a hand to his bleeding ear. "It bit me." He crashed through the thicket to where the raft lay rolled at the top of the shingle. The striped tails of several bojerts vanished into the undergrowth to left and right. They had been gnawing at his raft, working on the thick, soft stems that he had pulled from deep in the mud. Their sharp teeth had done considerable damage.

"Stupid. Brainless. Omnivores!" Earl shouted, running back and forth along the beach waving his arms. "Stinking canyon rats." He scooped up handfuls of pebbles and threw them after the bojerts. "Miserable stinking varmints. You're not going to eat my raft."

Pebbles spattered off leaves and rattled down rock walls. "That's the last time you get the chance, I promise you. The last time. Ever." Earl kicked up a spray of beach rock and then sank to his knees, gasping for breath with one hand pressed against his chest. "Rats," he muttered, stretching out on the pebbles and rolling over to look up at the sky. "Can't let them eat the raft."

That night and every night thereafter, Earl slept on the raft, drifting downstream, trusting the darkness to hide him. He spread leaves underneath him to stop water from splashing up through the cracks, and more leaves on top of him for warmth and camouflage, and he settled his hat over his exposed face. He found himself caught up on rocks every morning, or entangled in weeds, but he had no more trouble with bojerts, and even chuckled at times when he looked at the ragged ends of his precious craft.

One night as he drifted, listening to the gentle lapping of water, he watched the full moon edge past the lip of the canyon and slowly cross that river of sky. "I wonder if that's the same moon they're looking at in Cadogan Mills," he said, "It's two weeks since I came to Moerden. Two weeks in this blessed canyon and no end in sight. I wonder what Ellen is up to."

The silhouettes of three dragons passed across the face of the moon, flying west and high, and he held his breath.

Two days later, Earl noticed the canyon walls had dwindled, and on the third day, he climbed off the raft at the edge of the river delta and knew everything was about to change.

Chapter
Twelve

REMAINS
OF THE DEAD

"Wait!" Ellen raised a hand in warning. "What if something's in the circle at the other end? What if Javeer is sitting on it?"

Marise stood in the kitchen, cupping the relic sphere in the palm of her left hand. She was dressed in stained but freshly laundered blue jeans, a flower print short-sleeved cotton blouse she'd borrowed from Ellen, and her battered sneakers. A bandaged toe protruded from the open end of the right shoe. Except for bruises on her arms and an unseasonal suntan, she looked quite herself.

Bonner's backpack hung from her shoulders, bulging with clothing and supplies—a dark green hoodie, a pair of sunglasses, travel-size soap, shampoo, toothpaste and a toothbrush, fresh bandages with antibiotic ointment, a Swiss Army knife, and a small dissecting kit retrieved from Bonner's office. The two women had decided against packing food as Moerden provided plenty, but there was a box of crackers for Javeer.

Marise nodded at Ellen, her eyes wide. "Yes. I haven't forgotten. I need to look where I'm going!" She put the sphere down on the mosaic. "That'll help me visualize the other mosaic as well." Gazing into it, she pictured the cave with its high ceiling and tiled floor.

The pattern and circling dragons illuminated by afternoon sunlight came into view.

Nothing blocked the mosaic. She took a moment to check the entrances under the falls and the sloping tunnel to the surface, finding she could move her view from place to place with increasing ease. Javeer was by the lookoff on top, gazing out toward the valley. He tilted his head as though listening, and she knew he felt her gaze.

"Okay," Marise said with satisfaction. "The circle's clear, and Javeer's there waiting. I should go." She picked up the sphere. "Wish me luck."

Ellen's hands gripped her walker. "Be careful, dear. I'll be waiting to hear how you fare. I'll keep the kitchen floor clear."

Marise smiled and looked down at the floor. She placed her feet carefully, so that she saw most of the mosaic clearly. The white bandage on her right foot caught her eye.

Get this wrong and you're dead.

Her imagination summoned a gruesome image of her body protruding from a rock. She wondered how that would feel—or would she be killed instantly? How much of her would have to be in the rock to kill her?

She swallowed and took a shaky breath. Her heart was racing.

"Marise? Are you alright, dear?" Ellen's voice cut through Marise's panic.

"Uh. Yeah. Okay. Okay." She sucked in another breath, forcing herself back to reality. "Got to stay calm. Give me a moment." She went smoothly into her meditation exercise, recalling how terrified she'd been before her first flight with Javeer, how she'd managed to calm herself. *Breathe in perfect love. Breathe out perfect trust. Trust, trust, trust.* When she felt her heart slowing, she focused on the floor.

She envisioned carved dragons linking into each other and circling the mosaic in a red cave floor. Gazing at the center pattern, she imagined herself standing on it. Then she brought the sphere down in front of her and focused her gaze within it. Her mental image of the mosaic faltered, but she breathed in slowly and brought it back. She saw it inside the sphere. Her feet left the floor.

This time there was no awkward landing, just an adrenaline rush that left her breathless. One moment she was in Ellen's kitchen; the next, she stood in the cave by the falls. She sighed with relief and turned just in time to see Javeer bounding down the tunnel from above.

"I'm back, Javeer," she said as she hugged his neck. "I've lots to tell you. Did you find Kuvrema?"

A splash from behind and a lull in the roar of the waterfall made her spin with alarm. A dark form crashed through the curtain, splattering water over the walls and floor, setting the plants swaying. Momentum carried the form on, and it barreled toward them. Marise cried out and reached for Javeer, who drew himself up, half spreading his wings. As one, they moved backward, eyes on the intruder.

A large dragon advanced, shaking water off its scaly copper hide. The dragon's head came down, and their eyes met. Kuvrema had found them.

Marise and Javeer sat with their backs to the setting sun. Though she could have used her relic sphere, she held his for companionship. Their heads turned in unison from time to time as Kuvrema passed above. She flew in a zigzag pattern, searching in the rocky crags to the north, sometimes dropping out of sight for minutes at a time.

"Kuvrema didn't like it when she saw Dr. Bonner's pack and all his stuff scattered around in the cave. She didn't even ask about us."

'She looked even worse when you told her he'd disappeared from Cadogan Mills before you even came here,' Javeer replied. *'She wasn't*

surprised you knew him, though, was she? I think she knew him too. There's something she's not saying.'

"Kuvrema keeps to herself. Do you think she'll find him out there? She'll have to give up soon. It's getting dark."

As if she'd overheard, Kuvrema rose from behind the nearest peak and glided in to join them. She spat out a milky globe, opaque as bleached bone. Javeer jerked back with a grunt of disgust, and Marise leaned forward to get a better view.

'A relic sphere left in sunlight.'

Kuvrema's words made Marise go still, and goosebumps rose on her arms.

'His remains were not with it, so he may still be alive, but I am not hopeful. This sphere lay on a ledge no climber could reach. A dragon put it there.'

"But that means other dragons know about this place!" Marise looked around as if expecting a whole squadron of them to appear. "We're not safe here."

'No. My coming here may have made it less safe. We must leave in the morning. But first, we must decide where we're going. Tell me everything that's happened since you left my rhumba.'

Javeer filled in the details up to the point where Marise left for Cadogan Mills. Kuvrema cooed with surprise when she learned he had secretly carried a sphere in his stomach for over a year. When told about the house fire, she clucked, then shifted with apparent nervousness at the part where they'd planned Marise's trip back to Bonner's office.

'If I'd anticipated you'd find a relic sphere, against all odds, I'd have told you more. Warned you not to use it under any circumstances. Many have died. But did you go? You've been and came back safely?'

"Yep, but not without hurting myself." Marise pointed to her bandaged toe. She picked up the story, pausing often to answer questions. Javeer cringed when she described what had happened to her toe. He kept asking to hear that part again. She finished with her plan to return to the forbidden cave and dissect the mummy's skull.

Javeer and Kuvrema gawked at her, horror clear on their faces.

"I know it's gross," she said, "but it's the only way we could think of to prove a worm causes the stagger."

'You want to go back to the mummy? After what happened? Do you want to get us killed?' Javeer thrust his snout so close to Marise's face she had to pull her head back.

'And disturb the remains of a dragon who suffered a horrible death?' Kuvrema added. *'Cut his head open looking for worms? Do you know what you're saying? And if you find worms in the dragon's head, what then? No. This can't be. Is this what you do in your world? Pick apart the remains of the dead?'*

"Well, yes, sometimes." Marise was dumbfounded. *Don't they understand what I'm trying to do? What's wrong with them? I suppose I'd never dig up a dead person at home and smash their head open. Gross. But people do exhume bodies sometimes. Wouldn't it be worth it if we could save lives?*

"Listen." She chose her words with care. "If I'm right, we can save other dragons from dying. We just have to stop them . . . I mean, without proving it *is* the worm, we'll never convince dragons like Korpec it's not contagious. That dragons can't get it from dragons. It's easy. We can find out whether the dragon in the cave had worms in his skull. Without that, we're only guessing."

Kuvrema stayed silent.

'I can't go back.' Javeer sounded uneasy.

"Kuvrema, remember when you said you thought I might be able to help? I thought you were crazy then—sorry—but now I think you were right. We have to find out if I'm right about the worms. Do you think the dead dragon would really mind me looking inside its head if it meant we could save the dragons that are left?" She gestured at the two dragons. "He . . . it was *he*, wasn't it?

He would hate those worms even more than we do. I won't do anything more than I must to prove it. I promise. Kuvrema, I can do this. Maybe I'm the only one who can. Isn't it worth it?"

'And if you found the worms?' Kuvrema sounded undecided now.

'I won't go back in there,' Javeer said flatly.

"Javeer, I can't do it without you! I'll need light. You can look the other way. Just stretch out your tail near me so I can see."

'I'm not turning my back to that thing.'

'Oh! You males are intolerable,' Kuvrema snapped. *'If you won't do it, I will. Marise, what will you do if you find these worms?'*

"If I do, then we go to the coast, figure out what's spreading it, and tell the coastal dragons how to avoid catching it. Are there deer at the coast?"

'Yes!' Kuvrema and Javeer answered in unison.

Thoughts and images came in a rush. All Marise got out of it was that the deer at the coast were important in some way to the coastal dragons.

"That's probably it then," she said with satisfaction. "We go find the deer, use the microscope to prove they're spreading the worm. *Ugh*! Then we can explain it to the coastal dragons and get them all to move to the desert where there are no deer."

'What! Tell them they have to leave the forest? Move them into cliff rhumba? That will never work.' Kuvrema got up and walked to the edge of the cliff. *'Still, if you're right about the stagger, it would end this nonsense about killing humans and locking dying dragons in caves. Dragons can't catch it from dragons?'*

"No. If we're right, they catch it from deer. But once they have it, there's no cure."

Kuvrema looked off toward the horizon, her thoughts hidden. When she spoke again, it felt like she was merely thinking aloud. *'Something is not right about this. When would he have?'* She went silent once more.

She turned to face them at last. *'I had a son, Jigmae. He died of the stagger some time ago. He spent time at the coast—on Korpec's patrol—until he became what they guarded against, slowly losing his mind. Korpec realized it first. He had the males take Jigmae to the delta while he could still fly. They kept him there. Wouldn't let him come home.'* She spoke with bitterness.

'Krivic told me Jigmae died turning circles in the swamp, setting marsh gases ablaze with his breath.' She turned away, seemingly lost in her memories once more.

"Kuvrema, I'm very sorry." Marise remembered saying something similar to Ellen after Bonner disappeared. At the time, she'd just been uttering appropriate words, but now she'd never been more sincere—for both of them.

Kuvrema started and looked directly at Marise. *'Yes. I'm not telling you this to make you feel sorry for me. I'm telling you because I don't think Jigmae ate any deer. They don't hunt while they're down there. Fish only. They would have to venture further to hunt the deer. It would be an intrusion and take them into stagger territory.'*

"Fish?" Marise's thoughts were muddled. Javeer's memories of his father's death flashed through her mind. She thought about Jigmae's fate and regretted reminding Kuvrema of it, but she pushed those thoughts aside and recalled the details of the *Elaphostrongylus* life cycle. She was sure there had been no mention of fish.

"Well." Marise sighed. "I don't think I'm wrong, and there's only one way to find out. I'm sorry, Kuvrema, but I believe it's the deer. Jigmae must have eaten deer at some point. Don't they meet up with coastal dragons sometimes? He must have shared a deer with them, maybe?"

'It's possible, I suppose,' Kuvrema admitted. *'I hope you're right. If we do as you suggest and you don't find worms, I fear my rhumba will be destroyed. Tensions are too high.'*

'I don't want to go back into that cave,' Javeer said. *'But if you insist*

on going, I won't be left behind. What's happened at the rhumba? Things are worse? How will we get in and get away without being seen?'

'It will be difficult. As soon as Korpec learned you were gone, he put out extra patrols to make sure you don't come back. He's been working the rhumba, telling everyone you let the disease out of the cave. Dragons are leaving. Heading inland. Even I can't convince them Korpec is paranoid. They're terrified.'

"Wouldn't they be too afraid of the stagger to attack us?"

'They probably wouldn't touch you, that's true.' Kuvrema inhaled and blew a gust of flame at the sunset. *'They can still kill you.'*

"Oh. Right." Marise felt foolish.

'Darkness,' Javeer said. *'We go in late at night, leave before dawn. We'll be safe inside—from live dragons, at least.'*

Marise was spooked. "Go in there in the dark? Last time we didn't last two minutes, and it was broad daylight."

'It's dark inside, anyway. And this time we know what we're going to find. Kuvrema?'

'We have time to decide. Let's leave in the morning and follow the canyon. I want to look for the professor. If he's alive, that's where he'll be. By the time we near the rhumba, perhaps things will be clearer.'

Before lying down, Marise got the crackers she'd brought from Cadogan Mills. She opened a sleeve for Javeer and deliberately left the remainder on the floor in case he wanted to snack during the night.

In her dreams, she relived Kuvrema's sudden entrance through the falls again and again, but it was Korpec who came, carrying a dead sphere in his mouth. He stalked past the mosaic, leaving a slippery trail, and held the sphere so close she felt his hot breath. She smelled burning sugar.

Marise woke with a gasp. She stared into the darkness, listening for sounds over the roar of the falls. The burnt sugar smell remained, but she heard nothing. Eventually she nodded off again, curled against Javeer's warm side.

In the morning, cracker crumbs and damp patches littered the cave floor. Javeer looked mournful, and she wondered how he'd done that without waking her. But there wasn't time to ask. Kuvrema waited for them by the falls.

Marise shouldered the backpack, slung her sneakers around her neck, and wrapped the green cloak around her. Soon, they were off.

Kuvrema went straight out through the falls, leaping powerfully at the deluge, holding her wings tight against her body until she was clear. Marise noticed that Javeer watched the maneuver with interest, but she was sure she would be knocked from his back if they tried it. They hurried to launch from the lookoff and joined Kuvrema as she circled the turbulent bowl at the base of the falls.

Marise looked at the chaos where water struck rock and remembered how she'd nearly been swept over the lip above. The back of her neck prickled. *No one could survive that fall.*

An unpleasant odor drifted by, and the feeling of disquiet increased. The hairs on her arms stood up, and her fingers tightened around Javeer's halter. He passed close to the base, and the odor intensified. She suspected yet another cave lay hidden there, but she couldn't imagine what might live in it.

Kuvrema led them out into the canyon. The mingled scent of flowers and wet rock exploded around them, and Marise relaxed. Heading southwest, the two dragons flew side by side above the river.

For a while, a group of flashy green and yellow birds fluttered between them. Their cries reminded Marise of seagulls. Her eyes followed them, admiring their agility, and as they dipped, wheeled, and turned back, she saw a brilliant flash from the riverbank. She pointed with a shout. "What's that?"

Javeer descended, with Kuvrema close behind. Marise peered down, trying to identify the silvery object wedged between rocks. "It's a piece of metal or glass," she said when he landed. "Reflecting sunlight." She dismounted and reached down to pull it free.

"A watch. A man's watch." She held it up.

Kuvrema swung her tail sphere around. *'Is it Earl's?'*

"I don't know. Why would he leave it here?" She looked around. "If he was here, we might find something else."

They searched both riverbanks and worked their way back, finding numerous argar seed shells. Javeer whistled from the cliff wall, and they joined him. He'd found a pyramid of white firefruit seeds piled on a ledge like a little shrine. Swinging his head around, he overcompensated, smacked his nose into the cliff and sent seeds tumbling into the greenery. In seconds, just three seeds remained, rocking gently on the ledge.

"Javeer, are you okay?"

'I was clumsy again.' He hung his head. *'Sorry. That big pile of gral seeds. Only a human would do that, right?'*

"I saw them." Marise looked over her shoulder at Kuvrema, who shook her head in frustration.

'Yes, I saw them too,' Kuvrema said. *'Argar seed shells are all over the beach, too. Bojerts don't bring lunch to the river. I think Earl was here, but we can't be sure. It doesn't matter, Javeer. Let's move on and see if we find anything else. Look carefully. Keep an eye out above as well. I want to know if we're being followed.'*

Kuvrema flew high, moving from side to side. Javeer stayed low enough for Marise to watch for footprints. The stony beaches recorded no sign of Bonner's passing, but she had her first clear sighting of a bojert just before they arrived at the lake.

The animal gnawed at something at the edge of the beach. It fled when Javeer's shadow fell across it, and Marise watched the leaves shake in a straight line all the way to the cliff base. "Bojert."

'Yes. Lots of them down here,' Javeer said. *'They eat everything, even each other. But they're afraid of everything too. They run for cover if a fly buzzes. Look there.'* He turned and approached a bedraggled stand of tall plants at the water's edge. Prints left by human shoes

pocked the soft mud, as if someone had tramped around the area for hours.

Kuvrema took this as proof Bonner lived, but though they scoured the shore, they found no further sign of him, nor did they find anything as they searched methodically down the canyon. By early evening, they neared the rhumba and spent as much time watching the sky as they did scanning the ground. At last, they settled on the riverbank where Marise and Javeer had shared their first picnic and the conversation returned to the mummy.

Marise dumped out the backpack. A box of chocolate rosebuds slipped out of the rolled hoodie, and she oohed with delight. She hadn't seen Ellen slip them in. The chocolate was in a melted lump at the bottom of the plastic liner. She peeled back the plastic and offered the sweet to Kuvrema and Javeer, who sniffed it curiously but turned it down.

She put the chocolate aside and set about re-bandaging her toe. As she worked, she held the relic sphere against her right ankle with the uninjured foot, hoping to hear the dragons talk with her hands free.

'So, we'll go as soon as it's dark?' Javeer asked.

'I don't like it. I don't think we've been seen—yet. But I'm sure you will be spotted if you try to reach the cave tonight. Better to go in before dawn. I'll fly ahead to divert the patrol, if there is one, and you two can follow. You'll have to go on to the cave alone, do what you came to do, and get out. Head for the canyon, then the coast. I'll follow.'

"Yes," Marise agreed. "This way we can get some sleep before we go. And we won't have to spend the night in the cave. If we're fast enough, we can get out of the rhumba right away."

'Ah.' Javeer sounded relieved.

Marise shoved two glass bottles and a pair of surgical gloves back into the pack. She added bandages and ointment, the dissecting kit, and a sleeve of crackers. She debated taking the microscope, too. They must have that if they went south later, but she didn't want to risk losing it if their mission didn't go well. Several times, she put it in the backpack and took it out again, finally resolving to leave it behind.

She laid the hoodie and the chocolate on the beach, bundled everything else in her cape, and tied the fabric in a bulky knot. "Can bojerts climb?" She stood and tried to lodge the bundle in some high branches.

'No. They can jump, but they cannot climb. Give me that.' Kuvrema took the sack in a wing claw and flew up, stashing it on a high ledge. Marise took careful note of the location. *'Now,'* Kuvrema said, dropping back to the beach. *'I'm hungry.'*

Chapter
Thirteen

FUGITIVES

Marise and Javeer strove to remain silent and invisible as they winged across the desert toward the rhumba. She hunched on his back with her hood drawn tight around her face and the sleeves extended down over her hands. The hoodie covered the backpack so that the cold glow of moonlight wouldn't reflect and give them away, and Javeer stayed within the shadow cast by Kuvrema, who flew above and a little ahead.

As the cliffs drew near, Kuvrema veered left toward the outcropping of rock that concealed the ledge of her cave. She reached the closest end of the formation, and they watched her hesitate for a moment, letting her shadow blend with the pool of darkness at the foot of the cliff. She turned for home in a leisurely curve while Javeer and Marise turned the opposite way and began to climb.

Marise longed to look up, scan the sky for dragons, see where they were going, but she kept her face turned down. Her heart raced as they approached the mummy cave and she readied herself for the landing.

Javeer came down perfectly, but lost his balance for a moment, and pitched toward the cliff wall. To Marise's relief, he righted himself. He turned toward the tunnel entrance. She ducked, and he walked straight in. As soon as they were completely inside, he lit his sphere, and slid it out from under cover. She slipped to the floor, pulled the hoodie over her head, and shrugged off the backpack, then lifted the relic sphere out of it.

"You ready?" Despite her bravado earlier, Marise was reluctant. She felt like a grave robber.

'Not ready, but when you go, I'll go. I'll go around the far side so I can give you light.'

"I'm scared, Javeer! You scared?"

'Scared. But I won't leave you this time. We're going to do it and get out before the sun rises. Right?'

"Right." She took a deep breath and hoisted the backpack. "Let's go." She walked toward the mummy, Javeer's light trembling above her. Soon, she stood over the corpse.

The dragon had died with his wings partly folded, and wing claws extended as though he meant to push himself up but never found the strength. His neck lay curved in an S, his head turned away from the cave entrance. Marise studied the sunken eyes, the teeth poking through cracked lips, the bare cheeks where scales had fallen. She shuddered.

'Marise?'

Marise started. "Sorry. We need to change places so I can get at, um, see the back of his skull. Can you come over here?"

He shuffled around and turned so his back was toward the dragon's crumbling face. He held his sphere high above it. The circle of light quivered.

Trying to still her shaking hands, she thought, *If I was holding that light, it'd be shaking a lot harder.* She set the sphere down and found the dissecting kit in the backpack. She fumbled with its ties. The stiff canvas unrolled like a parchment to reveal an array of blades and other instruments, each tucked into its own narrow sleeve. Marise laid the collection on the cave floor.

"Bide the Wiccan rede you must," Marise muttered, pulling out a scalpel, a probe, and a pair of forceps. "In perfect love, in perfect trust." She laid the tools beside the mummy's right jaw. "Eight words the Wiccan rede fulfill." She groped in the bottom of the backpack for a bottle and a pair of surgical gloves and shifted closer to the corpse. "If you harm none, do what you will."

Javeer drew an enormous breath, and the light swung away for a moment, then jerked back. Marise put on the gloves and picked up the scalpel.

"Sorry, my friend," Marise said softly, scraping dry skin off the back of the skull with a shaking hand. The remaining scales slid away, and flakes of parched flesh followed. Bone lay beneath, hard and unyielding. "In perfect love, in perfect trust," Marise breathed, biting off the words. A cloud of fine dust brought a smell of musty basement, and she turned her face away, digging her nose into the crook of her elbow. *I'm breathing in dead dragon!* she thought, fighting the panicky feeling in her chest. *That's so disgusting!*

Javeer blew a thin jet of flame at the cave floor, igniting a pile of twigs and leaves that flared brightly, glowed, and went out, producing a curl of aromatic smoke.

"Thanks!" Marise suspected it was coincidence, that Javeer was just distracting himself, but the smoke smelled better than the mummy, and it brought her back to the moment. She went back to work, scraping lower to expose the base of the skull.

Suddenly, she knew she was being watched. She lurched backward, dropping the scalpel. It plunged straight down into the mummy's neck, crashing through brittle skin and protruding like a skewer.

"Someone's here! Who's that?" Marise twisted to look toward the door. "Javeer, someone's here." She grasped her sphere. "Someone's here! Kuvrema?"

'I don't know. I don't think it's Kuvrema. She said she would only watch the ledge outside.'

"Who then? Not Korpec. Tell me it isn't Korpec." The sense of another presence pressed down on her, and Marise imagined a malevolent spirit towered over her like a cobra poised to strike. Her heart raced, and her breath wheezed painfully in and out of her lungs.

'I don't know.'

"What should we do?" Marise couldn't think, couldn't stop looking around, trying to spot the intruder even though she knew she wouldn't find them. Sweat broke out on her upper lip.

'Whoever it is, they won't come in. Everyone is too afraid of catching the stagger. Our being here will make it look like Korpec was right to all the dragons in the rhumba. We have to finish, though. We won't get another chance. Go on. Do it.'

She whimpered, hugging herself. She held the sphere out in front of her with both hands and watched it jitter in rhythm with her heartbeat. The feeling of being watched stopped.

'They've gone. Quickly!'

"If you harm none, if you harm none, if you harm none," Marise repeated the mantra. She pulled the scalpel out of the mummy's neck and set to work, scraping and picking, until the lower edge of the skull lay exposed. It had a great U-shaped groove in the middle of the back to allow passage for the spinal cord. The backbone threaded into the head like a snake slipping into a mouse hole.

"*Ugh*," Marise forced herself to continue. She'd kept one hand on her sphere. "Javeer, don't look. Don't look, okay?" She shoved the fingers of her left hand under the mummy's jaw and tilted the back of its head up. Skin crumbled from the top of the snout, and the skull separated from the spine. All she saw was empty space inside. Hunched over, she reached for Javeer's sphere.

"Still can't see," Marise said. She pushed the dome of the skull higher, accidentally driving her thumb through the dragon's dead eye with a crackling sound. The musty smell grew stronger. "Oh, oh, oh, oh. This is awful."

The head tore off completely with a cracking sound. Marise bit down an exclamation and glanced at Javeer. Mercifully, he was looking away, but his tail went rigid.

She turned the skull upside down and held it like a bowl. A hard dry lump the size of a walnut, what must have once been the brain, broke free and rolled about. Tattered stalks, the remains of blood vessels perhaps, stuck out at odd angles. Filaments of dried tissue curled and peeled off the inside with each pass of the brain.

"Nothing. There's nothing in there. We were wrong." Marise felt tears of disappointment and fear burning the backs of her eyes. "I was so sure." She tipped the skull, letting the brain roll.

No worms. We haven't proved anything. We don't know what causes the stagger. This was all for nothing. Her eyes strayed back to the dragon's neck, fixing on the puncture wound made by the scalpel and tracing the spine up to the bony stump where the head once rested. The stump curved up slightly at the end, wrapped in something pale and wispy. She leaned down to look.

The structures came into focus, a knot of coiling filaments no thicker than dental floss, jumbled at the top of the bones like a tangle of Christmas lights. She pictured them alive, writhing against the inside of the skull and the underside of the brain. Marise hooted. "There they are! We were right! They must have been a lot bigger, too, before they dried out."

Reaching for the forceps, Marise plucked the tangle and shoved them into a glass jar, heedless of those that snapped with the rough handling. *All I need is proof,* she thought. *We're not gonna frame them or anything.* She dropped the jar into the backpack and placed the skull back in its original position. She gathered up her tools and sphere and turned away.

She froze, feeling an alien scrutiny lock onto her.

"Javeer!"

'I know. Look into your sphere. Look at the ledge outside. See if there's anyone there.'

Marise forced herself to stop obsessively scanning the darkness. She put the sphere down in front of her. Focusing on its center, she summoned an image of the outside. When the empty shelf materialized in the sphere, the sense of being watched faded.

'Good, they've stopped. Whoever it is knew you were looking for them and didn't want to be found. It means it's probably Korpec, or one of his cronies. And we don't know where he is. Anybody on the ledge?'

"It's still dark, but no, I'm sure he's not there."

'Are you finished? You found something, didn't you?'

"Yes! We were right about the worms! I've collected some to show Kuvrema and others. Now we can get out of here." Marise couldn't wait to leave.

'They may think we're still busy here. I think we should go right now.'

Marise scrambled to put everything into the pack and was soon on Javeer's shoulders, well covered as before. He rushed out and sprang into the air, descending toward the foothills. Dawn light glowed over the eastern peaks.

Three large dragons rose to meet them. From his size, she guessed the leader to be Korpec.

"Javeer! Look below. They're waiting for us." She wasn't holding his sphere, but Javeer's response told her he had seen them too.

He turned and dove between two peaks, emerging near the entrance to Kuvrema's cave. There was no help in sight, and he flew straight across and through another cleft. He banked sharply left, heading south.

All around them, cliffs rose to jagged peaks and plunging valleys cut further into rugged backcountry. Marise hunched down. Gripping with her legs, she looked back, watching for pursuit. A dragon came through behind them just as Javeer turned again, plunging deeper into the labyrinth. A bellow of rage echoed off the rock faces.

Javeer dodged left and right, racing up canyons, cutting around peaks. Marise was wrenched from side to side, and several times, she thought she would fall but was able to pull herself back up. She quickly learned to relax her upper body and go with it. She caught several more glimpses of the pursuit and cried out in warning, but Javeer stayed ahead of them. Smaller and more agile, he slipped through the winding canyons like an alley cat.

At length, Javeer wheeled and looked back. They'd lost their pursuers, and he settled to earth and helped Marise down. She stretched her legs and looked around. The ground was rough, strewn with boulders and slabs of rock, and she propped herself against one. No life was visible, and though it was cool now, she knew it would be roasting hot at midday. She was also lost.

She reached for his offered sphere. "Good flying, Javeer! You lost them."

'Good riding, Marise. I hardly felt you there. But we can't stay here! We have to get back to the river. The more daylight there is, the harder it will be. We'll head up and cross above Korpec's cave, then come downriver. They'll expect the opposite.' He curved his neck around Marise's shoulder and nudged the backpack with his nose. *'Have we got any crackers?'*

They shared the rest of the crackers, and Javeer agreed to try the chocolate. *'Mmm, a bit like kreel.'* He took another morsel.

She wondered what kreel was, doubting dragons were into making candy. Rolling a nugget of chocolate around in her mouth, she showed Javeer the bottle with the tangle of mummified worms.

He looked at them intently and even asked Marise to take the lid off so he could see them more clearly. Then he asked her to put them away.

The two set off again, flying slowly and deliberately, until they reached the last line of cliffs before the desert. Javeer hovered, and Marise surveyed the open space ahead. She allowed herself to hope they would reach the river undetected. As they hung there, the top rim of the sun edged past the jagged line of the horizon, casting bright rays across the expanse.

'If anyone's looking from the rhumba, the sun will be in their eyes. I'm going to fly very high. It might take longer to notice us. Okay? If we're chased, I'll come down.'

"Yikes. Okay, yeah. I'm ready for anything."

'Right. Time to go.'

Javeer circled back and climbed to a dizzying height before winging out over the plain. She clung to the bridle, white knuckled, terrified and thrilled at once. The view was spectacular. She gazed up and down the valley, seeing innumerable peaks stretching far on both sides. *A dragon near the ground would look like an ant from this height,* she thought. *It's like being in a plane.*

She quickly realized her perspective was off when three dragons lifted off to her left before Javeer had crossed even half the distance to the canyon. They looked much bigger than ants. So did three others, who came winging up the plain from the rhumba.

Javeer launched into a stomach-churning dive aimed straight at the rift where mist rose from the river. Marise was flung backward, and she clung desperately with knees and hands. Her face stung as grit struck her exposed skin. She closed her eyes but couldn't bear not seeing what was going on. Squinting, she looked down to her left. Six dragons sped below, flying to intercept them near the ground.

Javeer came down faster than he had ever done before. They had a slight lead and would reach the lip of the canyon first, but she wondered what good it would do to drop into the chasm with six determined enemies chasing them.

They gained the edge, with Korpec close behind. He was closing the gap. Fire scorched the air above Marise's head. She ducked, lurched forward, and turned her face away.

Javeer careened down between the canyon walls. He headed downriver, still descending. He turned, without warning, and she had to throw out one leg for balance. They hovered above the river in a bottleneck where the surrounding cliffs curved in and forced the river through a narrow gap. He dipped toward the water and bounced back up, dodging another blast of fire.

Marise realized it was an advantage to be in the canyon because the attackers were forced to crowd together. She glanced downriver, wondering if more dragons might come from that direction.

Looking forward again, she questioned why Javeer had chosen to turn and fight. Then she noticed the second trio of dragons were females, and one of them was Kuvrema.

The females bellowed and entered the fray, engaging the males in a firefight that cut the morning mist, flying as a writhing tangle of sinuous necks and tails, highlighted by blasts of fire. A chorus of screeches split the dawn air and echoed through the canyon.

Korpec broke away and advanced upon Javeer, breathing a steady roar of flame. Marise struggled to stay seated as Javeer dodged and ducked, answering with his own fire. One on one, he was no match for Korpec, and the larger male pushed them to the side. Javeer couldn't slip through the gap and flee downriver and was driven backward toward the canyon wall. They were trapped.

A screech from the clash in the background distracted Korpec, and Javeer seized the opening. He surged forward and aimed his fire at Korpec's eyes. The older male shrieked and dropped toward the river. Javeer turned tail and sped away, gaining altitude and speed on the other side of the gap. His sphere came around to Marise.

"Did you blind him?"

'Only temporarily. He won't be after us for a minute or two. I can out-fly him if we don't lose any time.'

Marise was both relieved and appalled.

Javeer bolted between canyon walls, making turns without

slowing. She kept an eye out behind. "Will Kuvrema and the others be okay? Shouldn't we help them?"

'We are the reason they're fighting. If we get away, the fighting will stop.'

At times, Javeer veered frighteningly close to the cliff walls, but always managed to avoid striking the rock. Marise suspected they were approaching the place where they'd left the microscope, and she watched for landmarks.

Javeer sped around a corner and slowed. She looked up, and her lips formed a silent O.

It was clear that in the few hours they'd been gone, a sandstorm had blown through, layering everything with pale grit. In this new landscape of dunes and drifts, nothing looked familiar.

Javeer slowed, and Marise felt Korpec's shadow growing steadily on her back.

"Leave it. We'll never find it! Let's just get out of here before Korpec catches up." She heard her shrill cries bounce back, as though the canyon mocked her. Then she saw a spit of gravel reaching out into the river, and her voice dropped back to a normal pitch. "Look! That's the beach. There's where we stopped." Javeer turned toward the left wall.

Time was running out. She knew Korpec would be on them any second. They flew back and forth, searching for the bundle.

Shadows hung everywhere, confusing her eyes. Ledges looked like tunnels. Cracks turned out to be plants. She swatted at every irregularity in the cliff face, bruising her knuckles. Sand rained down on the already loaded vegetation below. *Where is the ledge? Where is the bundle?*

"There!" She spotted a rounded heap of sand just above her head. Her hand grasped fabric underneath. "Yes! Got it."

Korpec rushed at them, bellowing and blasting fire.

Javeer backed away, colliding with the cliff wall, and she felt herself slipping down around his neck. She let the bundle go and fumbled for a second handhold on the bridle. Searing pain shot through her shoulders as she clung to it, swinging below Javeer, and she cried out. Javeer thrashed with his tail, driving his sphere into the rock wall, pelting Marise with shards of rock. He turned toward the cliff face, shielding her from Korpec's belching flame.

She saw the cliff face coming at her again and instinctively let go of the bridle with one hand to fend it off. Her fingers closed around a thick stem of waever vine. As Javeer pulled away, she released the bridle and clung to the living waever, scrabbling with her feet, gasping as her injured toe bumped against rock and pain shot up her leg. Finally, one foot hooked into a fork of the vine and the other found a purchase on the rock.

An odd popping sound came from above. She looked up as the waever separated from the rock and she fell. The vine snapped taut and halted her plunge. She slammed against rock, and almost lost her grip. A tangle of waever stems flopped down around her, and she wrapped her legs around them.

She looked up to see Javeer deliver a glancing blow to the back of Korpec's head with his sphere. The larger dragon lunged toward Javeer's tail, flaming jaws agape.

A storm of pops sounded, and the waever tore from the cliff again, dropping Marise closer to the canyon floor, bringing her up short with a jerk. Sand rained down.

Pop. Again. And again, until she swung just above the canopy, curled in a ball and gripping the tangle of vines around her with hands, arms, and legs, eyes clenched shut.

A faint sharp odor like vinegar snapped her senses into focus. The canyon was quiet. She opened her eyes. The dragons had carried their combat up, and the bright ribbon of morning sky above glowed blue. In the canyon, only the soft gurgle of flowing water and an occasional rustle of sliding sand broke the silence.

The vine dumped her through the canopy. A landslide of sand followed her through. She hung suspended in a bower of waever, crushed leaves, and twisted stems. Letting go of the vine, she brushed sand off her face with stinging palms. She looked up to the porthole of sky her entrance had created and relaxed with a grunt.

Marise knew she was lucky. *Should be dead. Again. If Javeer gets away from Korpec, he'll come back for me. If.* She couldn't be sure it was safe to climb down. *I should just wait for a bit more light. I'll lie still and listen for him. If he comes back, I can call out.* She closed her eyes and listened, straining to hear distant cries of dragons or other noises in the canyon, any sign she wasn't alone.

She meant to continue listening, meant to stay alert in case any of the dragons came around, but she hadn't considered the weariness brought on by too little sleep and too much danger. Marise felt more comfortable in her hammock of leaves than she had in days, and the musical rhythm of the river was pleasant and soothing. In minutes, she was asleep.

Chapter
Fourteen

ALONE
IN THE CANYON

Marise woke with a start. Sunlight filtered through the canopy, through the flesh of the broad leaves themselves. Even the air looked green. Stems rose around her, green pillars draped with brown gauze where old growth had died, spikes of young leaves still unfurling, and a tangle of waever vine throughout as if someone had cast a net.

"Phew." Marise wrinkled her nose at the smell of vinegar. "Where's that coming from?" Her words seemed muffled in the humid air, and she went silent. *I wonder how long I've been asleep.*

Something moved inside Marise's clothing.

She jerked to a sitting position, half expecting to find herself covered with biting ants. Innumerable aches and stings overwhelmed her, and she couldn't help crying out in pain.

A furry intruder had crept up the sleeves of the hoodie and the legs of her jeans. It wrapped around her neck and ribs and snaked underneath her waistband, circling her left thigh, coiling behind the knee, and it burned.

She stared at her ankle, where a dark cord disappeared beneath her jeans. She leaned forward, pushing waever from her face and shoulders. The vine sprang back, and she looked up, hands tracing a network of rough tangles. In a flash of comprehension, she realized the waever vine had sent out shoots all around.

A living lattice had formed. Cords stretched to meet, running up against one another from opposite directions, fusing together into an immense unbreakable web. She was trapped in a mesh sack, the openings too small for her to wriggle through. And worse, the plant had crept beneath her clothes, thin, and stealthy, and venomous.

The weaver vine was eating her.

Marise yanked her left sleeve up to her elbow and dragged a tendril out of her armpit. Where it came away from her skin, a crimson lesion wept tissue fluid.

"*Oooh*!" Marise gasped. "Ow! Ow, that hurts." With panicky, jerky movements, she pulled more vine from under her clothing, moaning with each extraction. Liquid ran down and soaked into her clothing.

A few vines refused to let go. She yanked and pulled but only succeeded in dragging more waever under her clothing from another direction. The pieces were inseparable. She tried shrugging the hoodie and her backpack off, twisting and turning, pulling at the straps, but it was useless. The waever bound everything together.

"You stinking piece of, of, twine." Marise cursed, trying to stay calm as the truth of her predicament sank in. "No wonder you have no freaking leaves—you *beast*, you hunt for food. I should have *known*. You're not even a plant. Well, you won't have me for dinner. You won't. By the Goddess, I'll carve you up like spaghetti. Just wait till I get that scalpel." She panted with exertion. *I've got to get the backpack off. Got to get into it.* She fought the cords that bound her, pulling with all her might, heedless of the pain. But the pack clung around her shoulders, as if riveted to her.

While she struggled, a blister formed on a length of waever near her face. It bulged and popped, revealing a wet woolly knob that unfurled into a tendril before her eyes. Looking about, she saw similar young shoots weaving themselves into the net, closing the trap even tighter. She launched into a frenzy of writhing and kicking.

Finally, she realized she was only wasting energy. She lay gasping and sobbing, pushing the waever away wherever she felt it touch her. Pain washed over her, and every swallow brought the urge to vomit. Drool crept out of the corner of her mouth and ran down her cheek.

She relaxed for a moment, thinking Moerden had won at last. *There is no escape this time.* She looked up at slivers of blue that shrank and grew again as the leaves swayed. *Empty sky. Even if a dragon flew over, it would not see me here in the undergrowth. Blue sky. Pure blue. Sky blue, the color of truth and wisdom, calmness and protection.* Sky blue, her favorite color. It seemed to tumble down toward her.

Her courage returned. She wouldn't let the vine win. She thought through all her belongings and remembered the Swiss Army knife Ellen had given her. *Where is it now?*

She groaned. *I left it in the cloak. In the bundle I dropped. Where did that land? It should be right here.* She sat up again, gasping in pain, and peered through green shadows in search of a more substantial, deeper green. She thought she saw it—lodged in the plants a few yards away.

Might as well be ten miles, she thought, but she resolved to get to it one way or another.

Shuddering, Marise pushed her arms and legs through gaps in the waever mesh and crept toward what she hoped was her cape. Gritting her teeth against the pain, she squirmed between plant stems, wriggling down toward the canyon floor. Sand fell onto her, and coils of weaver dragged behind. She felt a new tendril sneaking under the hoodie and paused to drag it out. It came away soaked in blood.

She worked her way forward, stopping frequently to pull waever off her skin. Her breath came in gusts. A continual rain of sand made her eyes sting and coated her raw wounds with grit. The pain grew worse as the tendrils rubbed. She felt one she couldn't reach, burning a trail up her back. Tears ran down her cheeks. Waves of nausea washed over her.

Poison. She clenched her teeth. *It's poisoning me. If I don't get it off me, I'm going to faint and die.* She struggled onward.

The shapeless lump lay wedged between sturdy plant stems and half buried in sand, but she grew more and more certain it was her cloak. She fought on, hands outstretched.

She grasped it at last, shook off the sand, and untied the knot with shaking fingers. "Where is it?" Contents scattered as she groped for the blade. Her fingers closed around it, fumbled it, felt it slip. She clawed empty air and watched the knife strike a plant stem and slide down. It disappeared into the roots.

"No! *Nooo*!" She chopped at the plant with bare hands, trying to break it. The stems were unyielding, woody, and tough, and her strength was ebbing. She shoved her hand into the roots but couldn't reach far enough.

Sobbing, she looked for something else, anything that might save her. Seconds slipped away. Her mouth tasted like vomit. Her vision blurred. She felt the ground tilt, and she fell forward. In front of her, a bottle lay amid the debris. The empty beer bottle she'd been using for water.

"Where's the other bottle? Where's the full one?" Her eyes darted back and forth. "There."

It was there, lodged in a plant by her knee. She seized it, felt its weight, and whacked it against the empty bottle. Not hard enough. She tried again. And again. Her strength was failing, but she summoned it one last time, fighting against the tension of the vine.

"Break, will you break!" She brought the full bottle down with all her might, shattering both. A geyser of beer shot up in a mass of creamy foam, but it was the brown broken glass, jagged and sharp, she focused on.

Marise cut an opening in the net of waever and scrambled out of the tangle. Grim and methodical, she severed tendrils that held her, pulling the last one with a whoop and a shudder. She lurched through the thicket and emerged on the beach where she had waited for sunset with Javeer and Kuvrema.

Gasping, she hacked at the vine that still held the backpack in place, slashing her fingers and her clothes in the process. The pack came loose, and she flung it away from her. Half moaning, half screaming, she lost all self-control and pulled and tore at her clothes, ripping off remnants of waever vine stuck to her skin, vomiting on the gravel. Naked and bleeding, she dashed for the water, throwing herself headfirst into the deepest pool, shrieking at the bottom with the last ounce of air in her lungs. A halo of bubbles boiled around her head.

Marise pitched a rock at a pointy nose protruding from the greenery. The missile sliced between leaves and stems and struck with a distinct smack. The bojert scuttled away, squealing. She'd aimed better than she thought.

"Stupid bojert," she said to the nearest leaf, working swollen lips despite the pain. "They are really stupid." All the same, she was worried. As the hours passed, the creatures grew bolder. She suspected they were attracted by her wounds and feared what would happen if she fell asleep again. After dark, she wouldn't be able to see them. *What if night fell and Javeer didn't return?*

She pushed the thought from her mind and used the remains of her hoodie to dab at bleeding cuts and welts as she picked through her meager pile of belongings. Finally, she stopped searching for something she knew she wouldn't find and accepted her only weapons were rocks and a broken beer bottle.

She eyed a heap of jagged boulders in the middle of the river. They baked in full sun now, but later they might make a refuge. An uncomfortable refuge. She'd have to last on the beach until sunset.

"Protection," Marise said as she mulled over what she knew about protection spells. Remembering how she'd used them to ward off unwelcome boys and homework assignments, she shook her head. "I was so serious. Me and Celeste. Where are my candles and my sea salt now?" She looked around. "Earth, air, fire, water. Well, water's no problem." Taking one of the small jars she had salvaged from the cloak, she eased to her feet, gasping as newly formed scabs cracked and beads of blood popped out. She filled the jar at the river and set it down on the beach.

"Earth." Marise collected smooth walnut-sized rocks, wincing as she bent to select each one. "And ammunition," she added under her breath, assembling a second pile of larger ones.

"Air." She thought for a moment before plucking the largest flower blossom she could reach, sniffing it first to confirm it was fragrant.

"Now fire." She had difficulty with that one. "Fire, candles, oil, lava rock, wood? What would burn?" She looked around.

"Well, why not?" She moved up the beach toward the greenery, gathering lengths of waever vine and taking care to align them so they didn't stick together. She realized if they were severed from the main plant, they were as harmless as shoelaces.

Having assembled what she needed, Marise faced north, or at least upriver, which she thought was north, and moved clockwise, tracing a circle in the sand with her fingertips. She made it about nine feet across and took it through the vegetation at her back. When she arrived at her starting point, she scooped up the small rocks and went around again, placing them one by one in the groove. She kept her eye out for bojerts. At intervals, she made throwing motions with her arm and occasionally grabbed for a larger stone to throw. Three more times she circled, dribbling water, laying out lengths of waever, and sprinkling flower petals. She carved three half circles within the larger one, joining ends at the periphery, recreating the Celtic knot pattern from the mosaic at the cave.

Finally, she stood at the center of her circle, facing north, and regarded the cluster of bojerts looking back. Ignoring them, she took three deep breaths and let the air out slowly. Focusing on her breathing, she cleared her mind. She raised her left hand and traced a pentagram in the air. Turning clockwise, she repeated the gesture to the east, south, and west.

She spoke softly. "Guardians of the watchtowers, earth, air, fire, and water, bear, um, raven, dragon, um, mermaid. I ask you to protect this sacred space." She sat cross-legged and closed her eyes, visualizing a sphere of blue fire springing up from the periphery of the circle and closing above her.

When Marise opened her eyes, more than a dozen bojerts gazed back at her, some just beyond the circle, some farther away. Careful to stay inside, she moved up the beach to be in the shade and settled with her back to the vegetation. *I won't throw rocks,* she resolved, eyeing the bojerts. *They're not crossing the circle, and if I throw things, I'll break it. I won't throw rocks. I won't throw anything.* Still, she reached over and tumbled the pile of larger stones toward her until they lay in easy reach.

She entered a staring contest with the bojerts, ignoring the certainty that more of the creatures were staring at her back. She scanned the striped faces aligned outside the circle, willing them to come no closer. And they didn't, though they milled about, and their numbers grew steadily. A musky, wild smell permeated the air.

As the hours passed, the shadows on the beach lengthened, and

Marise moved to the middle of her circle, as far as possible from the animals, to be in plain sight from above.

There's no point hiding under the leaves. I'd still be perched in the biggest bull's eye I've ever seen. She sat and felt like she and the bojerts were waiting for something to break the impasse.

The pain of Marise's wounds receded, but her thirst grew, adding an unpleasant sour edge to her lingering nausea. She longed to rinse her mouth and wished she'd filled more bottles with water. But she dared not break the circle to walk to the river. Some of the bojerts went down for a drink, and others turned to nibbling on plant debris. One or two curled up and went to sleep, covering their faces with bushy tails. Whenever Marise caught herself nodding, she stood up and stamped her feet, reviving the pain of her injuries.

The cliff faces upriver were aglow with late afternoon sunlight when something broke the monotony of ripples on the river. At first, Marise thought it was a large fish, or perhaps an object floating just beneath the surface. Then she realized she was seeing the reflection of something passing above.

She tipped back her head just in time to see a dragon pause in midair before plunging down, belching flame.

Seconds later, Javeer skimmed along the beach, searing it with his breath and scattering squealing bojerts. The acrid scent of burning fur exploded in the air. Marise sprang up with a yell of delight and pain, and sprinted clockwise around her circle with arms spread, shouting, "Guardians of the north, east, south, west, I thank you for your protection and bid you farewell!" She whirled around to face Javeer and found him crouched on the beach, staring at her.

Marise stared back. She knew how she looked; she'd seen her reflection in the river. Red wiggly lines like Chinese writing covered her skin, some raised and inflamed, others bleeding or oozing fluid. One zigzagged its way down the left side of her face, leaving the cheek so swollen her left eye was half-closed while her mouth looked pushed to the right. The injured toe had lost its bandage and the exposed stump was an angry mess. Blood clotted sand coated her in patches.

He moved closer and dropped his sphere into her outstretched hand. *I'm going for a cilirum.*

"Javeer." Marise managed to stop him before he pulled away. "Javeer, I've ruined everything. The bojerts have eaten everything. All the food and stuff, most of my cape, and they've chewed holes in all my clothes. The microscope is full of sand, and the sphere, Javeer, I left it! I left it in the cave."

She met his gaze, expecting him to be upset, at least disappointed, but he said nothing. He flicked his long tongue at her forehead.

We have my sphere and the other will be safe enough in the cave. The other things we'll have to do without. I'm going for a cilirum. I'll be back soon.

"Is it safe? Is Korpec after you?"

It's okay right now. I'll tell you everything. After. Wait here. No, stand in the river in case the bojerts come back.

Javeer sprang away, and she saw he'd lost a strip of scales on his left flank, and one of his ridge spines appeared damaged. She wondered what Korpec looked like. While she waited, she repacked the backpack, keeping a stone handy to ward off hungry bojerts. A hole the size of an orange gaped on one side, but the bag's contents were intact, and she'd found her toothbrush and sunglasses. Nothing remained of the things that she'd wrapped in the cape, except the soles of her sneakers and the microscope. She retreated into the shallows as he had suggested and stayed there until he returned. She didn't see a single bojert the whole time he was gone.

The cilirum slid over Marise's skin. The relief was immediate—heavenly—and the sharp odor of paint thinner unexpectedly revived her, clearing the last traces of vinegar and bojert musk, and easing the nausea. Javeer guided the creature over every welt and scratch, even the stub of her toe. He gave her his sphere and suggested she rinse away the sand and blood and did it all again.

'Did waever vine do this?'

"Yeah. Why didn't you tell me it eats you?"

'Waever eats insects and sometimes traps bojerts and birds. It's not dangerous to dragons or humans.'

"Like it's not! That piece of hairy poison ivy would have killed me if I didn't get away." Her tone grew wry. "I suppose no one has ever laid down in a nest of it before and gone to sleep."

'Ah.'

"It trapped a bojert after I got away. Over where the cloak was. It's all wrapped up in vine . . . looks like a giant potato with a striped tail."

'Potato? It will be nothing but a hollow pod of bones in a few days.'

Marise shuddered. She'd come very close to being reduced to a pod of bones, a skeleton in a hacky sack. She shook the mental image off. Feeling much better, she was anxious to learn what had happened to Javeer.

"What happened after I fell?"

'I was losing. Couldn't think right after I hit the rock, and you fell. All I could do was dodge and run.'

"So you got away?"

'No, but I stayed ahead of him long enough. Climbed above the canyon where I could fly faster. I aimed back upriver, looking for Kuvrema. Without Korpec, I knew the females would have finished with the other two males. But right away, I thought I'd made a mistake. Looking for them slowed me down. Korpec caught up.

He nearly knocked me down. He had me then, with his teeth in my back.'

Javeer drew himself up, and his voice took on a proud note. *'I got in a few good blows with my sphere. Got him right in the nose.'* The proud note wavered. *'But he still would have killed me if Kuvrema and the other four hadn't come.'*

"What did she do?" She leaned toward him, caught up in the tale. "Did she kill him?"

'Kill him? I've never seen her so angry. But Kuvrema is a steady flame. She didn't need to attack. As soon as he saw them, he backed off. He knew he wouldn't win alone.'

"You mean the males switched sides?"

'Those males are cowards.' Now Javeer had disapproval in his voice. *'They only fight when they can't lose. They might not have helped Kuvrema, but they wouldn't have helped Korpec either, not when they were obviously on the losing side.*

'Opinions are changing, Marise. Kuvrema has told the others that you and Bonner know what's causing the stagger, and you're going to get rid of it. They're timid and frightened, but most wouldn't hurt you. They hope she's right.'

"We don't even know if Bonner's alive! I don't think he is. How could he have survived in this canyon with the waever? And the bojerts. They're dangerous! He couldn't fend them off forever. We weren't looking for him wrapped in waever on our way down the canyon. We would have missed that. I think it's just you and me. What happened after that? Why didn't you come back for me?"

As she listened, Marise eased into the remains of her blouse and jeans, swapping Javeer's sphere from hand to hand and pulling garments gingerly over soothed skin. The clothes were ragged and blood-stained, but they still covered most of her. The bojerts had been busy with the cape and its contents for a while and hadn't bothered to destroy the things on the beach.

She learned one of the females with Kuvrema had come looking for her, but she'd given up and returned to the rhumba. Meanwhile, a host of dragons gathered as news of the battle spread. One scout group was met halfway to the canyon by Kuvrema's group, escorting a defiant Korpec and an injured Javeer.

"Oh! Javeer, are you badly hurt?" She chided herself for not asking sooner.

'No, I lost some scales. The first I've lost! But Eschla treated the skin and tended to the bite. It'll heal. Just a bit sore.'

Marise smiled at the pride in his voice. She inspected the wounds from below. A strip of grayish exposed skin on his flank looked ridged and puffy, but he didn't complain when she touched it. It felt like stiff rubber. The injured spine, close behind where she always sat on his shoulders, was ragged and listing to the side, and it looked as if a number of scales were missing. She wondered if he'd be comfortable carrying her.

"Your scales grow back?"

'Only if the skin below isn't scarred. It depends.'

She nodded. "So, Korpec?"

'Dangerous as ever. Boasted about killing Bonner at the falls. It was Korpec that left the sphere in the sun.'

"What?" she interrupted. "Bonner *is* dead? But we found his watch and those seeds downriver. And you said . . ."

'Kuvrema told them! That shut Korpec up. Took him by surprise. It scored a major point for Kuvrema because others now know Korpec is lying. He has little support left. Just Karkas and Folcom, who were with him here and only, I think, because they're his friends, and they don't want to get on his bad side.' Excitement lined Javeer's voice. *'Kuvrema told Korpec to leave, and he did. The other two followed. They may leave us alone, but I don't think so. If Karkas and Folcom are still listening to Korpec, I think they'll come after us.'*

"What now then? Where's Kuvrema?"

'Kuvrema sent three females downriver to look for Bonner, and to contact Wyvern Wood, the ocean rhumba. She and Vica, one of the other females, have gone north to the cave—it's called Darjugan—to look again for Bonner. We're to go to the coast like we planned. We'll find deer and prove they're infected? We'll wait at Tiderook if Kuvrema hasn't caught up.'

"Tiderook?"

'A cave in the delta. A waypoint safe from jeong, those brutes that killed my father, and out of the weather. Not a rhumba, but a hold like Darjugan. We may meet others there, but it's not likely in these days of the stagger. Kuvrema says few go there now. I've never been there, but Kuvrema says you can see it for miles. We'll find it.'

"How long will it take to get there?"

'We can do it in two or three days, even if we don't hurry. But Tiderook is the only safe place to spend the night in the delta, so we have to start into it early in the day.'

"Let's get going then." Marise wondered where it was safe to spend the night in the canyon, but she didn't voice her concerns, trusting Javeer to keep the bojerts at bay. He'd be okay, and she'd sleep on a rock in the middle of the river if she had to.

She released his sphere and picked up the remains of the cape, so full of gaping holes that she folded it in half, stuck her head through a gap, and wore the rag like a poncho. She reached for the backpack and the soles of her sneakers.

"Eat that!" She pitched the slabs of rubber into the vegetation with a disgusted sigh. "I hope it gives you a bellyache." She put a hand on her stomach and winced. "Worse than mine."

Javeer tucked his sphere back into her hand. 'Are you hungry?'

"The waever made me sick. Maybe in a while. Let's fly for a bit." She motioned for him to lift her up and took care to avoid his injured spine as she settled, cautious of her own injuries. The cilirum had done wonders again. Despite her queasiness and some tender skin, she felt remarkably good.

As soon as they were aloft, his sphere came around. *'I have to take this cilirum back to the bitterbush.'* He rose past the rim of the canyon.

Marise looked toward the rhumba and her jaw dropped. The sky above the cliffs teemed with dragons, so many they looked like a swarm of bats. Marise was amazed, frightened, and delighted all at the same time.

"What are they doing? I didn't know there were so many."

'There are hundreds of dragons in the mountains. We've stirred them up. Good! His wingbeats quickened. *It'll keep Korpec quiet for a while and give us extra time. I don't know what they'll do if he comes after us. Maybe stop him, but we shouldn't linger. They expect us to go downstream, and that's where we'll go.'*

Javeer veered toward the bitterbush on the opposite side of the canyon and dropped the cilirum. It disappeared in a puff of sand. They curved back to fly above the river and watch for signs of Bonner.

As the sun set, he landed, and they tucked up against the cliff base where an overhang offered some cover. They dined on houra and berries, and after the first tentative bites, she found she was hungry. When she finally announced she'd had enough, Javeer ventured out to nibble at the vegetation. A moment later, he cooed and motioned for her to join him. She picked up his sphere.

'Kreel! Look at them.' He licked a leaf.

"Kreel? You mean these little pearly things?" She looked closely. A multitude of glossy creatures in pastel shades like mother-of-pearl crept around on plant leaves and leaf litter on the ground. They were spherical, about the size of wild blueberries, and appeared to just roll along without the benefit of legs.

Javeer licked them up with gusto. *'I love kreel. Try some. Here.'* He spat a teaspoon of bluish goo into Marise's hand. Broken shells poked out of the creamy mess; empty transparent casings flashed in the last rays of sunlight.

"What are these little pearlies? Snails? Are they eating the plants?"

'Kreel. Snails? I don't know. Try them!'

When she'd arrived in Moerden, she would never have considered eating raw snails that came out of a dragon's mouth looking like blue snot. But he hadn't steered her wrong when it came to food, and she didn't want to hurt his feelings.

I'm going to do this, she told herself. To make the challenge less daunting, she plucked three intact kreel from a nearby leaf, and without giving herself time to change her mind, popped them into her mouth, biting down to break the shells.

A burst of sweetness hit her taste buds, followed by a flavor so like butterscotch she stopped chewing to study it, smoothing the gooey filling over her tongue. The shells melted in her mouth. She swallowed and breathed out, savoring an aftertaste of warm butter.

"Oh my. Those are delicious. Like candy. Butterscotch pearlies. Why haven't we seen them before?"

'They're rare along the river. Only in patches. I found some at Darjugan, by the pool, but only a few. There are millions in the delta. You'll see.'

She filled her palm with kreel and tipped them into her mouth. Letting them dissolve, she savored the clear sweet beginning and waited for the butterscotch. She sighed, thoroughly addicted. She collected another handful and went back under the overhang, eating them slowly like Smarties.

Wanting more, she returned with one of the small glass jars, sucked on more kreel while she filled it, and screwed the lid down tight.

The sun had set. Marise stooped by the river to wash her face and brush her teeth. She felt homesick, nervous, and kept expecting dragons to plunge out of the sky. On the opposite riverbank, a mat of waever vine grew thicker than any she'd seen. She looked down at her arms and traced a tender red zigzag up to her elbow with a fingertip.

Why is the waever so healthy here? Lots of bojerts, too? She lowered her gaze and spied two pairs of gleaming eyes and several trembling leaves that signaled the presence of more. Looking left and right, she saw the canyon winding in both directions, an endless tangle of leaves and vines, quivering with the coming of night. She wheeled and scrambled for the safety of Javeer's company.

"Javeer! Where will we sleep tonight?"

Chapter
Fifteen

MOERDEN'S DEER

Marise urged Javeer on. She sat rigid on his back, holding a little round mirror from the dissecting kit to watch behind without turning around. The small glass was no better than a peephole and squinting at it tired her eyes.

Korpec could easily be ahead of them by now if he'd gone straight across the desert. He might be lurking around any bend or waiting to ambush them in some narrow place. Marise and Javeer watched every direction. She scanned the canyon below for Bonner and the skies above for signs of pursuit. She saw neither. For Marise, this sometimes felt worse than knowing someone was there because her imagination worked overtime. She thought she saw dragons in the foliage, and dead bodies among the rocks in the river. As the hours passed, she grew anxious about Kuvrema as well.

They'd spent two days flying between canyon walls, and three restless nights fending off bojerts. They were far to the southwest of Honedrai. Marise was eager to see the delta, and she believed that they were getting close. The river, which had dwindled to a creek, swelled again as other watercourses joined it, rushing through tortuous ravines and plunging over cascading waterfalls. Wide beaches and tall plants clustered against the canyon walls hinted at frequent flooding. And the canyon walls were not so steep and tall.

Javeer, meanwhile, didn't share Marise's haste. He dreamily meandered, sometimes flying so low his feet dragged through the greenery. Occasionally, he snatched a leaf or flower as he passed and savored it, drawing it into his mouth bit by bit as he flew. This amused Marise—made her think of flying cows—but she wasn't amused when Javeer didn't watch where he was going.

"Javeer, are you feeling okay?" Marise asked him after a close brush with an outcropping of stone. "Are you tired?"

'Yes, tired, but we won't stop. We're near the delta. I think we need to go up so we can see. It's late in the day, and deer will be grazing in the open.'

"We'll be so visible up there. Deer don't come into the desert, do they?"

'No. Not the delta either. The ground is too soft.'

"I think we should go to the mouth of the canyon, then turn along the edge of the delta. That way, we can stay out of sight longer."

'Korpec may be waiting there.'

Marise pursed her lips. "That's true. Okay. Your way. Up and to the north, uh, toward the forest." She shoved the little mirror into the back pocket of her jeans and prepared to act as lookout. He ascended.

The land beyond the canyon walls here was nothing like the desert. They were out of the mountains, and a rolling line of forested foothills closed in behind them. Even the hills dwindled, giving way to flatter ground. The land west of the mountains was as green as the desert was barren. Below them, to the south, she saw a broad flat expanse of green wetland, intersected by winding waterways. To the north, a forest of greens and yellows. The woods seemed to blaze in the slanting afternoon sunlight.

Javeer climbed hundreds of feet so they could have a good look around, then dropped low and headed north. They were near the forest's edge.

'We can't go far. We need to get back to the canyon before night. The jeong hunt at sunset.'

A prickle run up the back of her neck. "They don't come into the canyon?"

'This close to the coast, nowhere is safe except Tiderook. They can smell you. They're clever, and they don't give up. The canyon is the best place.'

Looking down, Marise half expected to see a pack of jeong bounding through the forest below them. The trees were tall and widely spaced and the predators would be easy to spot, but all she saw was a flock of birds moving from one tree to the next.

"Can you find deer?"

'Deer graze near the forest edge. I'll circle around and come from the forest, so they don't see us.'

Javeer flew with confidence now, so Marise relaxed and scanned the horizon for other dragons, thinking about what she needed to do when they found a herd of deer. *They pass the larvae in their droppings, so to prove they have the worms, I'll have to collect some deer poop and look at it with the microscope to see if there are larvae in there. Gross.*

She had a good idea of what she needed to look for—she and Ellen had found pictures of the larvae—but she wasn't sure how she was going to pick through droppings to find the microscopic creatures. The microscope was her only hope, but it had sand in every groove. Changing the magnification caused an alarming grating sound and the light no longer worked.

Javeer pitched into a steep dive, sweeping around to the right, his tail straight out behind. Directly ahead, Marise spotted a herd of deer grazing in a meadow near the trees.

"Goddess! Red deer!" She knew she wasn't mistaken. Celeste's uncle ran a deer ranch near Cadogan Mills, and Marise had seen them many times. "What are red deer doing in Moerden? That's the deer, Javeer. The one that carries the elapho worm."

But she realized Javeer had no idea what she was saying because she didn't have his sphere.

She watched the alarmed herd wheel and race for the trees. Javeer angled to cut them off. The lead deer gained the safety of the brush, causing barely a quiver of the upper branches. A second darted after it.

Javeer lunged.

"Javeer, no! We don't need to catch one!"

He skimmed the ground, forcing the remaining herd to split and run to either side. The last straggler dodged right, eyes wide, nostrils flaring. It made a frantic leap for shelter.

Javeer's tail came around and swept it off the ground, a jumble of dark fur and crooked legs. Javeer tumbled the helpless beast back toward him until he seized it by the neck. He gave it a hefty shake, and its neck broke with a snap.

Marise sat dumbfounded as he lifted his head and looked at her, the deer dangling limp from his jaws. He brought his tail sphere up and put it in her hands.

'Dinner!'

Still, she was in shock and said nothing. She felt sad for the innocent, dark-eyed creature that had been grazing just moments before, but she knew this was the way of things. *Dragons have to eat. Me too. He's clearly so proud of his kill. I can't bear to scold him.*

"Wow! I never saw you hunt before. I can't wait to eat. We've had nothing but fruit and houra for days. But you can't eat it raw. We think the deer carry the stagger. Remember? We have to cook it. Okay?"

'I forgot. It's okay to eat it?'

"If we heat it till there's no pink left, it should be."

'We'll take it to the canyon. Not safe here.'

Again, a prickle raced up her spine. She looked around, probing the shadows under the trees.

"Right. But let me down before we go. The jeong wait for sunset, right?"

'The sun is going down.'

She dismounted and walked from the trees to the area where the deer had been grazing. Listening for any sound from the forest, she moved back and forth, glancing up occasionally to check how far she strayed from Javeer, who waited with the carcass at his feet.

Finally, she found what she was looking for: a scattering of deer droppings hidden in the grass. She rummaged in her backpack for a small bottle, then scooped up some of the pellets. They rattled as she screwed the top on.

She moved on, scouting for a second sample. With the sun approaching the horizon, she tried not to turn her back to the forest. A whistle from Javeer brought her running to pick up his sphere.

'We won't get back to the canyon before sunset. Time to go.'

She was too nervous to argue, and they were soon winging their way toward the river, the deer carcass dangling from Javeer's jaws. Climbing high enough to see a wide panorama, he pointed out landmarks.

'See that peak way in the distance, across the delta?'

Marise thought she could see it.

'That must be Tiderook. We'll be there tomorrow. Maybe Kuvrema will be waiting for us.'

Right. And maybe Korpec will be waiting for us, she thought.

'Look behind, four mountain peaks back. That's Jaceks Peak. Twisted Pass runs around the far side into the mountain valleys beyond. That's where the Whispern Caverns are, the shelter and cache of the coastal dragons.'

She was about to ask what he meant by *cache*, but at that moment, he dropped the deer.

The carcass plunged straight down into the scrubland, but Javeer kept flying. She looked down in amazement.

"Javeer? You dropped the deer."

'Huh? I dropped it? Oh.' He sounded confused.

"Don't you want it?"

'Oh, right. I dropped it, didn't I.' He turned in a wide circle and descended.

She wondered what was going on in his head. She scanned the ground but didn't see the carcass. *We won't be able to see a pack of jeong either, if they get there first.* She was worried but knew Javeer's eyes were better than hers in the dark.

He found the crumpled carcass without difficulty, landing beside it and nosing it about to get a good grip with his claws.

"Javeer, what happened? Why'd you drop it?"

'I don't remember. I forgot about it, I guess. I was thinking of something el—'

A shivering cry cut him off, so wild, and so close, Marise screamed.

'Jeong! Shhh! With luck, they're after that herd of deer, not us. They wouldn't give us warning.'

He grabbed the carcass and lifted off, pulling his sphere away from Marise to stretch his tail out for balance. She hunched on his back, pretending to be invisible. She looked back toward the forest and could have sworn she saw a cluster of gleaming lights some way off, like a many-eyed monster on the prowl.

Another howl rose in the deepening twilight, and he put on a burst of speed that quickly carried them over the river, some distance from the delta. She sighed with relief when they dropped into the canyon.

Seated on a rock near the canyon wall, Marise fiddled with the microscope, keeping an eye on the cliff top above and on Javeer, who was occupied with the deer. He held the carcass down with one foot and tore muscle tissue from shoulders and haunches with his jaws. His tail sphere lay in her lap.

"Can the jeong get to us here? Don't use your mouth. Can you just use your claws?"

'The jeong can get down here. We have to keep a watch. I'll be able to smell them before they get to us if they come from downriver, and they won't jump from so high. Use my claws?'

"Because of the worms. You might accidentally eat one. I think they're supposed to be in the deer's muscles." She winced at the sound of flesh tearing from bone. "Small pieces. We need to cook it."

He gestured to a pile of ragged steaks big enough to feed a family of ten. *'This is enough.'*

She chuckled, then turned her attention to the bloody carcass. "Can you open up its guts, you know, its intestine, so I can get another sample?" She walked over and looked down at the mangled animal, wrinkling her nose.

"Roll it on its back, maybe."

He flipped the remains and pinned them while he ripped open the abdomen with a wing claw.

"*Ugh.*" Marise turned away for a moment, repelled by both the grisly scene and the fact that the deer's intestines had ruptured. Its insides were awash with blood and dark, mushy dung.

'Ah.' Javeer eyed the mess. *'It's not good to drop them.'*

She pulled out a bottle and collected a sample, holding her breath and using a crisp dead leaf as a scoop. "Let's get rid of it," she said when she was finished. "Give it to the bojerts or, or the jeong."

As though in reply, a chorus of yaps floated down from above. She started and looked at Javeer.

'They've caught something. Good, they won't be interested in us.' He picked up the carcass and headed downstream, leaving a bloody trail along his flight path.

"Hurry!" Marise ran her eye along the tops of the cliffs, and the riverbank. *At least there don't seem to be any bojerts here. Too close to the jeong, I suppose.* She took a deep breath and busied herself gathering dry leaves for a fire. With a clean stick, she poked at a deer steak, scrutinizing it for worms. She wasn't sure she wanted the meat.

The fire wasn't necessary for cooking. Javeer flamed a couple of flat rocks until they cracked. When she tossed steaks onto them, the meat sizzled and steamed, releasing a tantalizing smell. He heated the rocks from the side till the meat was cooked all the way through. The small steak for Marise was ready quickly, but his meal stretched on for ages.

After they ate, she tried to get the microscope light to work, but gave up and used the fire as a background for studying her samples. If she looked directly down into the bottles, the sample blocked the light. If she looked through the curved glass, everything became distorted and blurry. She explained the problem to Javeer, who said nothing, and she thought he wasn't interested.

Javeer finally broke his silence. *'Use water.'*

"Huh?"

'Add some water. Maybe they float, or swim.'

"Brilliant!" Marise reached for the backpack. "I've got more bottles," she said, talking more to herself. "I can divide the samples, so I don't need to add water to the whole thing." She pulled out the bottle she had put kreel in days ago. They looked like glittery gray nail polish, but when she tipped the bottle, the contents rolled like slime. "*Ugh.*" She tossed it back in. "I forgot about that." She found two empty bottles.

The hard little pellets she'd collected in the meadow didn't yield much to the water, even when vigorously shaken. She poured the amber liquid off into the second bottle, remembering the manure tea her father used to fertilize his flower beds, and stood near the fire with the sample and the microscope. She tried focusing on anything floating in the liquid. A few bits of microscopic flotsam drifted by, but nothing that looked like it was alive.

"I wonder what magnification I should use. I don't want to keep adjusting it because the sand is grinding inside. I'm worried I'll ruin it."

'Worms are big,' Javeer offered. *'You can see them with your eyes.'*

"Yes, but the larvae aren't. You're right though, they'd still be big compared to bacteria or plant cells." She was thankful she'd made at least a halfhearted effort to learn biology. "I'll stick with sixty." She set the first sample aside and picked up the one she'd collected from the deer's gut.

This time, she had no trouble getting her sample to mix with water. She stood by the fire again, studying the microscopic world that revealed itself in the firelight. A heady odor of animal dung wafted up from the bottle, and she wondered if Uncle Reg's deer had elapho. *How did these deer get here? They're the first living thing I've seen in Moerden that I recognize.*

Javeer ambled over and suspended his lit sphere above Marise's head. It cast shadows where she didn't want them, but it gave her an idea. She reached for the sphere.

"What if we both look? You hold your sphere down where I can look into it, and I'll hold the jar above it. That way, the light will come from below. Then you look through the microscope, and I'll watch the sphere. Wait, will it work with your sphere lit?"

'I'll dim it a bit.'

After some fine tuning, with Marise being excruciatingly careful not to hold the sphere and look into it at the same time, they got a sharp view of the microscopic world in the bottle. Sheets of cells quivered in the liquid, tapering plant hairs, spiny objects that looked like seeds, transparent globes, metallic chunks, discs with intricate patterns. The bottle was awash with microscopic treasures. They didn't see anything they thought was a larva.

"Let's try another bit." She fertilized a plant with the bottle contents and made a new dilution from the gut sample. They went back to viewing. This lot looked much the same, but the floating treasures wouldn't stay still. Inevitably, when Javeer focused on something, it was swept from view by a tidal wave. She grew frustrated, and it took her a few moments to realize the significance of the turbulence. She seized his sphere.

"Javeer, something's moving down there. It's stirring up the water. We have to find it."

I'll see if I can chase it.' He moved the field of view slowly. Another surge washed past, tumbling everything end over end. She watched, holding her breath. Another wave. Then the coiled tail of a serpent lashed across the field.

"Oh! That was it. What was that?" She tensed with the thrill of discovery. She didn't take her eyes off the sphere as he attempted to follow the creature.

It drifted into view again. A long tapering beast with one pointed end and one rounded was coiled up like a spring. It sprang straight and was swept away in a wave of its own making.

"That was a larva. It had to be." She spoke as though she'd just witnessed a miracle. Again, she took the sphere.

"It *is* red deer. It *is* the elapho worm. We won't get any better proof. You saw it, right?" She felt a dark and reluctant surge stirring in him as she waited for his answer. With a shock, she realized he hadn't really believed in the worms until now.

If the deer have it, why don't all the coastal dragons have the stagger? They all eat deer.' He turned his head to the bloody patch of beach where he'd butchered the deer and blew a blast of flame as if to kill anything remaining there.

His question touched on a memory of something she couldn't put a finger on. "Ah . . . because only some of the deer have it, maybe?"

'Which deer did this come from?'

"Oh, the one we ate . . . it's okay. We cooked it."

Javeer looked up at the stars without comment.

Marise awoke to Javeer nudging her with his sphere. She opened her eyes to find him towering over her, holding her backpack in his mouth. The waning moon hung above his head.

"What. . ."

'Quiet. Jeong. Coming up the canyon. Take this and get on my back. Quick.'

"Where will we go?"

'Right over their heads. Hurry. They'll be here in a moment.'

She sprang to her feet and fumbled with the backpack. She put it on one shoulder, but her left hand tangled in the shreds of her cape when she tried to wiggle it through the other strap. The cape was wrapped around her wrist. Javeer whined.

Twisting, she tried freeing her hand. She heard the fabric tear. She tried once more to get the strap over her arm and turned toward Javeer. He reared, drawing his head back and opening his mouth. She looked downriver and saw a dozen pairs of gleaming eyes advancing along the canyon floor. She gasped and scrambled for the bridle.

Swept up onto his back, she could have sworn his eyes glowed scarlet. Even without his sphere, she sensed rage boiling from deep within him. She was barely secure on his back, the backpack hanging crooked off one shoulder, when he took to the air.

He rose above the advancing jeong but brought his tail around and knocked the leading third of the pack into the river. The water pulled them away, yelping and thrashing. The rest hesitated, turning aside.

The blow had thrown Javeer off balance, and he tilted to the right. She felt herself slipping. "Javeer! I'm falling. Help. Help me. No!"

Marise reached for the ridge of his spine but just brushed it with her fingers. She shucked off the backpack, but it was too late.

She was falling free. Javeer snaked his head around and grabbed the folds of the cape in his jaws. He dipped and deposited her on the beach, then turned to face the jeong.

She clambered to her feet and ran for the backpack, thankful Javeer had the beasts in retreat. One was on fire, screeching and trying to get to the river. The rest dodged left and right but couldn't get around him.

In the darkness, she tripped and sprawled on the sand. In seconds, she was up again, reaching for the pack. A dark shape with glowing eyes came charging from downriver.

Her scream cut through the yelps of jeong, and Javeer wheeled again, diving toward her, neck outstretched. The jeong lunged.

Marise threw a handful of sand in its face and brought her right knee up to kick the monster away. Her foot slid off wet fur. The beast staggered left, then lunged again with its mouth open. She screamed into its gaping jaws. A fetid odor of deer entrails and wet dog choked her.

Javeer closed in, seizing the brute by the back of the neck and flinging it at the canyon wall. It crashed into a tangle of waever vine.

She struggled to stand while Javeer flew in a tight circle before landing. He plucked her off the ground with a wing claw and deposited her on his back. She slid into her usual place, and he clawed the backpack off the sand. Seconds later, he was in the air chasing two more wet and bedraggled jeong down the canyon with billows of flame.

Marise sat on Javeer's back, heady with victory and relief, whooping and wiping tears from her face. "We thrashed them! Well, you did! They won't be bothering us for a while. Good for you, Javeer. Good for you."

She looked up as the scant light in the canyon dimmed and saw a heavy line of clouds cloaking the moon.

"I've never seen clouds in Moerden before." She noticed his sphere hovering in front of her and realized she was talking to herself again. She grabbed it and asked, "Where are we going?"

'Into the delta. It won't be comfortable, but the jeong won't follow us there.' He apparently didn't believe the pack had given up. *'We should be okay there until dawn. Then we'll make for Tiderook.'* After a pause, he added, *'It looks like it might rain.'*

They flew in silence for some time before he wheeled above a bog south of the river and settled gingerly, keeping his wings spread wide and his legs tucked up close to his ribs. A sharp scent of crushed herbs rose around them.

'Stay on my back and don't put your feet down in the delta.' He promptly went to sleep, leaving her to watch the light grow on the eastern horizon and listen to a chorus of peeps and rustles.

Okay for you, she thought, feeling a rush of tenderness for Javeer. *But I can't sleep like this.*

She felt him move beneath her as though taking a deep breath. The third time it happened, there was enough light to see the bog around them lift as well.

The wave of earth approached with a host of silvery creatures the size of silver dollars. They sprang out of the bracken and lined up at the front edge of his wing. They looked a lot like frogs except they had thick, forked tails. When the hump moved away, they warbled a descending tune and flipped back into the bog.

The fourth time the swell passed, Javeer woke, stretching his wings, neck, and tail and lightly shook before handing his sphere to Marise.

'Okay?'

"What is that underneath us? What makes the ground move?"

'Marsh traveler. They swim in the mud down there. Some believe they keep the soil stirred up all the time, so the whole delta is really floating on a sea of mud. It's probably true because the channels are

changing all the time. A branch of a channel can lead somewhere one day and be a dead end the next. The traveler is dangerous, but it won't come to the surface except in open water. We're okay here, as long as we don't stick a foot too far down.' He looked up at the low ceiling of clouds. *'A storm is coming.'*

Chapter
Sixteen

NO SAFE HAVEN

A heaviness in the air at Tiderook told Earl the weather had turned. He shuffled to the river's edge, wincing at the pain in his stiff muscles and aching joints.

The tide was out, and the water in the river channel was sluggish. It was so shallow launching the raft would be impossible. He would have to wait for the tide to come in. He stood eyeing patches of exposed riverbed, recognizing a crusted rubber boot and the metal frame of a shotgun and shook his head.

Earl followed a narrow shelf out through the cave's entrance and up the cliff face outside. From a ledge high on the north face, he looked out over the expanse of islands and channels. Yesterday, at high tide, the slender tree trunks had looked as though they came straight from the bottom of an enormous lake. Now, they rose in tufted humps separated by channels of slick mud. Immense root systems lay exposed, knobby and interwoven like tangles of snakes.

"Now there's a rhumba for you," he said under his breath and turned his eyes to the sky. Not a scrap of blue showed through the woolly clouds above. *There will be no sun today.*

"That could bring in every dragon between here and Twisted Pass. I've got to get away. But where will I go? Not down to the ocean with a storm coming. And the current won't take me north."

His eyes turned eastward to the fringes of the Lusus forest, all he could see of the vast southern forest. Sinking his hands into the pockets of his tattered pants, he considered his options. There had been no safe havens in the delta. He thought he'd been lucky to reach Tiderook without being spotted by the trio of dragons that passed repeatedly.

Earl had woken peacefully enough the previous morning, dawn birdsong and a rustle of leaves interrupting a light sleep. Warm sun filtered down through overhanging marsh grasses, and he caught a whiff of flowers and sulfur.

He stretched and heard what sounded like the patter of raindrops. He lifted his battered hat from his face and pushed away a blanket of leaves and rushes and saw dozens of glossy pearls tumbled out of the leaves, bouncing, rolling, and lining up in the grooves of the raft.

"Kreel. Eating my sleeping bag, you little gremlins." He brushed most of them off into the water and watched them float away. Many did not go far before a silver flash beneath the surface took them. The few that remained dissolved to greasy circles on the surface.

"A shame I've nothing to use for a hook," he mused, tossing in another kreel and seeing it snatched from below. "I might catch myself some fish. But then I'd have to eat them raw." He poked through the pile of foliage he'd been using for warmth and camouflage and located a couple of canyon grals nestled like purple eggs inside a coil of waever vine. They were turning soft and gray, but they were better than nothing.

A scaly froglike creature with a long-forked tail plunked down on the raft and sat opening and closing its ample mouth as though making fun of Earl talking to himself. Suddenly, the air hummed with the creatures. They came out of the water like flies off a refuse pile, landing all over the raft and even on him. Many clung to the curved blades of grass hanging out over the water, and there they glittered in shades of silvery pink and green. A swell rocked the raft, bumping it up against the bank.

He froze. Only his eyes moved, as he tried to look around without frightening them away. He did not look long before the throng plopped back into the water. One remained on the raft.

"What are you?" he asked the frog thing. "I've not seen you before." It opened its mouth as though to speak, but no sound came out.

"I need a safe place to think. A place to figure out how I can find a friendly dragon and borrow its sphere. Or even a spot in the forest where there's food, and it's safe from the jeong. Do you think I could build a tree house with this raft?"

The creature snapped its mouth shut and leaped back into the stream.

"No," he agreed. "I'm not too hopeful myself. Well, Earl, better get moving. Even the fork-tail frogs have left."

He jammed his hat on his head and went through his morning routine. He spread his collection of leaves and vines over the pale deck of his raft to camouflage it, adding fresh leaves from the bank. Then he draped vines over his head and shoulders, wrapping one around his neck several times to hold everything in place, and pushed off with his pole.

The raft bumped along the bank, then joined the bits of grass and floating debris in the center of the stream. Drifting in the labyrinth of streams and pools, Earl hoped he looked like a floating brush pile that occasionally extended a long branch to push itself from the bank.

He scanned the sky constantly. Any dragon flying this far from the rhumba would be one of Korpec's crew, looking for stagger victims or anything else of interest—and he would certainly be of interest.

The waterway drew his attention as well. On several occasions, he'd glimpsed a dark form pass just under the surface, as big around as a full-grown crocodile and at least twice as long as the raft. Now and then, he thought he felt something nudge the raft from below. He was careful not to immerse his hands or dangle his feet in the stream.

About half an hour after setting off, he saw the trio of dragons for the first time. Three dark arrows flew low near the eastern horizon. Squinting at the bright sky, he watched them closely.

They'd pass to the northeast over delta he'd already traveled through. But if they turned toward him, he might not have enough time to find cover. Extending his pole, Earl struck a mat of roots and mud hard enough to propel himself in the opposite direction. The raft hit the far bank and slid under a bower of overhanging grasses. Seizing a handful, he held the raft in place. He lay on his back, looking up through the cover of strap-like leaves just inches from his nose and waited.

Fifteen minutes later, Earl parted the canopy and allowed the raft to emerge. From horizon to horizon, he scanned the sky, but saw no movement. He rejoined the current, but from then on, until he reached better cover, he lay face up and only moved to dislodge the raft when it got caught up, or to choose a route when the stream forked. Always, he chose the channel with the strongest current.

A distant wall of green grew nearer. In the tidal zone, he knew, a belt of overhanging kantha vine shrouded clusters of leggy trees, creating a world of shadowy hiding places. Once he reached it, he'd feel safer. About midmorning, he caught his first glimpse of a massive solitary bluff sticking out of the flat green terrain as though dropped there by some passing giant.

Tiderook. I probably shouldn't go there. There is no better place to meet a dragon. But the weather's fair. No one will be looking for shelter, and the current is taking me there.

He passed under the first sparse kantha vines. As he lifted his head to note the position of the sun and Tiderook for the last time, three dragons burst upon the stream. He gasped and ducked as they flew straight toward him, so low the wind of their passing stirred the leafy canopy.

Earl stilled and held his breath. *I am a log,* Earl thought, willing it to be true. *I am a log, just a log floating in the stream.* He noticed his hat was askew, leaving his face exposed, but he dared not move to fix it.

The current ran slow, but the cover grew thicker. Perhaps it would hide him. He closed his eyes, then opened them again, afraid of being taken by surprise. He gasped as the throb of wing beats muffled the hum of insects busy in the shade. The dragons were directly above. The air rippled, fluttering the kantha leaves and opening small windows to the sky. He saw them, mere feet away.

I am a log!

They were gone. The dragons had missed him again.

Three more times, he saw or sensed the trio passing close overhead, always coming from a different direction. He was well hidden beneath the foliage, but knowing they passed above always made him huddle in frozen silence while his heartbeat drummed in his ears. On the last occasion, he caught his best glimpse of them. Medium-sized and black against a bright sky. Females perhaps. Earl chewed his lip, wondering if they might help him, but didn't take the chance and reveal himself.

The tide rose, and Earl made little progress for several hours. He poled along or rested, watching bright insects pass. At length, he felt the tug of the sea again. Soon, it became a steady pull, carrying him swiftly down dark channels through an otherwise impenetrable aquatic jungle toward Tiderook.

Earl sat up, watching for any sign that he was close. He would not go in without being sure it was deserted. Perhaps he wouldn't go in at all. Perhaps he would work his way around the outside instead.

When he saw the wall of rock loom in front of him, he realized he'd misjudged both the distance and the strength of the current. He snatched at trunks leaning over the water and felt them slip through his fingers.

Grasping one at last, he tried to stop his forward movement. He clung for a second, felt the raft being sucked from beneath him and let go. The river swept him through Tiderook's yawning mouth.

The opening at the far end lay submerged, but at the surface, water turned from the rock face and swept Earl around in a wide U-turn. He bumped against the rock wall of the channel and came to a stop.

He peered over the rock to check the cavernous interior of Tiderook. Seeing nothing alarming, he got off the raft and took a closer look. He saw nothing but bare rock. He rolled up the raft and scuttled into a shadowy alcove at the dark end of the cave. Huddling there, he waited for the pain in his chest to fade, then alternately dozed and tried to plan his next move.

The water lapped against the channel walls, and he relaxed and listened for the gurgling sound that would signal the exit tunnel opening, hoping when he heard it, he'd be able to launch again and get out. Instead, he fell asleep, curled against the rock.

He woke once during the night to utter blackness and stretched out, trying to ignore the ache of hunger and the pain of many small injuries. When he woke again, daylight had returned.

Now, perched high on the outside of Tiderook, Earl considered his situation. Bad weather meant he should stay in the cave, but bad weather brought dragons. Scouts and hunters probably, Korpec's gang if they were in the area, coastal males of the same mind. Tiderook wasn't safe. He'd have to take his chances with the weather, yet there was no way out until the water rose.

He walked back down to the tunnel and sat on the edge of a ledge for the next few hours, dangling his feet over the side. The rolled raft lay across his thighs. He'd thrown everything except the raft into the river, clearing away all evidence of his presence. He'd even discarded his hat, knowing he wouldn't need it in a rainstorm.

At midmorning, he knew he could not delay much longer. He must get out through the entrance before it submerged. Unable to see the bottom, he had to trust his memory to judge the depth. Water inched up the sides of both entrances.

A howl of wind sounded behind him, and he jumped. His arms wrapped tight around the raft, he belly-flopped in the water. The current took him.

Buoyed by the raft, he rolled, floating near the surface. He managed to get his legs wrapped around and bring his head up for a lungful of air before he was sucked under, enveloped in darkness. His fingers scraped the rock above. His legs were forced straight. He clung to the raft, screwed his eyes tight shut and held his breath.

In seconds, Earl felt the current slacken. He bobbed to the surface and opened his eyes to daylight. He let the raft unroll and dragged himself onto it. Laying on his back, he gasped and pressed one hand against his chest. A wild gust of wind spun him as the stream sped the raft through winding channels toward the coast.

He looked up at rolling black clouds, low and full of rain. He rested for a few minutes, too overwhelmed to care he lay exposed to the sky, but soon, he sat up to look south.

The bank slanted up to an undulating bog that ended a mile or more away with a line of tall trees. He wondered how long he had before sunset, and whether the jeong hunted early on cloudy days.

Earl seized a tuft of reeds to stop his forward drift. He staggered ashore, dragging and rolling the raft as the first raindrops pattered down. Crossing the bog was hard work. He tested his footing with each step. Several times, he broke through the upper layers and sank into the liquid sludge below. If he hadn't had the raft to cling to, the bog would have sucked him down. The muck claimed both his shoes and his socks, and he struggled on in bare feet.

Pulling himself out after one of these incidents, he unrolled the raft and rested on it. Rain washed away the grime in his hair and clothes.

"Thirsty," he said, and opened his mouth to catch rainwater. He turned on his belly and searched in the undergrowth for anything edible. He found a half dozen shriveled berries, probably from the previous season. They were fibrous and bitter, but he chewed them greedily. A caterpillar among the leaves caught his eye, but it prickled his lips, and he couldn't bring himself to eat it. A beetle he picked up clung to his tongue, and he spat it into his hand. A pool of open water lay just ahead, and he closed his fingers around the beetle. Dragging the raft to the water's edge, he peered into the depths.

"Good fishing while it's raining." He flicked the beetle onto the surface. Within seconds, something rose from below and snatched it.

He found another beetle and dropped it on the water. He held his hand poised above the surface, counted to three, and plunged it in. A slippery body escaped his grasp. Its fin sliced his waterlogged palm. He winced but didn't give up. Two more beetles went the same way before the fish stopped biting. He gave up baiting them and stuck his arm into the water, groping for houra, or anything else that lived down there. He reached down and down but couldn't find the bottom.

Earl thrust his head out over the water and turned on his side. Squinting against the driving rain, he thought he saw the ground heave on the opposite shore. He blinked, shook his head, and jerked farther out over the water, wrapping his feet around a bush beside the raft so he wouldn't fall in. He reached farther, deeper.

Something moved on the far bank.

Something pushed the bog up like a giant worm just below the surface. The moving hump approached the pool, and the rain seemed to reverse. Several oversized shiny droplets landed on his face like splotches of pudding. He recognized the fork-tailed frogs before they moved on, migrating from the water in the hundreds.

Motionless, Earl lay with his right arm and shoulder submerged, his head just above the surface. The mound disappeared at the edge of the pool, transforming into a swell that was visible even in the tossing waves. A boil of fish came to the surface, writhing and flapping as though trying to take to the air.

He twisted, reaching for a nearby bush with his free hand, pulling his arm out of the pool. The bush tore out of the ground, and he fell back. His right hand came down hard on the rounded snout of a head the size of a large roasting pan. He got a glimpse of flat black eyes and a gaping mouth that looked a lot like the maw of a great white shark before it sank.

It came right back, jaws agape.

Earl scrambled backward. He wrenched to the right, sweeping his right arm out of range and ramming the bush down the dark maw with his left. He grunted at the pain exploding in his chest, but he kept his eyes on the monster as he got clear of the water and sat up, hunched and panting.

The traveler snapped its jaw shut on brittle branches and shook its head. Sticks rained down. The head went down, and Earl watched the monster's long spine break the surface.

"A bloody sea serpent. Five meters long if it's an inch." The howling wind carried his words away, and the mud-colored head reemerged.

Earl jerked and moved to the far end of the raft, breathing hard. He returned the monster's steady gaze and sensed only cruel hunger. *If it catches me, it will tear me to bits.* It sank below the surface once more, and Earl felt even more uneasy.

"I like you better when I know where you are," he said between breaths. "What do you eat when you can't get a starving human?"

The head emerged again, this time with the tail of a fish protruding from one side of its mouth. It pointed its nose at the sky and opened its jaws wide. The fish disappeared down its throat.

Fish. He answered his own question in his mind, reluctant to speak aloud while the traveler's head was up. He dared not step off the raft lest his foot sink into the bog again. *Maybe if I wait and stay still, it'll go off somewhere else.*

It heaved the ground under Earl's raft as if making one last effort to pitch him into the pond. Earl watched it burrow in the direction of Tiderook until he could no longer see it through the driving rain. Then he rolled up the raft and staggered on, watching for heaving ground and flocks of leaping frogs, and avoiding water as much as possible.

Finally, the terrain rose. The ground became rocky and firm. Bracken, grasses, and mud gave way to small trees, then larger trees. By now, Earl was weary and desperately hungry. The ache in his chest was unrelenting, and he had to stop frequently to catch his breath. He paused under the spreading branches of an evergreen to rest.

His familiarity with the delta ended with Tiderook. The forest offered shelter from the storm, though, and he hoped he might find a tree he could climb. He ventured in until the wind and rain felt less strong, then aimed for the coast, but he became disoriented and unsure of where it lay. He looked up more than down, knowing he must be off the ground before dusk.

Finally, Earl found his tree. It had low limbs he could climb like a ladder, and a fan of sturdy branches about six feet off the ground. They were bare of leaves until they curved toward the sky, well away from the trunk. Above, a dense mass of shoots and interlaced twigs would provide him shelter from the rain. He clambered up and pulled the raft up after him.

With the raft lodged against the trunk, he unrolled it. He climbed down to gather sticks from the forest floor and worked them through on either side of branches and into forks to hold the raft in place. A few short lengths of waever vine survived in his pockets, and he threaded them through the raft and around the tree limbs.

The daylight faded, but he thought he had a little time, so he returned to a stream he had crossed earlier. It cut through the woodland, washing bare rocks and swirling into quiet pools. He stood in the stream with his face turned up and thought he had never been wetter, or hungrier, or more exhausted.

To mark the route back to the tree, he left a pile of rocks on the bank and moved upstream, foraging along the edge for edible plants. He didn't see much he ventured to eat, passing up mushrooms, beetles, and some lime-colored berries. The fresh spring seedlings numbed his tongue and he moved on. He poked under leaves and deadwood and lunged for shadowy fish in the stream without success.

He dredged the bottom of a pool and found an houra. "I didn't know they lived out here, but I suppose that river feeds the stream. Why not?" He stuffed the treasure into his pocket and groped around for another. "Ah!" he said when he found his quarry.

A shivering howl rang over the rising wind in the trees.

His head snapped up, and he spun in the direction of the cry, the houra dripping in his hand. "Jeong. Oh, Lord. I've stayed too long." He turned and hurried downstream, moving as fast as his bare feet would take him. He aimed for the smooth rocks along the bank, bounding from one to the next until he slipped and fell. The stream cushioned him, and he surged upright, scrambled into the shallows, and rushed on. He clutched the houra to his chest with his hand, as if it might ease the pain blossoming there.

Another howl pierced the deepening gloom. Nearer. They were coming. Earl scanned the trees on the bank and guessed he'd missed the pile of stones. Gasping, he raced upstream again. He thought he saw the stones and then realized he was mistaken.

There were too many stones. They all looked the same. He recognized the place where he'd nibbled the plants and knew he was wrong. The rocks lay downstream. He turned again and staggered into the center of the stream. Again and again, he lost his footing.

He finally found the rocks he'd placed and bolted past. Now tree roots battered his toes and stones grazed the soles of his feet. Branches smacked him across the face. He kept on, hands out to part the branches.

The gentle slope beneath his feet told him he ran in the right direction, but he couldn't see the tree. *No time.* Panicked, he spun around, looking for another tree. Any tree he could climb.

He spotted the pale raft right above his head. In the same instant, he realized the jeong surrounded him. He had a vague impression of a converging tide of coarse pelts and bared teeth as he grasped the lower branches. Earl leaped off the ground, scrambling higher with arms and legs that didn't work fast enough.

Hot breath hit his ankle a second before teeth sank into his heel. He called up one last burst of energy. He yanked his foot up, feeling flesh tear as he pitched onto the platform. "*Ugh!*"

He rolled onto his back, gasping for breath, then curled to his side. His face twisted in agony; he folded his arms against his chest. As pain consumed him, his left hand released the houra, and it slipped over the edge into the snapping jaws below.

When Earl came around, the pressure and pain in his chest had lessened. He was wet and clammy, and the heel of his left foot stung when he flexed his ankle. He peered through gaps in the platform, but the forest floor lay in darkness. Turning an ear to a crack, he listened for the sound of snuffling or panting, but heard only his own labored breathing in the think humid air.

He leaned his back and head to the trunk. *I won't survive much longer . . . . May not live till morning. Bad decisions. Should have stayed at Tiderook. Oh. I still haven't eaten.* He thought about the raw houra in his pocket. A wave of nausea surprised him, and he put it out of his mind. Curled up with his arms crossed in front of his chest, he found he was sweating despite his wet clothes.

His thoughts drifted, and soon, he was asleep

Chapter
Seventeen

TIDEROOK

'*Hold your breath. Don't let go.*'
Marise had seconds to react before Javeer's sphere left her hands, and he plunged headfirst into the channel, folding his wings into tight fins. Down he pulled her, under the heaving surface to the roots of the river delta, into the shadow of the incongruous bluff that thrust out of it.

She flopped above Javeer's back. Her initial horror of being in the water, easy prey for a marsh traveler, faded. Her lungs screamed for her attention.

Perfect love, perfect trust. Marise slipped into her familiar mantra. She clamped her teeth shut. Her lungs felt like putty—paralyzed, stuck. She forced concentration back to the words. She felt as though she was spinning, thought her hands had lost the waever. Her chest was caving in. Water rushed through her hair and clothes.

She could see nothing. Nothing. Darkness spiraled around her. A black fuzziness crept around the edges of her consciousness.

With a tremendous splash, Javeer heaved her through the surface, and she felt his wings open out. She inhaled with a tortured wheeze, grateful air, and not water, filled her lungs. The blackness remained. Water still swirled around her. She felt his nose pushing her up.

Fire lit a jagged ceiling high above her, and she knew she was inside Tiderook.

The flame came again, high above them. Javeer startled and scooted toward the river's edge. A light appeared, lower, closer. It seemed to move like a searchlight across the water. His tail flipped around, and Marise took it as she tried staying on his back.

'Quiet. Stay down! There's someone here. It isn't Kuvrema. Maybe we should go back out.' His words trailed off when a sphere's glow found them tucked up against the rock.

A female voice came through. *'Better get out of the water. There's a traveler.'*

Marise squeaked and drew her feet up. Javeer hesitated, apparently weighing the danger of staying in the water against the threat of the unknown dragon. Looking over her shoulder toward the stranger, she thought she saw a ripple cut across the water.

"Javeer! There's something in the water!"

He flapped his wings, raising a storm of wind and spray that reminded her of the foul weather outside. She kept her eyes on the surface but saw nothing. He cleared the water for a moment but slumped back, leaving her submerged to the waist.

"What's wrong? Get us out of here!" She tried to look in every direction at once, scanning the water and gauging the distance up to the rock shelf. Safety lay only a short leap away.

Bubbles broke the surface. In the light of the sphere, she looked past gaping jaws down a traveler's throat. She smelled rotten eggs, saw jagged teeth coming at her.

Water and air exploded around her, and Javeer bellowed flame at the back of the monster's head. He pulled her up with a frenzied flapping. Steam rose in billows, surrounding the three in a hot, glowing fog. For a moment, she lost sight of the traveler and tried to get to her knees on Javeer's back. He rose a third time, heaving and splashing.

The traveler resurfaced. Wind buffeted her from all directions as the monster lunged. Javeer blocked its advance. Its teeth scraped against his armored chest with little effect, and it submerged once more.

She felt something tugging at her backpack. She'd tied the straps together in front with waever. The pack clung to her shoulders, dragging her with it. She clawed at the fastening, trying to release it, knowing she wouldn't succeed. Wrenching her head around, she tried to see what grabbed at her, but whipped it back as the traveler burst from below, jaws agape.

Something pulled her across Javeer's spine, tearing her clenched fingers from the bridle. She flew backward, her feet slicing a trough in the water, then floated up, shrieking at the traveler, screaming at whatever had seized her, kicking her legs, and jabbing her elbows back in a futile effort to strike her captor. Through the steam, she saw the turmoil of water and scales beneath as Javeer fought with flame and claw.

Marise went stiff and silent when a glowing orb whistled down and struck the traveler a tremendous blow on the back of the neck. With an audible snap, the terrible head flopped backward onto its spine and the monster disappeared into the depths, leaving a lingering odor of sulfur in the humid air.

Javeer cleared the water at last. He turned toward her as she dangled from the claws of the female dragon. Something brief and indecipherable to Marise passed between the dragons, and they approached each other. Instead of attacking, the female hovered and carefully lowered Marise onto his back. Both dragons wheeled and flew toward the dark recesses of Tiderook, sphere lights blazing. As they crossed the channel, Marise leaned over and threw up into the water below.

They settled in an alcove where the walls and floor were worn so smooth that she wondered how many dragons had sheltered there in the past. A small pile of dead fish lay off to one side, near the charred skull of a small animal. The female picked up the skull with her wing claw, flew back to the river and disposed of it before settling again. She moved her eyes from Javeer to Marise with a pleased expression.

Marise huddled against his side while a puddle formed around her. Her skin felt clammy and sweaty, and her stomach still threatened to heave. The sodden cape and backpack lay by her side. Her hands were wrapped around Javeer's sphere to still their trembling.

She reminded herself female dragons were usually reasonable and peaceful. She waited.

'*I am Tochara, of Wyvern Wood,*' the dragon said in a melodious voice. '*You are Marise. And you are?*' She looked at Javeer.

'*I am Javeer, of Honedrai, son of Zalton and Senja of Wyvern Wood, the ocean rhumba. How do you know Marise?*'

'*Honedrai, yes. Ocean rhumba? Wyvern Wood. Zalton and Senja . . . I don't know these.*' Tochara looked from him to Marise and back again. '*How did you come to live in Honedrai? The stagger?*' She seemed to collect herself. '*I'm sorry, we'll talk more later. Messengers came from your rhumba to Honosa, our henne, to tell us about Marise and the stagger. We also heard about the trouble at Honedrai.*'

'*Knowing you were likely in the delta, I came looking for you.*' She pulled herself up straight. '*I'm a fast flier, and we thought I'd have time to do a quick search before the storm struck, but it came too soon. I barely made it here before the water closed the gate. You did well to get in. I don't know if I could have done that.*' Her tone and the way she looked at Javeer conveyed admiration. He tilted his head away, not meeting her eyes.

Marise noticed a delighted tingle float through her palms, and a look of surprise crossed her face as she realized it came from his sphere. *He's embarrassed*, she thought. *He likes her.*

Turning to Marise, Tochara provoked a second, more intense

tingle. *'You didn't know your caball is a great flier? Maybe one day, if your quest is successful, we'll celebrate the famous flight of Marise and Javeer.'*

Her voice turned softer and her tone more serious. *'There's trouble at Wyvern Wood, as well. Word of humans in Moerden doesn't please everyone, and some don't wait to hear the whole story before starting a fire. The headstrong males plan to find and kill you as soon as the weather clears. They are holed up at Whispern Caverns now while Honosa tries to keep everyone calm.'*

A puzzled look crossed her face when she turned to Javeer. *'That traveler nearly did it for them. You're lucky I was here.'* She looked at him for a long moment before speaking again. *'Well, we're safe enough for now. Fish?'* She gestured at the silvery pile off to the side. *'Eat. There are more in the river. Then you can tell me your story.'*

She flew back to the river, and Marise watched her hovering with her tail hanging down, her glowing sphere suspended above the water. After a moment, Tochara dove and rose again, tipping her head back to swallow a catch.

Marise remembered being hungry before they reached Tiderook, but her stomach rebelled now at the thought of food. Javeer barbequed the two largest fish in the pile, flaming them till their skin turned crisp and black, but she could only pick at them.

"Can we trust her?" She glanced at the river.

'I think so.' He swallowed two fish whole before going on. *'I think we're lucky. The messengers Kuvrema sent have changed things at the coast. It's safer for us now.'*

"Do you think Tochara's pretty? She's about your age, isn't she?"

They both looked toward Tochara. He ruffled his wings and shifted his feet, moving his gaze from Marise to Tochara. *'Yes, she's beautiful.'*

"Thought so." She felt uncomfortable and wondered why. "I think she likes you, too. Why don't you go fish with her? I know you didn't have enough to eat."

'You'd be left in the dark.'

"I'm okay. It's safe, right? Nothing's going to get in here without you knowing, and I'll be able to see you." She gestured toward Tochara. "Go on," she said, more of a command than a suggestion. He hesitated, but he went, keeping his tail sphere lit as he flew away.

As soon as Javeer had gone, Marise scooted over and put her back against the wall. Even though she was confident they were alone in the cave, she felt more secure knowing nothing could sneak up from behind. She leaned on the smooth, cool rock and watched the pair diving into each other's circle of light, plucking fish from the current. She felt dejected and alone and wished they were closer. Try as she might to relax, dark thoughts surfaced.

Look at them over there. They're friends already. I'm baggage here now. I'm not needed anymore. She picked up a fish bone and tried breaking it without success. *I could leave right now if I had a sphere. Go home. It wouldn't make any difference. We've solved the mystery. Javeer and Tochara can tell the dragons to stop eating deer and go off and live happily ever after. If I hadn't left that sphere in the mummy cave, I could go.* She stabbed at the rock floor with the fish bone. *Forget dragons, and travelers, and jeong, and bojerts, and bloody waever vine. Dear Goddess, what a place.*

But I don't want to.

She dropped the bone and clenched her fists between her knees, closing her eyes to shut out the sight of Javeer fishing happily with Tochara. When she opened them again, the scene hadn't changed.

There must be millions of fish in this delta. They could be at it for hours. Fish. That must be what the travelers mostly eat. She remembered how the traveler had appeared to know to go after her rather than the dragon. *I wonder what happened to that traveler. It must still be drifting around in the water.* She straightened, watching the dragons more intently. *Maybe it isn't dead. What if it isn't dead, and it comes back? It might attack Javeer.* She watched Javeer dive. In her mind's eye, she saw him thrashing in the water with his head trapped in the monster's jaws, jagged teeth working to sever his neck.

She sat up straight, staring toward the river where he hadn't relit his sphere. *Where was he? Why didn't Tochara do something?* Marise put a hand to her mouth. She blinked and shook her head, moving her hand to her forehead and rubbing hard. Through her fingers she saw his sphere light up, dangling above the water and illuminating him from below. Tochara prepared to dive.

Stupid, she chided herself. *Moerden's scary enough without imagining stuff.*

She'd had enough of watching alone from the sidelines. Despite her assurances to Javeer, she felt increasingly nervous and bad tempered. She got to her feet and started toward them, intending to sit at the cliff edge closer to the light, dangling her feet above the river.

The rock was worn smooth, and she kept her eyes on the light ahead. She slowed when she judged about a hundred feet remained before the edge and scanned ahead, hoping she'd be able to see it clearly. Before she'd covered half the distance, her bare feet splashed into water. She stopped.

I've walked into the river. No, there's a drop-off at the edge. I'd be swimming. A puddle then. Looking ahead, she saw glitters from Javeer's sphere reflecting off a rippled surface that stretched all the way to where they were fishing. Water crept over the tops of her toes.

The river's rising! Goddess. The river's rising, and we're trapped. This whole cavern could fill with water.

She went into frenzied action, jumping up and down and kicking up great splashes. She waved her arms and screamed. "Javeer! Tochara! Javeer. The cave's flooding. What are we going to do?" Her cries reverberated off the cavern walls. In seconds, she felt the river licking at her ankles. It was rising fast.

Both dragons turned and sped toward her, settling on either side. She reached for the nearest sphere.

"The river's rising," she said. "We're trapped!" Despite her anxiety, the sensation of peace and calm that came through the sphere steadied her. She realized she was holding Tochara's sphere.

Tochara's not afraid. It's going to be okay. She shook her head. *No, we're trapped. Maybe Tochara means for us to drown. She knew all along the water would rise.*

'This is Tiderook. *A sheltering place of dragons for generations. It has never filled with water. All we have to do is wait out the storm.*' She looked at Javeer. '*We should move Marise up. High water brings travelers.*'

Soon Marise was perched on a spacious ledge high above the river. She sat near the edge, looking at the spotlights below as the dragons fished and probably talked. She could see no way down to join them.

For the first time, she glimpsed what his life might have been like if he hadn't been orphaned. She thought he must have been lonely all that time in Kuvrema's cave, without other dragons his own age.

But she told herself she didn't care. Her hands closed into fists and her mouth set in a straight line, she glared. *They just left me up here. Stashed on a shelf like a doll they don't want to play with anymore. I can't even get down. It's been only Javeer and me for days, and now she's here, and I'm nobody. He doesn't even know her.*

A tremendous splash from below interrupted her thoughts. Javeer was in the water again. A few dim shafts of light penetrated the cavern near the ceiling, but the darkness below made it impossible for her to see how high the river had risen. She imagined the cavern had become a giant pool, patrolled by invisible travelers. She wondered if it was deep enough for her to jump into. *That would get their attention.* Looking straight down into blackness, she couldn't tell where rock ended and water began, and realized she had no idea what lay below. "Loser. Forget it. If you survived, they'd only stick you back up here."

Marise retreated from the edge and stretched out on the rock, bored and sulky, feeling safe enough to indulge in her sour mood. She lay ticking off everything that bugged her. Damp clothes, Tochara, the smell of fish on her hands, no lights. Tochara. No bathroom, no sphere. Tochara. Tochara.

The warm air high in Tiderook kept the dampness from chilling her, and her clothes gradually dried. Drowsiness crept in, mixing up her thoughts.

Marise woke to faint shafts of daylight. They penetrated Tiderook like spotlights, diffusing to a gray haze before they hit the water. She wondered if the tide had gone out. Peering over the edge, she saw the cave entrance was submerged. She turned to look for the dragons and found them curled up together against the far wall. She frowned. Their ridged backs were outlined from behind by a patch of daylight, and seeing it, she questioned whether there was an opening to the outside.

Making her way to the back, she found a natural tunnel no dragon would fit through, but large enough for her to navigate if she turned sideways. Gray light framed an opening a few yards away. She could get outside.

Squeezing through was difficult, but she made it and emerged high on the face of Tiderook. At the entrance, she steadied herself against the tunnel wall as the floor plunged toward the water far below. The rock under her bare feet crumbled when she rubbed it with a toe. She stepped back, put her back against the wall, and slid down. She crouched sideways in the opening, comfortable and secure. Letting her gaze run out across the delta, she saw a vast floating world all the way to the horizon.

The rain had ended, but the sky remained overcast, and the heavy air reeked of mud and wet rock. The tangled thickets that were all around her yesterday were gone or underwater. Only a few islands remained, with a mat of vines floating and undulating in the currents like a kelp forest at low tide.

Marise marveled at the transformation. *So that's how those vines stretch themselves from island to island. The delta is not actually floating because of the travelers, just parts of it are, or it would all be carried out to sea every time there's a storm.* She looked north toward the entrance to Tiderook but couldn't see the channel leading in. The opening lay far below the surface now, where only fish and travelers could find it.

A shimmering iridescence above the water caught her eye, and she studied it for a moment. The surface swirled as though something moved beneath it, and she jerked back into the tunnel. She waited for the ripples to subside before looking for the distant margin of the desert and the mountains beyond.

She knew the sun shone there, but here, dark clouds hugged the horizon and not a sunbeam reached the earth below. As she scanned the gloom, Marise thought for a moment she saw an even darker patch moving near the ground. She blinked and lost it, but she saw it again out of the corner of her eye.

"A dragon?" she wondered. "What else would be flying over the delta?" After a few minutes, she was no longer sure she'd seen anything. *Maybe,* she sighed, *my brain is conjuring up spots.* Her eyes felt strained and sore, and her head ached. She rose and slipped back through the narrow passage.

Tochara sat at the edge of the ledge, looking down at the river. Marise plunked down beside her and picked up her sphere. "I think there's a dragon flying over the delta."

'Hmmm,' Tochara responded but didn't shift her gaze from the river.

Marise leaned forward and peered down. She saw the swirling water and spotted Javeer, splashing about over the lower ledge, shaking drops off his verdigris scales and flapping his wings. He turned in a full circle, turned back again, ducked his head, and shook again.

"What's he doing?"

I'm not sure.' Tochara sounded sad. *'Marise, there is something wrong with your Javeer. Do you see it? He's not right. Clumsy. Disoriented.'*

A worm of fear wriggled in Marise's stomach. She said nothing.

'Look at him. He shouldn't have had trouble getting out of the river yesterday. He's more than strong enough to lift you, even in water. And I've noticed he's distracted at times. Blanks out sort of. Haven't you noticed this?'

Marise balked, defiant. "No!" Silently, she thought back over their adventures, recalling odd moments. Javeer knocking the firefruit pits off the shelf in the canyon when they were searching for Bonner. Javeer bumping into the canyon wall and throwing her off into the waever, narrowly avoiding collisions with the canyon walls on their way downriver, dropping the deer.

"He's tired and just naturally a bit clumsy," she asserted.

'I think he has the stagger,' Tochara said flatly. *'And I think he knows it and is trying to hide it from us. From you. He's told me all about himself and everything he knows about you. Wonderful. We will tell of the flight of Marise and Javeer when this is all over. But I fear he won't be here to enjoy it.'*

"No. You're wrong! Javeer's fine."

'It's not just the physical things. Javeer gets muddled a lot, forgets what he's talking about. I'm having to piece a lot of it together. You think he's just clumsy? That's how it starts—in small ways you hardly notice. As time passes, it gets worse and worse. Judging by the way he's behaving down there now, he doesn't have long before it's obvious to everyone.'

Marise sat speechless, staring into space. Her hand still cupped

Tochara's sphere, but her fingers lay slack. *She's right. Ever since Javeer dropped the deer and didn't remember, I've known it, too. I just didn't want to admit it.*

"It's not true. It's not. Javeer can't die."

'Marise, he has it. Javeer has the stagger, and there's no cure. He's going to die.'

"No," her voice broke.

A leathery softness surrounded her as Tochara enveloped her in a coppery wing. *'I'm sorry. I like him too. He's not the first I've seen go this way.'*

Marise pushed the wing and the sphere away and got up. She stalked over to lean against the rock wall. Blinded by tears, she no longer saw Javeer floundering in the water below. Sinking to her knees, she buried her face in her hands and sobbed.

In the hours that followed, Marise attached herself to him and refused to let him leave her. She couldn't bring herself to talk to him about her conversation with Tochara.

If he doesn't realize what's happening to him, I won't be the one to tell him. What's the point? There's nothing we can do.

A lump formed in her throat every time she thought it through, and she turned from him to hide tears welling up in her eyes.

To distract herself, she ducked out through the narrow tunnel at intervals to check for the approaching dragon. Soon there was no doubt. She kept Javeer and Tochara informed, but she never got a good sense of where the dragon was headed. Finally, it disappeared altogether, and they had no way of knowing whether it had moved on or settled somewhere nearby to wait out high tide.

Marise conjured a mental image of an enormous dragon perched atop Tiderook like a gargoyle. She couldn't shake it and kept looking up at the cave ceiling. Tochara used spheresight to look outside but saw no one.

"Maybe it's Kuvrema."

'Or maybe it's Korpec,' Javeer suggested.

'Every dragon who knows you were moving toward the delta will have guessed you are here,' Tochara said. *'And that you are trapped by the storm tide. There could be more than one dragon waiting by morning, and some are sure to want you dead. You have to get out of here. Worry about Kuvrema later.'*

The water level was dropping. The wide pool in the cavern inched down the walls. By midafternoon, parts of the lower shelf reappeared. Tochara predicted the entrance would soon be partially exposed. She said they must decide what to do before that happened.

The three spent the hours fishing while Javeer and Tochara debated their next move. The problem, Tochara reasoned, was no longer what caused the stagger, but how to stop it. Though Marise had seen larvae, and they all believed she'd proven how the stagger spread, they'd found no sign of Bonner and weren't certain they could safely go to Wyvern Wood without Kuvrema.

Eventually, they settled on a plan.

The natural light in the cave dimmed, signaling sunset outside, and Tochara made frequent circuits of the cavern, flying low over the water to monitor its progress. Marise sat curled in a tight ball beside Javeer, watching and waiting for the cave entrance to appear, dreading the night ahead.

A change in the murmur of the river announced the opening of an air space at the entrance. The three waited a few more minutes to let that space grow, then the dragons left, with Javeer in the lead. Marise, left behind on the high ledge, watched them settle in the water and swim against the current with just their noses and lit tail spheres exposed. She hoped Javeer's thoughts remained coherent long enough to get him through the short passage.

A long, dark shape breached behind Tochara. Marise stiffened and leaned forward, frowning. *Is that?* The shape turned toward Tochara. "A traveler!" Marise bounded to her feet. She nearly leaped from the ledge in her panic. Her voice rose in pitch and volume. "Traveler, Tochara, traveler!" Tochara swam on.

Marise waved her arms, though there was no one to see. The high reaches of the cavern resounded with her cries. She cupped shaking hands over her mouth to direct her voice, but her shout died.

The traveler wheeled and moved in the opposite direction as Tochara's sphere light disappeared into the passage. In the last daylight, Marise watched the monster slam into the far wall and come around again in a wide circle.

Her thoughts were sluggish. *Oh, it's dead. It's the dead one.* She took a deep breath to calm herself. A putrid whiff of decay drifted up in the gathering darkness.

With shaking hands, she donned the tattered cape and picked up the backpack. Feeling her way, she slipped out through the crevice in the back wall. It was only marginally lighter outside. The sun had long since set, and the crescent moon would not rise for many hours. She inched along to avoid stepping into thin air, and as soon as she had room, she put on the backpack to free her hands.

The cool air soothed her nerves, though she remained watchful. She heard the distant cry of a bird and a trickle of water, a whisper of wet leaves. A damp breeze carried a marshy smell ripe with the tang of bruised plants. She waited.

Marise felt something pass above. She tensed, knowing this could not be Tochara or Javeer. They'd be flying low and using their spheres to find her. Leaning out and looking up, she saw the shadow pass, a huge beast whose edges blended with the background, so it appeared to stretch across the whole sky. Her gargoyle was real.

"A dragon," Marise whispered. "Probably a male. I can't let it see me!" She tucked back into the tunnel, wishing she had some way to warn the others. Her eyes remained fixed on the small patch of gloom through a peephole framed by rock walls.

A tail sphere came on like a spotlight. It pinned her in a circle of blazing light and pitched everything behind it into darkness. She threw her hands up against the glare and lurched away, turning into the tunnel. With the backpack on, she could not fit through the passage. She pushed forward, heedless of the rough unyielding rock, trying to bend herself into a shape that would go through. It was too narrow.

She reversed direction and pushed backward until she could turn. She crouched; her hands extended as though to ward off a blow. The light went out, and she was left blind, perched in a crevice on the side of Tiderook.

Chapter
Eighteen

THE LUSUS FOREST

In Kuvrema's soft spherelight, Javeer offered his sphere to Marise. *'We've got Kuvrema, so the plans have changed. We'll spend the night by the water, south of the delta. We need to get going. There might be others about.'*

Kuvrema plucked her off the rock and placed her on Javeer's shoulders before gliding toward the ocean. The dragons flew in a close V as the last of the daylight faded in the west and patches of stars glimmered in the sky. Before long, Marise heard the roar of distant breakers and shortly after, she slid down from Javeer's back onto damp sand. With their backs to the night sounds of surf and whispering trees, the dragons surrounded her.

"Jeong?" she asked, wrapping her hand around Kuvrema's sphere and peering into the shadows beyond the circle.

'They're not stupid enough to attack three dragons, and they don't hunt the beach. They'll leave us alone.'

Marise knew a pack of jeong barely threatened one dragon, let alone three. She allowed herself to relax.

"We were worried. You haven't found Dr. Bonner? I found the larvae, Kuvrema! In the deer. Tochara was going back to the ocean rhumba to see if it's safe for us—me—to go. And Javeer and I planned to wait for her on an island off the coast. Now you're here, maybe we can all go to the rhumba. Or . . . maybe . . ." Her words faltered as she thought about how dragons at Wyvern Wood might react to a human riding a dragon who obviously had the stagger.

Kuvrema looked from Marise to Javeer. A jolt of terror blended with grief came through her sphere, plunging Marise into emotional blackness, and she realized she hadn't kept her thoughts private. Kuvrema shut her out with a snap that stung from ear to ear.

An agonizing, empty pause followed. Marise sat with her head bowed, not daring to look at any of the dragons, trying to swallow the lump in her throat.

When Kuvrema spoke again, her tone was level and businesslike. '*Yes, someone must go to the rhumba. We searched for Earl—Bonner—up and down the canyon and through the delta but found nothing.*'

As the tide advanced, the foursome shifted nearer to the forest, and Marise tucked herself into the familiar shelter of Javeer's leg. She relaxed in his steady warmth, breathed in the pleasant bookish odor, and laid her cheek against his rough skin. A tear trickled down the other cheek, closely followed by another. She cried herself to sleep.

Marise heard the cries of seabirds and smelled beached seaweed. She stood and stretched stiff muscles. Javeer slept with his neck outstretched on the sand, twitching and shuddering from some dream, or from his disease. Plump gray insects with too many legs jumped off the sand and crawled on his face, but he didn't wake. She shooed them with a cry of disgust.

Kuvrema and Tochara sat together a short distance away. Beyond them, the beach ran on, white sand littered with driftwood, piles of rotting seaweed, and massive slabs of black earth topped with bracken. Marise recognized them as chunks of the delta, their bright colors leaching into the ocean.

Turning to look toward the delta, she found it close at hand, a tongue of vivid green jutting out into the ocean. And like a tongue, it curled up at the end, its broad tip reared up in an enormous dike. She stared, thinking this rampart must have been built by humans. It looked so artificial. Then she understood that it was a great heap of earth and driftwood, a mash of mud and vegetation uprooted by travelers, carried out of the flooded delta and heaved back by storm waves.

I wonder what Kuvrema and Tochara are planning. We have to get Javeer some place safe where we can look after him. Now that we know he's not contagious, there's no reason to leave him alone to die. She felt a glimmer of hope. *Maybe with time, he might recover.* She looked at the empty sky, knowing that no dragon had ever survived the stagger.

As one, the females lifted off, gliding over the water side by side. In seconds, they were gone, leaving Marise and Javeer alone on the beach. She wheeled to face the forest. Shadows gathered beneath the canopy, growing impenetrable beyond the first few trees. She imagined wild, hungry eyes looking back.

"The jeong have gone to sleep for the day," she told herself. "They are not there." But she kept Javeer between her and the trees. The minutes ticked by. She paced the beach, staying within yards of him, watching in all directions, while the female dragons fished far out.

A cracking sound made her spin around. She backed a few steps toward the water but reversed direction and stood right beside Javeer. Silence. Marise's eyes moved left and right, her ears straining for any sound. Nothing moved on the beach or at the forest's edge.

She felt a gust of air at her back and spun around.

Kuvrema and Tochara swept in. They dropped two enormous pink fish on the sand before departing. The commotion woke Javeer, and he seemed delighted at the prospect of breakfast. He nipped off the fishes' heads and swallowed them, giving his lips a coating of iridescent fish-scale lipstick. He tossed the remains of the smaller fish onto a heap of dry seaweed and flamed it. Fish scales drifted up and sparkled like fireflies in the flame. Her pulse still racing, Marise giggled with tension and delight.

She plunked down on the sand and extracted the barbequed fish with a stick, peeling strips off with her fingers. She watched Javeer eat the other, pleased to see him looking so well.

The smile died on her lips when he arched his neck, vomited, and rolled over on the mess. He convulsed, throwing up sprays of sand, forcing Marise to cover her eyes. He pushed up piles of sand with his feet. His neck flexed, carving a deep arc in sand and seaweed, then he slumped, motionless.

"Javeer!" She jumped to her feet and bent over him. She brushed sand off his face and was relieved to see he was coming around. He pulled his limbs in and righted himself before offering his sphere.

'I have it, you know. The stagger. I ate some of the deer we caught that day at the edge of the delta. You saw the larvae. I ate some. I'm dying.'

"Oh Javeer. Javeer, I know. I'm so sorry!" Her eyes filled with tears. "But you know, I think you must have caught it before that. It takes longer than a few days to get sick. I think you've had it all this time. You know how you're clumsy sometimes?" She stroked his cheek. "Javeer, you can't die from the stagger. No! You must try. Javeer, hold on, okay? I'll get you somewhere safe and take care of you. I'll look after you. Hold on, okay?"

'Marise, I want to go back to the meadow where my father died. I need you to take me there. The jeong will find me, just like him. I should have died that night. I have to go back.'

"No!" Marise brushed tears from her cheeks. "You can't. You... can't."

'I don't want to die like that mummy in the cave. I want to go back to the forest.'

"No, Javeer, please. Not like that. Let me try." But another voice inside her head intruded. *'Honor this wish,'* it told her. *'There's nothing else you can do for him.'*

'I don't want to die like the mummy. Or like Jigme. Jeong is better.'

For a moment, Marise couldn't answer, but eventually, she drew in a tortured breath and croaked out a few words, her voice gradually growing stronger. "Okay. If that's what you want, I promise I'll get you there." Each word was agony. "I promise. I'll help you get back there, but hold on a little longer, okay? It's not that bad yet. There are lots of times when you're okay. Most of the time." She cupped his chin in her free hand. "We don't need to go yet, do we?"

'Soon.'

Her heart skipped a beat.

'I have to go soon. While I still can.'

Now that it was out in the open, Marise didn't have to hide her grief, and she let her tears flow as she leaned against her dragon, with her arms wrapped around his neck. They huddled together until Kuvrema and Tochara returned.

Kuvrema dropped a mat of tangled waever vine on the sand and offered Marise her sphere.

This was snagged on a floating log offshore. I believe it's a hat, and I'm thinking it was Earl's.

Marise poked at the mess. "If it's his hat, what does it tell us? He got swept out to sea?"

'Maybe. Or maybe he was in the delta as we suspected, and he lost it. He wasn't at Tiderook, and he isn't here, so where might he be?' She looked toward the forest.

"You think he's in the forest?"

'Where would you go in a storm?'

'He might have gone north,' Tochara said. *'We're going there next. Let's have a look on this side before we go.'*

Kuvrema led them along the edge of the Lusus Forest, her shadow undulating over the canopy like a ragged cloak. In the near distance, Marise spotted Tiderook poking out of the misty delta, and far to the north she thought she recognized Jaceks Peak.

They flew so low the dragons' wings stirred the leaves. Insects and birds moved about in the canopy. Marise caught only the briefest glimpses of the forest floor, and she wondered how they'd find anything that wasn't in the treetops.

They stayed parallel to the edge of the delta, three abreast, and were well past Tiderook before Kuvrema turned and led them back. A few birds flushed and flew away, complaining like chickens, but nothing else took any notice of them, until something much larger rose above the treetops.

Marise thought it was a small grotesque dragon, but she didn't get a good look before it plunged back into the trees and was gone. Kuvrema veered toward the spot.

The same moment, Javeer fell out of the sky. He crashed through the canopy, breaking tree limbs and opening a great gap. Leaves rushed past. A branch scraped up her left arm.

He hit the ground and Marise was thrown onto the spongy forest floor. She sucked in musty air as she rolled to her feet. Javeer staggered and surged forward, hitting his swinging head on a tree trunk. He collapsed, his legs and wings bent at odd angles like a heap of sticks. She ran to him, wrapped one arm around his neck, and cradled his head against her chest, weeping again. Kuvrema and Tochara descended to the understory.

Kuvrema helped him get upright while Tochara hung back, letting her wings go slack and stretching out her neck toward Javeer. Despite the crash landing, he appeared uninjured. Marise walked around to his sphere. She didn't feel pain through the sphere, but she did feel exhaustion and confusion. And fear. He huddled on the forest floor, taking in deep, slow, gusty breaths.

Marise heard Kuvrema's voice through the sphere. '*Plica! I think we may have found Earl.*'

Marise fought the urge to tell Kuvrema to shut up. Bonner didn't matter now. But she knew they couldn't abandon their quest. She looked into the forest, her eyes coming to rest on a smooth white rock the size of a human skull. If Bonner was alive, he might continue her mission to save the dragons while she looked after her dragon. He knew so much more than she did. Maybe he'd know how to help Javeer.

"That creature was a plica? What is it?"

A small creature that lives in the forest,' Tochara said. *'They aren't very bright. Small lizards that build big nests of sticks in the trees.'*

'But they like people,' Kuvrema added. *'If Earl is here, a plica has likely found him.'*

"Let's go find it, then. Is anyone coming with me?"

'I am.'

'And I will stay with Javeer,' Tochara said, meeting Marise's eye and holding it.

After a moment, Marise looked away. She forced a smile, though she felt the corners of her mouth quivering. "Yes." She took a deep breath. "You stay with Javeer and keep him safe." She turned to go but turned back. "Thank you."

"Javeer, you stay here and rest, okay? I'm going to look for Dr. Bonner." She wondered if her thoughts sounded as broken as her voice. "Maybe he can help. You'll be alright? I'll be back. Soon." She knelt by his head and kissed his long nose, wiped a tear as it slipped down her cheek, and turned away.

Making their way through the trees, Marise heard Kuvrema breaking branches behind her. *One thing these dragons aren't is quiet in the woods.*

A sound came from above.

The tree before her rose tall and sturdy, reddish like a pine. It had scaly bark and rings of radial branches, but its leaves resembled lily pads, balanced on long stems like a fleet of saucers. Fifteen feet or more from the ground, a jumble of sticks formed a structure that reminded her of a beaver dam.

Below it was a platform of some sort with a bloody human foot hanging over the edge.

Kuvrema came up from behind, and Marise bent to pick up her sphere. "Is that a nest? Is it safe to go up there?"

'Plica nest. Plicas are harmless. But Earl is hurt, I think.' She bounded ahead and reached the base of the tree well before Marise, stretching up to reach the body on the platform. Marise climbed the lower branches like a ladder. When her head and shoulders were above the level of the platform, her eyes widened.

Bonner lay slumped against the trunk like a broken scarecrow, clad in filthy rags. His breath whistled in a labored pant. His legs stretched diagonally across a blood-stained mat of canes and waever vine. His left foot dangled over the edge of the platform. It was caked with dried blood and a flap of skin hung from it. She gasped at the dreadful view of muscle and bone and wrinkled her nose at the nasty odor coming from the platform.

There was something stretched along one side of Earl. One unblinking eye turned toward Marise, while the other was fixed on Kuvrema. It had wings and a dragonish tail, but its neck was short and its skin a mottled camouflage of greens and browns. A string of diminutive pearly spheres shone atop its spine ridge, culminating in a larger sphere, upon which Bonner's right hand rested.

"Tree beaver?" Marise glanced up at the nest above her head and back at the creature. She pulled away as the plica's jaws gaped open and snapped shut again. Marise looked at Kuvrema for guidance, but her gaze was fixed on Bonner, nose poised inches from his face, wing claws flexing. Bonner looked back at Kuvrema with dull eyes sunken in a gaunt face.

The plica lowered its head to rest on the platform. Only its eyes were alert, constantly moving independently and turning in all directions on short flexible stalks. The nearest eye returned to check on her with disconcerting regularity. When she looked at Bonner again, she found him looking back.

"Marise? How?" He struggled to draw a breath. "I remember . . . I was careless. You saw the spheres. What a mess I've . . ." The words came slowly, and he paused repeatedly to catch his breath. Just listening to him made Marise feel breathless.

"I can't do it now . . . my darling . . . Kuvrema. I hoped you'd find me." His voice faded to a whisper, and the words came more slowly. "But too late. I think . . . heart attack. The old ticker . . ."

"A heart attack! We have to do something! Get you to a hospital!" Marise looked around, as if expecting to find an ambulance and a team of paramedics standing by.

He smiled weakly. "A hospital? One just around . . . the corner."

She waited for him to draw another tortured breath. It seemed like forever, but finally, he did.

"Do you . . . have a sphere?"

"Yes! Ah, no. Well, yes, but not here. It's back at the cliff rhumba in the mummy cave." With a sick feeling, she wondered how long it would take Kuvrema or Tochara to fly to the cliff and bring the sphere back.

"Mummy cave?" He took in air, and it made a wet gurgling sound in his chest. He gestured vaguely at Kuvrema, and something passed between them. Her tail sphere came up from below. He released the plica's sphere and gestured for Marise to take it.

She crawled onto the platform, ready to retreat if necessary. "Nice tree beaver," she said, sliding the backpack off her shoulders. She set it down on the platform. Both the creature's eyes fixed on her for a terrifying moment before swiveling away.

Marise tentatively brought her hand down on the milky orb, her gaze fixed on the plica's roaming eyes. She almost yanked her hand back when three things happened at once: the plica tipped its head back and made a low-pitched gargling noise, the orb grew uncomfortably hot, and Bonner's voice filled her head.

Better. No sphere, no way to get to a hospital. Probably no point going anyway. You can tell me about the mummy cave later, if there's time.

"Dr. Bonner, what happened to you?"

You mean since I left Cadogan Mills? Or why am I lying here like the living dead? I may give you the long story later, but the short answer is, the last thing I remember is running from the jeong. I barely made it up here. Pains in my chest. When I woke, I felt weak as a kitten, and that jungle space heater lay stretched out beside me.

She turned to the plica. It *was* warm. A steady heat emanated from the beast. Her hand was slippery with sweat. Combined with the moist air in the forest, it made the space around her feel like a greenhouse on a hot day.

Kuvrema, I must tell you what I've discovered. I can't finish the job. Can't prove I'm right, but I must tell you what I know.

"Dr. Bonner, I know about the stagger, and I know what causes it, I think. It's the worm, elapho . . . elapho—oh, I can't remember, but you know about it, right? The deer have it. I saw the larva. And I saw the worms in the mummy. I have them here in a jar. Dr. Bonner, do you know if there's a cure? Javeer has it, and he's really sick. We have to help him."

Goodness, Earl replied after a short pause. *You've been busy. You've discovered in a few weeks what took me two years to figure out. What to say first . . . No. No cure, I'm aware of.*

Marise squeezed her eyes shut.

The problem is that all the drugs act on the larvae and not the worms, but it's the worms in the brain that kill dragons. If we're right, that is. You say you saw larvae? And worms? In a mummy—a mummified dragon? Gosh, does that mean you've found another sphere? But it's the worms, the worms. If we could just stop transmission, find the intermediate host, that would be the way to go. It's what I was looking for. It won't help your friend, though.'

She gaped at Bonner, frowned, and sorted through the tangle of confusion he had created. *Another sphere? The mummy! Goddess, of course, the mummy must have a sphere. There all this time.* She raised her free hand to her forehead and choked on a half chuckle, half sob. Shocked and embarrassed, she said nothing about spheres. Bonner seemed to have already forgotten it. *What else did he say? Intermediate host? Deer, of course. It was deer, wasn't it?*

"What do you mean?" she asked, hearing the strain in her voice. "It's deer, isn't it? They need to stop eating deer."

'No. Yes. The deer have it, but that's not how dragons get it. Dragons are sort of accidental deer for the worm. They take the place of a deer. Other animals in Moerden may have it too, so just getting rid of deer may not work. No, there's another host, probably a snail of some kind. The snails get it from deer droppings. The dragons get it from them. But dragons don't eat snails, do they, Kuvrema?'

Kuvrema flicked his cheek with the tip of her tongue. *'No.'*

"So, how do . . . dragons . . . catch it?" Bonner's frustrated whisper was barely audible.

Marise's head spun. "We were wrong about the deer?"

Bonner coughed weakly and went back to speaking through the sphere. *'I've thought and thought. Could it be in the water? Maybe it's fish? Fish eat snails and dragons eat fish. Perhaps intact snails in a fish's gut, or the fish is a paratenic host . . .'*

Muddled by her confusion and lost in Bonner's scientific language, Marise couldn't follow. She stopped listening and tried putting the pieces back together. They'd focused on deer. Why had she thought it was deer?

She heard Ellen's tired voice, describing the life of the worm, "Eggs hatch in the lungs and larvae crawl up to the throat. Eventually, they get passed in the animal's droppings. Slugs and snails eat them, and the deer eat the snails, or whatever. But this time it's not deer, it's dragons."

Not deer, dragons. Snails, slugs. Yes! We figured that out, but we forgot it. Dragons don't eat slugs and snails, they eat deer and fish, so how do they . . .

"Yes, they do!" She spoke so loudly Kuvrema startled, and the plica poked both eyes toward her. "They do. Dragons eat pearlies. Javeer loves them. I ate some. Oh, Goddess, I ate some. That's how. He's probably been eating pearlies all his life."

'Pearlies?' Kuvrema and Bonner spoke in unison.

"Pearlies. Butterscotch pearlies. Uh, those little pearly things." She cast around for Javeer's name for them. "Kreel. Kreel! They taste like candy, like caramel." She rummaged in the pack, pulling out jars until she found one containing a mass of gray slime. "Yuck. I collected some in the canyon, days ago. Javeer and I were eating them." She tipped the bottle and watched the goo roll over itself toward the cap.

'Disgusting.' Kuvrema pulled away, looking at the rotting kreel remains.

'Kreel? Indeed.' Earl reached for the bottle. *'Dragons eat them, do they? News to you, too. Kuvrema?'*

'These are not snails. Kreel! Yes, I know the coastal dragons eat kreel. Desert dragons do not eat them. Kreel are scavengers of dead things, rotten things.'

"They're delicious!" Marise said. "Javeer adores them. We ate lots in the . . . in the canyon." Her voice faded as she realized the implications. The desert dragons were safe because they didn't eat kreel, and even if they did, there were no deer in the Darjugan canyon, or at the waterfall, to infect the kreel. But to end the stagger at the coast, they not only had to get rid of all the deer, but they also had to convince the coastal dragons to give up candy.

Tochara thrust her head through the branches. *'Javeer is feeling stronger. But he's asking to go to the foothills. He wants to go now.'*

Chapter
Nineteen

CABALLEROS

'*Think about it.*' The plica's sphere was cupped in Bonner's hand, and Marise's rested on top. '*Have you ever seen a pile of dragon dung? Has your dragon Javeer ever left a steaming heap in a campsite?*'

Alone with Bonner and the plica on the platform, she had to admit the answer was no to both questions. She'd been slipping around corners and stepping into nearby vegetation to relieve herself, but she had no idea what dragons did.

"Well, don't they then? Don't they . . . ?"

'*Poo? Of course, they do. They burn it. A good blast of flame, and there's nothing left but a whiff of dust and perhaps a few bone fragments. Perfect system really.*'

"So, even if they do pass larvae, they can't infect kreel."

'*Right.*' Bonner's closed eyes flickered open for a second. '*No, sick dragons aren't spreading the stagger, except possibly near the end when they don't know which way is up, but they're generally not eating much by that point. If you get them to stop eating kreel and get rid of the deer, I think the disease will disappear. Unless there's some other animal, but I doubt that. Get rid of the deer. They shouldn't be here in the first place.*'

"They shouldn't . . . Dr. Bonner, those are red deer?"

'*Right again, and they don't belong here. They came from our side.*

And the parasite came with them. Who'd have thought that would work out so badly? Let me think, now. Let me think. I can explain . . .'

Earl's thoughts went silent.

Marise fidgeted. She knew Tochara was waiting, ready to go with Javeer to the foothills. She wanted to put it off, didn't want to even think about it, but she knew the passing of time frightened him, and waiting for her while she talked to Bonner would make it worse. A sense of determination and excitement to have a lot of questions answered made her stubborn.

'I don't know how the first sphere came into human hands. I imagine some adventurous dragon tried sphere travel and landed on our side. Perhaps a long, long time ago. Dragon stories go way back in human cultures. I think someone got hold of that dragon's sphere and learned how to use it.'

"The dragon probably landed inside a rock or something. Dead on arrival, I bet."

'You know about that, do you?'

"*Oh* yeah. I know about it. Here, take a look." From her cross-legged position, Marise pulled out her injured foot, and he opened his eyes long enough to look at her toe. It hadn't bothered her much since Javeer had treated it with the cilirum, but the stump was still inflamed. "The rest of it and a piece of my sneaker, is in your office desk."

'You're lucky you didn't lose more. No, you have to use the circles. It's the only safe way to get home, or to get around in Moerden.'

"Get around in . . . wait. You mean there's more than one?"

'There are at least four circles, all different, and I wouldn't be surprised if there are more. Each is one of a pair.' He held up two fingers. *'One here in Moerden, one on our side. Like portals, if you like. You've seen the one in my kitchen?'*

"Yes."

'That's one of triplets. There's another like it, but with dragons, in a church in northern New Brunswick. The roses made it easier to

get home. My own idea.' He took a ragged breath that sounded as it if was meant to be a sigh. *'Which brings me back to how these confounded deer got here.*

'Fortunately for Moerden, the number of people who can come in has always been limited by the number of spheres. People collected spheres gradually, as dragons died, but I don't think there were ever many. People made friends with the dragons, formed partnerships, usually men with male dragons. They called the dragons caballs. Like caballus, *you know? That's Latin for horse.'* His eyes opened, and he looked at her, as though to gauge whether she understood. *'And they were caballeros, of course. It became a sort of secret society generations ago—very secret, with small enclaves all over the world.*

'About twenty years ago, a fellow by the name of Wyett Milne had the bright idea that it might be possible to bring people and animals to Moerden. He was a sportsman, this fellow, a big game hunter.' Bonner's hands mimed taking a shot with a rifle. *'And he thought it would be great sport to hunt deer on dragonback, so he bought a herd of red deer and talked the others in his enclave into letting him use all the spheres they had.'*

Bonner's thoughts went silent, and Marise waited patiently until he was ready to go on.

'I'm not sure exactly how he did it, but he made sure each sphere was in contact with a deer and sort of connected with them through his own sphere, pictured the destination, and bingo. He was vague about it all, but he told me it was odd linking with the mind of a deer. "Like dreaming of summer," he said. They brought a lot of red deer to Moerden that way. Never lost a single sphere in the process.'

"Were you in the society? Did you know Wyett Milne well?" Marise saw a spasm of pain cross Earl's face and felt a sudden ache deep in her chest. She watched the grimace pass, and his muscles relax, leaving him looking pale and strained. His lips had an unsettling bluish cast.

'No. And yes. Milne gave me the two spheres before he passed from cancer. He told me what he knew. And he told me how it all went wrong. He wanted me to figure it out and stop it. A year or so after they brought the first red deer into Moerden, the sickness hit the dragons.' He shook his head so slightly that Marise almost missed the gesture. *'The caballs got it first, but it spread, and dragons all along the coast died. Milne's dragon died, too. It broke his heart.*

'The dragons blamed men. Some of them started killing us. You see, they thought if they stopped people coming, they'd get rid of the disease. Every time they killed a human, they repossessed a sphere and destroyed it.'

"That's why Korpec wants to kill me! And why he tried killing you. And he ruined your sphere. But I don't even have a sphere."

'He probably didn't believe that. Why should he? He might think you have the disease.'

"It's deer that have the disease!"

'The dragons don't understand that yet.'

"So, why don't Javeer and the females hate me?"

'I suspect Javeer doesn't know the story.' Even though it came through the sphere, Marise recognized Bonner's biology teaching tone. *'He was young when Kuvrema found him. And she isn't stupid. She sees the disease remains even though all—almost all—the people have gone, and she hopes that if we did bring it, we can also make it stop. That's if she can prevent hot-headed Korpec and others from killing every human and cutting off all contact with our side.*

'She's been working quietly to solve the problem before it's too late. She's powerful! One of a long line of rhumba hennes. The dragons have great respect for her. Except Korpec. He's her brother! A twin hatched at the same time. Unusual in dragons. But he's not like her. Where she has wisdom and diplomacy, he is impetuous, greedy, and jealous.'

"Her brother! How do you know so much about Kuvrema?"

Bonner smiled. For a moment, he looked better, and his eyes

opened fully. '*Kuvrema is my caball, though that doesn't suit her any more than caballero suits you. I met her ten years ago when I first came to Moerden. It's rare for a female dragon to take a rider, but as I've said, Kuvrema's unusual, and she does as she pleases.*'

"She hasn't told me any of this."

'*She took you for a stray puppy like Javeer.*' Earl paused, drawing another deep, ragged breath. '*And she was right. Marise, we may not have much time. I may be dead by the time you come back to collect Kuvrema.*' He raised a hand, wincing at Marise's exclamation of denial. '*Never mind. What will be will be. I've things I want to say, so listen.*'

Marise's eyes opened wide. Then she slumped, causing both of the plica's eyes to pivot in her direction. She scowled at the creature.

'*Here's what the dragons have to do,*' Bonner shook a finger. '*Kill all the deer. They can eat them, there's no danger. Make sure they clean up after sick dragons.*' A second finger joined the first. '*Burn everything. You know what I mean. They must stay away from kreel everywhere where there are deer.*' Three fingers pointed to the sky. '*Kreel out in the waterways of the delta should be safe, and up in the desert along the Darjugan. If the dragons do this and the stagger doesn't disappear, it means there's another animal spreading it. Do you follow?*'

She nodded, a furrow creasing her forehead. "How will I make them listen?"

'*Kuvrema and Tochara will help. But Marise, you need to go home. And soon. How will you do it? Can't just step back into your old life. From what you've told me, they'll be looking for you as a possible . . . arsonist.*'

The chest pain returned, strong enough that she lifted her hand until the grimace on his face relaxed. "Kuvrema!" she yelled, hoping the dragon heard her.

Bonner let out a long breath and strained for another. '*I've an idea. Use the circles. Go to the church. It's in Cedar Settlement.'* His chest rose, fell, and didn't rise again for what seemed like an eternity. He gasped. *'Dragons, not roses.'* He closed his eyes and went silent.

"Kuvrema!"

The female dragon's head rose past the level of the platform. She looked at Bonner, slipping her sphere under his slack left hand. He wasn't breathing.

His chest rose suddenly as he sucked in a strained breath. *'Just show up there and let them find you. Don't remember anything. How you got there. How you escaped from the house. Where you've been. You don't remember.'*

Pain lanced through Marise's chest, and she jerked her hand away again with a grunt. She heard him gasp, but when she looked, he lay still and quiet. She slapped her hand back down. The plica shrieked, its eyes whipping around, so they both focused on Bonner. Through its sphere, she felt a wave of inexplicable joy.

Kuvrema turned to Marise. *'He said, "post-traumatic stress." Then, "you get an A in biology. Tell Ellen . . . "'*

"Tell Ellen what? Goddess! I get an A in biology? Tell Ellen that? Tell Ellen what?"

'What she needs to hear, possibly.'

"What? Is he dead, Kuvrema? Do something. Is he dead? No! He can't be. We just found him." Marise scrambled to her knees, eyes fixed on the professor's slack face.

'He's gone on.' Kuvrema's tongue flicked out, lightly touching the old man's forehead. She bowed her head. *'I'll miss him. But he's not unhappy.'* She brought her head up and looked at Marise. *'No need for you to go off without me. We'll leave him with the plica. Let's go.'*

"What?" Marise almost shrieked the word. She looked around wildly, not sure what she was looking for. "Leave him? What? You're going to let the tree beaver eat him? Can't we bury him or something? We can't just leave him here to . . ."

'The plica will look after things.' Kuvrema leaned across Bonner, draping a leathery wing across his legs, wrapped her wing claw around Marise and plucked her out of the tree.

Instead of lowering her to the ground, Kuvrema set her on her shoulders and dipped her head while Javeer slipped the waever bridle on.

Marise protested. They shouldn't be leaving Bonner's body lying in the woods. She wanted to ride Javeer. She wasn't ready to take him to the meadow and leave him. The stagger could wait.

But no one was paying any attention. In a moment, the trio of dragons lifted off and rose above the forest canopy. Turning northeast, they winged away, Marise twisting on Kuvrema's shoulders to look back.

A loud crack and a whoosh made everyone turn. A billow of smoke rose above the tree where Bonner lay, pushed up by a pillar of fire. The inferno boiled, consuming the tree and everything resting in its branches. A muffled whump shuddered up from below, and as quickly as it had ignited, the fire collapsed into the blackened hole it had carved in the canopy.

Marise watched openmouthed as a gust of wind settled the smoke like a broom sweeping soot down into the cracks of the forest.

The dragons wheeled, and Kuvrema's tail sphere came around, but despite Marise's loud protests only moments earlier, now she had nothing to say.

'At least it wasn't Korpec that killed him.' Kuvrema sounded calm and matter-of-fact, but Marise was certain the dignified dragon grieved for her caballero.

She wondered what to say. She wondered what she would say to Ellen if she ever got home. *I wish I'd known him better. I wish he'd lived a little longer.*

"Dr. Bonner told me people have probably been coming to

Moerden for thousands of years," she said at last. "That they've been pairing up with dragons, like you and him, and Javeer and me."

'No dragon alive today can remember a time before there were men in Moerden. Men. Always men, riding male dragons. You might be the first woman to ride one.'

"But they never built anything? No castles, no cabins?" She looked over her shoulder toward the ocean to the west. "No ships?" She deliberately sent images, thinking Kuvrema might not know what she was talking about.

'Nooo.' Kuvrema's answer came slowly. *'There were never enough of them, I suppose. They brought things, treasures, and gave them to dragons. We have lots of treasures from men. Collections in caves. Men made the circles and changed some of the caves. Like Darjugan cave. A man named Darjugan made that circle and built the path to the top. There are signs of humans all over, but you don't see them. Places were named by humans. The rhumbas too. I thought we'd always called them rhumbas, but Earl said* rhumba *is a human word for a nest of rattlesnakes. I don't know what that has to do with dragons, but Earl thought it amusing.'*

"Really? I thought it was a kind of dance." She tried in vain to think of a word for a nest of snakes. "A Spanish dance, maybe."

Kuvrema's head came right around, and she met Marise's gaze. She looked ahead again. *'I think I like that better.'*

"Kuvrema, where are the other circles? Dr. Bonner said there were four."

'One is in Wyvern Wood near the ocean rhumba.'

Marise received an image of three cords loosely twined around each other in an endless circle. They had spikes all along their edges, not unlike the ridges on a dragon's back, and in the center, a triad of square nails intersected each other, all pointing in different directions.

'Another is in the Whispern Caverns.'

This time a Chinese dragon filled the circle, ringed by Chinese characters. Marise found herself hoping she'd see the Whispern Caverns someday.

'And the fourth is in Korpec's cave at Honedrai. I have not seen it.'

"You've never seen the circle in your own rhumba?"

'We don't use them,' Kuvrema spoke simply. *'And I don't go there. Ooh!'*

Javeer pitched earthward and was dropping fast, his wings bent at a peculiar angle. Marise saw an embankment directly ahead of him, topped by towering trees and strewn with boulders.

Tochara and Kuvrema dove in pursuit. Tochara darted beneath him, as though to intercept his fall, while Kuvrema dropped from above, reaching for him with her enormous claws. Kuvrema wrapped her talons around the bony ridge supporting the leading edge of his wing.

Marise gasped as the big female dropped, dragged into Javeer's descent. *He's going to bring us all down.*

Marise squeezed her eyes tight shut, held her breath, and focused all her attention on Javeer through Kuvrema's sphere. No thoughts or images came from him, and she concentrated harder, willing him to spread his wings and fly. She imagined them cruising smoothly above the boulders, rising above the trees. For a long moment, she felt as if she was floating, then branches splintered, and she braced for an impact that never came.

She opened her eyes.

They were still aloft, skimming the treetops, with Tochara flying close beside Javeer, and Kuvrema gripping his wings from above. Marise saw a grassy slope ahead and held the image in her mind as she snapped her eyes shut again. She imagined coming down gently onto the grass, willing Javeer to do it. He wobbled beneath them and came down roughly, skidding across the meadow. Kuvrema let go and wheeled around, landing beside him.

Marise rushed over and picked up his sphere. She looked around, wide-eyed. "Is this it?"

'No.' Kuvrema sighed. *'But we're close. I'll see if I can find it while he rests. Stay here.'* She sprang away, angling toward the mountains.

Javeer pitched to one side and flung his neck out straight, blowing a gust of fire that left a comet shaped scar in the grass. Marise ducked and rolled as his head came around, spewing flame. She leaped to her feet, poised to run, but Tochara intervened, forcing his head to the ground, and holding it there till he drew a deep breath and slipped out of consciousness.

Marise forgot everything except that she was losing him. In the lonely foothills meadow, it wouldn't be simply goodbye. She threw herself at his heaving side, running her hands over his scales and breathing in the curious dusty smell of him. She sobbed, slumping to the ground and curling into a ball under the edge of his wing.

'Kuvrema is back.' Tochara's gentle voice cut through Marise's misery. *'If you'll agree, I'll carry you now. The meadow's just over the next rise.'*

Numbly, she allowed herself to be lifted onto Tochara's shoulders and sat with a bowed head as they lifted off. She hardly noticed the groves and clearings passing below as they covered the short distance to the meadow. When Tochara settled to earth again, Marise slid down and went straight to Javeer, picking up his sphere and tucking herself into the cleft of his leg.

"I'm staying with you," she whispered.

His head came around. *'You can't stay. The jeong will kill you.'*

"I'll climb a tree."

'And watch them tear me to pieces? Marise, it is terrible. Terrible. Say goodbye now. It's better.'

"No, I can't. I can't leave you here to die."

He kissed her cheek with his forked tongue, and she felt him gather as if to take flight. *'Marise, you're my best friend. Like part of my wings. But I won't let you stay here. There's no hope for me, and I've made my choice. Go now. Go, or Kuvrema will take you.'*

She had never heard him speak with such determination. She saw he meant it, and she knew he was right, but she couldn't move.

'Don't forget me, Marise.' He pushed her out with his nose and drew his leg in so she couldn't return. He pulled his sphere from her hands and turned to Kuvrema. Marise heard nothing as the two said their goodbyes.

Blinded by tears, she dimly saw them touch noses and sensed something pass between Tochara and Javeer. Marise strode back toward him, her mouth set in a straight line, but before she reached him, a claw lifted her from behind.

"No!" she shrieked as she came down on Tochara's shoulders and the females lifted off.

"No." She stretched her hand out, as if to touch Javeer from above as the dragons climbed and circled the meadow once. He grew smaller and smaller below. Kuvrema whistled, turned, and headed northwest. An upwelling of tears blurred Marise's last sight of Javeer hunched in the center of the clearing. "*Nooo!*" she shouted at the sky, then hung her head and wept.

"This is wrong. This is all totally wrong." She sobbed. "We can save the coastal dragons and the desert dragons, but not Javeer. Too late for him, no matter what I do. Just some worms crawling around in his brain. Damn worms that don't even belong here." Anger sputtered to life inside her, pushing aside the pain. "And what do we do? Leave him to be torn to bits by jeong. Without him, we'd never have learned the answer. He's a hero, and we've left him to die. And he *will* die tonight, even though he doesn't need to yet. He doesn't need to."

The sun descended into a bank of clouds on the western horizon. In minutes, twilight would come. The birds would roost. The jeong would rise from their beds and hunt.

She remembered the mummy in the cave back at the cliff rhumba. The terrible way he had died alone, with a cluster of worms wrapped around the top of his spine. She'd plucked them off the bone like loose hairs. *Finally gone. Removed long after they killed him. If only it was so easy.* Her chin snapped up.

She reached behind her and knocked on Tochara's ribs. Her sphere dropped into her hand. "Turn around," she demanded. "I think I can save him."

Tochara's wings missed a beat. Kuvrema turned her head toward Marise but flew on.

"Turn around! There's no time to explain. The sun is going down. Look! We have to get back there and get Javeer out of that death trap. Now! Turn around, or I'll jump." She swung a leg over Tochara's spine and hooked a thumb through the backpack's strap.

Tochara flew for another wingbeat, but she either sensed Marise was dead serious or yielded to her own desire to go back. She dipped and wheeled. Kuvrema continued alone, sending a fading thought. *'Meet me at the rhumba. I cannot bear it.'*

"Fly. Fly, Tochara. Fly! The sun's nearly down." Marise felt the air cooling already. The rhythm of wing beats picked up speed.

They got to the meadow just as the top rim of the sun sank into the clouds, and Marise heard the dreadful howl that had been echoing in her thoughts all day, like a nightmare that wouldn't fade. The hunt was on, and the jeong were nearby.

Javeer was gone.

"It's the wrong place." Her voice sounded high and shrill in her ears. "He should be right here."

'This is where we left him.' Tochara landed precisely in the middle of the open space, where the grass lay broken and flattened.

"Where is he?" She slid to the ground and ran around Tochara. "Javeer! Javeer!"

Tochara raised her head and whistled, long and piercing. "Javeer. Javeer."

An undulating howl answered.

Hoisting Marise onto her back, Tochara lifted off, doing a quick circuit of the clearing before going higher, whistling for Javeer. As they came around to the west, the red glow of the clouds on the horizon disappeared. The ground below lay shrouded in gloom.

Marise caught her breath and pointed. A jeong pack approached, moving fast and with purpose. "They know he's there. They're after him. Where is he? We have to find him now."

'We have.'

Marise saw him moving out from the trees.

Tochara dropped into the meadow, intercepting him. *'Stay on my back. The jeong are very close.'*

Marise immediately dismounted, stumbling as she hit the ground. She ran to seize Javeer's sphere. "Javeer, I think I can save you. Quickly. The jeong are coming. Lift me up."

'Go away.' He looked at Tochara as if willing her to do something.

She reached to grab Marise as another howl split the air. Marise dropped his sphere and ran forward, raising her arms and jumping up and down. "Lift me up. Lift me up."

The pack paused at the edge of the trees. Marise sensed their eyes upon her. She was defenseless. She assumed they would take her first. Trembling, she sidestepped another attempted snatch by Tochara. She thrust her arms straight up. "Lift me up, Javeer." To her right, she saw an enormous jeong separate from the shadows, with one on each flank.

"Lift me up!" Her plea turned to a shriek of panic as the jeong attacked.

Chapter
Twenty

DRAGON'S MIND

Javeer snatched Marise off the ground and dangled her from a wing claw. His tail knocked the leading jeong off their feet, but the rest of the pack had circled and now came at them from all directions.

Tochara shrieked and blew a gust of flame, driving the jeong on her side back into the shadow of the wood. Her breath set grass and brush blazing and lit up the clearing. She wheeled on another group of attackers.

Extending his wings, Javeer lifted Marise higher. She looked down on more than a dozen jeong, watched Tochara seize one and throw it into the flaming brush, and screamed a warning as one slipped in under his wing. He set the fiend alight, and twilight was rent with howls, bellows, and her wild yells.

Javeer rushed at the beasts in front of him, roaring and belching fire, his tail whipping left and right. The jeong dodged the assault and retreated long enough for him to place her on his shoulders. He sprang aloft and brought his sphere around, knocking the lead jeong senseless.

For a moment, Javeer lost his balance, teetering in the air, but recovered. He rose, circling above the blazing meadow. Cutting through clouds of smoke, he whistled.

A surge of exhilaration filled Marise when she saw Tochara separate from the melee and come up, tossing down a jeong carcass. "Woo-hoo! Yes, yes, yes." She threw her arms up, heedless of the height. She cupped Javeer's sphere in her hand, giving it a jubilant kiss.

'Marise?'

Her lips stretched wide in a confident grin. She let her excitement flood through the sphere and felt curiosity and hope returning. "You're going to be okay. Head for Honedrai. Tochara, you coming? I need your help."

'Javeer can't fly all the way to the desert rhumba. You've seen what happens.'

"Yes. Yes, he can. Javeer is fine, except when he's not. Javeer, you tell me if you feel weird or tired, and we'll set down, okay? If you falter, Tochara and I will help you to the ground. We'll stay low, so it's not far to fall." She looked down at the fire already dying below. "The rest of the time, we're going to fly. No stopping. I need the sphere I left in the mummy cave. Javeer, if I didn't believe we can do this, I wouldn't be on your back, would I?"

'What are you planning to do?' he asked.

She considered her response. "I need some help from home. That's why I need the sphere. I have to get you to the rhumba. I'll get you there if it kills me. I'm not letting you die all alone in a field. Even your father didn't die alone, right? I promise, if it doesn't work, I'll take you to any place you want to go. Any place. But it will work. I see how. Trust me, okay?"

Time passed. Marise grew tense. *They won't leave me. They won't leave me, so they're going to do what I ask.* She remembered how cold she'd been to Tochara. *She didn't deserve one bit of it. Now, my life and Javeer's depend on her.*

A howl from below brought goosebumps to her arms and reminded her that if Javeer crashed, only Tochara would escape. Javeer veered northeast and picked up speed.

'Okay.'

"Tochara?"

I'm here. You'll never make it without me,' she replied. *'I've always wanted to see the desert.'*

"Tochara, you're my friend for life." Marise sighed with relief. "I'm sorry I ever doubted it."

The trio headed across the foothills for Honedrai. As night deepened, Marise could see nothing below, but she knew the forest gave way to scrub, and scrub to sand. Soon, they would cross the lower reaches of the canyon.

Despite the uncertainty ahead, Marise was at peace. Riding on Javeer again felt right, and she told herself everything would work out. She said a quiet prayer of gratitude to the Goddess and relaxed, letting the wind cool her tear-reddened face.

They'd been flying for more than an hour when he dropped.

Marise gasped as he rolled sideways and nearly let go of his sphere but remembered this was the wrong thing to do. She'd anticipated this and planned for it.

"Tochara!" She took a deep breath, clenched her eyes shut, and summoned all her Wiccan visualization skills. Shutting out everything else, she gripped the sphere in front of her and focused on sending pictures and thoughts. She envisioned Javeer righting himself and leveling off. She poked at his mind, pushing the images at him, willing his mind to meet hers. Sensing a fuzziness, a deserted space where his thoughts should be, she pushed harder.

Marise exhaled as her mind expanded into the void. For a moment, she felt giddy, as though her brain was disconnected and weightless, floating in space. Then Javeer's great heart centered her, thumping behind her eardrums. She became aware of cool air swirling under wings, rushing over scales. It flooded the depths of cavernous lungs and rushed out again through flared nostrils, hot with a hint of fire. The sphere felt warm and sensitive to everything—the movement of air, the twinkle of starlight, Tochara a wingspan to the left, the ground rushing up to meet her.

Marise found wings hinged on her back and seized control. She stretched them, commanded them to work, to push against the air below and pull her up. Flexing her long neck, she lifted her face to the stars, eyes closed. She visualized a star she'd been looking at seconds before he faltered and mentally steered toward it. She felt herself level off, then climb. Her confidence escalated. She doubled her efforts to fly toward the twinkling star.

Buoyed by a sense that she was climbing, she felt a surge of exhilaration. She was a dragon, a real dragon, and she was flying. Flying! She was free and impulsive and wild.

'*Hang on.*' Tochara's warning cut through her reverie seconds before Javeer plowed into a crest of coarse sand and bitterbush and careened down a slope.

The impact unseated her, throwing her over his head and down the far side of the dune. She slid to a stop in the warm sand and tried to stand, but her jellied knees wouldn't hold her up.

"Tochara?"

The glow of sphere light illuminated the scene. Tochara stood beside Javeer's still dark form. He was splayed on the sand, his tail a dark line trailing up the incline behind him. His slack wings lay flat.

She scrambled toward the dragons and reached for Tochara's sphere. "Is he okay? How did we get down? Did you do it or did I?"

'*We both did it,*' she answered. '*I gave him support from below, but whatever you did helped as well. It got us to this slope—a good place to land. He'll be okay. What did you do?*'

"I tried to take over for him. Like I was doing the flying. I thought it was working."

'*It was. But I didn't know what was happening. It made me feel strange. I had to block you. How did you know to do that?*'

"Sorry. I didn't know for sure I could do it. I guessed, because of something Dr. Bonner said. He said you could get inside a deer's head to bring it to Moerden. I thought I could get inside his head, and maybe control him. I mean, to keep him safe—when he isn't thinking, having a worm spell, I mean. Not when . . ." She saw Javeer's head move. "Let's see how he is."

He was bruised and somber, but he sat up and folded his wings. He brought his sphere around by his feet and gave Marise light. Tochara kept watch, alternately circling their position on the ground, and lifting to scan more distant terrain.

'*Marise*,' Javeer said after Tochara passed above them for the third time. '*It will happen again. You've been lucky, but we won't make it to the cliff rhumba. You'll fall eventually. I'll fall and kill you. We have to go back.*'

"We're not going back." She tentatively pushed against his mind, exploring whether she could get in there while he was conscious. It was like trying to push through a stone wall.

'*What are you doing?*'

"There's something you don't know. Dr. Bonner told me you can use a sphere to get inside someone else's head. You know? To sort of take them over."

'*Why would you want to?*'

"Right, but I can do it when you have a worm spell and get you down. It's why we landed okay this time. I thought you'd be able to warn me, but you can't, can you?"

'*You landed? You brought me down, not Tochara?*'

"I tried, and it sort of worked. Helped. Tochara helped too. I think I can get to the rhumba, and everything will work out. I'll have my—your father's—sphere back and I'll get help from home. We can't turn back now. If we go back, there's no hope for you or anyone who's infected. We have to go on, okay?"

Javeer didn't answer immediately.

'*Did you have my memories while you were in my head?*'

"No! Well, I didn't look for them, but I don't think so. There was nothing there, just emptiness. I wasn't trying to be you. Only to get you down safe."

'I don't remember anything. Okay. We'll go on. But I'm tired. Let me rest a bit.' He laid his head in her lap.

She relaxed against his shoulder and looked up at the sky, willing the stars to see them safely to Honedrai. The constellations were unfamiliar, but she succeeded in building an enormous pentagram low down in the northeast sky. She imagined it poised above Honedrai like a welcome sign, and it comforted her.

Marise lay half-dozing, wondering about the noise she had been hearing in her sleep. *Strange. Haven't heard so much as a jeong howl since we landed.* After a moment, she realized the noise was running water, and it was real. She jumped up, waking Javeer, and called out for Tochara. The female settled beside her within seconds.

"There's a stream nearby. Do you know where it is? Let's find it. We can get water."

'Follow me. It's one of the rivers coming down from the mountains. We're not far from the canyon here.'

The river ran rapid and shallow, with rocky banks and lots of little waterfalls. Her way lit by Javeer's sphere, Marise walked down to drink and took the opportunity for a quick bath, her first since leaving Tiderook, while the dragons drank. There was a pool nearby where they rooted out houra and fed them to each other, accompanied by much splashing and low hooting.

Marise lined up her little bottles on the bank. She set the one containing mummified worms and the one where they'd seen the larva aside. The rest she washed in the stream. She filled them with water and screwed the lids on tight.

The trio crossed the Darjugan River within minutes and flew

northeast, crossing its winding path three more times before morning. Each time, the unmistakable sound of rushing water rose from the chasm. For a time, it ran below them, and Marise longed to set down in the lush shelter and sleep, but as long as Javeer was able to go on, she didn't call a halt.

He landed once and rested for a bit, saying he felt strange. Just as the eastern horizon grew pale, he had another episode, dropping beneath Marise without warning.

This time, breaking the fall was easier. She melded her consciousness with his vacant mind and simply took over. He wobbled and tipped as she worked at maintaining her focus, and Tochara dodged in and out, helping to guide him. The landing was easy, except she forgot to extend her great clawed legs until seconds before impact.

They leapfrogged through the desert throughout the day and into the following night, resting for short periods and pushing on in a straight line for Honedrai. As Javeer's energy flagged, worm spells came more often, but each time Marise had to take over for him, she found it easier. By dusk on the second day, Tochara only had to help with landing, and only because Marise closed her eyes to heighten her ability to focus.

He was sluggish and disoriented on waking from his short naps, and it took longer and longer to get airborne. She didn't know how to help him. She grew reluctant to force him to go on, but the farther they went, the more impossible it became to go back.

Marise sent prayers out to the universe. *Just let him make it to the cave. Then we're okay.*

Meanwhile, Tochara talked to Javeer during the worst times and somehow pulled him back into the world.

As they drew near Honedrai, Marise had Javeer lead them north to the river again, and they slept for a few hours where her protective circle of stones still marked the beach.

She woke to a pale sky in the east and paced at the edge of the water alone until Tochara joined her. The dragon dipped her head and took a long drink from the river, and Marise stooped to pick up her sphere.

"Have you eaten kreel?"

'Lots of them. All the young dragons at the coast eat them.'

"Not older dragons?"

'Yes, older dragons too, but not as much. That's why so many young dragons have died, I guess.'

"Aren't you scared? Do you think you have it?"

'I don't know. When you told us it was kreel, I was shocked. I believed, for a while, that I have it, and I'm going to die. I even thought about staying with Javeer in the meadow and letting the jeong take me, too.'

"Oh, Tochara! No. But you didn't."

'I'm not as brave as him. I don't think I'd have been able to follow through. But I thought differently by that time. I was frightened before you figured out about the kreel. Before that, we didn't know how dragons got it. Anyone could have it. Anyone might start showing symptoms any time. Now, I know. I may have it, but I'm not sick yet. Maybe I don't have it. Look at Javeer. He's not scared, and he knows he's going to die.'

"He's *not* going to die." She softened her voice, addressing the crooked strip of brightening sky above. "If my plan works, neither one of you will die.

"I don't think you should come to the rhumba with us. Javeer and I should go alone from here. Once we get into the mummy cave, I won't be able to get you out again. The dragons here don't know you, and Korpec will kill you if he sees you. Either Javeer and I make it, or we don't, but there's no reason for you to risk it. There's nothing more you can do. Sorry, I never meant to leave you alone out here. I didn't think that through. Maybe you should go back to the coast to find Kuvrema and tell her what's going on. Do you think you'd be alright on your own?"

'How will you and Javeer get to the cave? What will you do if he has a spell? I won't be there to help.'

"I think I can handle it on my own now. I'm tired, but it's a short distance, and I think we can make it if we go now, before the desert dragons wake. I hope Korpec isn't expecting us."

'I could help in a fight. I don't want to leave him again. I'll come with you. Please.'

"Tochara." Marise thought it through as she spoke. "If there's a fight, and we make it into the cave, you'll be trapped. The only way out of there for you would be sphere travel. Are you willing to risk it? Do you know what happens to dragons who make mistakes when they travel that way?"

Tochara tensed.

Marise hoped she wouldn't ask how she planned to get Javeer out of the cave if it came to that. She heard, again, Bonner's casual comment when he'd seen the stump of her toe, "You're lucky you didn't lose more."

Tochara turned her head toward Javeer, still asleep at the top of the beach. *'It's forbidden. Though it might be a better end than the stagger. Alright. I can still help. I'll go back to Kuvrema. We'll return to find you. But I'm staying here until you've gone. I'm not sure Javeer could fight off a bojert right now, let alone a rhumba of hostile dragons. I'll head down the canyon until I'm well away, so I won't be seen, then fly straight for Wyvern Wood.'*

Relieved, Marise flung her arms around her neck and hugged her. "Look for us at Darjugan cave, at the head of the river. I love you, Tochara. Be careful. If anyone comes after you, just fly, fly as fast as you can. I know you can fly faster than Korpec and his bullies."

They moved up the beach, and Tochara nudged Javeer, speaking gently until he was alert and paying attention. Marise explained the plan. They gathered some breakfast and drank from the river, after which Marise walked a little and had a quick bath.

Minutes later, they bade Tochara goodbye with hugs from Marise and neck rubbing between the dragons. To Marise, the clicks their scales made as they slipped past each other sounded like the hands of a clock ticking away the seconds.

They headed straight for the mummy cave. The faster they made the trip, she thought, the better. Making no attempt at concealment, she rode with the rags of her cape flapping around her like limp feathers in the cool morning air.

She watched intently for other dragons but didn't see anyone out and about near the rhumba. Javeer didn't suffer a worm spell as they covered the short distance. She believed they were going to make it to the cave without incident.

When they drew close to Kuvrema's cave, she asked him to help her reach Eschla. Together, they bent their minds toward the henne's cave, gambling that she would be there.

Her voice was thin and reedy, but distinct. *'Javeer? Marise? Where are you?'*

"We're just outside," Marise answered. "Javeer's sick, and we need help. Can you go to the cave at the head of the river? Do you know where it is?"

'Just come in.' Eschla sounded as gruff as ever. *'Why do you want me to go to the river cave?'*

By then, Marise and Javeer had passed the end of the great outcrop of cliffs separating Kuvrema's cave from the mummy cave, and Eschla's voice faded to a whisper.

"No time to explain! Will you go? Say you'll go!"

If Eschla answered, she didn't hear.

They aimed for the third level of cliffs where the cave lay, but as they rose above the second level, Marise saw movement out of the corner of her eye. She twisted to look and gasped.

An enormous male dragon launched and sped toward them. Korpec was even bigger than she remembered.

"Keep going. Make him chase us."

But Javeer turned toward his enemy, giving Korpec the seconds he needed to dodge ahead and cut them off. The bully swung around, hovering huge and beastly between them and the cliff.

'So, you're back. Where's your friend from the coast?'

"What friend?" she hedged, giving herself time to think. *How does he know about Tochara? Has she been attacked in the canyon?* Her fingers tightened around Javeer's sphere.

'Do you think I'm so stupid I wouldn't know you were coming? I spotted you a day ago, limping across the desert.'

I . . . he didn't say we. *Does that mean he's on his own now? The rest of the rhumba's on our side? If that's true, Tochara's all right, and no one will come to help him.*

"Let us pass," she demanded, allowing a surge of frustration and anger to push against her outward calm.

Korpec lowered his head as though preparing to charge.

If no one's on his side, why doesn't he give up? Why doesn't he listen? What an idiot. She clenched her teeth.

He opened his mouth, and she drew back, anticipating a blast of flame. Glancing around for a means of defense, she decided to gamble. "Korpec, we're going to the mummy cave. Let us go. If another dragon dies and turns to dust in that cave, what do you care? You know there's no cure. Once we're in, you can block the entrance, set a guard, whatever. Let us go. If you harm us, I don't think Kuvrema and the rest of the rhumba will be pleased."

'Kuvrema's not here, and the rest of the rhumba will see I was right all along. The last thing we need is a bunch of soft-hearted females trying to nurse the sad little orphan through it. That overgrown bojert you befriended has the stagger. I'm not about to let him bring it here.'

Overgrown bojert! The coil of anger she was holding down sprang loose. "Overgrown bojert. Overgrown bojert? You asked if I think you're stupid." Her voice rose to a shout. "Yes, I think you're stupid. I think you are so stupid you wouldn't know a real enemy if she stuck a spear up your nose. Look at you, you flying rattlesnake, bullying a girl and a sick dragon like we're a threat to anyone. You are nothing but a coward. A great big—" Something twisted in her head, and Javeer went into free fall.

Marise's attention snapped from Korpec and locked onto Javeer. Following a now-familiar routine, she closed her eyes, hijacking his wings and steering him away from the rocks. The fall was under control long before they were in any danger of hitting the scree, but now she had a problem. She couldn't deal with Korpec and remain focused on keeping Javeer in the air. She had to know where the big male was, and she couldn't see him with her eyes closed. Marise looked up.

Korpec plunged toward them, his angle and speed implying deadly intentions. Javeer dropped, and she clamped her eyes shut again, bringing her focus back to him. They had lost altitude in seconds, and she knew they now hovered perilously close to the scree.

Okay. She righted herself as he wobbled beneath her. *It has to be through Javeer. I am Javeer. I am.* She opened her eyes. He tilted to one side and slid down through the air. The tip of one wing carved an arc in the scree, pulling them around and setting off a landslide.

She glimpsed Korpec, just above and too close, but lost him again. Javeer hit the scree facing down and slid, setting tons of rubble in motion. Barely able to keep her seat, she snapped her eyes shut and pulled up, up, away from the scree, gliding out over the foothills.

Through Javeer, she told herself. *Through Javeer's eyes.* She probed his vacant mind, unsure but envisioning his skull encasing hers like a helmet. She imagined her eyes peering through his eye sockets.

At last, the blank screen behind her eyelids gave way to a view of the cliffs, sharply outlined and multihued in the morning sunlight. And Korpec, lunging toward her belching flame, only yards away. Already she felt the heat on her face. She screamed.

A noise burst from Javeer's mouth, loud and high pitched, like the squeal of rusty train brakes. Shocking and unfamiliar in the quiet of the desert morning, it bounced off surrounding cliffs and escalated to a chaotic roar.

Korpec faltered and drew back, flapping his wings in reverse. He stood straight in midair. Equally surprised and shocked by Korpec's retreat, Marise stopped screaming. The clamor died away, and she realized what had happened. She laughed, a great belly laugh, surprise and relief and power overcoming fear.

If the scream had been shocking, the laughter, coming from a dragon's throat not built for it, was terrifying. A shrieking gargle, half death rattle, half war whoop blasted the canyon walls. It summoned every horror movie she had ever watched. It was awe-inspiring. It was ridiculous. She laughed harder, and the bubbling whoop intensified.

Now filled with a reckless glee, she rushed headlong at Korpec, a maniacal grimace splitting her human face, her dragon jaws stretched wide. The movement of her human arms matched the sweep of her dragon wings, making shreds of her cape float around her like a halo of writhing tentacles. She threw herself at her enemy.

Korpec hung in the air, his expression of malice transformed to uncertainty. He jerked backward, opening more distance between them, and allowing her a clear line of sight to the mummy cave.

She shrieked, creating a crescendo of dissonance. Korpec increased the distance again. At one with Javeer, she raced for the heights, easily outdistancing Korpec, who seemed to have given up the pursuit.

Marise aimed for the third level until she saw the cleft of the cave's entrance. She made for the tunnel without looking back. Encouraged by her flying accuracy while navigating through Javeer's eyes, she hardly slowed when they reached the ledge. She extended her dragon legs to meet the rock, folded her dragon wings, and disappeared into the mountain like an enormous bat coming home to roost.

Chapter
Twenty-One

A COLLECTION
OF BONES

Marise's hands shook, and her legs felt as though they were made of rubber. In the gloom of the cavern, her laughter faded to a nervous giggle followed by a series of hiccups, making Javeer gag.

She stiffened. Had someone been here? Something felt different. Then she realized she had never seen it through his eyes before. She hadn't understood how well dragons could see in the dark.

The mummified dragon was still an undefined heap in the far reaches of the cave, but the animal bones and dry plant litter scattered across the floor were clear. She was still in control of Javeer, so she used his claws to pile up a heap of debris, dragging it all midway between the doorway and the mummy.

She whispered, "I've wanted to do this for days." Breathing in, she filled his lungs, then huffed the air back out, willing it to ignite. It did not. She tried again, closing her eyes and humming deep in her own throat as she forced air out of his mouth. A growl echoed off the walls, but no fire. She switched to a squeal, but it worked no better.

"Goddess, help me. I need light." She considered the challenge, then pressed her lips together.

Sorry about this, Javeer. Blame it on crackers. Here goes. She thrust his nose into the pile of brush, inhaling deeply, drawing in dust and plant debris.

A burning, tickling sensation roared down her nasal passages and throat, making her eyes water. As his ribs expanded, she fought an impending sneeze.

"Oh. *Achoo!*" They sneezed in unison. She, hunched with a hand over her face, he, blasting the floor at his feet. She heard brush scatter as a second sneeze followed on the heels of the first. Jolted off balance, she scrambled for a handhold, sneezed again, and righted herself in time to brace for another heave. The irritation in her chest grew worse with every breath, and she consciously turned the next sneeze into a cough.

Javeer produced an impressive flame.

She coughed uncontrollably, tears and nose streaming. She coughed until she gagged, and Javeer coughed with her, lighting up the floor for yards around.

Still coughing, she hustled him toward the mummy and had him gather a new pile of kindling. She set the brush alight. She expected it to burn fast and fill the cave with smoke, but she didn't care. Her intention was to be out of there in just moments. She slid down from his back, pulling out of his head.

To her relief, the urge to cough died, but her legs buckled as her feet hit the rock. She was thankful to be on the ground a second later when Javeer's head passed above her, still belching fire, huffing and snorting.

She fumbled with the backpack's straps, dragged the bag off her shoulders, and pulled it open. In the flickering light, she reached for the mummy's skull, heedlessly hooking her thumb through an eye socket to get a firm grip. She shoved the skull into the backpack. Dried flesh scraped against the rough fabric. She reached for the mummy again, snapped the top section off its neck, and shoved it down beside the skull.

Marise crawled, following its spine with eye and hand. Where she judged the end of its tail to be, she dug in the debris on the cave floor. The fire was feeble now, and she searched mostly by feel.

"Be here," Marise said. "Be here. Be here." Her hand passed over diminishing tail bones for the last one, the one with three talons holding a sphere. Finally, her fingers found a smooth, cold, curved surface. She pulled it up into the dim light. It was a sphere, still attached to the last vertebra of the tail.

"Yes!"

She jammed the sphere into the pack, tail segment and all. She slung the bag onto her shoulders and reached to pick up her relic sphere, which lay in the dust where she'd left it days ago.

With her free hand, she tossed more debris on the fire. When flames licked up, she turned her gaze to the sphere, setting it down in front of her and summoning an image of Darjugan cave. The cavern swam into view, sunlit and empty, the mosaic illuminated by light from above.

Marise breathed an *ah* of delight when the illuminated image produced light from her own sphere to add to the dwindling firelight. She studied the pattern in the mosaic, recalling every detail. She let the image fade, scooped up the sphere, and turned toward him.

"Javeer?"

He lay slumped on his side, but she felt his ribs rise and fall under her hand.

"Still in the worm spell. That's good." She draped his tail over her arm and tucked herself under his wing just as the fire went out.

Marise scratched a circle on the floor with her index finger. Working blind, she added the three-pointed symbol from the mosaic, not caring how good it looked. She ducked forward, feeling around in the dirt, letting the warmth of charred kindling guide her hand. Her fingers found a handful of ashes, still warm but cool enough to touch. She held them to her nose and inhaled the sharp aroma of burned wood to help her focus.

"Bad thoughts be gone. Be gone." She drew a deep breath and thought about the protection symbol she'd scratched on the ground. Methodically, she filled it in with color and sunlight and conjured the sound of the falls. She added intertwining dragons around the outside.

Marise stilled and sent out a brief prayer. "So mote it be."

Keeeyah! The call of a dragon cut the air. It sounded very close.

Forgetting all caution, all uncertainty, she held Javeer's sphere in front of her with her own and closed her eyes. She pushed into his mind with her mental image of the mosaic in Darjugan cave. She held back a second longer to double-check the image, then imagined herself and Javeer hovering millimeters above the mosaic.

The call of a dragon came again, closer.

She took a deep breath, opened her eyes, and shifted the image smoothly into the depths of his sphere.

The floor beneath her heaved.

A pillar of morning sunlight lit the mosaic, and water roared past the cave mouth in a glittering curtain, misting plants that clung to the wall within. The humid air soothed her irritated breathing passages and dry, dusty skin. The cave at Darjugan felt like home.

Marise wasted no time getting Javeer off the circle. Then she let him slump and gathered her focus. At the bottom of the ramp, Marise pulled the backpack open. She looked down at the mummy's sphere and rounded skull.

"I really am a witch," she whispered.

She pulled out the sphere, prying with her fingertips to work the globe free of its claw-like tail. One talon broke, and the orb came away. She strode to the falls with the remnants of the tail and dropped them into the cascade.

"Deep peace of the running water to you."

Returning, she paused where the cave branched and looked toward the pool. "Dr. Bonner says 'Hi,'" A lump formed in her throat. "He thought you were cool." No soft footfall or distant splash replied.

She stood, remembering the elderly man, and thinking about what she would tell Ellen.

Lifting her tattered cape off over her head, she arranged it on the floor. She took the mummy's neck bones out of the backpack, wrapped them in the cape, and tucked the bundle against the cave wall. Everything else in the pack came out, and she piled it into a jumble next to the cape. Only the skull, sphere, and Bonner's watch remained within. Marise was ready.

Javeer still lay where she had left him, but when she put a hand on top of his head, he half-opened his eyes.

'How did we get here?'

"We made it, Javeer. That's all that matters now, and you won't have to fly anymore." She stroked his scaly cheek and smiled.

"Now you rest. I have to leave for a while. Go back home. But I'll be back with help, okay? You stay here and sleep. Don't go up to the top, okay? You might fall if you . . . ." The lump in her throat returned. She swallowed. "Eschla should be here soon. And maybe Tochara and Kuvrema. You'll be alright. Don't worry about the crackers creature. It won't hurt you."

His eyes opened wide, and he lifted his head to look at her. She chuckled. "Dr. Bonner told me about it. You knew all along, didn't you, but you didn't know how tame it is." Marise sighed. She was wasting time. She curled up in a ball, hugging her knees, and peered past her kneecaps at him.

"I promised I'd get you back to the meadow if I couldn't help you. If I don't come back . . ." She tucked her face down behind her knees for a moment. "If I don't come back, use sphere travel to get yourself back there . . . if you want to, that is." She saw Javeer jerk his head back and blink. "No. You can do it. Just visualize the meadow and go there. But you won't have to. I'll be back." She jumped to her feet and leaned forward to give him a kiss on the forehead.

She gave herself no time for second thoughts. Slinging the pack onto her shoulders, she crossed to the center of the mosaic. She went through the steps of checking the mosaic in Cadogan Mills before building a perfect image of it in her mind. Seconds later, she stood in the spring sunshine in Ellen's spotless kitchen.

The smooth ceramic felt plush under her travel-worn soles. She blinked at all the finished wood. The stainless steel sink. The polished chrome taps. She looked down at herself, at her torn stained clothes, her bare feet, and the purplish stump of her toe. She imagined how others would see her. Her hair was in tangles, her knuckles grazed, her fingernails and toenails chipped and dirty. She wondered if she'd ever feel comfortable in human surroundings again.

Ellen shuffled around the corner, pushing her walker, with an empty teacup dangling from one hand. She came to a sudden halt.

"Marise."

She was jolted into reality. "Ellen. I'm back. But I can't stay. Javeer's dying! He has the stagger, Ellen. I need you to help me."

"Oh. Oh dear. Me? Help?" She frowned. "But what have you been doing? What can I do? Have you found—"

"I need you to go to The Witch's Cupboard on Airlie Lane. The Wicca shop, you know? The owner, Lupin, she's tall and thin with purple hair. I need you to talk to her. Tell her Marise Leeson sent you, and I'm calling in my last two favors. Right now. Tell her to come here, and she needs to bring surgical tools. And say not to tell anyone! No one can know I'm here. How are my parents?" She shook her head. "Never mind, you can tell me later. Tell her to come as quick as she can. Today. Now."

"You expect her to just close up shop and run over here? Marise, why would this woman do this for me, just because I claim to bring a message from beyond the grave?"

Marise assumed a stern expression and crossed her arms over her chest. "She'll know it's me. Tell her, *if* she refuses, tell her '*because you can.*'"

Ellen glared at her. She glared back, a silent battle of wills. Finally, Ellen turned away. "I'll call a cab."

Minutes later, they stood by the window in the living room. Ellen wore a light spring jacket, and her purse hung from her forearm. She watched the street through the sheer curtains. Marise, tucked behind heavy taffeta drapes with the backpack at her feet, combed her hair with her fingers while she waited.

"Did you find Earl?" Ellen asked again.

"No. We found his watch and some footprints." She pulled the watch out of the backpack. "I brought it for you."

Ellen eyed it and took it. "That's his watch alright. Put it on the mantel when I've gone." She handed it back. "By the way, they did not, of course, find your remains in the ashes of your house. They have no clues, no leads, and most people believe the investigators didn't look hard enough. You're dead.

"Ah, here's the cabbie." Ellen turned to push off with her walker. "Your parents continue to search and ask for tips. Good luck to them, eh? Are you ever coming home?"

"Here." Marise stepped toward her. She held out a tangle of hair. "Give these to Lupin."

Ellen took the hair with a look of bewilderment. She rolled the strands into a ball and tucked them into her coat pocket.

Marise stood silent as Ellen went through the front porch and onto the front step with surprising speed. The cab driver, who clearly knew the elderly lady, strode up to the steps and took her walker, collapsing it and tucking it under his right arm while offering her his left.

She watched the taxi until it turned right at the end of the street. She walked to the mantelpiece and dropped the watch over the head of a rearing ceramic horse.

Marise left the room and walked down the hall, opening doors until she found a den with comfortable furniture and heavy curtains. She flopped onto the couch with a grateful sigh. The smell of leather hit her, and she thought of Javeer's bookish smell. She wondered if he was alright, if he was sleeping, if Eschla was on her way.

It felt like only seconds had passed when she heard voices in the hall.

"Where is she?"

She recognized Officer Wheaton's voice, strong and resonant.

"I, I don't know," Ellen said. "She was here when I left."

"Well, maybe she's disappeared again. A fly-by-nighter, that one. I hope we don't need to report her missing . . . again."

"You still don't believe me, do you? You think me crazy? She's here. You'll see, and she has no intention of going home or even being seen by anyone else."

Marise tried sitting up but found she couldn't. She knew hiding behind the door was pointless this time. They would find her. Where to hide? Her only thought was to get behind the couch. She thought there was just enough room, but her limbs wouldn't obey. *I've got the stagger. I have it. People can get it after all.*

"We'll have to search the house room by *room.*" Wheaton's voice came from the hall, "until we winkle her out. *What's* in here?" The doorknob turned. A shaft of light broadened as the door opened inward toward Marise. Then the light was blocked by a tall silhouette.

She thought she would explode with panic. She tried flinging herself over the back of the couch.

Sitting up with a jerk, her dream shattered, and she became wide awake. *I'm okay. I don't have the stagger.* She felt a surge of dizziness.

A tall figure advanced upon her, followed by Ellen, pushing her walker. Cornered, Marise looked up.

Lupin's quizzical blue eyes met hers. No one could resemble a police officer less than Lupin at that moment. Dressed in a baggy green sweatshirt and tight leggings, with a wide leather belt, she looked more like Peter Pan. A bulky satchel hung from her shoulder with a strap so long the bag dangled by her knee, and her windblown hair formed a ragged violet halo around her head.

"Lupin! I thought you were . . . I thought." Her gaze shifted from Lupin to Ellen and back again. She was disoriented and confused.

"You've been asleep dear," said Ellen. "Take a minute. There, dear, you must be exhausted. I'll make some tea."

"What *have* you been up to?" Lupin ran her cool eyes down Marise's bedraggled frame. She sank into an armchair and reached into her bag. The hair picture of the Green Man emerged, much more complete than when she'd last seen it. The billowy waves around his face had solidified into leafy hair and beard. Veins in red—Celeste's hair, perhaps—ribs of brown-black, and lobes of gold. The leaves looked as though they actually moved in the breeze as Lupin turned the work toward herself, picked up her dangling needle, and poked it through the fabric.

Marise couldn't help but notice that there was none of Lupin's hair in the picture. Then she thought she saw the Green Man's black eyes move, turning to look her over, and she gasped.

Lupin glanced up. "With the Green Man, the gold *can* stay," she said.

Marise gaped at her. She had no idea what that meant.

"What do you want from me?" Lupin asked.

Her head cleared, and Marise knew exactly what she wanted to say. She reached into the backpack with both hands and pulled out the dragon's skull first, followed by the sphere. She held them out to Lupin. "I want you to do brain surgery on a dragon."

Chapter
Twenty-Two

DETOUR

"Did you hear anything?" Marise leaned forward and peered down the passage to the pool, resting a hand on Javeer's taloned toe. Her eye ran along the trail of crackers and crumbs they'd laid down the center of the floor. Other than the waterfall at the end, nothing moved in the tunnel.

From where they sat, Marise had a clear view of Eschla and Lupin. The two sat facing each other near the mosaic with the mummy's skull and neck bones arranged on the floor between them. Marise noticed Lupin pick up the skull and turn it over, peering inside the dome. Eschla leaned forward to look as well.

Javeer seemed to avoid looking at the pair, looking down the side tunnel instead. *I can't hear anything over the noise of the waterfall. What will you do when you go home?*

She leaned back against him and looked up. She was in the powder blue tank top she'd been wearing when she first arrived in Moerden. Stained and torn, it was hardly recognizable as the same garment. She had soiled it anew with dirt and plant stains since returning to the cave, concealing the fact Ellen had washed it. She'd be going home in tattered jeans and without any shoes.

"Dr. Bonner said to go to the circle in Cedar Settlement," she said. "It's a long way from home. He told me to act like I don't remember anything and something about stress. I asked Ellen. She says he meant I should say I have no idea how I got there. That'll be easy enough. Even if I tell the truth, no one will believe me. They'll think I have amnesia or something." She pulled another cracker out of the package and sailed it down the passage like a Frisbee.

"Here, Crackers. Come and get it," she called, then spoke more softly to Javeer. "I'll go find my family. They're living with my uncle and aunt since the house . . . since I burned the house down. Everything's gone, Javeer. Everything I owned before the fire. But you know what? I don't care about that. I just want to see my parents and Celeste, and my other friends.

"What will *you* do if you . . . after the operation?" She glanced at Lupin, recalling the relief she'd felt when she and Lupin had arrived in the cave to find Eschla already there.

'*I'll go back to Wyvern Wood, find Tochara, and help them get rid of the stagger. I should go back, anyway. There it is,*' he said, yanking her attention back to the side tunnel. A dark hump rose past the lip of the pool.

She held her breath. Intent on watching the dark shape grow larger, she didn't notice a long tentacle snaking across the floor until it snagged a cracker and reeled it in over the ledge. "Oh! Dr. Bonner said it looked like a catfish with legs, long whiskers, and bulgy eyes. He never said tentacles."

'*Will you tell other people about Moerden?*'

"Nope. Well, maybe Celeste. And Lupin knows." She sighed. "It will be hard telling lies all the time. I feel like I'm always straightening out the lies I've told. I told Lupin about the crystal ball. The sphere, I mean. And I told Ellen the truth about Dr. Bonner. That was hard. I lied to you, too. I sort of tricked you into this, and we don't even know if it can work. But I think it can. I believe Lupin can save you."

'*I'm glad I'm here with you. I'm glad you came back to get me before the jeong. If I don't die, will you come back?*'

"Yes, of course. Look. Crackers!" Her voice was barely audible.

The pool grue climbed out of the water, plum colored and about the size of a punching bag with stumpy legs. It nodded a head, the shape of an overturned mixing bowl, with two eyes bulging near the top, giving it corners. A crescent of long whiskers waved like feelers across the top of a mouthless snout.

"Look." One of the whiskers reached for a second cracker, stretching like an elastic string. As though equipped with a sticky tip, the whisker plucked the cracker up and reeled it in, tucking it under its chin where it disappeared. The pool grue advanced several paces, and a third cracker vanished.

"I'll look for you at the ocean rhumba?" She wondered if this would be difficult since she'd never been there, but she didn't want to worry him, so she didn't bring it up. She'd be able to find Kuvrema, or Eschla, she thought, and they'd help her. She remembered Tochara and hoped she was safe. She should be near the rhumba by now.

"Javeer, do dragons get married? I mean, do they mate for life . . . or you know, would you and Tochara . . . ?" She didn't know how to ask the question.

The pool grue was halfway up the tunnel, clearing up the crackers like an automated broom. Marise reached into the box for more, passing one up to Javeer and tossing several more about a meter out.

She tried again. "You were with your father when he died, but I haven't met any dragon families. Like a father, mother, and young dragons all together. Do dragons do that?"

'Some have mates, and they stay together and look after their young. But they don't have their own cave. Lots of dragons don't have mates. Can I have another cracker before he gets the rest of them?'

The pool grue abandoned caution and advanced upon them with an odd undulating motion like a giant caterpillar. Flat black eyes with silvery rims turned to Marise as though demanding she pass over the cracker supply.

Without taking her eyes off the beast, she reached into the box, feeling for a cracker. She took in four-clawed feet, beads and rivulets of water on finely wrinkled skin, and a ridge of coarse hairs running down the spine. Her hand trembling, she held out another cracker.

Lupin jumped to her feet and strode toward Marise and Javeer. The grue wheeled and darted toward the water with a slap of wet feet and a splash, disappearing before Lupin had covered the distance. She paused and turned her head to the tunnel. "*What* was that? It smells like burnt sugar."

"Crackers, the pool grue. Have you figured it out? When will you start?"

"We cannot do it," she stated in a tone that rang with finality. Marise's chin came up, and her hand tightened around Javeer's toe.

"Not without more help. The anatomy's clear enough. It's possible. Theoretically *possible*, but how do we anesthetize the patient? How do we knock the dear fellow out?" She looked at Javeer.

"Wait till he has a spell."

"Yes, and have him come *around* while his head is cut open? And why shouldn't he once the worms are removed? No. No, that is *not* a good idea. Eschla thinks we might take control of his brain, but this *might* be painful for those taking part. We need more help if we're to attempt it. You alone might fail, and I need Eschla helping me." Lupin stood looking at Marise as though she had all the answers.

She nibbled on a cracker as she considered this latest roadblock. When the cracker was gone, she spoke with a calm that hid inner turmoil. "Well, I'd better go to Wyvern Wood."

No one spoke for a dozen heartbeats until Javeer broke the silence. '*How? It takes days to get there, and who will take you? Eschla?*'

"Eschla," Marise called. The older female turned toward her. "Have you ever seen the circle at Wyvern Wood?" She pointed at the Darjugan mosaic.

'Never. This is the only one I've seen.'

Marise closed her eyes and took a deep breath. "Ok." She rose and crossed to the circle where she sat cross-legged and placed the sphere on the ground in front of her, her hand resting on its upper curve.

'Marise, what are you doing?' Javeer rose and moved toward her. *'Don't. You don't know where you're going.'* She pretended she didn't hear him.

Eschla looked poised to prevent her from using the sphere as well, but when Marise raised an imperious palm, she hesitated and moved to Javeer instead. She planted herself in front of him, his neck curved over her spine ridge. Lupin joined them, and the three stood in a tight cluster watching Marise.

She sorted through her memories of her flight with Kuvrema. She remembered the mosaics—one a Chinese dragon surrounded by Chinese writing, one a strange twining circle with spikes and arrows in the middle. *Which was which?* She knew one lay at the ocean rhumba, the other in the Whispern Caverns. She tried to remember the order in which Kuvrema had showed them to her. Her thoughts flitted from one to the other, unable to settle. She felt her heart racing.

"The Whispern Caverns," Marise said to herself. She remembered Tochara mentioning them. *"The headstrong males plan to find and kill you . . . . They are holed up at the Whispern Caverns now while Honosa tries calming everyone down."* The wrong choice could be deadly if the males were still there.

The dragon, she thought. *It makes sense—there are dragons in the mosaic here—it makes sense there'd be a dragon in the other rhumba as well.* She built an image of the Chinese circle Kuvrema had shown her. She'd liked it, and her memory of it was much clearer than the other one. It was beautiful, intricate. It drew her. She prepared to move the image into the sphere.

Doubt made her pause.

But this isn't a rhumba. The rhumba's hours away, and I don't know what the circle in Korpec's cave looks like. The carved dragons probably don't mean a thing. She rubbed her palms on her knees and licked her lips. She glanced sideways at Lupin and the two dragons.

Once more, she closed her eyes and tried to recall Kuvrema's exact words. She remembered a longing to see the Whispern Caverns, the mysterious hideout in the mountains. It had been the Chinese dragon mosaic that inspired her desire. She was sure of it. The other mosaic was what she needed now.

"A two-stranded cord in a circle. Strands wound around each other with thick spikes on the edges. Shades of brown. Yes. White inside? White, I think. And three nails. Big solid nails in the center, pointed, uh, eleven o'clock, two o'clock and four o'clock sort of . . . doesn't matter, as long as they're close together."

She built the mental image piece by piece, as accurately as she remembered it. She pushed it aside. "Have to use Kuvrema's memory. That's what's real."

Marise stood up and paced around the circle with her arms crossed. She looked at Javeer and the others, and a movement behind Lupin caught her eye. She watched Crackers fish a cracker out of the abandoned box. Smiling, she turned, looked into the sphere, and summoned Kuvrema's memory. An image of the mosaic formed in the sphere, indistinct and shadowy. She picked up the sphere.

Dim light illuminated the cool stone of the mosaic beneath her feet. She smelled incense and heard muffled voices. She was inside a building. A vaulted ceiling rose high over her head, and through an arch to the right, Marise saw row upon row of polished church pews. A handful of people were there, seeming oblivious to her unusual arrival. They faced a massive altar of carved wood, marble, and gold, their heads bowed as though in prayer.

She took in towering pillars, stained glass windows, displays of religious artifacts, and a legion of dust motes drifting in filtered sunlight. Never had she seen such an ornate church, and she gazed about openmouthed.

Voices came from behind her, and she turned, finding a couple standing close by with their backs to her. They spoke and gestured at an object in a glass case, but she couldn't make out a word of what they said.

Apart from the foreign language—Spanish, perhaps—she found no clue in her surroundings to tell her where she was. Nonetheless, it dawned on her she'd gotten the wrong one. *I've found another mosaic on our side, somewhere. At least I know what it looks like now. Better get out of here before someone notices me.* She looked down. '*Yellow, not white, more like one-thirty, black and gray spike nails.*' She studied the pattern briefly, transferred the image into the sphere, and left the cathedral.

This time, when she felt solid ground under her feet, she had only seconds to take in a forest clearing and lots of movement around her before something hit her hard in the chest and knocked her staggering backward off the circle into knee high grass.

Marise clutched the coarse bulgy object that had hit her and recognized its tough exterior at once. She held a sack of matted weaver vine with a collection of hard objects rolling about inside. She shook it.

This is full of bones, she thought. *Bojert bones, most likely.* Hearing a low chittering, she looked up. Three young male dragons hovered yards away.

"Is this yours?" She held out the sack.

The largest of the youngsters darted in and took it with a wing claw. He ascended at once. The dragon let the sack drop, brought its tail around, and whacked the falling sack, sending it sailing across the clearing. Two smaller dragons turned to speed after it, racing and whistling. The first dragon remained, winging past Marise to land behind her.

'Are you Marise?'

"Oh! You know my name. Um, what's your name?"

'Valcke. My mother says you're going to be the most famous caballero ever, but Riekor says Tochara's missing, and you're the only one who knows where she is. You're not allowed near the circle.' He looked at her sphere and then met her eyes again, as if waiting for an explanation.

Well, I know where I stand. And this is obviously Wyvern Wood.

"Tochara should be here, or she should be here soon. Valcke, do you know Kuvrema? Is she here somewhere? Can you take me to her?"

'I know Kuvrema. She's fun. Tells us stories. But this time she's been with Honosa in the great hall since she got here. My mother's there, too. I want her to tell us about you and Javeer. Javeer came from Honedrai, didn't he? My mother says he's a hero, but now he's dead. She says Kuvrema changed everything by saving him, but now her heart is broken. She says—'

"Valcke, Javeer's not dead!" She was amused by the chattery little dragon, but anxious to move on. "Not yet anyway. I need help right away to save him. Will you take me to the—where did you say Kuvrema is? The great hall? Now?" The two smaller dragons approached, batting the sack of bojert bones between them.

'Where's Javeer? My mother says no one can save a dragon with the stagger. I'm not allowed to eat kreel anymore.' The bone bag passed so close Valcke ducked his head. He twisted round and trilled a rebuke.

She seized the opening. "If you take me to the great hall, I'll try to get you some kreel that are safe to eat. If it's okay with your mom, of course. How about it?"

'*Sure, I can take you. You can follow me. You know where there's kreel that are safe to eat?*' Valcke lifted off but stayed close.

"Yes, I do. Look, you can fly above me. We'll still be able to talk."

Valcke landed again and looked at the sphere. He showed none of the revulsion the older dragons held toward it. '*That's a relic. I've never seen a relic. I thought they were all gone. Riekor says the relics didn't work for talking to men. Did you use the relic and the circle to get here? No one's allowed near the circle. It's dangerous. Riekor says some of the males use the circles sometimes, especially to get to the caverns. Everyone knows they do it, but no one talks about it. I'm not going to do that when I get older. I don't care about treasure. I want to hunt. Our hunters have gone to hunt deer. My mother says they're going to hunt all the deer and get rid of them.*'

"Yes, that's right. Deer spread the stagger. Look, I'm not holding your sphere, and I can still hear you, see? It does work. At least it works for me. Can we go now? To the great hall? Is it far?" She wondered where this great hall could be. She didn't think there were any mountains nearby, and imagined it might be beneath her, perhaps an underground cavern.

'*Not far, but you'll have to walk. We'll take the circle path. It leads straight there.*' He lifted off again and flew toward a gap in the trees.

She had to run to keep up. When she reached the opening, she saw it was the end of a track, as straight as an *i* with the circle for a dot. Tall trees bordered it on both sides, but at ground level, it was overgrown with bushes that gave off a pungent, spicy smell when she brushed against them.

She pushed through, ignoring the damage to her bare arms and imagined the circle path cleared, a wide green avenue for dragons and caballeros arriving at the circle. Though she tried to keep up with Valcke, her progress was slow. He circled back repeatedly, often advising her from above about the best route through.

Before long, the trees on the verges grew taller and spread their boughs farther across the opening until they joined overhead like an arch. Though the undergrowth thinned so Marise could move more freely, the light dwindled, and she had to pick her way with care. The canopy above grew so thick she found it hard to keep Valcke in sight. She called to him and asked for light.

'*You should be quiet,*' Valcke scolded her. '*Some of the males would kill you if they knew you were here. They think the stagger is your fault. Riekor says now we know how to get rid of it you should go back where you came from and leave us alone.*'

His tail sphere barely illuminated the ground as they continued down the circle path. Meanwhile, the woods around her grew darker. From time to time, she glimpsed light far off and imagined it traveled down tall narrow corridors straight through the dense forest. She heard distant calls of "*keeyah*" that seemed to come from everywhere, and once she thought she heard movement close by in the darkness. She wondered how many dragons there were in Wyvern Wood, and how many already knew she was there.

Chapter
Twenty-Three

EMERGENCY SURGERY

Marise stepped into a vast open space and jumped back to the shelter of the circle path. The clearing was more twilight than dark, with dim light filtering down from above and a cluster of glowing spheres in the distance. Valcke surged ahead, his sphere a searchlight illuminating the ground, but she hung back.

The floor was polished bare earth, without so much as a footprint, save here and there a dry brown leaf large enough for Marise to stretch out on. The canopy was far above, a black dome pierced by beams of sunlight. Where the shafts of light shone brightest, animals, huge insects, or perhaps plica flew about. Marise wondered how enormous the trees must be to form a roof over such a huge space.

Valcke returned with a rush. '*Come on, they've seen us. Look.*'

She saw only two lit spheres remained on the far side of the clearing. A flash drew her eyes upward as a dragon burst out through the canopy, the brief shaft of light glinting off the scales of three more dragons in the air. They closed in on her near the ground.

Marise looked for Kuvrema among the trio. She could not see any of them clearly. She tried to look at all three at once but was always forced to turn her back to one.

The relic sphere in her hand felt gruesome and inappropriate, and she lowered it, wishing she could put it out of sight. She thought these dragons must know who she was, but were they friend or enemy? She wanted to start talking, to explain herself, to convince them they must help her save Javeer, but she held her tongue.

The nearest dragon was a female, with patches of shiny copper glinting in Valcke's sphere light. The dragon's manner was so commanding, Marise guessed she was Honosa. To the henne's right was a smaller dragon. The third remained behind Marise, hidden in the deeper shadows near the forest's edge.

The silence weighed on her. She took a deep breath and invoked the Goddess for some guidance, some inspiration. She put the relic sphere down by her feet and held out her hand to Honosa. The large female granted her request, placing a warm, half-lit sphere in her palm. Through the sphere, she felt friendliness and curiosity.

"Honosa? I am Marise Leeson of Cadogan Mills, daughter of Carol and Dean Leeson."

'And I am Honosa, henne of Wyvern Wood Rhumba. Welcome, Marise. We were not expecting you, especially in such young company. Tochara returned today and told us she left you in the desert. She has flown without stopping. I wonder how you came to be so close behind her.' Honosa's gaze turned to Valcke. The young male fluttered and bounced.

Excluded from their conversation, she felt certain Valcke was describing her arrival and protesting his innocence in a series of rapid-fire sentences. She smiled and waited a moment before interrupting.

"Is Tochara okay? She wasn't attacked in the canyon? I worried about her flying back alone."

'She is well. She wants to return immediately with Kuvrema, but maybe that isn't necessary now?'

The silence grew heavy again as she tried deciphering what Honosa was asking her.

'What has happened to Javeer?'

The dragon behind Marise moved closer, and she suppressed the urge to turn or dodge away. She fervently hoped it was Kuvrema. *For Javeer's sake, I must find the right words now. I must convince them to help me.*

"Javeer is alive." The dragon at her back moved closer. "Javeer is safe for now in the river cave. I've got help from home, another woman who can remove his worms. A . . . a surgeon. But we need more help, more dragons to keep him, keep him . . ." She paused and cast about for the right words. "Quiet and comfortable during the operation. Eschla is there, but we need more. Quickly. That's why I've come. Why I used the circle." Marise turned at last, looking directly at the third dragon, who now stood close on her right.

"Kuvrema! It is you. You showed me the circle. Do you remember? When we flew with Javeer? If your memory of the circle here in Wyvern Wood was good enough to get me here—I couldn't have got here without it—surely your mental image of the circle in the river cave is good enough to get you back there. You can even see it with spheresight first."

'What?' Honosa's tone and sphere were less friendly now. *'Use the circles to go to the desert? Humans using circles is one thing. Dragons is another. We do not travel by sphere.'*

Marise wheeled on Honosa. "It *can* be done! I moved Javeer from the cliff rhumba to the river cave using spheres. It worked."

Honosa's head whipped down so her face hovered inches from Marise's. She said nothing, but Marise felt the dragon's breath on her forehead and goosebumps rose on her arms. In her peripheral vision, Kuvrema drew herself up as if about to belch fire, and she wondered who, or what, the blast would target if it came. The third dragon hustled Valcke away under a folded wing.

"The males use the circles, don't they? I bet Korpec uses them, doesn't he, Kuvrema?"

Kuvrema spread her wings, threw back her head, and screeched. The rising cry flooded the clearing and filtered through the forest, a heart-catching feral shriek. Marise renewed her grip on Honosa's sphere, trying to still her shaking hands. She was reminded she wasn't talking to people. These dragons were not pleased with her, and she was alone among them.

She glanced toward the knot of dragons on the far side of the great hall, and her breath caught as more emerged from the wood. The shriek died away, but the air reverberated with answering calls from near and far. Her heartbeat thudded in her ears, and she spoke breathlessly.

"Males use the circles to get to the Whispern Caverns. And they've used them to track down all the people in Moerden and kill them. I'm right, aren't I? Dragons use the circles all the time. You just won't admit it." Her hand had gone cold and clammy. What she sensed from the Wyvern Wood henne now was hostility and fear.

"You dragons are the bravest creatures," she rushed on. "The bravest creatures I've ever met. You're not afraid of anything . . . except those circles. I've seen Kuvrema stand up to Korpec when he's spewing fire everywhere. Javeer took on a swamp monster that could have torn his head off. But you freak out about something you're *supposed* to be able to do! The spheres are part of you. They're a gift. Why not use them?" She realized she was holding Honosa's sphere up like a trophy, and it gave her an idea.

She addressed every dragon in the great hall. "Those circles were created so people and dragons could use the spheres to travel safely. Think about it. You can get home from anywhere instantly. Anywhere in the universe! You have a brilliant way to travel, and you don't use it!"

She turned to Kuvrema, and back to Honosa, holding the henne's sphere over her head in her right hand, reaching out to

Honosa with her left. "The circles are safe if you use them properly. Totally safe. Use them for something good! Use them to save the dragon who's risked his life over and over to save all of you. How can you refuse? He is waiting for you. Waiting for your help. If he doesn't get it, he will die. Help Javeer, or he will *die!*" She stopped talking and counted her heartbeats, scanning the clearing. *Twenty dragon, thirty dragon, forty dragon, fifty dragon, sixty dragon, dragon, dragon . . .*

'Forbidden,' Honosa said, her sphere dull, radiating doubt. *'The circles are forbidden. No dragon will follow you to Darjugan through the circles.'*

Marise sank to her knees, drawing Honosa's sphere in against her breast. Her head drooped.

'I will.'

Marise's head jerked up. She thought she recognized the musical voice. The newcomer's sphere blazed, illuminating the whole knot of dragons with Marise at the center.

'I will do whatever Marise asks,' Tochara said. *'She never meant to come here. Never meant to get mixed up in the stagger and our . . . disagreements. She might have gone home long ago. She has good reason to go home and leave us to die until the rhumbas are graveyards of withering dragon corpses. Look at her. Is she a threat? She's saved us and now she's trying to save Javeer. I think she can do it.'*

'Tochara, I forbid you to use sphere travel. You don't understand the danger.'

'I understand indeed, and I'll take the risk. For Javeer.' A ripple passed through the growing crowd of dragons. There were at least a hundred. The shifting mass, males and females, pressed closer.

'You will not.' Honosa spoke with finality. She drew up and leaned over Tochara.

Tochara looked at Marise with a steady, meaningful gaze, and Marise understood.

If Honosa refused to bend, Javeer would get no help from Wyvern Wood. The dragons would let him die. She remained hunched before the henne, staring at Tochara in mute silence. In all the vast clearing, not one dragon moved or spoke. Marise felt a scream rising from somewhere deep within her.

'Javeer.' The voice came from the crowd.

'Javeer son of Zalton and Senja of Wyvern Wood Rhumba,' another said.

A cry erupted near the edge of the wood, rising to the canopy, and fleeing across the great hall. It faded, changed pitch, returned. "Javeeeeer." Others picked up the call. "Javeeeeer. Javeeeeer!" Each time it died away, the chant rose again from somewhere else. It swept around like a haunting wind, wild and mournful. Marise watched as dragon heads rose and dipped in synchrony with the song.

'Honosa.' Tochara drew the henne's and Marise's attention. She postured as Honosa had done and looked her henne in the eye. *'I've decided, this is not the time for fear for my own safety. I'll take the risk. For Javeer and for them.'* Her eyes flicked toward the crowd. *'We'll bring Javeer back alive, and we'll end the stagger. He has a right to be part of that.'*

'I will go also,' Kuvrema said, breaking her silence. *'I will use the circle.'*

Marise dropped Honosa's sphere and ran to Kuvrema. "Thank you, thank you." She stoked her coppery scales.

Something passed overhead, and she looked up to see Valcke cutting circles over her head, crying, "Javeer! Javeer!" as if the young male he'd never met was his hero.

Marise laughed and wept, stretching a hand toward him in gratitude.

The chant roiled to the front of the crowd like an ocean swell, crushing Honosa's resistance. The henne had lost.

Marise and Tochara watched in horror as Eschla struggled to keep Javeer from bashing his head against the wall of the Darjugan River cave. The blows she stopped looked powerful enough to break bones.

Marise breathed a sigh of relief when Kuvrema materialized on the circle. Then she focused on Javeer, and Lupin, who waited beside his crumpled back legs. His tail sphere whistled over Lupin's head and smashed into the cave wall, showering the witch with rock fragments. Kuvrema caught the end of his tail with her wing claw.

Trusting the dragon to hold it still, Marise wrapped her fingers around it and delved inside Javeer's head. The stark contrast from the chaos in the cave only seconds before was shocking.

She relaxed, beginning at her toes, and working her way up, guiding his body to relax as well. His muscles went slack one by one until he slumped. She sensed the others' tensions ease. Kuvrema's grip and Eschla's weight drew back. Her lingering reluctance to put him through the surgery evaporated. Either they saved him now, or he would die.

She lifted her dragon head and directed a question at Lupin, who held Eschla's sphere. *'Ready?'*

"As ready as *I* will ever be. But are *you* ready? Can't you feel what the dragon feels? How will you bear it when I cut through the flesh at the back of your neck and *peel* back the skin to reveal your skull? Will you hold still while I tilt your bleeding head over a rock and poke around the muscles and vessels at the top of your spine looking for worms? How long will you last? What if the worms cling to your nerves? What if they are *embedded* in your brain?"

Marise wanted to smack her. Her teeth clamped together, but as she answered through the sphere, she tried to hide her irritation and fear. *'Maybe it won't hurt all that much. I'll meditate. I'll use a mantra. There's no other way.'*

"It will *hurt* more than anything you have ever experienced. You will likely be unconscious before I *even* finish chipping the scales off at the base of his head. *Then* who will keep Javeer still?"

'Kuvrema and Tochara will! That's why they're here! Just get on with it. Just do it, okay? Do it!'

Eschla snorted. *'You are the most courageous, and possibly the stupidest human I've ever met,'* she said. *'Everyone stay here. Don't do anything until I return.'* She rushed through the waterfall's glittering frills.

No one said anything. Lupin put down the scalpel she'd been gripping, and Marise looked at Kuvrema through Javeer's eyes. A tear welled up and spilled over, taking a zigzag path down his scaled face.

'Kuvrema and Tochara, you might as well see if you can get into his mind with me. You still want to do this?'

The females brought their tail spheres around. Marise waited to feel their presence, but they couldn't make it work, so they put their spheres together with Javeer's, and Marise held them like a bouquet of balloons. She sensed their tentative mental pushes and tried guiding them into the space where her consciousness nestled.

Kuvrema slipped in first, her calm resolve bumping against Marise's hard determination. Tochara arrived anxious and heartbroken. The meeting of minds felt awkward and disjointed.

Marise stiffened as images and feelings tumbled around her, a myriad of experiences of dragon life, Moerden's mountains, the desert, her own appearance, and after a minute or two, a predominance of memories of Javeer. She knew he was the glue that would hold them all together through the operation. They all loved Javeer, and they trusted each other.

Faintly, Marise became aware Eschla was back, and she bent her muddled powers of observation toward her. In one wing claw, she held a dripping cilirum, which she extended above Javeer's head and poured milky fluid down the back of his neck.

'Go,' Eschla said.

As the sharp odor of paint thinner caught in Marise's throat, Lupin pushed a rock under Javeer's jaw, tilting his nose down, and dragon scales struck the floor.

Melded with Kuvrema and Tochara, Marise worked to keep Javeer motionless and relaxed. Mercifully, she felt little more than nudges and touches at the back of his head, save for a swelling ache whenever Eschla left to rinse the cilirum. The pain receded as soon as she returned and reapplied it.

Lupin murmured while she worked. "Should be here. Where's that skull, Eschla? I need to see....Yes, that's what I thought.

"Not just . . . no, that's a vein. Can't see. Some light Eschla? There. No, under the brain. A little lower. Lower. Ah."

Marise felt dizzy. She opened her dragon eyes and tried focusing on the mosaic, but it was too far away. Nearer, something long and thin fell to the floor in a splatter of blood.

"The little ba—Look how they've damaged that membrane. Two, three, no, more. There. Where are the forceps? That stuff is keeping the bleeding in check, isn't it? Amazing. Seven. Eight."

'Marise!' Tochara's voice sounded weak and distant.

Marise tried answering but felt herself slipping, sliding into shadow at the edge of Javeer's mind. Worms and monsters lurked there, and she knew Kuvrema and Tochara could not follow. The shadows dragged her under.

Chapter
Twenty-Four

MARISE'S PEARLIES

'*You changed Moerden forever.*'
Javeer's voice came as if through a closed door.

"All we've done—you did it, too—is put Moerden back the way it used to be. Almost. Before people. Before the stagger."

'*You made it happen. Dragons will never forget. We will hunt the deer down and kill them all, and I'll tell everyone not to eat kreel at the coast till there are no more deaths from the stagger. We'll rename the canyon kreel* Marise's Pearlies. *The ones that are safe to eat. And we won't let people bring any more animals from your world. Not ever again!*'

She smiled. "I want to stay and help you. I want to fly down the canyon with you again and eat pearlies. And go back to Tiderook and Wyvern Wood. But right now, I can't. I have to go home. There's trouble there, too, and it's my fault. I have to fix it."

'*You'll be back. We'll watch for you. You're famous now. We all love you. I love you.*'

"I love you, too. No. Not everyone. Korpec doesn't love me. But you're the famous one. You and Kuvrema, and, and Toch—"

Marise gasped and jerked into a sitting position, looking around in alarm. Someone was watching them. Someone was spying on them with spheresight. Javeer's voice gone from her head, she looked to the other dragons, but all were looking toward the falls.

Javeer lay on her left, splayed on the cave floor, his wings slack, legs stretched behind. A band of bare skin at the base of his skull was red and swollen where Lupin had made an incision to remove the worms. A neat line of stitches ran like an ant trail to the corner of his mouth.

Tochara handed Marise her sphere and nudged Javeer's cheek with her nose. *'I think he's gone. It didn't work.'*

"No. No. I was just talking to him. He was okay, and he said he'd wait for me to come back." Listening to her own words, she realized they couldn't be true. She hadn't even been holding a sphere. She hadn't been awake.

"He's there. I know he's there." She turned to Kuvrema. "Who's that? Who's watching us?"

'It can only be Korpec. No one else would look into this cave. No one else would be rude enough to keep looking, knowing he's been detected.' She sighed, turning to the prone Javeer and then to Eschla.

"But if he comes here, he'll kill Javeer." Hysteria tinged Marise's voice. Scrambling to her feet, she started toward the waterfall, but reversed to drop Tochara's tail sphere and pick up her own relic.

"Javeer's alive. We have to protect him. I was just . . . . What happened? I don't remember anything after I saw the worm . . ." The sensation of being watched intensified, and she groaned, covering her face with her free hand. She peered out between her fingers.

Eschla reached into the shadows beyond Javeer's shoulder. She lifted up a limp cilirum and placed it on the back of his head.

Her fingertips sliding down to her lips, Marise watched Kuvrema stride over to the circle. "No! Kuvrema, Korpec might use the circle."

'If he does, we will both be killed. He won't.' She carefully took up as much of the circle as possible.

"What if he doesn't look?"

'He is looking now. This will slow him down. Marise, you and

Lupin must go. We'll deal with Korpec, and it will be easier if the two of you are not here.'

"I'm not ready to go. I have to say goodbye to Javeer."

"*I'm* ready to go." Lupin tossed a few remaining items into the gym bag she'd brought from Cadogan Mills and stooped to pick up her relic. "I'll need the circle, though."

"You're just going to leave him like that?" She couldn't believe Lupin was so eager to go. "He might need you." She noticed the sensation of being watched had gone, but it brought no comfort. *If Korpec isn't watching,* she wondered, *what is he doing?*

"There is nothing *more* I can do. He's alive, I think, but he teeters on the edge. Either he will live, or he *will* die. Eschla can look after him."

Marise gazed at Javeer; her lip trembled. "I suppose we have to go, don't we? But I'll be back! I'll be back, Javeer." Her fingers went white around her sphere as she tried convincing herself she had to leave him without knowing whether he lived. "You first Lupin. You know how to get back? Just visualize the circle in Mrs. Bonner's kitchen. Don't forget to look first."

"I've got it, yes. But Kuvrema will have to let me see this one."

'You move on, and I will move off. We must not leave the circle empty.'

Marise drew her breath in through her teeth. Her eyes met Lupin's. "Don't rush it. Be careful."

Lupin and Kuvrema exchanged places, and Lupin prepared herself in the middle of the mosaic. Marise squatted and put her relic sphere on the ground. She visualized Ellen's kitchen until the room materialized in the sphere.

"You're okay to go Lupin. See you there." Her attention remained locked on the sphere, but in her peripheral vision she saw Lupin vanish.

Kuvrema leaped back into the circle as soon as it was clear, and

Marise waited for Lupin to appear in the kitchen. She counted the seconds as they ticked away. "One-one thousand, two-one thousand, three-one thousand . . ."

Lupin did not materialize.

How long does it take? It feels like two seconds. She waited and waited, eyes fixed on Ellen's empty floor. At least a full minute passed before she tore her gaze away and looked at Kuvrema. She stood up, searching the cave's recesses, as though the witch might have simply stepped into the shadows.

"She's not there," Marise said, stooping to cup Kuvrema's sphere in one hand. "She didn't appear."

Marise bent over and focused on the relic sphere again, summoning the kitchen in Cadogan Mills. The room remained empty.

"No. She's not there. She didn't make it." Marise covered her mouth with the back of a hand, still gazing at the sphere. How could everything go so wrong, she wondered, just when she thought she had it all figured out?

This was where she'd imagined stepping into the circle and blowing kisses to the dragons, with Javeer conscious and recovering. Instead, he lay dying, Lupin was lost in sphere travel, and Korpec was stalking them.

Kuvrema and Tochara stood in silence while Eschla kept her back turned, adjusting the cilirum, now pallid and limp, on Javeer's incision.

Marise's mind cast around for some way to find Lupin but couldn't think of anything. Spheresight only worked if you knew where to look. She sank to the ground, staring into the sphere, watching Ellen's kitchen as though Lupin might yet show up there.

'You must go.' Kuvrema jerked Marise back to reality. *'We need to be ready if Korpec comes here, but you must get out of here now. Go, Marise.'*

She picked up her sphere and stood. She turned to retrieve

Bonner's backpack for the last time, then moved toward the falls on legs that felt weak and wooden. Mentally off balance, she missed the moment when the light filtering through the falling water dimmed. She started when a dragon's head drove through the glittering curtain, bringing a splatter of water and a blast of flame.

"Korpec!"

He almost landed on top of her. Stumbling, she fumbled the sphere with wet hands. It slipped out of her grasp, hit the floor, and rolled toward him. He reached out with a scaled foot and knocked it toward the side passage. Marise watched in horror as he brought his own sphere around and struck the rolling relic. It sailed down the side passage.

"No!" she cried out, pitching forward as if to go after it.

The sphere hit the cascade at the end of the tunnel and disappeared.

Tochara shrieked from the other side of the cave, but Marise already knew she stood well within range of Korpec's incinerating breath. She felt as if she was moving in slow motion, trying to outrun the flame.

But no blast came. Instead, he turned on Kuvrema, bounding forward, and Marise found herself staring at his ridged back. He had the dragons cornered.

Tochara shrieked again, and it sounded to Marise as if the cry faded to bubbling steam when Korpec blasted fire. The temperature shot up, and a wave of hot air rolled over her. Kuvrema returned fire of her own, and the temperature increased again.

Marise felt faint. She scrambled toward the falls and crouched as close to the plunging water as she dared, hoping the mist and spray might protect her.

The dragons blasted each other with red flame. The cave belched scorching air that rushed down the passage and made her cry out.

The spray from the falls and a current of fresher air did cool her, and she pressed her back against the wet rock. She inched closer to the brink, reaching toward the water to wet her hand and wipe her face and neck. As she leaned out, a crack like a gunshot echoed through the cave and she sprang back, only to find dust and debris raining down.

A great fissure zigzagged across the ceiling. It ran from above her to the edge of the chimney, with cracks branching off to either side. Korpec delivered another scorching blast, and the fissure widened. More cracks appeared. Fine sand mixed with rocks fell on her. The ceiling looked ready to fall at any moment.

"Stop!" Marise choked, crawling from the brink. The dust burned as it entered her lungs. She put her hand up to her face, covering her mouth and nose. She could not stop coughing.

Her chest heaved with her efforts to breathe. Through blurred vision, she saw a dark object move across the floor. It drifted in front of her, traveling in a wide arc. It came close, and she reached for it.

Her fingers closed around Korpec's sphere. His unguarded thoughts made her gasp, setting off a renewed coughing attack.

Reckless, mindless, violent panic; her fingers stiffened into rigid claws. She could feel nothing but towering fear and helplessness.

Suddenly, any action, no matter how destructive, looked better than no action at all. It didn't matter if the mountain fell and crushed them, as long as the danger was removed.

Kill them. Kill them all. Kill them now.

Marise retched, spitting out grit. She forced the panic down. *Korpec is afraid. He's terrified. And he's going to kill us.* Her hand tightened around his tail until she felt the edges of his scales bite into her palms.

She breathed in dust and gagged. Her stomach heaved, but nothing came up. Retching, she cupped his sphere in one hand and tapped it with the other, then rubbed it lightly.

She felt a shudder run through the crazed dragon. He turned on her, but she kept on tickling. Korpec huffed as though to incinerate her, but no flame came out. He twitched his tail, pulling her forward so she lay on her belly, arms outstretched, hands gripping the sphere. She rubbed and tapped. With her eyes locked on Korpec's, she mercilessly tickled the sphere.

Her gaze moved beyond him. The three females emerged from the dust storm, hustling Javeer's limp body across the circle and up the ramp toward the open air. Just before he passed beyond her range of vision, she thought she saw Javeer turn his head.

Korpec collapsed on the floor, flapping his wings in futile resistance. They stirred up a dust cloud as they slapped the floor. She crouched, aching to follow the others, wondering whether she had time to gain the relative safety of the ramp before Korpec recovered.

She was poised to make a wild dash for the ramp when a sensation of being watched intruded again. *One of the females?* She hesitated. *Are they telling me to hang on? Are they coming back?* She looked toward the ramp, through dust swirling in sunlight, waiting for some sign from above.

Burnt sugar. She tasted it as she breathed in through her mouth. She frowned, trying to place the odor so out of place in the chaos. Something wet and cold touched her ankle.

"Oh!" Marise looked down and yanked her foot back. Crackers hunched beside her. Dull disc-like eyes blinked from an inscrutable face. A facial tentacle that had begun exploring her lower leg stretched, reaching toward her as she inched away.

She got to her feet, her eyes moving back and forth from Korpec to Crackers. She tapped the sphere and readied herself to make a rush for safety.

Crackers made a guttural choking noise, and she put more distance between herself and the pool grue. She watched, open-mouthed, as Crackers retched and spat out a relic sphere. The creature turned and took off down the side tunnel, leaving a trail of wet rock and a lingering sweet odor.

Marise ran for the sphere, taking one shaking hand off Korpec's tail. As her fingers touched it, she heard Tochara's voice.

'Get out of there. Take the sphere and go. Javeer is okay. He's awake, and he says go. Remember . . . What? Marise's pearlies. Marise's pearlies. He says it's okay for you to go now. Let Kuvrema deal with Korpec.'

"Pearlies?" For a second, she couldn't remember why that was important. Then she remembered his promise. *'We'll rename the canyon kreel* Marise's pearlies. *The ones that are safe to eat.'*

"Yes!" He'd been talking to her after all. He was really okay. Elated, Marise moved toward the mosaic, dragging Korpec's tail behind her. As the brute stirred and tried pulling away, she delivered a fresh tickle attack.

The circle lay hidden under fallen rock and sand; the bright pattern beneath remained barely visible. Marise knelt and let go of the relic to brush the closest section clear with a grimy hand. She took her eyes off Korpec while she studied the mosaic, getting a fresh image of the dragons carved around the periphery, focusing on dragons instead of roses. She put a hand on the relic.

Her gaze shifted from sphere and mosaic. She directed her thoughts to Javeer and the females, wrenched by having to leave without proper goodbyes. She didn't feel ready.

"Bye, Javeer. I'm glad you're okay. I'll be back soon. Get well. Bye Tochara, Kuvrema, Eschla."

Marise took her hand off the relic and built an image of the mosaic in its depths. She imagined the carved dragons, studying the one that lay exposed beside her on the floor. She mentally brushed the dust from the cave mosaic and made the pattern clear and sharp.

Holding the image inside the sphere, she focused all her attention on it. She reached to take up the sphere, laying Korpec's tail on the cave floor, but she didn't look into the depths of the sphere.

A thought nudged at her, telling her she had forgotten something, something important. She paused.

"Oh, Tochara, Javeer, take some of my pearlies to Valcke. I promised. I owe him. Will you do that for me?"

'Yes, Marise. Go.' The reply was barely a murmur.

She raised the sphere to eye level, concentrating on the mosaic she held in its depths.

Carved dragons swam up from the center of the sphere, rising in a slow spiral. She blinked, and they dove back into place in the mosaic. She frowned and focused once more, holding the dragons still with her will. They shifted as though trying to rise toward her cupped fingers. Worried, she held back, willing them to be still. They quivered, heaved, settled again. She brought all her concentration to bear on the image.

Something struck her hands like a sledgehammer, sending bolts of agony through fingers and wrists. Marise pitched forward, crying out. Her body catapulted into the void. Beyond the agony in her hands, her only thought was that there was nothing there. Nothing. Her hands were empty.

EPILOGUE

Marise opened her eyes. From the coarse texture of rock against her cheek, she knew she lay face down on a stone floor. She couldn't make out the detail of the stones because a pattern of colored light was superimposed upon them, like sunlight through a stained glass window.

Lifting her head, she saw a curved gray tile with a dragon carved in it just beyond the lit area of floor. She moved to raise herself but slumped back as pain raced through her hands. The left hand throbbed, and she gasped at the sight of a twisted and crooked thumb. With both hands held in front of her body, she rolled over and sat. She climbed to her feet, bringing the left hand close to protect it.

Dark wooden pews and a red carpet center aisle decorated the church she stood in. Tinted sunlight slanted down onto the mosaic through windows behind the altar. She had no trouble recognizing the pattern now that she could see all of it. For a moment, the incongruity of sinuous Chinese dragons carved in a church floor distracted her, but she did not doubt that this was the church in Cedar Settlement that Bonner had told her about.

Marise watched dust motes float in the air, feeling the pain fade in her right hand and blossom in her left. She thought about looking for the relic sphere in the church, but knew it was pointless. The sphere was not beneath a pew or lying in the shadows. It hadn't come with her. Korpec probably had it now, and Lupin was lost with the other one.

She bowed her head and allowed herself to feel her misery. A small shudder shook her; how lucky she was to have arrived safely. The shudder returned when she wondered where Lupin had gone. She was likely dead, but she might still be out there too, trying to get home. At least she had a sphere.

The throbbing pain in her hands helped her focus on what she must do—get help, let her parents know she was alive, and as soon as she could, look for Lupin in Airlie Lane. She turned and strode down the red carpet toward the church doors. She found them unlocked and threw the right-hand door open wide, stepping out into a breezy May morning. Glancing left and right, she waved at a woman pushing a stroller.

Running the fingers of her right hand through her matted curls, Marise walked down to meet her. "So mote it be," she said under her breath.

ACKNOWLEDGMENTS

This tale took a dragon's age to reach a finished state, and on the way I gathered lots of invaluable comments and advice from fellow writers. Many thanks to Russ Barton, Alex Boutilier, Stacey Cornelius, Gwen Davies, Susan Drain, Russell Fralich, David Johnson, Susan LeBlanc, Brett Loney, Sheila Morrison, Sue Murtagh, Gordon Perks, Judith Scrimger, Nathaniel Southwell, and Valerie Spencer. You made it better.

A handful of other friends and family were unfailingly generous with comments, suggestions, and the magic of encouragement. Your support made it happen. Thank you Kayla Bates, Vic Drisdelle, Lex Gingell, Beth McClelland, and Kat McClelland.

Please note that I've resorted to alphabetical order to avoid the dilemma of wanting to put everyone first.

ABOUT
THE AUTHOR

Rosemary Drisdelle has written on various nonfiction science and professional topics. A fascination with parasites, where fiery serpents are not unknown, inspired her science book *Parasites: Tales of Humanity's Most Unwelcome Guests*. She's always had a weakness for reptiles and hopes to meet a real live dragon some day; however, there don't seem to be any in Bedford, Nova Scotia, where she currently lives.

SELECTED TITLES FROM SPARKPRESS

SparkPress is an independent boutique publisher delivering
high-quality, entertaining, and engaging content that enhances
readers' lives, with a special focus on female-driven work.
www.gosparkpress.com

Caley Cross and the Hadeon Drop, J. S. Rosen, $16.95, 978-1-68463-053-0.
When thirteen-year-old Caley Cross, an orphan with a dark power, is guided by
a jumpsuit-wearing mole into another world—Erinath—she finds a place deeply
rooted in nature where the people have animal-like powers and she is a Crown
Princess—but she soon learns that the most powerful evil being in *any* world is
waiting for her there.

The Goddess Twins: A Novel, Yodassa Williams. $16.95, 978-1-68463-032-5.
Days before their eighteenth birthday, Arden and Aurora's mother goes missing
and they discover they belong to a family of Caribbean deities. Can these goddess
twins uncover their evil grandfather's plot in time to save their mother, themselves, and the free world?

The Blue Witch: The Witches of Orkney, Book One, Alane Adams. $12.95, 978-1-
943006-77-9. Nine-year-old Abigail Tarkana has a problem: her witch magic has
finally come in, but it's *different*—and being different is a problem at the Tarkana
Witch Academy. Together with her scientist-friend Hugo, she face off against sneevils,
shreeks, and vikens in a race to discover the secrets about her mysterious magic.

Red Sun: The Legends of Orkney, Book 1, Alane Adams. $17, 978-1-940716-
24-4. After learning that his mom is a witch and his missing father is a true Son
of Odin, 12-year-old Sam Baron must travel through a stonefire to the magical
realm of Orkney on a quest to find his missing friends and stop an ancient curse.

The Rubicus Prophecy: Witches of Orkney, Book 2, Alane Adams. $12.95, 978-1-
943006-98-4. As Abigail enters her second year at the Tarkana Witch Academy,
she is up to her ears studying for Horrid Hexes and Awful Alchemy. But when an
Orkadian warship arrives carrying troubling news, Abigail and Hugo are swept
into a puzzling mystery when they help a new friend go after a missing item—one
that might spell the end of everything they know.

Kalifus Rising: The Legends of Orkney, Book 2, Alane Adams. $16.95, 978-1-
940716-84-8. Sam Baron's attempt to free his father brought war to Orkney.
Now captured by the Volgrim witches, Sam's only hope lies with his friends—but
treachery shadows their every step.